Date: 3/8/16

MYS COONTS
Coonts, Deborah,
Lucky break : a Lucky
O'Toole Vegas adventure /

LUCKY BREAK

Lucky O'Toole Vegas Adventure

Book Six

A Novel By

DEBORAH COONTS

Book published by Austin Brown, CheapEbookFormatting.com

Cover Design by Andrew Brown, ClickTwiceDesign.com

ISBN-13:9780996571272

PRAISE FOR
DEBORAH COONTS' NOVELS

"Deliciously raunchy, with humorous takes on sexual proclivities, Vegas glitz and love, though Agatha Christie is probably spinning in her grave."

—*Kirkus Reviews*

"Complete with designer duds, porn conventions, partner-swapping parties, and clever repartee, this is chick-lit gone wild and sexy, lightly wrapped in mystery and tied up with a brilliantly flashing neon bow. As the first in a series, *Wanna Get Lucky?* hits the proverbial jackpot."

—*Booklist*

"*Wanna Get Lucky?* is a winner on every level. Deborah Coonts has crafted a first-class murder mystery coupled with a touching and unexpected love story. Against a flawlessly-rendered Las Vegas backdrop, Lucky's story is funny, fast-paced, exuberant and brilliantly realized."

—Susan Wiggs, *New York Times* bestselling author

"Get ready to win big--with a novel that will keep you glued to the pages all the way to the end. *Wanna Get Lucky?* is as entertaining as the city in which it's set."

—Brenda Novak, *New York Times* bestselling author of *Trust me, Stop Me, and Watch Me*

Wanna Get Lucky goes down faster than an ice-cold Bombay martini—very dry, of course, and with a twist.

—*Douglas Preston, New York times bestselling author of Impact.*

Wanna Get Lucky? Is an amazing debut novel, a mile-a-minute read, with fantastic characters, dry wit, and the gritty neon feel of Las Vegas. Bravo to Deborah Coonts—I see a great future ahead.

—*Heather Graham, New York Times bestselling author of Night of the Wolves.*

NOVELS IN THE LUCKY SERIES

LUCKY NOVELLAS

CHAPTER ONE

*M*E, getting married. I still couldn't believe it. We hadn't set a date, but still... married!

When Jean-Charles asked me to marry him, I had said yes.

One simple word. I'd said it a million different times, in a thousand different contexts, with no life-altering consequences ... well, except for the whole Teddie thing. That hadn't worked out quite as I'd hoped, but about like I'd feared.

He'd loved me and left. If I'd listened to more country music, maybe I could've avoided that.

For good or for ill, I paused one last time in front of the full-length mirrors in my closet that caught all sides. Normally, I avoided the things like I avoided my mother, both for good reason. At six feet and, shall we say it, fully fleshed-out, I fell far short of my mother's dream that I would become a dancer on the Vegas Strip. Alas, I became something much worse, a hotel executive, specifically the Vice President of Customer Relations at the Babylon, Vegas's premier Strip property. But, despite my lofty rung on the corporate ladder, Mona still made me feel guilty that I didn't live down to her expectations.

Why is it we all want what we can't have?

Teddie.

As if hearing her lead-in or something, Mona breezed into my boudoir. "Well, don't you look every inch the virginal bride?" Mona said with her barbed tongue planted firmly in her cheek.

Resplendent in a rich shade of burnt orange organza that darkened and lightened as she moved, one shoulder bare, the bodice fitted, the skirt flowing, she looked every inch the hotel magnate's wife. To further fill her days, she also was the mother of month-old twins and a candidate for public office—the County Commission—if the voters didn't wise up soon. With the vote almost a year away, she was ahead in the polls, which frightened the hell out of me, but also made me grudgingly proud. My 24/7 job would never allow the time for a family and a job as servant of the people—I don't know how she did it. The wear-and-tear showed in added crow's feet and a subtle weariness dimming her normal wattage. Her brown hair was pulled into a chignon with tendrils of hair left to softly frame her face. The baby weight had almost disappeared. What was left softened her angular features and rounded her in an appealing, maternal way. Recent motherhood had made her even more stunning, a cross I bore. Her blue eyes, round with hurt and accentuated with black liner, put me on guard. "Red does suit you," she added as she eyed me with the calculation of a children's beauty pageant momzilla.

I'd chosen a strapless sheath of fire engine red with tiny gold threads running through the bodice just in case the red was too subtle. The five-carat emerald-cut diamond sparkled on the ring finger of my left hand. Every now and again I'd look at it just to make sure. Still, I couldn't believe it.

Me. Getting married.

Holding onto my mother's shoulder, I used her to steady myself as I donned first one low-heeled strappy Jimmy Choo, then the other. "Is this a social call?" I asked my mother, knowing her wounded doe-eyes provided the answer, but hoping just this once she'd let her bet ride. But she'd gone out of her way, making the trip from the Babylon, so the odds were against me.

"What?" She feigned offense. "Lucky, you act as if I don't want to check on my daughter every now and again."

Yes, my name is Lucky. Last name O'Toole, and, to be honest, I have no idea where either name came from and I'm too scared of the answer to ask. "Well, since this is your first visit in ages, it does make me wonder." I leaned close to the mirror to check my make-up one last time. I still wasn't used to the whole lipstick, powder, blush routine, but I did like the result. Especially the shadow and eyeliner that accentuated my blue eyes—even if they still carried a hint of shell-shock in them. I applied one more swipe of pink gloss, then pressed my lips together. "I know you well enough to see an ulterior motive lurking behind your innocent act."

She gave me a hint of a smile, a kid caught with Black Cats at school. "I want to talk to you about Jean-Charles."

"None of your business."

She ignored my frosty tone and eyes that had gone all squinty. "Are you sure about this? Are you sure Jean-Charles isn't one of those boomerang things?"

"Boomerang?" The visual was interesting. "You mean rebound things?" I corrected before my brain kicked in, shutting down my mouth. She knew perfectly well what she meant—and she misspoke to get me to engage. Would I never learn?

"Exactly. You're not over Teddie and what he did."

"So you don't want to talk about Jean-Charles; you really want to talk about Teddie."

"And your father."

That one whirled in out of left field, tripping my heart. "The Big Boss? He's okay, right?" Ever since he had that heart scare not too long ago, I hadn't been able to shake a feeling of impending doom. A dose of mortality to puncture his Mount Olympus aura.

"Of course, he's fine." Mona shrugged that suggestion away, a horse shaking off a fly. "It's what he's doing to Teddie."

Teddie.

This was my night, Jean-Charles's night. Tonight's party celebrating the opening of Jean-Charles's restaurant, J-C Vegas, would be the kickoff to a ten-day celebration of the grand opening of my very own hotel, Cielo. And she had to bring Teddie into it. I gave her a look that I hoped would instill terror. "Curiously, Mother, when Teddie left he ceased being my problem."

Mona rolled her eyes.

"Did you just roll your eyes at me?" A hand on my hip, I felt like the parent here. "Really? Keep doing that and maybe you'll find a brain in there somewhere."

I grabbed my purse, a sweet little evening bag in red and gold to match my dress—who knew love could turn this tomboy all girly-girly? If I started giggling, I'd hate myself. Mona dogged my heels as I strode through my bedroom and into the main room of my apartment. "Now where did I put my wrap?"

Mona's voice held the tinny notes of a whine fraying my already on-edge nerves. "Lucky, you have to deal with Teddie."

Taking a deep breath, I counted to ten ... twice. My gaze wandered around the room as I drank it all in: the view of the Strip through the wall of windows, the white walls, the burnished wood floor, the white leather furniture and the splashes of color on the walls—original paintings depicting the glory of the Mojave. My home. My sanctuary. Me. "I have dealt with Teddie, Mother. Done. Over. Finished."

"But your father." Mona trotted after me breathless. "He's cancelling Teddie's contract." My father had offered Teddie his former theater to develop and stage a new show—one based on Teddie as a singer rather than The Great Teddie Divine, Vegas's foremost female impersonator, his previous gig. I was glad that was behind him. I'd tired of him rooting in my closet for "costumes" and stretching out my shoes. Especially my shoes.

When my father had invited Teddie back into the fold, he hadn't consulted me. Both of my parents considered it their duty to meddle in my life. Up to now, they'd been irritating but not hurtful. Jerking the contract out from under Teddie, that was a knife to the heart. Teddie would wither and die without his audience. And, no matter what he'd done, how much he'd disappointed me, I didn't want to see him broken. Punishment, like revenge, wouldn't ease the pain. Oh, maybe in the short term ... but I didn't want my future to be burdened with guilt. *The high road, Lucky. The high road.*

I stopped and whirled on Mona, almost meeting her nose-to-nose. "What do you mean 'cancelled his contract'?"

She drew up, shoulders back, chin at a defiant angle, the look in her eyes a slap—a trait she'd taken from my father. He wore it better and could back it up. "Teddie's out with no place to go, and it's all your fault."

This time *I* rolled my eyes. And I knew that no matter how many times I did it, I wouldn't find a brain in my hollow head. "Of course it's not my fault. I don't know anything about it. So, stop doing that." Wow! Apparently I had shucked some emotional armor and exposed a backbone.

"You have to fix it." Mona wrung her hands. She used to

campaign against Teddie, telling me he'd leave me for a life on the road. She'd been right. He'd broken my heart. And now he and my mother were best friends? Unlike her daughter, *he* had lived down to her expectations, so I guessed she had a soft spot. There was all sorts of wrong in that. "Without you and Teddie being an item," her eyes slipped to the ring on my finger and then back to mine, "your father has less incentive to keep him around."

"Don't be silly, Mother. This is *all* about money. You know the Big Boss." With a hand on one hip, I eyed Mona, as I plotted my battle strategy. Brush her off or look into the problem? Which would be the least painful path? To ignore her would bring out her inner piranha. She'd keep biting off chunks of my resolve until I finally caved. Easier to get it over with. "I'll look into it, Mother. First, I have to know what the deal is and why the Big Boss is cancelling it."

Mona opened her mouth, but I heard Teddie's voice.

"He got a better offer." Teddie strolled in from the kitchen looking like a million bucks before taxes. Spiky blond hair, blue eyes rimmed with lashes most women would sacrifice body parts for, broad where he should be, trim where he shouldn't, a tight ass, and a voice like honey, the guy was a walking, talking, singing pheromone.

I whirled on my mother. "You asked Teddie down? So you two could gang up on me? Tonight?" Teddie's apartment connected to mine through a back staircase, which used to be convenient. Now it was a violation ... and a betrayal. I narrowed my eyes at my mother and wondered what the punishment for matricide was these days. If everyone's mother was like Mona, it couldn't be that bad. But everyone couldn't be so lucky.

Mona didn't look sorry. "A stacked deck is the best kind," she said, parroting her husband.

"In business."

She met me glare-to-glare. "This *is* business."

"My business, I should think," Teddie said. "Look, if it's any consolation, I didn't want to mention this at all. My presence here is as much a part of Mona's set-up as your help is. But, here it is, short and sweet. Your father cancelled my contract because Holt Box said he'd do thirty weeks a year for five years, coup of epic proportions getting him to come out of retirement. He'll be a huge draw for the Babylon, much more than I would." Although Teddie adopted a casual air, he was angry. It boiled just below the surface. His smile was taut with the effort to cover it.

I was blindsided. Ten years ago Holt had left country music at the peak of his career, devastating his legions of female fans and making himself into the stuff of legend.

And now the Babylon was hosting his coming-out-of-retirement tour? How could the Big Boss have inked such a deal without me being in on it? Considering my parents made me and my life their business, I didn't have to think on it too hard. In a way, Mona had been right. It was my fault, of a sort. Business and pleasure, almost impossible to separate, and my father didn't have enough confidence in me to do so.

Grudgingly I admitted, in this case, he was probably right. If I'd been left to negotiate the Holt Box deal, I would've been hard-pressed to do so. But that wouldn't stop me from letting my father know how I felt … about all of it.

Promises were promises.

And when it came to love, I didn't need him riding in on his white horse to vanquish the unworthy. Or to save me from my own mistakes.

Teddie.

Teddie had a lot riding on his new show; he'd put his heart and soul into it. And he'd given up his spot on his newly rejuvenated tour. Finally, the rage burbled to the surface, coloring his face and hardening his voice. Holding up his hand, he stopped the platitudes I was going to offer—I didn't have anything else, and he knew me well enough to know it.

"Don't fret, not that you would. Your father had the legal right to do what he did."

"Being legal doesn't make it right."

Teddie's anger cooled. "You always tilt at windmills, don't you? One of the things I love about you. In a gray world you see black and white."

"Principles."

I left it to the Harvard boy to fill in all the rest. Principles applied to life and love.

Hiking up the flaps of his tux jacket, he stuffed his hands in his pockets. "This whole thing is my own damned fault. In such a hurry to get back here, back to—" He gave me an open, vulnerable look that tore at my heart. "But that was a pipe dream. In my haste, I agreed to stuff Rudy went apoplectic over." Rudy Gillespie was his entertainment lawyer, one of my good friends, and married to an even better friend, Jordan Marsh—the Hollywood heartthrob who had finally come out, dashing hopes of young women worldwide.

I knew what Teddie had left out, what he wanted to say: He'd been in a hurry to get back to me. Back to us. After having thrown me over for a line-up of groupies.

Trust, an emotional Humpty-Dumpty.

"Don't forget Holt Box had a hand in all of this," added Mona.

Teddie's anger sizzled as it flared anew. His shoulders rose toward his ears, as his face closed. "Yeah, that dude is on the top of my hit list."

"If you want to kill him, don't do it tonight. Murder has such a chilling effect on fun and frivolity." I spied my gold pashmina on the couch. Grabbing it in one swoop, I headed for the elevator. One advantage of having one of the top floors was a private elevator that fetched me from the middle of my great room. "I'm late. And, Teddie, I'm sorry. I really am. I'll see what I can find out. But right now I need to go. You two have a fine time. It's well past pumpkin time and I've got to hurry."

"Holt Box will be there tonight?" Teddie's voice lost any hint of nice.

"What rock have you been living under?" I wrapped the pashmina around my shoulders—Decembers could be cool in Vegas. "He's cooking with Jean-Charles. Apparently he loves to cook, has a cookbook out or something, I don't know." In my world of late nights and early mornings finding a meal involved finding the time to grab something quick and convenient. "Holt asked to assist. Jean-Charles said yes."

"And you went along with it?"

"Not my purview. And, trust me, having him in the kitchen during the opening might sound like a great media play, but it's been a nightmare of epic proportions. For weeks, gaggles of female predators looking for their hunk of country music flesh have been stalking the well-guarded perimeter of the Cielo property."

Too late, I realized I'd added fuel, igniting Teddie's slow burn into a raging inferno. Hate flushed his face, a new look. I didn't like it, but I got it.

Mona chose that moment to wade back in. "I have Paolo waiting downstairs." She studiously analyzed her fingernails as she dropped that little bombshell.

"But, I have Paolo waiting downstairs," I said as the realization that my mother could now overrule me at the hotel hit me like a bucket of ice water. I jabbed at the elevator button. Thankfully, the thing was waiting.

The doors opened and I stepped inside, followed by Mona and Teddie, rounding out our awkward trio.

When the doors closed, Teddie's reflection half-smiled at mine, an appreciated effort to cut through the ugliness. Still, I felt he was contemplating burying a knife in my back. How fun to have all of the blame and none of the authority.

In the closed space, the subtle aroma of very good Scotch, or very bad bourbon, competed with his Old Spice cologne. Apparently he'd gotten a head start—some joy juice to deaden the downside.

From the look on his face, I could tell he wanted to change the subject as much as I did.

"Now, *that* is a dress," he said, a hint of warmth melting the ice in his tone.

While he looked appreciative of the wrapping, I knew he liked the package as well. A bit of sad longing brushed over my heart. We'd been so good together. Until we weren't. His smile dimmed when he caught the flash of my ring. He reached around my shoulder, pulling me close, shoulder-to-shoulder in a one-arm embrace. Catching me off guard, I fell into him. My hand braced against his chest; the other grabbed his waist as I struggled to get my feet back underneath myself.

"Sorry," Teddie said, not sounding the least bit as he helped me right myself.

Mona, looking a bit uncomfortable, had put as much space as possible between her and me, which wasn't much given we were in an elevator. Teddie stood close enough that I could feel the heat radiating off of him. Anger? Passion? Didn't know and didn't care. Straightening my gown and my thoughts, ordering the outside to cover the muddle inside, I focused on the party ahead and ignored both of them as the elevator whisked us downstairs. As we pushed into the night, Paolo was indeed waiting by one of the Babylon's limos wringing his hands.

He snapped to attention when he caught sight of me. A small man with jet-black hair slicked back, an always-impeccable uniform, a normally ready smile, and enough energy to light Vegas for a year, tonight Paolo looked uneasy. Another hapless male fallen prey to Mona's charms, and I'm sure her veiled threats. He rushed to open the back door for me. "Oh, Miss Lucky, Paolo is so very sorry. Mrs. Rothstein ..."

"I know, threatened to boil you in oil or something. Don't worry. It's fine." I stopped before I disappeared into the dark confines of the car. "Just ignore them," I whispered. "Maybe they'll go away."

Paolo nodded, his smile forced, terror in his eyes.

He situated Mona next to me and Teddie in front, then slid behind the wheel, I checked the clock. Ten minutes until a press conference my father had arranged. If I wasn't there, heads would roll.

I toggled the switch that would allow Paolo to hear despite the glass window raised to cocoon the back. "Paolo, the time."

"Yes, Miss." Paolo pressed his cap on tight as he gripped the wheel, his knuckles white. "Hold on."

I reached for the looped strap near my left ear and held on.

Mona tapped me on the leg to get my attention, like we'd been having a nice conversation and I'd gotten distracted. She recoiled when I looked at her with my not-so-happy face.

"This is my night, Mother. How dare you?"

She looked crestfallen, her best gambit. I didn't cave.

Teddie lowered the window separating the front seat from the rear compartment. "Lucky, I'm sorry. Mona said—"

I held up my hand, cutting him off. "Playing the hapless stooge in a game run by women is getting old, and it is not attractive. You know Mona. And you know our rules. We are friends, but you are not allowed in my apartment unless you have a specific invitation from me."

"At least you're talking," Mona said with more than a little gloat.

"This is wonderful," she said with bright eyes.

A bit late to wise-up, Teddie ignored her. "Mona said you'd be okay with it."

"Mona lies," I said, transfixing my mother with a stare. But Teddie knew that already. "Paolo, step on it before I kill somebody."

Tires squealed as he did as I asked, fishtailing the big car onto Koval, then accelerating south. The forward momentum of the large car pressed me back in my seat and scared Mona into quiet.

In less than five minutes, with several tourists terrified but still breathing, Paolo turned up the grand drive to Cielo. Huge trees lined the curved entrance, giving the hotel a secretive feel, as if one had to be in the know to find the place. Like The Mansion at MGM, Cielo was a decadent hideaway for those who valued their privacy or just needed a respite from the constant pulsing energy of the Strip. The front entrance, normally protected by large gates and armed security, stood open, ready to receive all tonight. Protected under a copper porte cochere, and softened with pots of riotous flowering plants, the entrance was welcoming and warm with understated elegance. The architects had bent under my supervision and used rock, wood and other natural building materials where possible. The effect was stunning, warm and welcoming like a Japanese sanctuary. Frosted glass with images of reeds etched into them separated the large space into smaller vestibules. When the hotel officially opened, hosts would greet each guest, escorting them to a desk where the registration process would be handled with a glass of Champagne. The waterfall on the far wall lent a comforting sound as well as humidity, to the parched desert air. Yes, the place had turned out exactly as I'd hoped.

When the Big Boss and I had bought the property out of foreclosure, I had imagined this, dreamt of it, but never really thought I'd pull it off. The building, which we'd taken down to the bare bones, then built out, adding on where we could, had housed one of the grand dames of Vegas past, The Athena. Irv Gittings, the former owner, would never recognize what had been the diamond in his crown. Life had taken a hard turn for Ol' Irv. The rest of us moved on, and he went to jail.

Through the glass, I could see Jean-Charles just inside the front entrance talking to a group of reporters. Resplendent in his chef's whites, the trousers black-and-white striped, he looked at ease amid the well-liveried crowd milling about the lobby in their formal dress. His brown hair curled softly over the collar of his jacket. Trim, with broad shoulders and a slightly formal bearing, he made my heart melt.

When the limo eased in next to the curb, he moved to meet us as if he'd been watching, which he probably had. He opened the door, extended a hand, and pulled me into his embrace. Flash bulbs popped as I lost myself in his kiss. For a moment the world disappeared, and it was just the two of us. "You are late," he whispered against my cheek. "I was worried."

I kept my arms looped around his neck. "Shanghaied by my mother. I'm sorry. Shouldn't you be upstairs?"

He gave me a Gallic shrug and an irresistible smile that lit his robin's-egg-blue eyes. "This is more important."

"There's just something about the French. Romance oozing out of every pore," Mona cooed.

Even though her words sounded benign, I felt the prick of her jab.

Apparently, Jean-Charles didn't; his eyes warm, never drifted from mine. "You look good enough to eat. This is right, *non?*" On a never-ending quest to learn American idioms, Jean-Charles never missed a chance to trot one out. Tonight, he got it right. Most of the time, not so much, with charming consequences.

"High praise indeed from a master chef."

He beamed, until he caught sight of Teddie with Mona now leaning possessively on his arm, claiming her horse in this race. "Your mother and her games." While the words were light, his tone was not. "Mona, how good to see you," he said, slipping into a well-honed insincerity.

Mona smiled, unaware of the frost chilling his words.

"Theodore, I didn't know you were attending." Jean-Charles acknowledged Teddie but didn't extend a hand as he ushered us all inside. "Your father is waiting. He is a bit angry."

"Why?"

"The reporters, they only want to talk to you." He led me to the half-circle of chairs bookending a couch and lighted for the media. "I will be upstairs. The food ..."

"Needs your attention." I gave him a quick kiss. "Go. I'll be there as soon as I can."

I watched him as he worked his way toward the elevators, admiring the ease with which he made each person he spoke with shine ... like they felt like the most important person in the world. Where did sincerity end and civility begin? With the French, it was hard to tell. So polished. So smooth.

"Lucky?" A light touch on my arm rescued me just before I slipped into insecurity.

Kimberly Cho, one of the P.R. people who had been helping me with a sticky problem at the Big Boss's Macau property, looked up at me, her eyes a bit too wide, her normal polished perfection a bit ruffled. "Do you have a moment? It's important. I won't take much of your time." Her black hair drawn back in a soft chignon, her porcelain skin lightly blushed, her eyes kohled, she'd chosen a one-shoulder sheath of exquisitely embroidered Asian silk in turquoise. I envied the ease with which she carried her elegance. Although short and trim, she had the presence of someone much taller. "You know I wouldn't ask unless it was important."

"I know." I checked the time. I glanced at my father, a light sheen on his face from the heat of the kliegs. The interviewer and her attendants shifted nervously—everyone waiting on yours truly. "Will it wait until after my interview? Everyone is waiting."

Her hand shook as she tucked in a strand of hair that had the audacity to wander loose. "There's this man. A very bad man. You must be careful."

"What? Who?"

"I knew him. From before." Her eyes stared past me. Her face went slack.

"Kimberly, what is it?"

When her eyes again shifted to mine, they looked dead. "Be careful." With a nod, she backed away.

"Find security, then meet me at the elevator," I called after her. "We'll ride up alone. You'll have my undivided attention, and we'll have some privacy."

I turned to go. Something in the way she looked bothered me. The paleness of her skin, the slight haunted look in her eyes. She wasn't scared; she was terrified. Why did I let her go? I whirled around to call her back.

She was gone.

I scanned the crowd. Nothing.

I couldn't wait any longer. Kimberly would be waiting at the elevator, I told myself as I painted on a smile and mentally shifted, grinding a few gears and threatening to throw the transmission.

My father waited, his smile firmly in place, his eyes questioning. "You look like you've seen a ghost," he said, half-joking.

"Once-removed." At his confused look, I said, "A friend, she looked troubled."

"You can help her." My father stated that like a certainty.

Helping people, solving problems, was a yin and yang kind of thing. Sort of like the push and pull of life. I loved helping people, then I resented them for needing too much. Drawing boundaries was not a tool in my toolbox.

"I'm sorry I cut it rather close," I said, settling myself. A perfunctory peace offering as a young man worked to find a place for the mic on my minimal bodice.

Seated next to my father, with Teddie and Mona stashed somewhere in the back of the crowd, the lights hot and unforgiving, I felt like a captive awaiting interrogation. While I was often the spokesperson for the Babylon, I wasn't used to having the spotlight turned on me, on my personal life. Everyone wanted to see my ring, which I though odd, and an invasion of a sort.

My father chuckled at my discomfort. Tonight, sharp in his tux, his salt-and-pepper hair perfectly groomed, his square jaw thrust slightly out as if begging for a fight, my father looked every inch the hardscrabble hotel magnate he was.

"Throwing me to the wolves, how ungallant of you," I pretended to grouse.

"It's your show, kid. I'm old news."

ACCORDING to those present, I had managed to sidestep the most invasive questions, keeping the interview on topic, and I didn't offend anyone in the process. A clear win in my book, but I didn't remember much of it. Panic derails any ability I might have to remember clearly. The pain was so great, if I remembered it I'd never do it again.

Like love.

Pain and pleasure—emotional triggers separated by perception.

Having Teddie around scratched at the thin scab over the tear in my heart. I wished he'd leave, which, had I chosen to listen, should've told me something. But I didn't.

I paused to speak with a few colleagues and old friends. Even though two million people lived in Vegas, in many ways it still was a small town. The power elite, the casino owners and representatives, the few local professionals peddling regulatory connections or perhaps insight earned from years in the business, and the requisite attorneys to create messes where there were none and the P.R. people to repair the damage—it was a small group. We hung out at the same parties, knew the same people, fought the same battles, often on opposite sides. But if one of us succeeded, Vegas succeeded. So, when the contests were over, the winner declared, we all settled back into being wary combatants always looking to realign allegiances to better our positions. Nerve-wracking and exhausting. The Big Boss was a pro, I an unwilling acolyte, strictly third-string.

At the elevator, I waited, surprised Kimberly wasn't lurking close by. Since we'd talked, I couldn't shake the feeling that she was in some sort of trouble. Silly, I kept telling myself. But I'd seen enough trouble to know how it looked, and how it felt, worming its way inside, coiling, cold and dreadful in the pit of your stomach.

I'd seen it, felt it, when I'd talked to Kimberly.

She didn't show. *Get a grip, Lucky.* As I stepped into the cab of the elevator, I shook off the odd feeling. Okay, I pushed it aside and tried to ignore it.

I had a party to work and a man's arm to grace. So nice for once not to be in charge, to be able to relax and enjoy the fruits of someone else's labor.

Amazingly, no one pushed in with me and I had the elevator to myself as I rode to the top floor. Teddie and Mona had left me to the media wolves, preferring to be early at the party. Mona loved to stake out the best spot in a room. From there she would work the party like a well-seasoned debutante. The thought of Mona with the high-society crowd made me smile. Teddie's parents wore the blue-blood taint, and Mona had put them where they belonged. I wished that kind of moxie, that ability to dissect someone without them realizing it, was genetically transferred, but no such luck. Either that or it had skipped my generation. Either way, I came out on the short end.

Pressing my back to the cool metal at the back of the elevator car, I let it hold some of my weight as the doors slid shut, cocooning me inside.

I used the quiet to breathe, the smooth ride to make a mental transition from being the lead dancer to a member of the corps. As the elevator slowed, I brushed down my dress, arranged my hair, wiped under my eyes, and relaxed ... ready to enjoy the part of the evening where Jean-Charles could showcase his brilliance and I could stay out of the limelight. The doors opened. My luck held—the hall to the restaurant was empty.

Visible through the glass doors, a Van Gogh hung on the wall, spotlighted perfectly, the personification of perfection and elegance of execution—like Jean-Charles and his cuisine. Jean-Charles and I had had a bit of a tiff over the painting—actually, it was the ace up my sleeve that I held until Jean-Charles had capitulated on a few expensive requests. He'd been played, and he'd handled it well.

Somehow we'd managed to be business partners as well as a team in life. I had no idea how we'd dodged the bullets that flew at us from every direction, but we had.

The noise of a party in full swing buffeted me as I pushed through the double glass doors fronting the elegant foyer. A few steps to the right and around a corner, then I stepped into the crowd. I loved seeing the Vegas glitterati turned out for a formal gathering. A quick scan of the room confirmed everyone who was anyone or who thought they were someone was here, including the political contingent. Not the governor, but some Gaming Commission members, as well as the mayor of Las Vegas and a few local politicos. If I remembered correctly, the lieutenant governor had hinted at putting in an appearance. With campaigns ramping up toward next year's elections, he just might. That would make sure we got some press in Carson City and Reno, never a bad thing. Even though the northern part of the state was further from Vegas than L.A., San Diego, and Phoenix, those folks still popped down for a taste of the bright lights.

The men looked brilliant in their fitted formal wear. The women, many of them powerful businesspeople in their own right, dressed to showcase figures and surgery, rather than their innate loveliness and quiet competence that made them truly interesting and set them apart. Superficiality—a Vegas thing that didn't make me proud.

Most days I felt like I waded alone in my quest for something a bit more solid than pretty outsides and relationships measured in hours. As Teddie had likened it, Don Quixote and his windmills, considering this was Vegas, where one could try on a different life for the weekend.

Excited voices competed with lively tunes from a quartet in the corner. Sinatra. *My Way.* Perfect. Mouth-watering aromas drifted from the kitchen each time a waiter pushed through the swinging doors. The tables and chairs had been hidden away, leaving the expanse of wooden floor open for gathering, dancing, and whatever. Bar tables with high stools ringed the floor, except that the far wall of windows overlooking the glory of the Strip was left unobstructed. The dark green walls, the wooden beams overhead, the brass sconces casting a warm glow, and the wrought-iron light fixtures above, each with a tiny flame in glass where a light should be, gave the space the comfort of a French country house, just as Jean-Charles had wanted.

"Food is pleasure," he told me, "to be enjoyed and shared with good friends. I want my customers to feel like friends here."

From the looks of it, he'd accomplished that in spades.

Many turned to greet me as I worked my way across the room. Mona and my father were encircled against the far wall of windows, the multicolored lights of the Strip backlighting them. My former assistant and now the Head of Customer Relations at the Babylon, Miss P, nuzzled her intended, the Beautiful Jeremy Whitlock at a table in the corner. Their wedding was set for Christmas Eve, only a few days from now, it would be the first to be performed at Cielo. Brandy, my assistant, had corralled a few important media-types, presumably stroking their egos as she spoon-fed them the story we'd like to see printed.

Still no Kimberly Cho. I tried not to be worried. But, no matter how hard I tried, I couldn't shake the feeling that tonight was going to be anything but routine.

Waiters passed trays of delectables, which I waved away for the moment. Me? Passing up a feeding opportunity? I was either sick or the apocalypse was imminent. I should wear tight clothes more often. Perhaps one day I'd fit comfortably in them and pigs would fly.

The Babylon's head bartender, Sean, appeared at my elbow with a flute of bubbly. "Schramsberg rosé. Medicinal. Chef's orders."

That I didn't wave away, thanking him with a smile as he stepped back behind the bar. I spied Jean-Charles across the room and began working my way toward him.

The back of a man walking away from me caught my eye. For a brief moment my heart went cold.

Irv Gittings? It couldn't be. An old, old flame, back when I was young and stupid, the thought of him usually had me reaching for a deadly weapon. One of my proudest accomplishments had been to play a large role in seeing him put behind bars a few months ago. There were nights I fell asleep picturing the problems he would be having in the general prison population. He'd tried to frame the Big Boss for murder, and then steal the Babylon from him. A capital offense in my book. And this was Nevada, one of the last outposts of the Wild West, where the death penalty was considered fitting punishment.

The guy easing out of the kitchen and striding away from me was dressed like Irv used to: a white dinner jacket with the crested gold buttons glinting on the sleeve as he raised his hand and a red tie that I could just catch a corner of as he angled away. The cut of the jaw, the arrogance in the exaggerated shoulder-back posture ... I narrowed my eyes. No, not Irv. Shorter, maybe. And hair more pepper and less salt than Irv's. But close enough to be spooky. I got ahold of myself. Irv couldn't be here. He was playing games with the inmates at Indian Springs.

Jean-Charles was engaged in animated conversation with a couple I didn't recognize when I stepped in next to him. Without missing a beat, he snaked an arm around my waist and pulled me close. Pausing, he introduced me. His fiancée! I never tired of hearing it, and, to be honest, it still shocked and delighted me each time he referred to me that way. With the pleasantries over, he picked up the conversation where he'd left off. Parking my head lightly near his, I let the words recede and my thoughts wander.

Just the nearness of him tingled me in places long dormant if not near dead.

Teddie was nowhere to be found. A minor blessing, all things considered. I didn't know why he came anyway. Nothing but bad for him here. He'd left this life. We'd moved on. I'd moved on, despite what my mother said.

The unease from my brief talk with Kimberly Cho had lessened to a low thrum, like distant traffic, my joy eclipsing that niggling feeling that something was off. Of course, being bushwhacked by Mona and Teddie hadn't exactly started my evening down a smooth path. Swaying to the music just a bit, making Jean-Charles grin as he tried to concentrate on the people in front of him, sipping my Champagne, I began to relax into the joy of life.

Big mistake. Tempting Fate had never worked out well for me.

Detective Romeo materialized at my elbow. Nodding to the others, he leaned in close to my ear. "We have a problem."

"Nope," I said, enjoying the happy bubbles that tickled my nose as I took a big sip of my Schramsberg. Then they tickled and warmed all the way down, settling into a nice pillow of contentment somewhere deep inside. "No, Romeo, we do not have a problem."

"Lucky, this is serious. And yes, we have a problem." He tugged on my arm, sloshing a bit of my Champagne. After counting to ten, twice, I gave him my full attention.

Even though spit-and-polished in a slim-cut dark suit and Hermès tie, his sandy hair cut and combed, even his recalcitrant cowlick bending to propriety, he looked a little ragged around the edges. His blue eyes dark, his smile absent, a frown puckering the skin between his eyes, he looked at me as a friend, which doused that warmth I'd been enjoying.

This was personal.

Brandy, my assistant and his girl, squeezed his arm. Her eyes big as saucers, she remained mute. Not good.

As I disengaged from my chef, handing him my glass of Champagne, I gave him a reassuring smile. This was his party, his time to shine, and whatever it was Romeo was dragging me into, I'd keep it to myself.

Yeah, I'm a dreamer.

Weaving through the crowd, I noticed security was guarding the exits. At this point, I doubted anyone wanted to leave as the party was just getting started, so the fact that they couldn't hadn't yet caused any alarm.

"Lucky. Come on." Romeo, one hand on the kitchen door, motioned to me with the other.

I joined him. "What's going on?"

"You are not going to like this."

"You always say that." I followed him into the kitchen.

Two steps inside, I stopped in my tracks. "And you're always right."

Holt Box lay on the floor, a red stain spreading across his chest, soaking his chef's whites. His face, slack. His eyes, sightless. His skin losing the ruddy flush of oxygenated blood.

Teddie stood over the body, holding a knife.

My father pressed to his side, blood on his hands.

CHAPTER TWO

*F*OR a moment time stopped. My heart, too. I tried to process the scene in front of me. Two of Romeo's off-duty guys working security for the party bracketed Teddie and my father and kept else everyone back. Not hard to do, since the kitchen had come to a standstill. Waiters, cooks, and prep staff stood rooted, open-mouthed.

Something burned on the stove. Water bubbled in a large pot, billowing steam. I thought I caught the hiss of butter in a hot pan. The roar of a party reaching a crescendo filtered around the swinging doors as they opened and swung back behind me, then opened again, repeating the cycle.

"I'm assuming he's dead?" I asked Romeo, my voice a squeak of its normal timbre. A stupid question, really, but, with me, hope was the last thing extinguished by reality.

Romeo didn't bother to answer. Instead he started barking orders to the officers who had filled in the tight space behind us, explaining the opening and shutting of the door. Movement restarted; so did my heart, pounding against my chest. My father gave me a tight look and a shrug, which I couldn't interpret. Teddie avoided my eyes, which spoke volumes.

Brandy moved in next to me—a vision in a white sheath, her face needing only the lightest touch of makeup to enhance her natural beauty, her long dark hair pulled back, her face tight, her eyes big.

I leaned down and spoke softly. "Go back to the party; work damage control. Get Miss P onboard. You two know what to do. Tell Jeremy to meet me at the office later. I'm sure he'll be there anyway. This is going to be a shit-storm of epic proportions." Just the thought made me want to run and hide.

A presence loomed behind me emitting a low, feral growl. The hairs stood on the back of my neck. I turned barely in time to catch his coattail as Jean-Charles hurtled by me. "Whoa. Whoa." Digging in my heels, I hung onto him with all I had, using my weight as leverage to stop his considerable momentum. "That's a crime scene. You really don't want to go adding your DNA do you?"

That stopped him, but I held on, unsure as to whether he'd stay stopped. He raked a hand through his hair as he worked for control. A man in whom emotions ran deep, Jean-Charles had a temper, but the level of sheer hatred I saw in his eyes surprised even me. Love and hate, two passions equally strong pulling in opposition, like the moon and the sun.

His mask fell back in place as he turned and glared at me. "I will kill him," he muttered, the tone of his voice leaving no doubt he meant it.

I assumed he meant Teddie. "Not if I get to him first." The level of joy in the anticipation left me breathless. For the first time I understood what the bard meant when he said revenge was best served cold.

And my father standing there, bloodied and a bit unnerved, sobered me up. Seeing him that way ... Dear God, he couldn't have had something to do with this, could he? An irrational thought, of course. My father wasn't prone to killing, at least not that anyone had proven. But, even if he had that proclivity, why would he kill his prize pony? If Teddie was right, Holt Box was worth millions to the Babylon.

Teddie.

"Somebody get that pan off the stove," Jean-Charles shouted, then turned on his heel and pounded through the swinging door so hard it reverberated off the outside wall. If some hapless soul had been on the other side, Jean-Charles's exit would have doubled tonight's body count.

Brandy followed him out, tossing a worried glance back at me over her shoulder as she disappeared.

"Fetch me a plastic bag large enough to hold that knife," Romeo ordered, extending his hand toward the kitchen staff. Someone managed to locate one, and Romeo held it open in front of Teddie.

"Put the knife in here."

Teddie's eyes found mine. He shook his head slightly, then did as Romeo asked. The knife looked old, with a long, narrow blade, the tip angled only on one side. The metal had a green tinge. "I know how it looks," he started.

My father elbowed him. "Wait. You need a lawyer." His eyes found me. "Lucky, will you make the call?"

I nodded, but the trouble was, I had no idea who to call. We had the requisite team of corporate pitbulls, but none of us had a personal defense attorney.

"Your mother will know," he added, as if reading my thoughts.

"Mother!" I'd better find her before the news of this mess did. "Am I free to go?" I asked Romeo, unsure exactly why he wanted me to see the scene in the kitchen—he knew how much I hated dealing with dead people. Holt Box wasn't a personal friend. Hell, he wasn't even an acquaintance. We'd met a couple of times but that had been years ago. I'd met his wife then, too, but could barely remember her. A slip of a thing, practically mute, but stunning. And I had no idea if he'd kept her or tossed her back, or vice versa. As I turned to go, I stopped, then whirled back around, scanning he room and the small crowd gathered there. My eyes searching, cataloguing.

Holt Box. Years ago. When I'd been Irv Gittings' arm candy.

"What is it?" Romeo watched me.

My lips pinched into a thin line as I took my time, taking in every detail. Nothing seemed amiss—well, except for poor Mr. Box. "Let me think on it. I don't know exactly. Not yet."

He nodded like that was a normal thing. *"That's* why I wanted you here," he said, in answer to my unspoken question. Lucky me. "Any idea why somebody would want to kill Holt Box?" He directed the question to me, but his gaze encompassed my little posse of Teddie and the Big Boss.

Nobody said anything.

Even I clammed up despite being privy to a very damning motive Teddie had, including his admission that he'd like to kill Holt Box. Said in the heat of anger, he hadn't meant it literally. At least that's what I chose to believe. It'd come out. But later. Not with an audience who I'm sure was videoing the whole thing on their phones and salivating over being the first to upload it to YouTube. Maybe they'd even cash out with an exclusive to one of the gossip rags.

Satisfied no one felt compelled to blurt out an ill-advised comment, I left them to Romeo. Pushing back through the swinging doors, I knew how Dorothy must've felt going to bed in Kansas and waking up in Oz. On this side, everyone partied on, oblivious to homicide in the kitchen only steps away. I snagged two flutes of Champagne from a passing waiter and slugged one, depositing the empty on his tray. The other I clutched so tight I risked breaking the stem.

My mother held a group of men under her spell. I shouldered my way through until I got her attention—it took squeezing her arm.

"Oh, Lucky. How nice. Perhaps you'd care to weigh in on whether we all should admit that sixteen thousand hookers and nine vice cops is the equivalent to non-enforcement of the archaic law that makes prostitution a crime in Clark County. Wouldn't it be better to legalize what's already happening here? Collect taxes and protect not only the johns but the girls as well?"

Prostitution. A divisive topic even in Vegas, especially in Vegas. From the clenched jaws and hard eyes of some of the men ringing her, Mona was working on a homicide of her own.

All eyes turned in my direction. I felt a drop of sweat trickle down the side of my face. Holding my Champagne, I swiped at the drop with the back of my hand. "Sex. A potent drug, with the argument for legalization equally as unclear." I grabbed Mona's elbow as I forced a smile. "But someone once told me that sex and politics were not topics meant for a cocktail party." I pulled mother away from her fans.

"Lucky, really. If I'm to make any changes in this town, I need to bend some ears, get people to listen."

"Not here. Not right now."

"What's all this about?" Curiously, she didn't adopt her normal huffy tone; in fact, she sounded amused. Maybe her running for office wasn't a bad thing on top of the whole late-in-life twin thing. Dealing with Mother was like handling a two-year-old: keep them busy, keep them tired, and they can't do you any harm.

I held a chair for her at a table off to the side in a corner by the window, then joined her. "It's Father and Teddie." I lowered my voice and made sure no one was listening. Then I explained the scene in the kitchen. "Father said you'd know who to call."

Mona sat like a statue, immobile, her smile fixed by fear. "Of course, Squash Trenton."

I blinked a few times, looking for the punch line. There wasn't one.

"He's in the book." The color drained from Mona's face. "You don't think your father ..."

"Of course not. Knowing him, he was trying to help. Unfortunately, someone had already permanently retired Mr. Box." I could say the words, couldn't admit the possibility. Instead, I gave Mother a pointed look that even she was clever enough to read.

A hand snaked to her throat. "Teddie," she whispered.

I leaned back and drained most of my Champagne as I looked at the Strip through the windows, the lights painting the night sky with bright, fun come-ons promising loose slots, cheap food, and fun. None of that here. "I don't know. Something's not right." I chewed on my lip as I tried to find the way out of the maze without success. Murder didn't mesh with the Teddie I knew. Of course, neither had duplicity and cheating, yet, he'd proven both were part of his skill set.

"I wonder what Teddie has to say for himself?"

THE large atrium-style vestibule of the Clark County Detention Center was virtually empty, which seemed odd for a Saturday night, especially with Christmas so close I could feel it breathing down my neck. Decorated in early institutional, the space held little warmth and hints of fear. A few lonely decorations hung from a string of lights over the intake desk, a token effort in rather bad taste. Even the few plants bent under the weight of hopelessness. My footfalls echoed eerily, like the last walk of the accused.

The evening had taken a bit to unravel, but unravel it had. Questioning by the police has such a chilling effect on frivolity. The police worked through the guests, taking statements, trying to get a handle on who exactly had come and gone from the kitchen. Not an easy task, and it took time. But, with alcohol plentiful and flowing freely, the mood had remained calm and even a bit excited—it's not everyday the average upper-crust denizen was invited to a murder, even in Vegas.

So I was later than I'd thought I'd be. I'm sure Squash Trenton had the meter running while he waited. But, never having met him, I didn't know what kind of man he was; but he was a lawyer, enough said.

I assumed the man chatting up the night staff as he leaned on the counter, his butt toward me, was the lawyer I was looking for. Something he said got a rousing chuckle from his rapt audience.

I cleared my throat.

Squash finished his joke before he rose and turned. Younger than I thought—I figured he'd be my father's contemporary—he lazily took me in, focusing on parts below my chin, which I'd thrust out in challenge.

Red hair, longish, seductively curly. Blue eyes—I was expecting green. Warm, with a laugh lurking. No freckles—they wouldn't dare. A whittled face supported by a strong jaw.

By the time he'd finished his visual assessment, I was more than a little steamed, which I think might have been his point. So I tamped it down. "You done?"

His eyes rose to meet mine. He didn't apologize. "That is some dress."

"So I've been told."

Dressed in jeans so old and soft that, excepting the seams and stitch lines, they were hardly blue anymore, a pair of Topsiders minus the laces, and a T-shirt a tad too tight for his toned and buffed torso, no belt, no socks, no ring, Mr. Trenton didn't seem too upset about being called out on a Saturday night. Nor did he seem to be in much of a hurry.

"Who am I here to see?" he asked, shrugging into his lawyer manner with the ease of donning a comfortable sweater.

Good question. "I guess it depends on who they arrested." Romeo had been hip-deep when I'd left what was left of the party. As I'd calmed Mother, keeping her from clawing her way through the cops to get to her husband, and directed Miss P, Brandy, and every staff member I could corral as to how to handle the mushroom cloud of impending publicity fallout, I'd seen him escorting Teddie and my father out through the back entrance. Jean-Charles had been doing damage control as well. I'd wanted to join him, rush to help, but I had my hands full with my own responsibilities. Such was our life. We both got it, not that we liked it.

I felt so alone. More alone than I'd ever been when on my own. Used to being two, his absence cut deeply.

As Squash grabbed his jacket, suede, worn to old-shoe comfort, with tattered fringe, he gave the officer behind the counter a quick nod. Apparently, that was the magic signal to unlock the doors.

Stepping to the side and sweeping his arm in front of him, he ushered me through the door, then fell into step at my shoulder. I knew where I was going.

Romeo met us at Interrogation Room One, his shoulders slumped under the weight of the murder of a country-music icon. I didn't have the heart to tell him the vultures were just beginning to circle. "Your father is free to go." The young detective, with eyes far older than his years, raked a hand through his hair, standing his cowlick at attention. Then he wiped tired eyes. "God, what a shit-storm."

Romeo had been a bright-eyed kid when we'd first met, not too long ago. I didn't even want to count the days, mere months, I thought. I knew they shouldn't have been sufficient to age him as they had.

"Has Mr. Rothstein been charged with anything?" Squash asked.

"No, not yet." At my look, he hastily added, "Most likely not at all. We'll give the evidence to the DA. He'll decide what to take to the Grand Jury. But I don't see any reason to hold him right now. It's not like he's a huge flight risk."

"And Teddie?"

"He's going to stay at the insistence of the great State of Nevada. Lucky, I don't need to tell you, it looks bad."

"We'll see about that," Squash said.

Romeo grew into his boots as he stared down the attorney. "Take your best shot, counselor. And, for the record, we're on the same team. I want to find who killed Holt Box, perhaps even more than you do, but right now, things are pointing to Mr. Kowalski."

Squash shifted to all-business mode, a tic in his cheek the only hint of the intensity running underneath the surface. "We'll see."

Romeo gestured down the hall. "I've had them bring Teddie into one of the attorney conference rooms. He wants to see you," he said to me.

Teddie, a turtle without his shell in an orange jail jumpsuit, sat in one of the metal chairs cozied up to the metal table. Exposed, unprotected, he stared down at his hands. Romeo had been kind enough to forego the handcuffs. Looking up, he gave me a slight tick-up of one corner of his mouth when I walked in. "I knew you'd come." His smile, if that's what it was, fled when he caught sight of Squash Trenton behind me.

"Who's that?" His voice was flat, lifeless.

"Your lawyer."

Squash held one of the chairs across from Teddie for me, and then eased into the other one. He held out his hand. "Kirk Trenton, folks call me Squash. Mr. Rothstein asked that I offer my services." He cocked an eyebrow at me.

"The Big Boss says he's the best," I confirmed, as I glanced around the room. No camera. No one-way glass.

Teddie looked like he would've laughed if the circumstances were different. "You really want me to hire a lawyer named Squash?"

"If he earned it in the courtroom, then not a bad thing." I tried to adopt a hopeful tone. "How did you earn that nickname?" I asked the lawyer.

He ignored me.

I turned back to Teddie. "The Big Boss would know who's the best." He'd had his share of legal scrapes, although so long ago Squash probably wasn't even a gleam in his mother's eye. But my father kept his finger on the pulse. If anyone would know, he would.

Teddie's face shut down in resignation as he looked at Squash. He didn't want a lawyer, didn't want to need one ... that much was obvious. But nobody promised we'd get what we wanted. "You going to get me out of here?"

"I'll give it a shot," Squash said as he cocked his head and evaluated Teddie with the narrow-eyed savvy of a bettor gauging a racehorse. "First-degree murder isn't normally a bailable offense in Nevada; but you tell me what happened, and I'll find someone who can strong-arm the DA."

That would be me, but I didn't say so. The Clark County District Attorney, Daniel Lovato, known as Lovie to his friends and enemies alike, owed me big-time. Like kept-his-ass-out-of-jail big-time. Nice to hold his marker. And I wasn't completely convinced this was the time to play it. Not yet. And not for Teddie.

Teddie.

Curiously, the anger and the hurt had fled only to be replaced by worry so strong it made my heart race and my breath come in shallow gasps. Not exactly what I'd been hoping for. Teddie could be a self-absorbed ass for sure—he'd proven that on multiple occasions. But a killer? That was taking things to a whole other level, one I tried to picture, but something in my heart wouldn't let me. As if my body was conspiring against my brain, my gut also weighed in, siding with my heart. So heart and gut voted to acquit, but my brain wasn't so sure. Ever at war with myself. Nothing new there. And no winner.

Of course, it didn't matter what my body parts were telling me. Teddie's fate hinged on what we could prove.

"I didn't kill him, for what it's worth." Teddie shivered, his confidence leaking from him like a trickle of water through a dam. With time, it would erode the structure from the inside, until the whole thing crumbled. "Even I know that motive, means, and opportunity usually seal the deal, and I got all three," Teddie finished, staring at his hands as he tapped them softly on the table.

Squash leaned forward. "You've been watching too much television." He turned to me. "I'll have to ask you to go. Anything Teddie says with you here can't be protected under attorney-client privilege."

I rose to do as he ordered, my chair scraping back across the floor with the nerve-grating screech of fingernails on a blackboard.

Teddie reached out and grabbed my wrist, stopping me. "The weapon, Lucky. Whatever it was, it's unique, old. Maybe you can find out where it came from."

As I loomed over him, I wondered how we had come to this. "You didn't carry it in there?"

"No." Emphatic, not a trace of waver in his eyes.

"No one gave it to you?"

"Of course not. I gave you a hug. If I'd had that thing, surely you would've felt it."

He had a point. He'd held me close to him, tight ... I remembered every inch where our bodies connected.

He let go of my wrist, the flare of fight gone. "I've been a fool in so many ways." He waited until I looked at him. "Although I've not been the man you wished I was, I promise you I'm not the man you think I am."

CHAPTER THREE

ROMEO held up the wall in the hallway. He looked up when I stepped out of the room. Hands in his pockets, he used a shoulder to lever himself upright then walked in my direction. "Anything useful?" he asked.

"Says he didn't do it." A chill shivered through me. I readjusted my pashmina, which had slipped from my shoulders to my forearms, wrapping it tighter. "He promised."

Romeo was kind enough not to point out Teddie had made promises before ... and broken them. "Do you believe him?" Romeo had to ask even though he knew me well enough to know I'd give Teddie every possible benefit of the doubt.

"Despite everything, I do." I wondered briefly where my limits were with Teddie. So far I'd bent to the point of breaking. "Did he tell you about the contract the bib boos pulled then gave the venue to Holt Box?"

"Yeah. Not looking good for him. You know that, don't you?" Concern warmed the young detective's voice.

With nothing to say, I shrugged.

Romeo looked pained, like he wished he could run and hide. I knew the feeling. "I want to believe him, too. But that doesn't change what I have to do. You do remember it's not what we think—"

"It's what we can prove," I finished for him as I'd done so many times before. Nothing like bonding over dead bodies to solidify a friendship. "So let's start proving he didn't do it. Any idea why someone would want to kill Holt Box, besides Teddie?"

"I've got my guys digging." Romeo rubbed the back of his neck, then rotated his head as if on a swivel, loosening tension. "Nothing so far."

"Did Teddie tell you why he went into the kitchen? It's not like him to go looking for a fight in such a public venue." That's the thing that struck me the oddest about the whole situation. Teddie hadn't been drunk. No one had goaded him, at least not that I knew about. Bracing someone in the middle of a chaotic kitchen wasn't his style, not that he had a style when it came to murder, but you know what I mean.

"You know the guy the keeps talking about? The one in the white dinner jacket with the gold buttons?" Romeo paused for my nod.

"The Irv Gittings look-alike."

"What?" Romeo said, clearly not following.

"Something about him reminded me of Ol' Irv. I know, weird, but Irv used to dress that way—white dinner jacket, red bow tie. Random thought. Don't mind me." My past haunted me from time to time.

"Teddie said that guy, your Gittings look-alike, came up to him and whispered that somebody wanted to see him in the kitchen."

"Who?"

"You."

I reared back as if he'd slapped me, which he sorta had. "You know I didn't!"

Romeo held up his hand. "Never a doubt. I'm just telling you what Teddie said."

"We need to find the guy in the dinner jacket." I pointed out the obvious—I didn't have anything else; grasping at straws made me feel better.

"No luck so far. I'm hoping Jerry has something on the security tapes."

"What about the murder weapon?" I could picture Teddie telling me to check it out. The memory sent a chill through me. "This is real, isn't it?" I asked Romeo.

He gave me an awkward hug. "We'll figure it out; don't worry." He stepped away and back into detective mode. "The murder weapon is being processed into evidence."

"Can you give me a look?" Raised in the wilds of Pahrump, Nevada in my mother's whorehouse, I knew a few things about weapons.

"Sure. Wait here." He stepped to the door, pulled on the handle and then stepped back, holding it open for someone on the other side.

My father, accompanied by a uniformed officer, stepped through, buttoning the sleeve of a fresh shirt—apparently he'd summoned a Babylon clerk to bring him a new set of clothes. Romeo spoke softly to the officer, who listened, then turned and followed the detective back through the doorway, both of them disappearing and the door closing behind them. My father looked like himself, his cool and control back in place as he reached for a smile. But subtle lines of stress bracketed his mouth and worry clouded his eyes.

"Hell of a thing, this." He gave me a hug, holding me tight. "How's your mother?"

Shorter than me by a head, he still gave good hugs. I didn't linger in his embrace. Fatigue and fear eroded my control. His hug would do the rest if I let it. I needed my strength for a bit longer ... for me ... for Teddie.

I eased away, putting a bit of distance between us. "Holding up. I dropped her by the hotel on my way here. She took some convincing, but I told her she couldn't do anything and would only make things worse. And then there were the babies; she couldn't just run off. I'm sure she's apoplectic by now, though."

"You haven't heard from her?" My father seemed amazed, and with good reason. It was a wonder she hadn't called out the National Guard or something.

Frankly, I was surprised Mona hadn't at least gotten the governor out of bed and down here to fix things. "I turned off my phone."

My father grimaced, anticipating my future. "Long-term pain for short-term gain."

"The worst she can do is kill me."

My father graced me with a smile. "Oh, child, that's far from the worst she can do."

He was learning. We shared a moment of familial bonding.

"What did Teddie tell you happened?" I asked him, since I'd been ushered out of the first-hand telling. Something I understood, but I'd love to watch Teddie's face, look into his eyes while he recounted his evening. Of course, my incredible powers of deduction and intuition had let me down before.

Grabbing my elbow lightly, my father steered me toward the entrance. "Not here."

Those words, acid on the steel of my resolve. My knees grew a little wobbly.

Teddie couldn't have done it—could he?

I eased my elbow free. "I'm waiting for Romeo. He's going to give me a look at the murder weapon. Paolo's outside, if you'd like to wait." Romeo was terrified of my father. Things would go better if he weren't peering over my shoulder making Romeo feel the need to posture, as threatened men are wont to do.

As if my father could read my mind, he nodded and went to the entrance to claim his things. I hoped Paolo had remembered to stock the single malt. If he hadn't, he'd be looking for a new job tomorrow... until the Big Boss found his smile and rehired him.

Romeo didn't leave me cooling my heels for long. "Here it is."

Already logged in to preserve the chain of evidence for trial, the knife was secured in a thick plastic bag. Lighter than it looked, made of metal with a patina dark and old. The blade long and thinner than most knives, the business end had been sharpened to a single edge terminating in a long point. The other end had a small wooden handle.

My eyes met Romeo's. "What is this, any idea? Unusual for a normal blade."

"Old, too, from the looks of it."

I spread the plastic so I could see the metal more clearly. I leaned close. Scratches in the patina on the edges. I pulled my iPhone out of my evening bag. "Mind if I take some photos?"

"Go for it."

I photographed and then recorded the dimensions as best I could. "You know what this looks like? A bayonet."

Romeo pursed his lips. "From an old rifle? How would you know that?"

I looked at the blade. 1859. The year was right. I had a sinking feeling. I flipped the blade over. G.G. I knew it. Gresham Gittings, the patriarch of the Gittings line—his statue atop a horse graced the grounds of some capitol building in the South; I hadn't bothered to remember which one.

"I have a good idea where this came from." My tone indicated I wasn't happy about it, which I wasn't.

Romeo's head jerked up, his pupils dilated. "What?"

Irv Gittings was the eight-hundred-pound gorilla in the room and I was the only one who saw him. "I knew a guy once who had a rifle he was very proud of. A family heirloom, rich with tradition and tales of derring-do to hear him tell it."

"You always have a guy you once knew." Romeo thought that funny; then he sobered.

"Be thankful you didn't have to live through my bad choices." I gave him a look intended to shut him up. "Remember Irv Gittings?"

His eyes bugged. "Shit, really? Isn't he in jail?" A girl shoved out of a tour helicopter and landing in the middle of the Pirate Show in front of TI had brought Romeo and me together. And together we had put Irv Gittings in jail for it.

Which is where I thought he still resided. "As far as I know. But it wouldn't hurt to check." In my gut I knew the answer, but I wasn't ready to accept it or believe it just yet. As if the metal had suddenly grown hot in my hands, I tossed the bayonet back to Romeo. "When you get the crime scene stuff from the coroner, can you forward the photos and measurements to me?"

He caught it and looked at it with renewed enthusiasm— enthusiasm I didn't share. I'd put Irv where he belonged once.

Romeo seemed to be thinking the same thing. When his eyes met mine, they were dark and angry, his smile a memory. "You got it."

"And when the techs finish with the crime scene?" I didn't need to elaborate. We'd worked together long enough for a bit of verbal shorthand.

"The full report, you got it." He turned to go, then paused. "And what are you going to do?"

"With Irv in jail, his hotel gone, and his apartment and hotel foreclosed on, I'm going to try to figure out what happened to his gun collection, who bought it, where it went."

"And how this," Romeo held up the bayonet, "could've ended up buried in Holt Box's stomach."

"Precisely. And I want you to figure out who other than Teddie might've wanted Holt Box dead."

"The wife might be able to help with that."

"A good place to start. But in the meantime, let's shake some trees and see what falls out. Maybe his manager, his P.R. person."

"His wife has been his manager for years. His P.R. firm is in L.A. A gal by the name of Kimberly Cho handles his account."

I grabbed his arm. "She was the one at the party."

"What one at the party?" Romeo clearly wasn't following.

"She came up to me in the lobby before my interview. She wanted to talk to me. She was scared."

"What did she want to talk about?"

"I don't exactly. She warned me to be careful."

"About what?"

"A man. " I remembered her expression, her warning.

"Which man?"

"I don't know. She said he was someone she'd known from before." I tried to remember her exact words. "She told me to be careful. That's all." I felt a horrible sinking feeling, that disappointment in myself. "I didn't have the time to talk right then. She was going to catch me after the interview, but she never showed."

"How do you know her?"

"She handles PR for a lot of folks, big names. She's doing some work for us in Macau."

Romeo pulled out his pad and flipped through the pages, shaking his head. "She wasn't at the party." His eyes met mine. "Or she left before talking with anyone at Metro. How do you know her?"

"The Big Boss has a large operation in Macau that is scheduled to come on line next year. The thing has been a morass of cultural clashes and palm greasing. Kimberly knows her way around Macau, knows the right people to get things done. She's been incredibly helpful."

Romeo slowly folded his notebook closed, stuffing it back in his pocket. Lost in thought, it took him three tries. "Do you have any idea where she might have gone?"

I thought for a moment. "Yes, I think I might."

PAOLO waited nervously by the car. He seemed unscathed as he opened the back door and ushered me inside, so he must've remembered the single malt. My father lounged, head back, legs extended in front of him, a crystal double old-fashion glass cradled in both hands on his lap. "What do you think?" he asked, knowing I had no more answers than he did, perhaps fewer.

"I'm trying not to." I pointed at the glass in his hands. "Pour me one of those."

He handed me his, then leaned forward to pour another.

"Tell me what Teddie said," I asked, as I popped off my shoes—even the flats killed my feet.

My father raised the privacy window and made sure the intercom was off, as Paolo settled behind the wheel. His Old Spice cologne filled the small space.

Teddie wore Old Spice.

Fuck.

I sucked down half the Scotch. It burned its way down, then exploded white-hot in my belly, but it couldn't dissipate the chill of dread permeating deep to my bones.

My father didn't speak right away. I didn't know whether that was good or bad, but I knew not to press. Paolo eased the big car out of the parking lot, leaving the darkness behind as he aimed the machine toward the bright lights of the Strip.

"I've been going over and over the whole sequence of events, and I just can't make sense of it," my father began, his voice husky, roughed up by the grit of emotion and the medicinal sting of the Scotch.

Moving down in the seat, pressed by the weight of worry, I lay my head back and closed my eyes, letting his story unfold over me.

"Teddie found me pretty quick. He'd been into the booze; I could smell it on him. But he appeared himself, under control, modulated, so I figured the liquor was just enough to put a mouth on him and give him a bit too much courage. I didn't think he'd do anything stupid."

"Stupid? You mean like kill someone?" I didn't try to hide the snark. Had my father been a bit more aware, all of this could've been avoided. Of course, put in his position, would any of us have thought Teddie would kill? "You think you know somebody ..."

My father shot me a look—I didn't have to see it; I could feel it. Father-daughter connections. Aren't they wonderful?

"I'll be quiet, let you finish."

"How did you ... ?" He slurped from his glass. "Never mind. You and your mother terrify me sometimes. Anyway, as I was saying, Teddie clearly wanted to chew on me over the whole Holt Box thing. We both knew I was within the letter of the contract, but I didn't think it would hurt to give him a shot at me, make him feel better."

Although I found fault in his logic, it still shouldn't have led to murder. "By the way, what you did ... the contract thing? It doesn't make me proud."

"It was legal," my father said, as if hiding behind the law could clear one's conscience.

I didn't need to tell him that was a dead-end. "You dangled a carrot, knowing Teddie would do anything to get it. You had all the power. He's a singer, not a tough guy. And just because it's legal doesn't make it right."

His sigh spoke volumes. "No, it doesn't. If it helps, I'm not proud of myself either. In some way I must've been punishing him. Clearly, I didn't understand that at the time."

"Punishing him? For what he did to me? Don't make this my fault."

"Well, *I'm* not the one on trial here." He threw the words at me.

"But, curiously, in all of this, you're the one feeling guilty." I thought about sipping more Scotch, but that meant I'd have to raise my head, and open my eyes, and that would make all of this real. "Anyway, Teddie's story?"

"I let him have his say, about everything: the contract, you, me. The guy unloaded. He was angry, sure, but in control. I put him off. Told him I didn't have anything to do with his personal life ... that was between you two."

"Pretty much a lie."

My father paused. I could feel the heat of his anger spike, but he didn't argue. "As to the contract, I gave him the old, tired story about trying to find a solution, an alternative."

Part of me wanted to hear what Teddie'd had to say about me, but the part of me that didn't won. "What did he say to that?"

"He wasn't interested. Said he had another gig lined up."

My heart sank. His tour. He was going back on tour. Now that horse had been shot out from under him.

"And then?"

"Then Benton shouldered in. You know Benton?"

"Head of the Gaming Commission?"

"Yeah. He wanted to bend my ear about putting some tables and machines in Cielo. I told him he was talking to the wrong person."

Vegas, still a good ol' boy town, even if it wasn't still run by the wiseguys.

"We'd only chatted for a few minutes. Over his shoulder I saw Teddie making for the kitchen. It took me a minute to put together exactly what he meant to do."

"And what was that?"

"There were two men in there he probably hated equally. I wasn't sure which one he might be after, but I thought it wise I take a look." His voice was taut with emotion when he said, "You have to believe me. I had no idea he'd try to kill one of them."

"I wouldn't have jumped to that conclusion either."

That seemed to placate my father; his voice settled. "I excused myself from my conversation, and I followed him." The ice clinked in his glass as he took another hit. "By the time I pushed through the door, Holt Box was slumped in Teddie's arms."

"What was Teddie doing?"

"Shouting for help."

"No one had noticed anything?"

"The kitchen was on overdrive. Everyone was busy with their own tasks, in their own world."

I knew exactly how it would be. His reputation on the line with each dish, Jean-Charles was a tyrant in the kitchen. His staff, highly trained and equally anal-retentive when it came to quality, would've been lost in their perfectly choreographed dance, their own piece of the symphony. "Jean-Charles didn't miss his new sous chef?"

"Jean-Charles wasn't in the kitchen. His executive chef was. What's his name?"

"Rinaldo."

"Yes, Rinaldo was running the show while his boss worked the room."

"Did you notice anything else, anyone standing around watching?"

"Things sort of got crazy after that. Teddie did say there was a man in a white dinner jacket, which I though odd and dismissed. Everybody in the kitchen wore a white coat of some kind. But Teddie was very insistent."

"Did he happen to mention the dinner jacket had gold buttons?"

My father's sharp intake of breath told me he had. "How did you know?"

My blood froze. "I saw the guy, just from the back. In a way he reminded me of Irv Gittings."

My father choked, then spluttered and coughed. Scotch going down the wrong pipe was painful. I sat up, then pounded him on the back, while he tried to suck in some air. Finally, he got control. Pulling a handkerchief out of his inside jacket pocket, he dabbed at his eyes.

"Are you okay?"

He nodded. Then, when his eyes caught mine, he slowly shook his head. "Irv Gittings got out of jail two days ago."

"What?" Air rushed out of me as If I'd been sucker-punched, which I sorta had. Blindsided more like. But a few pieces of the puzzle seemed to be lining up. Knowing Irv, I knew enough to reserve judgment. He was full of surprises and quite good at the sleight of hand, leaving someone else to shoulder the blame for what he did.

I bolted the rest of my Scotch, bringing tears to my eyes. "And you didn't tell me because?"

"Your mother and I thought it best not to spoil the party, the opening, all of that. Besides, you haven't really been all that available."

He knew I'd come like a dog when he called. Padding a weak

argument just made it look even weaker. But, Irv was out of jail; somehow I'd missed that tidbit, and beating my father over the head with it wouldn't help spring Teddie or find the real killer.

I'd start with Irv Gittings.

A protective undercurrent crept into my father's tone. A bit late, but nobody asked me. "You need to be careful. Irv certainly could have you in his sights."

As analogies went, that one was pretty spot-on. "Now you tell me?"

"He got out on a technicality with the help of a dirty judge. Daniel was apoplectic. We both thought he'd keep his nose clean, at least for awhile." Daniel, as in Lovato, the District Attorney. I'd known him all my life and still wasn't sure which side of the fence he preferred. Guess that's the way it goes with attorneys who turn to politics.

Irv was out. I needed to talk to Daniel about that. But right, now, there was nothing I could do about it, so I dropped it. "Okay, you walked into the kitchen, saw Teddie holding Holt Box. And what happened next?"

"I rushed to help. When we lowered Box to the floor, the knife came out in Teddie's hand. There was blood everywhere. Box was already gone." My father sounded relieved to be talking about homicide rather than Irv Gittings. I got that—Irv was a far bigger problem. I closed my eyes and assumed my previous position, head back and trying not to think about past mistakes. "How much blood?"

"You saw. His shirt was soaked. Blood had run all over his hands and forearms. It had pooled on the floor."

"If Teddie had just stabbed him ... " I let the thought hang. My father didn't need to be led by the nose.

But it took him a beat or two longer than I expected. "There wouldn't have been that much blood. At least I don't think there could've been, even if the knife had hit something vital."

A positive idea to hang my hope on. "That's something we can take up with the coroner."

"Did you call Squash?"

"Yeah, he's on the case."

"Then leave this up to him. You're not thinking right about

Teddie and all this. It would be best if you left it alone. You could screw this up rather than make it better."

That brought me upright; my eyes wide open as they clapped on my father, pinning him in my glare. "I am so sick and tired of you and Mother telling me what I'm not thinking right about." I raised my voice enough that Paolo shot a big-eyed glance my way in the rearview mirror. I withered him with a glare until he focused on his driving. "I will not let a friend rot in jail because I did nothing."

"You think you're better than the police?"

"Please, we're talking about Metro. And you and I both know I can come through in a pinch."

I'd saved my father's ass a time or two. He was smart enough to shut up.

"And, if you think about it, had you and Mother not meddled in my life in the first place, perhaps none of this would've happened."

"I see your point." Curiously, my father didn't sound like he was patronizing me.

"Great. You two learn a lesson, and Teddie pays the price."

I scrolled through my contacts in my phone, found the one I wanted, and dialed.

Dane answered on the first ring.

"I've got something I need you to do."

CHAPTER FOUR

EVEN though it was pushing toward 10 p.m., my office was a beehive of activity, everyone at their battle stations when I pushed through the doors. Animated chatter filled the air. Red lights on the phone blinking as callers held. All the lines were busy. Miss P, sitting at her former desk in the front office, held the phone against her ear with a shoulder. She gave me a quick glance.

I waited until she had finished, then handed her my phone. "I turned it off. Would you mind?"

She grabbed it, then pressed the "on" button. "We're already getting calls from Europe, death threats from Texas, and sobbing females unable to talk. And it's just beginning."

"It is juicy stuff. I can only imagine the lies they will fabricate, if that's not redundant." My heart hurt for Teddie. The media would mercilessly tear into every corner of his life, only to publish half-truths and innuendo.

"Bad news sells." Miss P stopped for a moment. "News." She gave a derisive little laugh and a shake of her head.

I knew what she was thinking—what passes for news these days in truth has little resemblance. "Gossip sells. The more salacious, the more tawdry, the better. Doesn't matter if it's true or not." Some wiseacre once said, "All publicity is good publicity. He was either stupid or way too optimistic. I'm sure Teddie would gladly trade places. Want me to take a phone?"

"We're just giving them all the standard line: we can't say anything as it is an ongoing investigation. So far, we've been able to keep up. Jeremy's waiting in your office."

"Why don't we just automate the answering with a recording to that effect?"

"Then those who need our help couldn't get through."

I looked at all the lines lit up and blinking. "They can't now."

I turned to go. A thought stopped me mid-stride. "The Shooter Show, how's that going? Any problems?"

One of the world's largest gun shows currently occupied most of the larger venues in town, with the aficionados filling most of the rooms. Regardless of how one felt about gun ownership, the annual convention was a huge draw and a financial boon to the city. The Babylon hosted the sales pavilion and the antique portion of the show.

Miss P gave me her full attention. "No complaints that I know of. Why?"

"Tomorrow is opening day?"

"Yes. We have it under control." She gave me a measuring look. "And how about you? The holiday party for the whales? Need any help?"

"On my list of things to put finishing touches on today. We'll be ready. Thankfully, we have a couple of days—I'm not at the top of my game." Every year we had a holiday celebration for our whales, our bettors that kept one hundred million on deposit with the house to fund their gaming activities. We had forty. Our operation in Macau, despite undergoing a major expansion, had four hundred. It didn't take a crystal ball to see where our corporate energies needed to be applied, but that was a continuing discussion with the Big Boss. He wanted me to spend some time overseeing operations there. I didn't.

"And," Miss P said, stopping me as I turned toward my office, "you are the honorary starter for the Elf Run on Christmas Eve morning. Do you want me to cancel?"

A citywide event eagerly anticipated by locals and holiday visitors alike. Christmas in Vegas normally didn't attract a huge crowd; we weren't exactly family-friendly. Christmas was usually seen as just a blip in the run-up to New Year's debauchery. Except for the Elf Run. "To be honest, I had forgotten. Don't cancel. I would say something stupid here like life goes on, but even I'm not that banal, despite my cliché addiction." Clearly, even though charging around at full-throttle, I was unable to keep all the plates spinning.

"Thank you for that."

"I'm hurt." The banter helped me find true north again. Life had been wobbling off track, and I was glad to have my feet pointed down the trail. Teddie's problems had solutions. We just had to find them. "What time is the race again?" I cringed, awaiting the answer.

"Race starts promptly at seven. They ask that you be there by 6:30."

"A.M.?" Mornings were not my friend. And lately I'd noticed a profound immunity to caffeine. The more I relied on it, the less effective it was—like my mother. "Why do people want to run? And at such an ungodly hour?"

"For fun and health."

"Aren't we supposed to drink for our health?"

"Milk."

I hated milk. "I'll keep my vices. They make me happy, and happiness is good for my health." Before she could shoot a hole in my justifications, I retreated. Out of habit, I started toward my old office, now Miss P's, then rerouted. With her at her old desk out front, she'd thrown me off. Perhaps we both were having a tough time adjusting to the new musical offices thing. Old habits.

My new office looked a lot like my old office, just larger, in a different location, and still under construction. I'd gotten so used to the two-guys-with-one-hammer crew who came each day to entertain me with their lackluster finish-out efforts and creative excuses that I wouldn't know what to do when they actually finished. Adoption was a possibility. That or find them a stand-up gig.

My burled walnut desk anchored the room, and me—my ship on the stormy seas. Two chairs fronted it. The walls were bare but for some paint splotches, as I tried to decide which color suited me. A difficult proposition as my choice changed with my mood. And right now, I was favoring something dark and dismal.

Jeremy, his tux wrinkled, his tie undone, lay on my couch, one arm across his eyes. I took a moment to enjoy the view. Over six-feet of well-muscled Aussie with gold-flecked eyes and wavy brown hair, the Beautiful Mr. Whitlock was indeed serious eye-candy. And, once he trotted out that delectable accent, truly swoon-worthy. The fact that he loved Miss P beyond measure, a woman fifteen years his senior at that, put his perfect-male score off the charts. She was one lucky gal.

My desk chair squeaked as I sat, then toed-open a lower drawer, put my feet on it, and leaned back.

Jeremy's body twitched, the only hint he was aware of my presence. "You okay?" he asked.

"Been better, thanks." I reached for my version of worry beads, a paperweight on the corner of my desk. Lucite encasing a golden cockroach, it had been a gift from the hotel staff after I'd dealt with a particularly odious guest intent on loosing thousands of the bugs.

"What can I do to help?" Jeremy eased his legs around, putting his feet on the floor as he levered himself to a seated position, then speared me with those eyes as he flashed his dimples. His wavy hair mussed from the impromptu nap begged to have fingers run through it.

Good thing I was genetically hard-wired to not go play in someone else's sandbox, but I had no idea how he fended off the hordes of less-principled women.

I motioned him closer, then I remembered I needed my phone. I buzzed Miss P.

"On my way with your phone."

I'd quit asking her long ago how she could anticipate my every need, but it still creeped me out a bit. Breezing through the doorway, a cloud of chiffon and a fresh floral scent, she stopped next to the desk. "Here you go." She held out my phone. "Twenty messages from your mother. I assume by now she is either dead or has found someone else to shoot. Several from a few of the reporters who have your personal number. And an odd one."

"Odd? How so?" I took my phone, not so sure I wanted it.

"A strange sort of chuckle, then a hang-up."

"Male or female?"

"Male. I left the message on there. Maybe you can recognize the voice."

Jeremy and Miss P huddled closer as I pressed play.

Short, low, with a hint of madness, the chuckle was worthy of a Halloween spook house, giving me goose bumps.

"You recognize him?" Miss P asked, angling a look at me over the top of her cheaters.

"Can't be sure. But did you know Irv Gittings was released from prison a few days ago?"

Shocked looks from both of them answered that question.

"Pretty light sentence for murder," Jeremy said.

"Apparently, he got out on a technicality. And something about a judge on the take. I plan to take it all up with the D.A."

"Wish I could be a fly on that wall," Miss P mumbled, as she tore the top sticky note off the stack on my desk. I handed her a pen. "You'll want to see him first thing?" She didn't even pretend she expected an answer as she made a note to herself.

"Don't bother. Tomorrow is Sunday. I know where to find him."

She tore off the sheet of paper she'd been scribbling on, wadded it up, and launched it across the room at the trashcan. A swish.

I focused on Jeremy. "Find him. Find Irv Gittings."

"Anything to go on?"

"Start with the phone number from the message." I scribbled it on a notepad, tore off the sheet, and handed it to him. I stared into the paperweight, as if looking into a crystal ball, hoping to divine answers. No such luck. "His trail went cold when he became a ward of the state. My bet would be to start with known associates, that sort of thing, but you're the pro."

"I'll run the number, but I'd be willing to bet that's a burner phone, a dead-end. But forward me a copy of the message. I'll see if I can pull anything that might help from the tape. I'll try the facial recognition software, too. Any security tapes from Cielo tonight?"

I grimaced; my stomach hurt. High-octane Scotch on raw flesh with no food to protect it. "Security is minimal there right now. We're not open yet. Still working out the kinks in the system, but ask Jerry what he has." The Head of Security at the Babylon, Jerry had been helping me refine the security system at Cielo. With no gaming on the premises, Cielo's security wasn't as sophisticated or refined as the system at the Babylon, but maybe he had something that might help. "Maybe you could get a bead on Kimberly Cho as well." I gave him the skinny of our disappearing P.R. agent.

Jeremy stood. Stepping behind his chair, he held the back in both hands. "What about the prison? Maybe he said something to a cellmate."

"I'll take care of that. I am at the top of Ol' Irv's hit list. Maybe somebody might like to tell me how much he hated me and what he planned to do about it."

SATURDAY night, the energy level at the Babylon at full-throttle, I decided to swing by Security to see if I could catch Jerry. The man worked almost as much as I did, so the odds were good. I fielded a couple of texts from Jean-Charles. Having someone check on me was a new thing—I think I liked it. No, I did like it; it just took some getting used to. We'd meet back at his restaurant when I'd finished with Jerry, if I found him.

Jerry kept the main room in Security dark, so after stepping inside, I needed a moment for my eyes to adjust. Monitors tic-tac-toed the far wall, each showing different views of the gaming tables: the players, the dealers, and a bird's-eye view where experts could watch the hands dealt and the player's movements, looking for a card drawn from the bottom or one pulled from a sleeve and all the more subtle tricks I didn't want to know about or think of. Other clusters of monitors huddled in groupings around the large room, each showing different parts of the hotel and each monitored by one staff member. Safety, not only for the house's money but also for those who donated to the cause, was a top priority.

My luck held. Jerry, his back to me, his hands clasped behind him, his feet spread, watched the ever-changing landscapes in front of him. He tossed me a sideways glance as I stepped in beside him. "Man, bad stuff tonight." The stale smell of cigarettes clung to him, which always intrigued me, given the Big Boss had turned every square inch of the hotel into a non-smoking environment. Scratch that—the great State of Nevada, with local assistance, had pulled off that bit of illogic. Like hotdogs and mustard, gambling without smoking just wasn't the full experience. The men groused, but the ladies in their Dolce and Chanel No. 5 on the way to a fancy evening loved the new, perfumed Vegas. I still straddled the fence.

Jerry and I had worked together so long we were family. When I'd had problems with the Big Boss, I'd turned to Jerry. When Teddie had taken a powder, Jerry had been the one to help me put my pieces back together. Tall and thin with dark skin, a bald pate that he shaved and waxed, a bright, infrequent smile and tired written all over him, Jerry still wore yesterday's suit and today's problems. He ran a hand over his head—a habit ingrained long before the hair had departed.

"They ever let you go home?" I nudged him with a shoulder.

"No reason to; wife's out of town."

"And you decided to wallow in a vice or two while she's gone?"

"That bad?"

"Eau de Ashtray. Not sure you want to go hang with my mother. She'll make you wish those cancer sticks had already killed you." I didn't understand, in light of all we knew, why people kept smoking. Of course, I often overindulged my affinity for Wild Turkey, so crawling up on a soapbox would subject me to the same scrutiny. Not a good plan, considering my collection of vices was as big as my backside.

Jerry took the last pull on the cigarette he'd been holding at his side, then mashed it out in his hand. "I avoid your mother at all costs."

I cringed. "Wise man. Doesn't that hurt?"

He gave me a look. "What? Avoiding your mother?"

People and their habits—he really didn't know. "Never mind." I watched the flickering images on the array of screens. Even on a Saturday night inching toward Sunday morning, folks were drinking and letting their bets ride. "Did Romeo find you?"

"Oh, yeah. He's been calling me every ten minutes or so." As if on cue, Jerry's phone at his hip rang. He tilted it up, looked at the number, then showed it to me before directing the call to voicemail. "See?"

"It's Teddie's ass on the line." A hard thought to swallow, even harder to say. "Sorta ups the ante."

"Yeah." Jerry switched to all business. "I had a few cameras working at Cielo. We're going through the tapes now. Got a hit on the guy in the white dinner jacket with a red bow tie and gold buttons. A short clip in the lobby. You want to see it?"

My heart tripped, then raced. "Seriously?"

"Veronica," he called. One of his techs looked up, her face

painted an interesting cascade of colors by the screen in front of her. "Cue up the feed and roll it to my office."

A small cubicle defined by walls of glass on three sides, so Jerry could have privacy and still monitor his fiefdom, Jerry's office was barely large enough for both of us and his desk, too. He turned the monitor around so we both could see. I leaned against the wall, my feet thankful for the easing of their load. My job took its toll. If I didn't change my ways, I'd work myself into a motorized scooter and a permanent ticket to rehab.

A few blinks and sputters, then the screen leapt to life. The lobby of Cielo, people milling.

"There." Jerry pointed to a white splotch. A man, half-hidden by a potted palm. He was watching someone. I followed the direction of his gaze.

He was watching me. "Shit."

He took a phone call, standing there a minute longer. The other people in the frame moved, greeting friends, collecting for the interview I'd given, or filtering toward the elevators. Everyone looked happy, normal. Except one.

Kimberly Cho.

She stared at the man in the white jacket and looked as if she'd seen a ghost.

The man terminated his call, then looked up at the camera with a chilling smile, keeping half of his face hidden. The feed ended, capturing him in freeze-frame.

I stared at the image. An Asian version of Irv Gittings, especially dressed as Irv always had. I could see why I thought he might have been that nightmare from the past when I first glimpsed him. Dark hair slicked back. A simian brow, small eyes and a mean mouth above a weak chin. "What about the cameras in the service area?"

Jerry gave a hacking, phlegmy cough.

"You're killing yourself."

He doubled over for a moment, fighting for breath. The spasms passed. His eyes teared as he looked at me. "I know."

I wondered what I could say that would make him hear. At a loss, I gave up. "The service area cameras?"

"Not working. That feed went down just as the crowd was

gathering. Still not sure what happened."

I pointed to the image now frozen on the screen. "He happened."

"You want a shot of him, I'm guessing." Jerry fingered a pack of cigarettes, then flicked them aside. "It's pretty blurry and only a half-face shot. Not going to be much help."

"I'd really like a shot *at* him, but for now, one *of* him will have to do."

CHAPTER FIVE

NEWS of a celebrity murder travels fast. The Holt Box faithful were beginning to gather even though we'd almost turned the corner into a new day. Candles, flowers, cards, stuffed animals ... expressions of grief clustered to the side of the main entrance of Cielo. The police had cordoned off the drive and manned a checkpoint, checking people in and out. A serious-faced youngster playing dress-up as a Metro cop leaned over to peer inside—no privacy with the top down. "May I help you?"

"Lucky O'Toole, I own this place. Well along with several banks and a hedge fund, but you get my drift."

"Some identification, please."

"You really think some bad guy is going to roll up here in a fire-engine red with the top down?" I'd let Paolo go home at the end of his shift and had borrowed a car from the Ferrari dealership in the hotel.

"You'd be surprised."

"And discouraged," I muttered as I dug through my Birkin, an extravagant gift from the Big Boss. I'd abandoned my evening purse— a small showpiece short on functionality. "Everything important seems to hide at the bottom." My hand brushed the butt of my Glock that I'd tossed in at the last minute. My father told me never to carry a gun unless I was ready to use it. I was ready and wishful.

The cop seemed nonplussed by my explanation and steadfast in his demand. A few curious Holt Box devotees, as identified by their T-shirts in garish hot pink and gold, took an interest and wandered over. One guy snapped a few photos, doing little to help my abysmal mood. If tonight got any worse, I would hop the next jet to anywhere

... if only I could find my credit card and ID.

My hand closed around my wallet. "Aha!" I shouted as if I'd discovered the pot of gold at the end of the rainbow. But, alas, my luck had run out some time ago, and with no leprechauns in sight, I doubted that would change anytime soon.

The cop waved me through.

This time, when I walked through the lobby of Cielo, it had lost its energy. The party was over. The police clustered in the corner comparing notes. Romeo was back, listening, occasionally asking a question as he jotted in his notebook. A couple of security guys seemed to be on the hot seat.

Romeo stepped away from the group after silencing the questioning so we could talk and he wouldn't miss anything. We met under the Chihuly chandelier of bright glass swirls in the center of the lobby.

This night so far had added years to his face. Still, he looked all of twelve. "Man, I am so dogged. Getting too old for this," he announced, a beleaguered pro caught in the vise.

"Barking up the wrong tree, kid. I've got empathy, but running real short on sympathy."

"This totally sucks."

I refused to be sucked into despondency. If I didn't keep steering the boat through the storm, I'd be swamped by a wave and sink to the bottom. "You got anything?"

He closed his eyes and pinched the bridge of his nose. "Nobody saw Teddie's white-coated guy."

"I did."

His eyes snapped open, and his fatigue vanished. "Why didn't you say that before?"

"I did. Told you he reminded me of Irv Gittings. Remember?"

"Yeah, that's right. Man, this case has me chasing my tail." He gave me a worried, distracted look.

I knew the feeling. *Teddie.*

"Anything to go on other than you saw him?" Romeo asked, trying to do his job. "Could you recognize him again?"

"I only caught him from the back, with a slight profile. I'm not sure I could recognize my own father if that was the only view I got."

Romeo deflated.

"But there is a bright spot."

Romeo didn't rise to the bait. He was really taking this Teddie thing personally.

"Kid, if we find the real killer, then Teddie's home free."

"But what if ... ?"

"No what-ifs." I pressed his copy of the photo Jerry had given me into his hand. "Start here. This is the guy we're looking for."

Romeo focused on the photo. "Not a very good photo. It almost seems like he knew exactly what he was doing, giving us something but not enough."

"Like maybe he's in the system?"

Romeo shrugged. "You know him?"

"No. But I just can't shake the feeling he's dressed like that for a reason." I didn't mention Kimberly Cho. I needed to find her first.

"Any luck on tracking down the gun?" Romeo gave me his best wishful-thinking look.

My face snapped into a frown, I could feel it crushing my joie de vivre, assuming I had any left. "It's heading toward midnight on a Saturday night in Vegas. What do you think?"

"Short of paying Mr. Gittings a visit, the answer would be no?"

"And, while many of my choices are suspect, I'm not foolish enough to go charging into Irv's lair, assuming I knew where he was hanging his hat, with nothing to go on other than a curious coincidence and armed with nothing but my sharp sword of sarcasm."

"So, you still think this could be personal?" Then what I'd said seemed to penetrate Romeo's haze of fatigue. "Isn't Ol' Irv in jail?" Irv always referred to himself in the third person, a very irritating habit, one of his many.

"Murder is always personal, kid. The question is personal to whom." I rooted in my purse for my phone. "Guess you didn't know Irv Gittings was sprung a few days ago? Some legal technicality."

The tip of Romeo's pencil broke.

"I'll take that as a no. Something about the guy in the white dinner jacket reminded me of Irv. Can't put my finger on it. Irv had a dinner jacket like that, monogrammed gold buttons. And he loved red bow ties." The whole idea that Irv could be behind Holt Box's murder seemed a bit out there. If he was after me, why didn't he just kill Teddie or the Big Boss? Now, here I go, making myself truly terrified rather than just marginally so. "Maybe I'm seeing monsters where there are none."

Romeo fished another pencil out of his pocket. "Murder is pretty monstrous."

"All I know is, somebody's playing games." I palmed my phone between us. "Not sure if this is related to the murder, but it's worth checking out." I played the message for him.

"Creepy." He jotted down the number.

"And awfully coincidental." I turned my phone off, then dropped it in my purse. "I've got Jeremy trying to trace it."

"Once again, you are at the vortex of a shit-storm." Romeo said it with a resigned groan.

"It's a gift."

"I'm assuming you didn't call him back."

I pretended to be offended. "What, and give him the satisfaction?"

"Good. We'll reach out when we're ready."

"And the same rules, okay?" I touched him lightly on the arm as he glanced over his shoulder at the men who were waiting.

My touch brought him back. Romeo gave me a grin filled with energy. "Same rules. You get to shoot him."

His flush of energy arced between us, jump-starting hope. We were on the hunt.

"Any preliminary from the coroner?"

"Stab wound killed him."

"I'm shocked."

He smiled, a cat playing with a mouse. "There was a blood trail. Stabbing occurred around the corner from where he died. Near the walk-in refrigerator."

"Teddie's in the clear?" I pressed, trying to tame my hope. Nothing this bad was ever that easy to fix.

Romeo confirmed my cynicism. "You know how this is going to go down. The media, all the hype, we'll have to take extra care that we are not only exploring every possibility, but that we actually look like we're doing exactly that. The world will be watching. It's been what, a couple of hours? I'm sure you saw them out there—the sharks are already circling."

"Extra scrutiny." I knew the drill. That weight was on my shoulders, too, but unlike Romeo, I was used to the load. "Like running the gauntlet, kid, there is an end."

"If they don't kill you before you get there."

"There is that." Although it'd be easy to jump on the Irv Gittings' bandwagon and go tilt at another windmill, there was another angle. "Anything on Holt Box? Any reason why someone would want to kill him?"

"The wife is in Texas. The local Mounties notified her. She'll be here tomorrow. Maybe she can shed some light."

"Will she be staying at her husband's place in the Kasbah at the Babylon? I think he had Bungalow 7."

"That's what I've been told. Want to be in on the questioning? You always seem to have a lighter hand than I do."

"Need you ask?"

Romeo returned to his men. He seemed to take my confidence with him, so I took a moment to let things settle, absorbing some of the tranquility I'd built into the lobby.

My hotel. Heady and terrifying, a high-octane mix of emotions that kept me putting out fires before they lit me up. Sleep was hard to come by; alcohol and caffeine were my drugs of necessity. A limited solution, but for now it kept the lid on.

The opening only ten days away, we were booked solid for the holidays and beyond. Casinos with their filtered air and carefully controlled party vibe, windowless rooms, and money-driven excesses weren't everyone's idea of a vacation. I was banking on the folks who wanted to separate pleasure from table play. And, to be honest, Vegas had cut its teeth catering to men with the gambling, the sportsbooks and the strip clubs and topless revues for the tame crowd, the full-monty strip joints for the rowdier bunch. Time to even that playing field. Women made up an ever-increasing percentage of Vegas visitors. And it was long past time to cater to their sensibilities.

Turning in a full circle, I savored the warm tile floor laced with wood, the blown-glass light fixtures in all the colors of the rainbow, the art, modern, but not too, bright and lively, gracing the beige walls. Even though it was costly, I went with a wallpaper of grasscloth. Desks clustered on thick rugs in oranges and greens, serving as a personal reception area. The concierge desks were opposite reception. The far wall opened into a casual piano bar and restaurant simply called the Lobby Bar. Long planters of bamboo and other grasses I didn't know the names of separated the area into smaller conversation areas filled with comfortable couches and chairs clustered around large square tables with marble tops. The entrance to the Spa was tucked into the far corner. Glass and brass, clean and comforting, where a squadron of fresh-faced experts in relaxation and comfort would greet customers and whisk them to paradise one floor up. The Spa comprised the whole of the second floor, half of it the swimming pool area with a retractable glass roof. If life would just slow down, I could set up shop by the pool and never leave.

Designed in the European style toward pleasure, pampering, and fabulous food, Cielo had no gaming—a risky move in Vegas, but one true to my heart ... in many ways. Jean-Charles's restaurant was our calling card, lending just that perfect bit of European flair.

My blood pressure eased, my mind stopping whirling, life receded enough for calm to ooze in. Hotels I could do. Life, not so much.

I clapped my hands, getting the attention of some staff that had been on hand to help with the party and now huddled in the corner. "Smiles. And get some music playing in here. I'm feeling the need for some country. I bet you guys can find the right playlist." Someone had stolen Holt Box's chance to make more music; the least we could do is honor him by playing his hits. Briefly I wondered it that would be in bad taste, but what better way to honor the singer? Either way, someone would complain.

That much I knew. And that I could handle.

The elevator waited, its maw open. Techs from the coroner's Office shuttled their equipment using the service elevator, then wheeled it through the lobby, the metal carts clattering on unsteady wheels. So much for subtle.

And so much for calm. Real life had an ugly habit of intruding into my Las Vegas make-believe where fantasies were our job.

With an eerie sense of déjà-vu, as the first strains of Holt Box's deep voice singing one of his hits about trucks and Texas filtered over the sound system, I stepped into the elevator and made another solo ride to the top floor. No excited voices greeted me, no Frank Sinatra songs ... no party. Someone had even turned off the light illuminating the Van Gogh. I flipped it back on as I walked by.

Jean-Charles stood behind the bar, his smile back in place—it brightened when he saw me. He popped the top on a longneck Bud and placed it in front of his only customer, Dane. The long, tall drink of Texas smooth had stepped back into my life as seamlessly as he'd left it. We had unfinished business. And, as with most of the relationships in my life where trust had been broken, and even some where it hadn't, I had no idea how to find an equilibrium again, or even if I wanted to. Not everyone deserved to be a part of my adventure—a lesson I still had trouble with.

Dane had turned when I walked in, his gun at the ready. When he saw it was me, he lowered his gun, then his hand closed around his beer. I could see the questions, the unfinished issues between us, in his emerald eyes. Time had given me some perspective, but I no longer felt the need to smooth those waters. His dark wavy hair had grayed a touch at the temples in the intervening months. It looked good on him.

Without the party excitement to mask them, my steps echoed off the hardwood. A much more somber air filled the room, although Jean-Charles seemed to have once again found his footing. Filling the crystal flute next to his on the bar with matching rosé bubbles, he gave me a look with a flicker of horror in his eyes as I took a stool across from him. "Such a bad thing, this. How is your father? And your friend?"

"My father is in the clear. Teddie, not so much."

"Did he kill Holt?"

"Means, motive, and opportunity," I muttered, mimicking Teddie. I caught Dane's sideways glance. For a moment, our eyes met. We were thinking the same thing: barring divine intervention, Teddie was screwed.

"What is this? Means, motive, what?"

I gave him the Hollywood version of police work.

"But you do not think he did this?"

"No." I didn't go into the details. No matter what I believed, it was still nothing but theory. Even someone who failed geometry knew that wasn't enough.

"You will fight for him, *non?*" Jean-Charles's voice remained impassive, but I could tell from the tic in his cheek that he wasn't feeling the love. "If I had only said no to Mr. Box."

I grabbed his hand, fisting it in mine. "Don't for one minute think this was your fault, or that you had anything to do with it. Whoever killed Holt Box would have found another way." Or another victim, if my theory held water, but right now it was just that, another theory. I'd be careful, but not paranoid.

He looked stricken. "I know that is to make me feel better, but I'm not sure it does."

Crestfallen, I let go of his hand. "I know what you mean. Evil finds a way."

"You must fix that." The conflict in his eyes wasn't mirrored in the tone of his voice.

"Me? This is Romeo's little problem. And what ever happened to you wanting me to stay out of the fray?"

Dane snickered, and I elbowed him.

Jean-Charles motioned to the cowboy to my right. "See, he sees this also. While I do not respect Theodore, nor do I like him, he doesn't deserve to be guilty if he is not."

"A matter for the police." The color rose in my cheeks; I could feel the warmth. I had no idea why this got my back up, but it did. All three of us knew that I couldn't keep my nose out of the investigation even if the fate of the world hung in the balance. So why was I arguing?

"Romeo is a better detective when you are with him." Jean-Charles looked to Dane for agreement. He got it—a quick nod. "But..." Jean-Charles stopped, waiting for my full attention. He didn't have to wait but a nanosecond. "You must not go where you will be in any danger. Just talking. Okay?"

Ah, there was the payoff. I wanted his concern. Was I still that needy, that insecure? No, but I wasn't above liking the expression of his concern. "Sure."

Dane choked. We all knew I lied, but somehow we all felt better. I knew I did, and I could see it in the men's faces as well. Jean-

Charles had said what he needed to. I'd heard it. And Dane had gotten a laugh out of it.

Jean-Charles dusted his hands, as if dispensing with an unsavory topic. "Then, a toast." He raised his glass. "To Holt Box."

We clinked and fell quiet for a moment. A man had died here. And not just any man. An icon of the country-music world died here. I wondered if Jean-Charles had any idea what that might mean. Rabid fans, like true believers, would make pilgrimages from far and wide to offer homage in a mecca of this sort. Country music and fine dining—an interesting Venn diagram. How large would the overlap be? Or were they mutually exclusive?

"Let me cook for you." Jean-Charles smiled, a look of understanding softening his eyes. "It will make us both feel better."

"Our own wake for Holt Box?"

"Or a celebration of our life, which is short. Our own little party, *non?*"

"A celebration." I clinked my flute with his. "Every moment of every day. Even the not-so-good days."

"*Vraiment.*"

The bubbles brought some happy back, not much, but enough to know we'd get through this and life would still be wonderful.

Teddie. Now, he was another story. Too many had been railroaded in the court of public opinion. I couldn't let that happen to him.

Dane swiped his beer off the bar as he backed off the stool. "I know my exit cue. I'll be out front."

I relented and gave him a smile. "Thank you."

He nodded and made himself scarce.

"You called this man to come sit with me. Why?" Jean-Charles adopted a conversational tone, but his eyes told me the question was anything but casual.

"A momentary weakness." A perfunctory reply to stave off worry. Then I stopped. He needed to know my suspicions, even if they proved to be false, as I so desperately hoped. "Not true. A man who hates me was released from prison a few days ago. No one bothered to mention it. I'm worried he might be targeting people close to me. You need to be careful."

Disbelief rearranged his perfect features, puckering his kissable lips. "Who could hate you? That is silly."

"And that is why I love you. Well, that and a million other reasons." Avoiding my flute, I leaned across the bar and kissed him. With my lips still next to his, I murmured, "And that's why I called Dane." Carefully finding my perch once again, I put my phone on the bar between us and played the message. The evil laugh still raised the hair on the back of my neck.

It also sobered my chef. "I see. And the phone number?"

"I gave it to Romeo and I have Jeremy tracing it."

"You haven't called it back?"

I drained my bubbly, then motioned for a refill. "Didn't want to give him the satisfaction. But you need to get used to hanging around with Dane."

"He is to be my shadow? This is right, *non?*"

"Yes. And yes."

For once, he didn't argue. "I am hoping he knows how to use a knife."

"One can only hope." My Frenchman and I were picturing different uses for that knife, but I didn't mention it.

"Papa!" The excited voice preceded by a fraction of a second a tiny human projectile who startled us both. Christophe Bouclet, followed by his aunt, with Dane rounding out the trio.

As Jean-Charles stepped from behind the bar and squatted, opening his arms for his son, I gave Dane a nod and he disappeared back to his post out front.

The boy launched himself into his father's embrace almost toppling him over. The laughter, the joy on Jean-Charles's face drove away the demons. The love between the two of them was something special, perhaps enhanced by the loss of Jean-Charles's wife in childbirth.

Desiree, Jean-Charles's twin sister, slipped in next to me, her breath coming in rapid gasps. "That boy. He sneaked out while I wasn't looking. He is a Bouclet, never wanting to miss the party. *Mon Dieu!*" As she caught her breath, realization dawned. "Where is the party? It is now, *oui?*"

I gave her the low points, but not the particulars. With Teddie and jail weighing heavy, I just couldn't go through it again.

Desiree sobered, her delicate features pressing into a look of horror, her blue eyes dark and serious. So much like her brother. "My brother, he is safe? This man, the killer, he does not want Jean, does he?"

I really couldn't say, so I told her what she wanted to hear. "No."

"This is good." Relief smoothed her concern, and her face returned to its previous perfection. With all her easy French sophistication, I wanted to hate her, but that would just prove I was as shallow as I feared. So I didn't. "If anyone wished to kill my brother, all they would have to do is take his child. He would perish."

A horrible sinking feeling hollowed my chest. "Don't even say such a thing!"

She crossed her other arm across her stomach, then rested her elbow on it. "I am sorry. When I see them together. How much my brother needs his son. How he almost did not survive losing his wife. And now he has opened his heart to you. We did not think he ever would. You see, my brother, he is a man of passion. He loves deeply. So loss is lethal."

I heard the subtle warning in her words. If I left him, perhaps it would kill him, but she would kill me for sure. I could live with that. My heart filled as we watched father and son giggle and tease.

Jean-Charles, his son in his arms clinging to him like a monkey, joined Desiree and me. As if leaping from one tree to another, Christophe launched himself from his father toward me. Prepared, I caught him, grunting theatrically with the effort. "You have been eating too much of your father's cooking."

The boy giggled as he raised his shirt. "I am still skinny."

I staggered a bit, pretending my legs buckled. "Then I am old and weak."

The boy howled in delight. "But, Papa, where is the party? I want to dance." Sometimes the tone in the boy's voice so matched his father's it was eerie.

"You should be in bed dreaming the good dreams," Jean-Charles said, trying for stern and failing.

"But I want to dance with Lucky." The boy pouted as his eyes flirted—the art of manipulation, a French birthright and a game he already played well.

The quartet had packed up, so Jean-Charles cued some music through the system. *La Vie en Rose*. My eyes met his, finding the joke there. A cabaret song roundly despised by the French and loved with equal passion by the Americans. Personally, it was one of my favorites. Life through rose-colored glasses. My kind of life.

And so we danced, with me holding the boy tight to my chest, his legs around my waist, and his arms around my neck. He hummed to the tune, exposing his father's affinity for the song. His breath soft on my cheek, his hands fisted in my Pahmina, he touched a side of myself I didn't know. A fluttering near my heart. Something primal, deep ... maternal. Me. The one who couldn't be trusted with a pet.

As the last strains of music drifted around us, the boy tightened his grip, almost cutting off my air. "Again!"

Ah, yes, *just* like his father.

Thankfully, Jean-Charles plucked the boy from my arms. *"Non.* One is enough. You must get to bed." Jean-Charles's voice turned stern. "And mind your *tante.* You leave without her again, and you will be punished."

The boy knew when the battle was lost. Besides, it was three adults to his one half. On a normal day, the adults probably still would lose, but today was far from normal. Perhaps the boy could sense that in our faces and our voices. "Yes, sir."

"How are you finding your accommodations at Cielo?" I asked Desiree.

"It is a lovely hotel. So European in its refinement, in the special touches. You have thought of everything. It is a bit—how do you say it?—odd to be staying here alone. Last night, the building it makes noises, *oui?* Very late I thought I heard the elevator running. My imagination, it plays tricks. I know there are guards and we are safe. I am used to hotels being full of people and sounds."

"The guards, they patrol," I said. "And tonight there will be some police here, watching."

"As children, she never liked to be alone. She has not outgrown this." Jean-Charles teased his twin.

"You'll be all right tonight?" I asked.

"Of course. I have my nephew to protect me." She tickled

Christophe and he squirmed in laughter, pretending to push her hand away.

With kisses and hugs in the dramatic fashion of five-year-olds we all said goodnight and bid Christophe *adieu*.

"Come." Jean Charles extended his hand as he stepped around the bar. "Now, about that party; you must be hungry."

"Famished." I let him lead me toward the kitchen. Careful not to disturb the crime scene, we wove our way around the yellow tape to the stove.

I perched on the stool he pulled next to the stove, out of the way, but where I could be close and watch a master at work. "The cops have released the crime scene?"

"*Oui.*"

"So we're waiting on the clean up," I muttered to myself. Given what Romeo told me, there wasn't anything to be gained here.

Jean-Charles gathered food from the various refrigerators below the counter to his right, presenting a very fine French backside. While I valued him for the intangibles, I wasn't above enjoying the package they came in, so I took a moment to enjoy the view. Arms full, he deposited his load on the prep table and set to work. When it came to food, he had a single-minded dedication reminiscent of my own. He cooked it, I consumed it—a great team.

"They dusted for fingerprints, took a few knives that my staff indicated Mr. Box had been using. The staff was still prepping and serving the chilled appetizers. The stove was not yet in use. Holt worked over there." He motioned toward the prep area near the walk-in refrigerator with a wooden spoon dripping something dark that smelled delicious. "We were not yet cooking, so they saw no need to keep me out of this section of the kitchen."

I knew what he wasn't saying, what he didn't want to say—the cops didn't find any blood here. No blood. I shuddered and closed my mind to visuals.

Teddie.

Watching Jean-Charles prepare dinner, I was glad there'd been no blood and the space had been cleaned back to its normal spit-and-polish perfection.

While he was occupied, I stepped over to the taped-off sections of the kitchen. The pool of blood, now a dark maroon ... almost brown in color, with tiny dark drips leading away. The drips were elongated, the thin tail of them pointing toward the back of the kitchen. My eyes followed the trail as I imagined a scenario, leaning so I could see the trail extending around the corner. It looked like it disappeared through the hanging curtain of thick plastic vertical strips, into the refrigerator.

"Is the walk-in normally only covered with the plastic curtain?"

Jean-Charles didn't turn to look. "When we are cooking, yes."

Someone could've waited for Holt Box in the fridge or near, stabbed him, then filtered into the flow of a still-new staff, and worked their way out of the kitchen unnoticed.

I'd love to know how my theory shaped up with the one the coroner would pull together—and how the timelines gelled. Did I notice the man in the dinner jacket easing out of the kitchen at about the right time to have murdered Holt Box? What time had it been?

All good questions with answers yet to come. So now I went back to my stool and focused on my life, my chef, and our party of two. Life gave us precious little time alone as it was.

Hard to believe it took a murder for this to be possible.

My life needing fixing in the worst way.

Wracking my brain, I searched for a happier topic—one that didn't involve blood and knives and dead country-western singers ... and implicated former lovers.

"I loved dancing with Christophe. I'm sorry he couldn't have stayed a bit longer."

The tension in Jean-Charles's shoulders eased. We'd both had enough murder for the evening. "He is my life, but he had to get to sleep."

"Then you'll have to settle for me."

"What is this 'settle'?" he asked, his back to me as he lost himself in the comfort of cooking. His flute was getting low; mine was dry. So I went to the bar, filled an ice bucket, and grabbed a new bottle of Schramsberg.

After adding a dash of water to bring the temperature of the ice even lower, I nestled the bottle, knowing Jean-Charles wouldn't want any more until he'd finished his preparations, and I could wait.

"Settling means you take a lesser option," I answered, as I busied myself setting a table for two in the kitchen.

Jean-Charles glanced over his shoulder. "You and Christophe would be the best choices."

"So, not settling." I gathered knives, forks, and other utensils we might need, then paused. "I really don't want to eat in here. Death is too close."

He put his hand over his chest as he paused in his cooking. "My kitchen is my heart. Here is for family." He took a long look at me. "But, perhaps you are right. Tonight we will eat in the restaurant."

"Thank you." I set a table for us next to the window. When I returned, he motioned me next to him. Busy with spatulas and spoons, he couldn't hug me, so I looped an arm around his waist, settling my head on his shoulder, breathing him in.

"You, like Christophe, are my heart," he said. Simple words, such complexity.

"There's room for both of us?" Normally I could keep my vulnerability, my fears, at bay, but tonight had knocked me off-center.

"But, of course. Powerful love, but different. Sit. You must let me plate this and serve you."

He didn't have to demand twice.

Over amazing food, we stayed on safe topics, repairing the day. The Champagne gone, the food enjoyed, Jean-Charles leaned across the table presenting one last bite on his spoon—the dregs of a heavenly chocolate pot de crème.

Leaning back, I shook my head, my hand pressed to my stomach. "I can't eat another bite."

He shrugged and, with a smile, licked the spoon clean. "Chefs get very angry when their food is not finished."

I leaned into him. "And what is the punishment?"

"For you? Very bad." Leaning in, he met me halfway. The touch of his lips on mine still fired every nerve ending. He deepened his kiss, consuming me, taking my breath, and stealing my heart. His forehead on mine, his whispered, "Dance?"

I giggled and pulled back to get a better look at him. "What?"

"I will make a plate for your friend, then I will put the pots to soak, and then we will dance. It is life, *non?*"

"Indeed."

Dane sat in a chair under the Van Gogh. Two works of art—one a vision, the other a reality. I wasn't sure which was which. I handed him the plate and some silverware still wrapped in a napkin I'd swiped off a table. "You must be hungry." I pulled a fresh Bud from a hidden pocket in my dress. "And thirsty."

Dane took the plate and bottle with a smile. "Thanks."

"Peace offerings in a way. I'll only say this once, and I don't want to discuss it further. What you did was wrong, not only to me but to your wife. I hope you've learned, and I'm sorry you didn't get the chance to fix it with her."

Pain flashed across his face as he swallowed hard. "Can I fix it with you?"

I'd thought and thought about that, and I still hadn't reached a conclusion. "One step at a time, cowboy. What do you say? Friends?" I figured I could get that far, even if trust remained an issue. Hell, Mona was my mother and I didn't trust her past noon.

Dane nodded, looking relieved. "Friends." He tilted his head toward the interior of the restaurant. "Lucky guy."

"Nice guy. Make sure no one gets to him or his family. Once we leave here, I'll have him covered. Romeo is leaving a couple of guys here, in addition to your guards and mine so Christophe and Desiree should be good." Dane didn't give me a leer, which was unusual. Most of the time he was creepy that way. "And he lives in an armed guard-gated community. So get some sleep tonight. Can you be ready in the morning to provide escort, should Jean-Charles decide to wander about? Given the events of this evening, I have no idea what his plans are tomorrow."

"I'm sure you'll be working." So sure of that he didn't even pause for confirmation. "So give me a shout when you get ready to leave."

"Will do."

"I'm thinking I might get one or two other guys so we can tag-team a bit. That okay?"

"Sure. As long as they're as good as you."

"Better. First one I'll call is Shooter Moran, if that's okay?"

"Shooter? Sure, but remind him this is an ask-first-shoot-later kind of gig." Shooter was an old Army buddy with a Pavlovian response when it came to his former Captain, Dane. Shooter also had a twitchy trigger finger and an over-developed sense of loyalty. But he was a good guy to have your back.

I left Dane with his food and his thoughts.

I owed a man a dance.

CHAPTER SIX

MORNINGS. Like I said, we don't get along too well. But today, a certain Frenchman worked to improve my attitude. Spooned in bed, one arm thrown casually across my waist, his breath soft on my cheek, I savored the heat where our skin touched. Jean-Charles shifted. His fingers brushed the back of my neck. The warmth of his lips pressed to the exposed skin. Soft, warm kisses sending warm shivers to my core.

"You are awake, *non?*"

"No. Dreaming."

A warm chuckle as he nibbled on my ear, his hand drifting to my breast, teasing. Reaching back, I trailed my hand across his skin, a light caress. His breath caught. Easing back, insistent, he rolled me over. His mouth found my breast, nibbling, biting. I arched into him, my hands fisted in his hair. His need fueled mine. His lips found the hollow in my neck, licking, tasting. Want unfurled, a warm, desperate need. His lips captured mine, his tongue plundering my mouth. Tangling, wet. Shifting his weight onto me, I opened to him. My hand guiding, he pressed into me. Taking, owning. I moaned as he filled me. My need joining his, a syncopated rhythm of desire. Slow, tantalizing, he toyed with me. Slipping in, then out, warm, slick. Pleasure, a building need, drove me. I wrapped my legs around his back, pulling him deeper, urging him faster. Arching, open. Waves of pleasure, building, consuming. Head back, my breath caught, held. Muscles tightened. I exploded in shattering spasms. With a groan, he pulsed into me, his body taut with pleasure.

Time stopped. Neither moved as we both tried to capture the

pleasure, hold it. When Jean-Charles raised-up on his elbows, his arms shook. Leaning down, he gave me a sweet kiss. "I am still amazed at the connection between us. Our friendship, our partnership, strengthens the love."

"The fact that you are a great kisser and have a great butt doesn't hurt."

He smiled as he eased down next to me, making sure our bodies, hot and slick, still pressed together. "You always do this."

"A joke to diffuse the emotion? Yes." I rolled into him, our faces close, our legs entwined. I nibbled on his lower lip. "Sometimes I am afraid," I whispered, uncomfortable with my own weakness.

"Of course. Love rips us open, leaves us bare. It is the most wonderful part of life and the most devastating. I love deeply, completely. I do not wish to do this, but my heart, it is its own master. If you do not love me the same, you need to tell me this. I lost my first love. My heart, it broke. I did not know if I could go on. I cannot do this again. You and Christophe. To lose either of you ... " His face crumpled with hurt, a memory, a fear, lashed him.

My heart opened. My fear fell away. "I do love you just as you say. I'm not going anywhere."

We both jumped at a soft knock on the door. "Papa? I am hungry."

Jean-Charles pressed his forehead to mine as he chuckled.

"Round two will have to wait until later."

"You have a date. This is right, *non?*"

"It'll do." I pulled the covers to my chin as he rolled off of me, taking his warmth with him.

Jean-Charles eased to the edge of the bed, leaning back to give me a deep kiss. Then he stood, stretched, and headed toward the closet. "I'm coming, Christophe." He stepped into a pair of gym shorts, then tugged a T-shirt over his head, working his arms through the holes. "What do you want to eat?"

"Lucky's happy-face pancakes. She will make them." A small boy with no shortage of confidence, he had adopted his father's habit of making a question into a demand. Sentence structure—one of the casualties of segueing from one language to another.

Jean-Charles gave me a lopsided smile and a shrug. "She needs to get to work," he said in answer to his son. Then turning to me, he said, "Even though it is Sunday, I can see the 'I have things to do' look on your face."

"And forego pancakes and little boys?" I threw the covers back and rolled to my feet.

Jean-Charles's eyes lazily roamed what he'd already had. Admiration lit his smile. He took a deep breath. "A high price, indeed. The cleaners delivered all your clothes back. I hung them in the closet. Now, you, to the shower, before I change my mind."

"Promises. Promises."

SUNDAY morning. December. Christmas right around the corner. And Teddie had dropped coal into my stocking. Fixing his problems would go a long way toward restoring my holiday cheer. Get him out of jail, then he could get out of my life. Better for both of us.

Daniel Lovato, our esteemed District Attorney, if he still adhered to his normal schedule, would be taking his daughter, Gabi, to play at the playground just off the Summerlin Parkway, which was on my way.

With the Ferrari grumbling at having to idle through the neighborhoods to maintain the child-friendly speed, I tried to absorb the warmth of the sun to chase the chill away. Murder did that to me. And this wouldn't be Daniel's and my first murder. We'd crossed swords over the murder of a particularly odious odds maker named Numbers Neidermeyer—a devil in a pretty package. Daniel's wife was collateral damage—she did a swan dive off the top of the Babylon, almost taking me with her. Not that eliminating her from the gene pool was anything to cry over. This particular Glinda was not a good witch. I shoved the memory aside—too pretty a day for such ugly thoughts. The long and the short of it was this: I let Daniel off the hot seat so he could raise his daughter.

So I figured he owed me.

The parking lot was empty except for a particular white 911-S Cabriolet I recognized. Déjà-vu washed over me. A different Sunday not too long ago. As I killed the engine and levered myself out of the car, Daniel turned and looked. He didn't wave. He did, however, move over, making space on his bench for me.

Gabi swung from the monkey bars, her long dark hair plaited down her back, a smile on her face, which grew when she saw me. "Hi, Lucky!"

"Hey, Cutie. You sure are getting strong." I watched in amazement as she swung from one rung to the next with ease. If I tried that, both my arms would be torn from their sockets. But being nine was so far in my rearview I couldn't even see a hazy outline in the distance. And today I didn't mind that. Each facet of me had been hard won through the years.

Daniel didn't look up when my shadow blocked his view of the sun. "You're here about Teddie." A statement, not a question. His voice hard, unapproachable.

Taking the space next to him, I settled back, then glanced at his profile. Patrician, stoic, chiseled features, he was Italian through-and-through with olive skin, a Roman nose, and carefully styled black hair. Beautiful was an adjective that often accompanied any reference to him. Beauty and a charm often accompanied by a bright smile, which he didn't bother to waste on me today, had allowed him to cut a wide swath through the double X-chromosome set. To hear tell, he'd more than earned his nickname of Lovie, not something I admired. He'd been married, and promises were promises as far as I was concerned. But, this being Vegas, people like me were in danger of following the Dodo into oblivion.

"Yes, but we'll get to him in a minute. Were you going to tell me about Irv Gittings?"

He shot me a shocked look, fleeting, but I caught it. "What about him?"

"You know he carries a pretty big grudge."

"He didn't make any overt threats. Nobody had any reason to believe he'd come after you." He swiveled a bit to give me a one-eyed stare, the other eye squinting against the sun behind me. "Are you saying he did?"

"I don't know. Just running the theories. How'd he get out?"

Daniel turned back to watch his daughter, his hands on his knees. "Good lawyer. Judge Jameson." He gave me a look that filled in the blanks.

Even I'd heard the rumors of judicial misconduct. Nobody'd caught him in the act, but everyone figured it was a matter of time.

Daniel smiled and clapped when Gabi called to him to watch her flip off the monkey bars. "A stupid technicality—most judges wouldn't have sprung him. Nothing to do with you. We'll get him on the retrial."

"You convicted him once. You can't take him back to trial."

"Conviction was overturned. No double jeopardy. We can and will try him again. This time we'll get him good."

I too watched Gabi as she climbed and swung with youthful abandon. Did I ever feel that free, that unburdened by life, its expectations, its unfairness, and its disappointments? Having been raised in a whorehouse, I doubted it. Life was pretty real when I was young. Even more so now.

"Who posted bail?"

"You'd have to ask the bonding company, Quick and Easy." He spat the words.

Oh, joy, the bottom of the barrel of a very bad kettle of fish—yes, clichés and mixed metaphors. Sue me. Stress has interesting effects on me. "Bail, a nice segue," I said. "Now Teddie." My tone matched Daniel's, getting a quick sideways glance. "What amount are you going to ask for?" I didn't even try to argue against charging him. Given the circumstances and the victim, Daniel would present the facts to the Grand Jury and an indictment was as close to a certainty as the sunrise tomorrow.

"Capital murder is not a bailable offense in Nevada."

So we were going to play that game. "I'm not a lawyer, true. But, in my job, I've got quite a few in my back pocket, and they've taught me a trick or two through the years." That sorta sounded like a threat. Unintended, I nevertheless let it lie. "You really want me to quote statutory chapter and verse? You know as well I do there's wiggle room."

He shifted, uncrossing his legs so he could turn and partially face me. "That's how it's going to go? You're going to squeeze my balls on this one? Grapevine tells me Teddie didn't do you any favors. You think he'd do the same for you now?"

"It doesn't matter. Other people's standards, or lack thereof, don't dictate my behavior." I fixed him with a stare. "You know that first-hand."

For the first time, he looked a bit uncomfortable. "So that's what this is? Payback?"

"No. I know what kind of scrutiny you'll be under." I stared into the distance, squinting against the sunlight. Traffic rushed by on the Parkway. I wondered about the people in the cars. What kind of problems did they have? Did murder ever touch their lives? I hoped not. And I watched Gabi. Carefree, happy, she was growing strong and true without her mother to break her. Choices. Life put us all to the test at some point. And, more often than not, the right path wasn't the easiest. Not by a long shot. "I'm just asking you to listen to me, to read the reports, to keep an open mind. And, in the end, to do the right thing. Teddie's as much a victim here as Box."

Daniel let out a sigh. His hand moved like he wanted to rake his fingers through his hair, then stopped, thinking better of mussing a two-hundred-dollar haircut and style. His hand dropped onto his thigh, where his fingers drummed. "The statutory standard is proof is evident or the presumption is great. So get me something; can you do that?"

"I'll give it all I got."

"I know that." He gave me a rueful smile. "Can't complain about that. But Box is dead," he said, reminding me of something impossible to forget.

"You lower the boom on Teddie, and *he* might as well be."

Daniel thrust his chin in the direction of his daughter, who played happily, letting us talk. "Gabi's really growing, isn't she?"

I knew what he was thinking. Had I not stuck my neck out, had I not made the difficult choice, his life and his daughter's would've taken a drastically different path. Teddie was at the same crossroad, and Daniel held the key. But I couldn't press him. While I'd be willing to post the bail, putting my money on the dark horse in the race, Daniel would be betting his job, his livelihood ... his ability to provide for his daughter. Only he could place that bet. "I can see hints of the beautiful woman she is becoming."

Fatherly pride puffed his chest a bit. "She's blossomed since her mother died."

"As have you." Peace had made Daniel even handsomer, if that was possible. And, while I didn't admire, I could appreciate.

"Not a priority anymore, but thanks."

From the Italian cut of his light wool suit, the French tie, and the Ferragamos on his feet, he was lying to himself, but didn't we all? I let him have his little self-delusion—mine comforted me all the time.

Daniel squinted against the sun behind me. "So you don't think he did it?"

"You've read the witness statements and the coroner's prelim, I'm sure. What do you think?"

Daniel shrugged. "Probably same as you: it looks real bad, but I think someone else designed it that way."

Relief flooded through me.

Daniel raised one knee. Rocking back, he hooked his hands around it. "With all the media attention, the Grand Jury isn't going to no-bill him."

"You arguing for bail in court and supporting a theory of his innocence will go a long way toward helping keep his life and his career intact. Just support bail and try to make it something I can afford, and I'll be happy."

"Okay. But let me ask you this: why are you sticking your neck out for the guy?"

This time, I waited until his eyes caught mine and held. "Because it's the right thing to do."

Daniel was a smart guy; I could see he got my subtext. "Lucky guy."

"That makes two of you."

AT some point in life, one must face their mother. Apparently, today was my day. Mona lurked just inside the front entrance to the Babylon and pounced the moment I walked through the glass doors.

"Lucky!" She grabbed my arm, squeezing tightly as if I'd been marooned on an island and just now returned to the fold. Which, come to think of it, I had. Warmth flooded through me as I paused in a memory of this morning: waking up, Jean-Charles ...

"Lucky?" Mona's whine burst my little moment of *joie de vivre*. She tugged on my arm, pulling me in the direction of the casino. "I need you to come with me. They just won't listen."

I knew better than to resist or to ask who; both would make this little interlude longer than it needed to be. Instead, I let her loop her arm through mine and shepherd me where she wanted me to go. As she led me through the lobby, over the marble floors inlaid with bright patterns, past the reception area with multicolored cloth tented above it, past the Lucite windows in front of our indoor ski slope replete with snow and the other trappings one would find at any alpine destination, I paused, looking up. The arcing flight of Chihuly blown glass hummingbirds and butterflies always brought a smile. To me, they looked like they were making an escape, winging toward a future that didn't involve murder and Mona. Perhaps I could sprout wings and join them? I could only wish.

Mona led me across the footbridges arcing over our version of the Euphrates and its reed groves and various fauna and fowl that seemed to be breeding like crazy. I'd have to talk with our vet about that. Birth control for ducks. The thought made me smile. God, I loved my job.

We marched up the stairs into Delilah's bar, an oasis in the middle of the casino. Surrounded by gaming tables, slot machines, and an ever-present crowd of hopeful donors that ebbed and flowed with the time of day, Delilah's, with its bougainvillea-draped lattice work and merrily trickling waterfall behind the bar was exactly that—an oasis with a secret cave kind of feel. I'd always found peace here. Of course the free-flowing Wild Turkey 101 often helped with that. Today the white baby grand in the corner where Teddie had often played sat alone, abandoned, reminding me of less than pleasant realities far removed from this fantasyland. I turned my back to the piano.

And came face-to-face with a coven of conspiracy.

Mona had gathered together a trio of terror. My aunt, Darlin' Delacroix as she liked to be known though her real name was Matilda, was the first female to own a casino in Vegas. And she was as daunting as that implied and then some. Today, Matilda—I seemed genetically incapable of calling anyone Darlin' (much to my aunt's irritation)—wore her ubiquitous black mini skirt, fishnet stockings, five-inch heels, and a jacket with Elvis patchworked on the back in varying colors of leather. Pancake makeup accented the creases and folds of skin ravaged by a lifetime of unfiltered cigarettes. Her fake eyelashes, so thick they looked like fallen eyebrows, weighed her eyelids down so she had to tilt her head back to see. I didn't even know they still sold blue eye shadow with glitter in it—a future trip to the Doc-in-a-Box waiting to happen. The woman was eighty and still hadn't quite conquered the nuances of good taste—not that she had ever aspired to that.

Flash Gordon, my best friend and ace investigative reporter for the *Las Vegas Review Journal*, would never be sitting quietly in my mother's presence unless a really great story lurked under the surface. I narrowed my eyes at her. Dressed in a tube of lime green Lycra that displayed her tiny body and huge boobs in alarming fashion, she wore equally high heels as Matilda, a tad bit less make up, large hoop earrings, a cascade of red curls and an innocent smile. She extended her arm across the back of the chair next to her as she looked like a pit-bull eyeing a rabbit.

I decided to zig when she thought I'd zag—keeping her off balance was the only effective strategy I'd found to keep her from ragging me until I bled information. "I expected about eighty phone calls from you last night. Doesn't Holt Box's murder have you salivating or something?"

She lowered her eyes for the briefest moment. Pity, I knew it. She was going easy on me because of Teddie. And I appreciated it. "I probably should be hounding you, but I don't see how that's going to get either of us what we want. When you have something for me to chase, you'll tell me."

Despite her words, I still felt like the rabbit. "Okay."

Mrs. Olefson, a lone beacon of style, class and Midwestern common sense, anchored the group. Today was red-white-and-blue day for her in her St. John's separates, pearls at her neck and earlobes, sensible Ferragamos gracing her feet, and Milo, her Bichon, curled in her lap. Mrs. Olefson had wandered into the hotel after the death of her husband and had liked it so much she prevailed on us to let her stay. She'd also wanted to marry her dog, so despite her exterior, she did fit in with this little gathering.

Mona tapped on the empty seat, and then took hers across the table between Darlin' and Flash.

I eased into the chair and leaned into Flash. "I'm not going to like this, am I?"

"It depends."

"I knew it. I'm going to hate it." I leaned over to Mrs. Olefson, who smiled at me as if we were bridge partners or something. Sometimes it took her awhile to catch on to Mona's schemes. "We have to stick together."

"Honey, I don't know what you mean." She stroked Milo. The dog opened one eye, saw I had no food, then promptly snapped it shut and started snoring.

"Remember the phone sex idea?" I prodded her memory. "And the virginity auction?"

Her face clouded. "Oh, but I don't think this is anything like that."

"What is M planning this time? What ill-advised scheme to bolster her campaign? She has to be planning something." My mind on adrenaline overload, and filled with thoughts of murder and the death penalty, spun-off into its own dark place. "I know! She's going to sell the twins? Or the right to name them, perhaps?"

The three women watched me with expressions running the gamut from Mona's exaggerated patience to Mrs. Olefson's confusion, Flash's amusement, and my aunt's haughty displeasure.

"Or are we running on a legalize prostitution platform? Such a popular issue to force into the light of day. What's the tagline? Vegas, where you can get a piece of ass with class?"

"Are you quite done?" Mona asked, not even rising to the bait. "Lucky, do be quiet. This isn't about me at all."

I looked at the faces around me. "No?"

Mrs. Olefson patted my hand. "No, dear. It's about Miss P."

"Miss P?" I so needed a drink. This early on a Sunday morning called for ... what? "Champagne," I said to the waitress hovering nearby. "Five glasses." I turned back to my little coven of conspirators. "This is about the bachelorette party, right? What are you guys cooking up?"

Everyone eyed me with blank stares. No one said a word.

"I hate surprises." I stared down each one in turn, but nobody broke.

Just as I was about to go cross-eyed, the waitress arrived with the Champagne, which did sort of perk everyone up. Or maybe just me. I knew Miss P was fine; I'd just spoken with her on the phone. She'd sounded a bit off, but not terribly. I'd chalked it up to last night being what it was.

"Matilda," I addressed my aunt. She'd been Matilda before she'd adopted the Darlin' costume, and she'd always be Matilda to me. She didn't like it, but she tolerated it. Since I tolerated her, I figured we were even. "Tell me what is going on."

My aunt gave me the stink eye. "As Mrs. Olefson said, this is about Miss P."

"I know. What are you all planning?"

"It's not about her wedding, Lucky," my mother broke in. "Well, not about this one anyway."

"What?" I glanced between the faces. Finally, I arrowed Flash with a look she would have no trouble interpreting.

"Right," she said as she sat up, bolted the whole of her flute of Champagne, then set the glass back on the table with studied, irritating care. "You know the wedding?"

"Miss P's and the Beautiful Jeremy Whitlock's?" I leveled my voice, pretending to play nice.

"Yes." Flash motioned for more Champagne.

"For God's sake!"

She jumped at my raised voice. "There's been a hitch."

I smelled a rat. "Those two are the biggest lovebirds on the planet. If something happens to them, I'm giving up on love. What is going on?"

"Not a what, dear." Mona adopted her patronizing tone, which of course made everything so much better. "A who."

"A who?"

"Yes, a who. Cody Ellis, to be more precise."

"What is a Cody Ellis?"

"Who, Lucky," Mona instructed, as if talking to a child. "He's a who."

"Second cousin to Cindy-Lou Who, I suppose?" I asked Flash. Panic tended to bring out my snark. Nobody else seemed to appreciate that, even though I thought it was one of my best qualities.

Flash relaxed with a grin. "Wasn't she the one who made the Grinch's heart grow three sizes?"

"Lucky!" Mona whined. Fidgety and anxious, she clearly had a bombshell she couldn't wait to drop.

"Go for it, Mother. After last night's shelling, one more tossed on the rubble won't even make a dent. But, give me a moment." I took a sip of bubbly, savoring being in the dark for a moment longer, gathering fortitude. "Okay, I'm ready. Who is Cody Ellis?"

Mrs. Olefson patted my thigh. "Cody Ellis, *Doctor* Cody Ellis is Miss P's husband, dear."

CHAPTER SEVEN

"**S**HE'S married to a doctor?" Praying this was one of Mona's jokes, I looked at each one of the women gathered around me, pausing for a few seconds on each. They each looked stricken.

No joke.

"I think we ought to gather up the good doctor and get rid of him," Mona said, folding her cocktail napkin with studied care, so she didn't have to meet my scowl. "But nobody will listen to me."

"That's because you are suggesting commission of a felony," I explained, which added to the whole surreal thing I was feeling. "No, two felonies—kidnapping, murder and maybe bigamy."

"Picky," Mona muttered.

All eyes turned to me, looking for answers. Unfortunately, answers were in short supply, but boy did I have questions. Questions that tumbled through my brain like those little numbered Bingo balls, the whole who-what-when-where-how-and-why thing. All good things to ask, but knowing Miss P and how close to the vest she held her personal life, I doubted any of the women around me had answers.

Trying to marshal logical thought, but knowing it would be an impossibility, I instead contemplated alternate careers in faraway locales as I stared over Flash's shoulder into the casino.

A figure standing against the far wall, immobile, stared at me.

I bolted to my feet, knocking over my flute, breaking it.

The man at the party. The white dinner jacket. He still wore it. And that empty, evil smile.

"Lucky, what is it?" Mona asked with a hint of worry.

Flash swiveled to look behind her.

The man pushed himself from the wall, nodded at me, then turned and melded into the patrons drifting from one table to another.

As I turned, I shouted to Flash over my shoulder. "Find Irv Gittings. Be careful. Jeremy's gone after him, so maybe find him first."

Questions flashed in her eyes, but I couldn't wait. I bolted through Delilah's, startling a few men nursing drinks at the bar, down the stairs, and onto the floor of the casino. Thankfully, I was tall and the crowd thin. I caught a glimpse of the man as he ducked through the entrance leading to the private area of the hotel. Dodging and darting as nimbly as I could, I still dislodged a cocktail server's tray. Glasses clattered and tumbled, but she managed to keep them on the tray.

"Sorry."

She gave me a tired smile.

I ducked into the passageway and, lowering my head, I ran. The hallway ended, dumping me out into a huge atrium area known as the Kasbah. A loose grouping of bungalows, each with its own swimming pool and all nestled under glass that allowed sunlight to nourish the tall palms and the lush flowering undergrowth, the Kasbah was reserved only for our most important guests.

The security guard behind the desk rose as I appeared, looking like he didn't know whether to stand his ground or run. I didn't blame him. I skidded to a stop. Out of breath, I managed to gasp out the words, "Man. Running. Where'd he go?" Hands on my knees, I sucked in huge gulps of air, hoping I didn't stroke out while my heart beat against my chest.

"Not, sure, Ms. O'Toole. He waved the key then headed around to the right."

"Have you seen him before? Any idea who he is and where he's staying?"

At least the man had the decency to act ashamed at his lackluster performance. Security guard, my ass. I made a note of his name and vowed to bring him up to Jerry, knowing I'd probably give the kid another chance. But, seriously, keeping those who didn't belong on the outside was the guy's only job. How hard could it be?

"You should get everyone's name and bungalow number, then cross-check them with registration, you know that, right?"

The guy developed a curious interest in his feet, which he shuffled a bit, rocking from side-to-side. "We have a lot of Asians staying here right now. Sometimes I find it difficult to distinguish them." He looked up at me, clearly stricken. "And they go everywhere in packs."

Finally, I straightened and could take a normal breath. "Do better, okay? I know our guests can be demanding, but it's our job to keep them safe. But I also understand the difficulties. I cut my teeth behind a desk like yours and not too long ago."

"Yes, ma'am."

Flash skidded in beside me, not even huffing.

I twirled my finger at the security guy. "We're just going to take a spin around."

"Yes, ma'am."

I walked slowly and, yes, peeked in windows where I could. Although I felt like it, I couldn't just go banging on doors. The guy could be anywhere. He could've jumped in one of the limos waiting at the back entrance, idling, ready to whisk a bungalow resident anywhere at a moment's notice.

"What can I do to help?" Flash asked. She sounded serious.

"I need info. Can you dig up anything on Irv Gittings that might have a tie to any of the players so far? Holt, his wife, Kim Cho, and anybody else you can think of. I need some connections."

"Sure." She put a hand on my arm. "How well do you know Kimberly Cho?" Her voice dropped to a hush. She glanced around, as if looking over her shoulder.

"Well enough to know anybody who has influence in Macau has interesting friends."

"Who make their own rules," she said, in case I was slow on the uptake.

I patted her hand. "Thanks. I'll watch my back. But, I won't run from a fight."

"I know. Just be careful." I seemed to be getting that same

advice a lot.

She'd been the third person in the last twenty-four hours to give me the same veiled warning. I shook it off as I watched her step to the curb and whistle for a cab, usurping the bellman's job and negating the need for a tip. I grabbed my phone, then hit Jerry's speed-dial.

"You looking for trouble or already find it?" His cough sounded worse than last night.

"You coming down with something?"

"You mean besides emphysema or something?" His voice held an edge.

"That was a joke, right?"

"Sure." He drug air into his lungs between hacks. "What can I do you for?"

I paused. Should I, or shouldn't I? "A one-way ticket to Paris, first-class and a suite at the Ritz for as long as my recovery takes."

That dulled the edge. "You know what I meant."

"Is there a twelve-step program for innuendo addiction?"

"Anything for a cheap laugh, right?" Jerry chuckled.

"Hey, made you smile. I heard it." I plucked a few dead flowers off a gardenia bush. Even wilted and brown, they still smelled divine. I'd strolled halfway around the Kasbah and not seen a soul. That would change. The whales were nocturnal, preferring the darkness to gamble by. I never could figure that out—the casino had no windows and no clocks, as if time was irrelevant and sleep an unnecessary impediment. "Listen, a guy just blew through security at the Kasbah. He flashed a key, but I'd like to know where he went."

"Gimme a sec."

He was back almost that fast. "He peeled around the perimeter then jumped into a Lambo. He looked like you guy from the party."

Not what I wanted to hear. "Yep. The one and the same." I'd love some nose-to-nose time with that guy to convince him to come clean. I couldn't prove he'd killed Holt Box, but I would. "Man, everything that happens in Vegas is memorialized in digital form. How'd he have a key, then?"

"Another mystery for you to solve."

The guy was gone, but I bet not forgotten. Somebody would remember him. "Anything to distinguish the Lambo?"

"You're kidding, right? It was a Lamborghini. I'm thinking that's distinguishing enough." Jerry covered the microphone on his phone, but I could hear the hacking coughs he tried to hide.

A tickle of worry touched the back of my neck. "You sure you're okay? Maybe you should go home." I reversed my course, doubling back to talk to the valets.

"I'm fine. So all you have to do is round up all the Lambos in town. Shouldn't be too hard."

I'd have rolled my eyes if he was standing in front of me. "You're serious, aren't you? You know all those kids that have been rolling into town? The ones buying table service and bottles of Cristal at Babel and Pandora's Box and keeping the Babylon in the black?" The question was rhetorical, so I motored on. "They all have serious iron, at least one car for each day of the week."

That left Jerry speechless.

"So not as easy as you might think."

"And a lot of them are from the Far East," Jerry said, sounding a bit more subdued.

"Just like our white dinner jacket guy. Keep an eye out for him, would you? I have a feeling he'll be back." I stared out at the circular drive, the private entrance hidden behind huge gates and sheltered by lush foliage, far from prying eyes. Even the boldest paparazzi hadn't yet pierced our veil of secrecy. The Babylon prided itself on jealously guarding the comings and goings of our top-tier clients. For once, I wasn't sure that was a good thing.

"Anything else?"

"Not right now. I'll get Jeremy working on the car, see if he can narrow the pool of possibilities down a bit. And you need to go home."

"I'd just be miserable there."

"Yeah, well, if you're carrying the plague or something, and you decide to share, there will be no place you can hide." I disconnected, then hit Jeremy's number. The call rolled directly to voicemail. Odd. I stared at my phone for a moment, trying to remember the last time I'd not been able to get in touch with Las Vegas's premier private investigator. I think he'd been shot or something—at least that had been his excuse. That cold ball of dread in my gut grew heavier.

"May I call a car for you, Ms. O'Toole?"

"What?" Jeremy's voice stopped; I heard the beep. I didn't leave a message. Instead, I killed the call and put my phone in my pocket.

"Do you need a car?" The valet looked like he'd just graduated eighth grade. A Dennis the Menace doppelganger, his innocent face hiding a youth spent cutting his teeth on taking the family Suburban for joyrides. Books and covers, I wasn't one to judge. But the kid wasn't exactly one to instill confidence in a Ferrari owner leaving his car while he gambled or dallied ... or killed a country-music legend.

"The guy who just left in the Lambo, you know him?"

"The yellow one with the black dragon logo?"

A bit more to go on. Not much, but I'd take it. Although I doubted the DMV kept note of distinguishing logos on registered automobiles. "Yes. That's the one. Do you know the gentleman?" I almost choked on that word. Of course, strip clubs were routinely referred to as gentlemen's clubs, so perhaps the term didn't carry the class it used to.

"Not personally, but by reputation, yes. He's the son of some bigwig from Macau. Throws his money around but is a real george when it comes to the staff."

"Dropping a ton at the tables and the clubs but stiffing the staff. Not a stellar character. And not very bright." Anyone who even brushed up against Vegas knew the town ran on tips. You grease the right palm with enough green, the world would be delivered to your suite. What was it the Big Boss had said on national television? "You can get anything you want at my hotel?" I'd about had a stroke, but the Earth kept spinning, the cops hadn't raided our facilities, and Vegas remained the adult playground it had always been.

"No, ma'am."

"Would you have a name?"

"Goes by Sam."

"Sam?"

"He says just Sam." The kid, his hands clasped behind his back, nodded. "He thought Joe was too..."

"Clichéd?"

The kid didn't have an answer, and I had the vague feeling he had no idea what I was talking about.

Not that I expected to find anything, but I made one more circuit of the Kasbah as I called Romeo and gave him the little information I had.

"We'll work through the DMV, see if we can narrow it down. Fancy wheels, shouldn't be too hard. "

I didn't feel like educating him, so I simply said, "Thanks," and rang off.

At a dead end, I set a course for Registration. Even though I doubted our dinner jacket guy would have given his particulars to our computer, a guest list for the bungalows at the Kasbah might prove insightful. Since he had a key, I assumed Sam, or whatever his real name was, had at least a passing familiarity with one of our guests. Of course, this being Vegas, physical intimacies didn't necessarily mean information was exchanged. Short on threads to pull, I decided to give it a shot. But one of the main services we sold to our Kasbah guests was privacy protection. So poking around would be a tightrope walk between privacy and murder to figure out who might know Sam.

TEDDIE'S phone call caught me skulking through the rows of slot machines as I worked my way toward the lobby, without alerting Mona and her coffee klatch to my presence. For a moment I wavered. Teddie didn't deserve instant access, but I suspected friends were in short supply for him about now.

"Hey. How're you holding up?" I tried for cheery. Stupid, it came off sounding forced, which it was.

His sigh wavered through the connection. "Your buddy, Squash, has scored me a suite of my own. Of course, it could use a woman's touch: it's a bit Spartan." Even though he was trying to keep it light, tension stretched his voice tighter than the high-C string on his baby grand. I said a silent thank-you to Squash Trenton. Teddie's stint as a female impersonator was no secret. Assumptions would be made. Mixing and mingling with the general prison population would've been problematic for the guards and painful for Teddie.

"That's good."

An awkward silence rode on an undercurrent of everything that didn't need to be said between good friends ... best friends of a time.

"I have a bail hearing in the morning." He didn't ask. He didn't have to.

"What time?"

"We're third on the docket at nine, but you know how that goes. Have you spoken to Daniel Lovato?" A tremor of fear vibrated the last word. He cleared his throat.

Was he worried that I would refuse or that Daniel would? "Yes." His breath rushing out gave me the answer I wanted. "No promises. I don't want to raise your hopes. You have to know what a FUBAR this is."

"I know. I didn't do it. I swear."

"We have to prove it, Teddie."

He started to talk. I shut him down. "Don't say anything. You don't know who's listening, and I don't want to get dragged into court to testify. I'll take my lead from your attorney."

"Okay." His tone suggested he didn't believe me. "For once, I'm glad that you don't take direction from anybody."

I knew it, but there was a time and place for breaking rules, and this wasn't either. "Teddie, this one is different. One misstep and you're on a death row suicide watch. Hang tight. I'm doing all I can. I'll see you in the morning." Wanting the connection, needing to know he was all right, I clutched the phone, pressing it to my ear long after I knew he was gone.

A hand grabbed my elbow. I yelped and jumped. And turned to look into the eyes of an old friend. Hank Pascarelli. He wrapped me in a bear hug, which I enjoyed. Then, hands on my shoulders, he leaned back. "Let me get a look at you."

Still in his Hawaiian shirt and khakis, but filling them out better than the last time I'd seen him. "You look terrific, Mr. Pascarelli."

"Happiness will do that to you. I got you to thank."

Joy hit my heart. "Mrs. Paisley? She feeding you some of her pies?"

Hank let go of me and patted his burgeoning stomach. "Too many."

"And how is Griffin, Indiana?"

He looked happily confounded. "Who knew I'd find my happy in the fat-big middle of nowhere?"

Hands on my hips, I gave him a smile. "Indiana is hardly the middle of nowhere. Don't tell me you two are living in sin?"

"Yep. Damned proud of it, too. But I decided she needed to make an honest man out of me."

"You're getting married?" At the blush in his cheeks it was my turn to give the hug.

"All the family is coming. Even her Harvard-boy grandson. Good kid. Nice thing you done."

I put on my best innocent face. "I don't know what you're talking about. What's he studying?"

"Government. Politics. Communication. Something like that. He's just started."

"Dear God, don't introduce him to my mother."

"Too late. Those two have been scheming."

Raising my hands in mock supplication, I said, "I don't want to know. When's the big day?"

He gave me the particulars, and I meticulously entered them into the calendar on my phone, the one I could never remember to look at. "You give your bride a hug for me. And best wishes to both of you." With a song in my heart, I said goodbye. Challenging Fate and my mother, I threw back my shoulders, thrust out my chin, and walked on air all the way out of the casino, through the lobby, arriving in front of Registration just as my confidence flagged. A one-woman army against the forces of evil—daunting odds even for a betting woman—and I wasn't holding up well.

Sergio Fabiano, our front desk manager, paced behind the long registration counter like a caged lion contemplating his opportunities for escape. His dark hair, which he wore long, angled across his face. Looking up, he flipped it out of his eyes and gave me a tight smile. With his flock of adoring females absent, lacking the glow of their adoration he looked almost human ... a Greek god dropped to Earth to walk among us mere mortals. A bit fastidious for my tastes, though—I drew the line at a boyfriend who was prettier than me. Teddie came perilously, close and, yes, he looked better in my clothes than I did. His legs weren't bad either.

Teddie.

"I'm very sorry about Mr. Teddie." Sergio took a step back. My eyes must've gone all slitty. Loosely interpreted, that was my body language for "run." "He did not do this."

"Of course not." I tried to loosen up. As Mona always said, worry did nothing but make you look like a Shar Pei. And anger would get you ten to life. Neither good end goals—not that I made a habit of listening to my mother. That could land me in jail or an asylum.

Slipping between two queues of guests, I basked in the buzz of several languages swirling around me, excitement burbling in each curious word. All shapes and sizes and in various states and styles of dress, our guests were united in holiday cheer, each of them clutching a free beverage of their choice.

Leaning on the counter, motioning him close, I lowered my voice. "I need a list of the guests in the bungalows."

Sergio's eyes widened, but he knew better than to ask. "Many of them register under false names."

"Vegas, where you can buy an alternate identity for the weekend. So helpful."

Sergio leaned into me, getting too close for my comfort. The nuance of boundaries and personal space still eluded him. "That depends on what you're looking for."

My flat stare pressed home the point.

"Right." He moved back, leaving a cloud of Aramis or one of those other cloying colognes men often hoped would render females weak-kneed and compliant.

They only made me sneeze. I held my breath, hoping to maintain my dignity. When I thought the urge had passed, I took a tentative breath. The sneeze had been hiding, and it was pissed, now doubling me over in a flurry of horrible honking like geese heading south for the winter.

One upside—the lines on either side stepped away, giving me elbow room. One kind woman offered me a tissue.

Apparently clueless as to his guilt, Sergio waited for one of the agents to finish checking in a couple, then eased her aside. His fingers flew over the keyboard, then he relinquished the machine back to his agent. "I've printed the list to my terminal in the back." As he disappeared through the doorway, I understood his logic as I watched the agents printing and grabbing papers from the various printers. The list couldn't fall into just any hands—access to the bungalow list was coveted by the media sharks always circling, looking for a tasty celebrity morsel.

While I waited, I turned and faced the lobby, leaning back, my elbows braced on the counter. Christmas had come to the Babylon. Festive greenery bedecked with rainbowed glass balls laced the countertops and railings. Evergreens sprouted through piles of brightly wrapped packages in every available nook and cranny and bookending the various couches and furniture clusters. Children, high on rumors of Santa's imminent arrival and the obligatory holiday sugar overload, rushed around like terrified cows being herded by helicopter, darting this way and that, bouncing off each other and the legs of strangers.

Holidays pressed home the point that parenthood should not be entered into lightly, a mantra I made my own.

Music provided a soundtrack to all the chaos. The familiar strains of *Grandma Got Run Over By a Reindeer* filtered through the hubbub, making me smile. Somebody had a sense of humor. I liked it. Laughter made everything better.

Except murder, the black cloud following me around. So far, I hadn't seen but a hint of a silver lining. Tomorrow's bail hearing would either brighten the sky or bring a deluge.

Sergio cleared his throat behind me, saving me from a mental stroll through that dark wood. His face clouded as he scanned the names on his list. "I am not so sure this will help."

I took the list to make my own assessment. Unknown names. Several Sams, as suspected. You'd think those intent on some reputation-damaging fun might be a bit more creative.

I sucked in my breath at the last name on the list.

Mrs. Holt Box.

She'd checked in last night. "I need a copy of this signature, please."

MISS P hunkered behind her old desk in the front office, wearing yesterday's clothes, her eyes red, her hair flat, and her smile absent. Guess life had given me my moment of happiness. Now it was back to business.

"If we have a bungalow available, will you move Mr. Pascarelli and Mrs. Paisley? They're back and getting married and bringing all the family."

Miss P didn't perk up like she usually did with good news and a fun job, but she did nod and make a note as she dabbed at her nose with a tissue.

"Did you go home?" I parked my butt on the corner of her desk and resisted the Siren call of the messages overflowing my in-box.

All hang-dog, she shook her head.

"You hang that head any lower, you're going to be drooling on the desk. You know how much I don't like that." I boosted myself from my perch. "Come with me. Some medicinal spirits are in order."

She still sat where I'd left her when I returned with two breakfast portions of Wild Turkey, each in its very own Flintstone's jelly-jar glass. I balanced the two glasses in one palm, and with a hand under her elbow, I encouraged Miss P to her feet, then guided her to the couch in my inner sanctum. Thankfully, Tool One and Tool Two were not taking turns with the hammer today, so we had my office to ourselves. The lone light bulb added ambiance, the weak light masking the layer of dust covering everything. "Sit."

She perched on the edge of the couch, her knees pressed together like a pious schoolgirl, the jelly jar I'd thrust into her hands cradled in her lap.

"Down the hatch."

She threw back her drink like a pro, only gasping a little as the firewater lit a path all the way down. "Dear heavens."

"As invectives go, a bit on the weak side." My need a bit less, I sipped my drink. While I loved my joy juice, the breakfast bit was a stretch. My desk chair groaned as I sat. "Can you add to the punch list oiling the springs in this thing? It's giving me a complex."

Owl-eyed, Miss P blinked at me.

Toeing open the bottom drawer, I put my feet on it and leaned back. "Feeling any better?"

Staring at her feet, she shook her head. "I guess you heard," she said, her voice thin, her shoulders slumped in defeat.

"All I heard was something about some guy—"

"Cody Ellis." She squared her shoulders a bit and met my eyes.

"Right. Mr. Ellis—"

"Doctor."

"Really?" So the ladies had been right. And I'd been thinking some Iowa farm boy. A youthful indiscretion. Life never missed a beat to show me how wrong I could be. Color my interest piqued. I tried to hide it, but Miss P had encyclopedic knowledge of my quirks and nuances. "Okay, some doctor asshat shows up—"

"He's not an asshat." Miss P's cheeks flushed, either from anger, embarrassment, or a firewater kick start ... or all three.

"He's not?"

She shook her head, looking like she'd lost her last friend. Or had found an old love.

I squinted my eyes, as if that would help me read the answer in her aura or something. Silly, but an undercurrent ran beneath this conversation, if it could be called that—and undercurrent I couldn't quite get the drift of.

Oh, this was not good. "So is he your husband?"

"That's what he says."

"And this is a bad thing, right?"

She plucked at an invisible speck of lint on the sleeve of her sweater and looked up over my left shoulder. "Of course."

What was it the experts said? If a person looks up and left while answering a question, they're lying? This time I slugged the rest of my drink. "What about Jeremy? I'm taking it he knows."

"He was there."

We both had empty glasses. I solved that problem with a quick trip to the kitchenette in my old office. This time Miss P didn't need any encouragement. My day still in front of me, and Teddie's life on the line, I decided to throttle-back on the high-octane and put my jelly jar down, then moved it out of reach. "And you're sure you don't know where he is?"

"No. He said he needed some time. So I haven't tried to reach him, not that he'd answer."

That could explain my inability to reach him, but there also was another explanation. I called Dane.

He answered on the first ring. "I'm following Jean-Charles to the Babylon. That guy works almost as much as you do."

"Once he's here, I'll get Security to ride herd on him. I need you to find Jeremy."

"Has he gone missing?" Dane's tone turned serious.

"Don't know, but he's radio silent, which makes me worried. There's a benign explanation that I won't go into, but also some that aren't." I stared at a spot on the wall, avoiding Miss P's stricken look.

"Got it. I'll let you know." He rang off.

I tossed my phone onto a stack of papers on the desk, then waved at the resulting small dust cloud and returned to Miss P. "So, why now? Why did Cody Ellis show up now?"

"He grew up." Miss P said that matter-of-factly, as if was a legitimate explanation.

I was so at sea. "What? Help me out here. How could you have married him if he wasn't grown-up before?"

"The difference between chronological and emotional maturity." She leveled her gaze. "I know you know all about that."

Ouch. "Obviously, I'm still learning. Maybe you could start at the beginning?"

With studied care, she set her jelly jar on the floor by her feet, then rubbed her hands down her thighs. When she looked up, a bit of the worry was gone, replaced by something else, an emotion I couldn't read.

"It all started in Kenya."

Blindsided once again. I was getting used to it, which didn't make me happy. "Like Kenya in Africa?"

"No, like Kenya in Iowa. Jesus H. Christ." She took a deep breath. "Sorry, this has thrown me off a bit."

The Mistress of Understatement. Leaning forward, I raised my hands and opened my arms. "Finally! A bit of piss and vinegar. Every problem has solution, but you got to man-up and face it head-on."

She looked at me from under lowered brows, one side of her

mouth ticked up.

A familiar look; no interpretation necessary. I grabbed my cockroach paperweight, turning it over and over in my hands. "As you are dying to point out, if running from problems was an Olympic event, I'd have more gold medals than Michael Phelps and Mark Spitz put together. If experience is the best teacher, I have a gold-clad Ph.D. If—"

"I get it." This time I caught a fleeting smile, or maybe I imagined it. Regardless, her posture softened. Leaning back, she tucked her feet underneath her.

"And I love you, so you should listen to me." I'd saved the best for last, and I could tell it worked.

"Okay. But just let me get through this. Don't offer a running commentary. I know I've been a fool. I can't outrun my past. Hell, by that standard I'm one of your beloved clichés. But, admitting that?" She raked a hand through her hair, spiking it back up and perhaps unwittingly showing a bit of her normal moxie. "Well, a bitter pill, that's for sure. I pride myself on being so ... "

"Contained? Enigmatic? Perfect in a way us mere mortals couldn't possibly attain?"

Her eyes narrowed.

"One step too far, huh?"

We both knew I was jerking her chain on purpose. Pissed off, she had a chance.

"Yep, too far, but too true. Now just be quiet and let me tell you a story."

"Sure. No more. Not until you're finished. I promise." We both knew I had agreed to an impossibility.

"So, as I said, it all started in Kenya. We were both young, stupid. I was doing basic nursing duties for one of those volunteer doctor organizations. They do such incredible work, really make a difference. It was all very empowering, satisfying in a way nothing since has been. Cody was—"

A voice shouted from the front office. "Lucky! Lucky are you here?"

Shit, just when Miss P was getting to the good part. "In here."

Kimberly Cho ran into my office. She too still wore last night's party costume although she looked even worse than Miss P. For once I wasn't the one on the short-end of the sleep spectrum. How had that happened? Had I gone mainstream? Old school? Or just old? Perish the thought.

"Oh, thank God!" Kimberly shot a glance at Miss P, then slapped me with worried eyes. "You have to stop him! Now!"

"Who?"

Kimberly stepped around my desk, grabbed my arm and started tugging. I had her by about eight inches and forty pounds. If she wanted me to move, brute force wasn't on her side.

"He has a gun, and he's after your father!"

CHAPTER EIGHT

"WHO has a gun?" I grabbed my phone.

Kimberly waved my question away. "Too hard to explain. We must stop him. I saw him from the balcony just outside your door. We must hurry!"

Miss P and I both leapt to our feet. Kimberly turned and ran with both of us hot on her heels.

"Where is he?" I panted the words as I ran. We hit the door to the stairs, then pounded down the stairs and burst into the lobby.

"Baccarat room." Kimberly didn't even pause, turning to the left, then regaining speed as she raced over a bridge over the lobby stream, scattering guests. Ducks flapped in a cloud of feathers as they skittered out of the way. As I loped after her, I caught the flash of yellow out the front door.

A yellow Lamborghini. With a black dragon logo behind the front wheel well.

I keyed the walkie-talkie feature of my phone as I ran. "Jerry? Tell me you're there."

"Right here." All business, he knew serious when he heard it.

"The dinner jacket guy is in the building. His car's at the front curb. Get a license plate. I've been told he has a gun and is after the Big Boss." I raced over the bridge, keeping Kimberly in sight. "I'm en route to the high-stakes Baccarat room. Get eyes open. I need to know where my father is. And, goddamn it, locate that ass playing games with us. And do it now." Technically, after my last promotion, I was Jerry's superior, but this was the first time I'd used that attitude.

"I'm on it. Keep the channel open."

I lowered my head and summoned my after-burners. A flame-out, but I managed to close the distance slightly. I could hear Miss P's ragged breathing as she pounded behind me. Heads turned as we raced by. The crowd parted, jumping out of the way as we dodged, darted, and ran.

Jerry's voice. "Confirm your father is in the high-stakes Baccarat room. Several whales, a lot of money in play. Three teams closing. ETA two minutes."

"Got it." My heart pounded more from fear than lack of oxygen. My father. A guy with a gun who had most likely killed before. And nothing I could do about it other than run.

I angled to the left. With a two-fingered whistle, I got Kimberly's attention, redirecting her. Now in the lead, I whipped around the corner and burst through the doors into the quiet decorum of high-stakes gaming.

A carefully controlled environment, the high-stakes rooms were kept library quiet, the staff unctuous, obsequious, and invisible unless summoned. No one ever bolted through the doors. Ever.

So, when I did just that, everyone froze in indecision.

Time slowed. "Father!"

He gave me a quizzical look.

Two burly men with "goon" written all over them stepped forward. Important people, impressive muscle, an unwritten requisite. The men paused, assessing my threat level. Several Asian men seated at the tables gave me little attention as I skidded to a halt—as a woman and an interloper, I was a trifle for someone else to sully themselves dealing with. My father, his arms crossed, his head lowered, was engrossed in heated conversation with an Asian man I vaguely recognized. Neither looked happy, my father in particular, a deepening glower on his face. His interest shifted at my intrusion.

Where was the dinner jacket guy?

Think, Lucky. Calm. What did he look like?

Short, dark hair, an arrogant bearing.

There. Across the room, at the far table.

He looked calm, unhurried. His eyes darting my way, the only chink in his unruffled exterior. My presence had upset him.

Where was his gun? Was Kimberly right?

With no immediate threat, I willed myself to calm. To restore decorum, I adjusted my features to a smile, even though my fingers itched to grab the little shit by the neck and squeeze. I moved in his direction.

Kimberly Cho skidded in next me. "There!" She gasped. "Oh, my God."

Activity in the room stilled. Except for me. I advanced on the dinner jacket guy. Sam Asshat.

The man reached into his coat. His eyes, dead hollow holes, caught mine. An evil smile as he pulled his hand out.

A gun.

He wanted me to see, to watch.

Chairs scraped back as players scurried for shelter. Someone upended a table. No one shouted. Odd.

Fear catapulted me to action. Fear and a mile-wide urge to commit homicide. One stride. I honed in on him with laser-like precision. He raised the gun. I threw a chair at him. He ducked. It glanced off his shoulder. He steadied his aim. Another step. Close now. Blood pounded in my ears. He pointed.

The Big Boss. Out of the corner of my eyes, I saw him flinch.

The gunman threw me a look, toying with me.

I flicked another chair at him, hitting his shoulder again.

"No!" I took a step and leapt.

The gun jerked in his hand. A silenced pop.

I barreled into him. Both of us crashed to the floor. One hand on his throat, I scrambled to straddle him. Squeezing soft flesh, I delighted in the pulse that beat under my fingers, in the dimming of the light in his eyes. My bulk held him down; my right knee pinned an arm. Frantically, he tried to work the other loose.

"Oh, my God!" Kimberly screamed. "He's been hit."

I whipped around. My father!

That moment of infinitesimal focus shift was the opening the guy under me was looking for. He pulled his left hand loose, then swung his elbow. With little weight behind it, his strength was still enough to stagger me. Stars peppered my vision as I blinked and tried to shake it off. Another punch to my solar plexus, and the air rushed out of me. He rolled me off of him, bolted to his feet and ran.

On my hands and knees, I struggled for air, my oxygen-starved muscles slow to respond. "Call Security. Get him. Warn them about the gun," I shouted as best I could. Two of the staff jumped to action.

On the far side of the room, I could see my father's legs extending from behind a table. I scrambled and crawled my way through the jungle of overturned chairs and tables until I reached his side.

A red stain bloomed across his chest. Blood.

"Call an ambulance!" I shouted, as I clutched his arm, pressing my fingers to the hollow in his throat. "Hurry!" A thready pulse whispered under my fingers. I tore at his shirt. Someone dropped down next to me. "I need to save him. He can't die." Panic ripped at me. Tears raced down my cheeks. "Don't touch him." I slapped at the hands that reached to help. Strong male hands.

"I can help." A calm male voice.

"Father," I said, loudly like a rude American willing a non-English speaker to understand. "Come on. Talk to me. You have to stay with me. You can't die. I need you."

The male hands grabbed mine, stilling them.

"Let me do this. I'm a doctor." The voice calm, reassuring.

I glanced up into warm brown eyes, a kind face exuding a calm confidence. A handlebar mustache, graying hair pulled back and caught in a ponytail. Something about him. I stopped my frantic desperation, and eased back. "You're a doctor?"

"In New York, Emergency Medicine. I've handled a lot of this."

"Don't let him die."

The kind face turned serious, the eyes focused. "I'll do my best."

I sat back on my heels, helpless, terrified. "Are you a good doctor?" I whispered. But intent on my father, he didn't hear, or couldn't answer. I raised a shaking hand to brush the hair out of my eyes, but it was covered with blood. Unable to process, I stared at it like it belonged to somebody else. Blood splattered my pants, my shirt.

The doctor barked quiet orders to those who hovered.

I didn't understand. The scene in front of me grew distant, my vision fuzzy, the world kaleidoscoped.

A hand on my shoulder, warm, strong, stopped the spinning.

"Lucky." Miss P's voice, steady and strong. "Come with me." She grabbed my arm and tugged. "Please. Give Cody room. If he's anything like he was, he knows what he's doing, and he's good at it. We just have to get out of his way."

"Cody?" My weight shifted back. I let Miss P help me to my feet.

"I was behind you when I heard the shot. I called him. He was nursing a drink in Delilah's."

"Drinking?" Panic pulsed, a heartbeat restored. I jerked my arm from her grasp.

"A soda." Miss P wouldn't let go. "Come on. We'll meet them at the hospital."

"Where's Security?"

"Chasing the shooter."

"God, a gunman loose in the hotel. What the hell is going on?" Miss P held my arm tight, then looped an arm around my waist to steady me. "First, Holt Box, which could've just been a fifteen minutes of fame kind of thing." Life. Mental health. A delicate balance. "But why the Big Boss?" A distant connection filtered through the adrenaline. A contract connected the two of them. But was it worth killing over? Who would care?

Besides Teddie. Unless somehow he'd been sprung on a technicality, too, and I had been left out of the loop once again; I was pretty sure he'd been in jail for this one, a pretty airtight alibi.

EMT's rushed into the room. They knelt beside the doctor, Cody, Miss P had said, deferring to him as he explained. In seeming seconds, they had my father hooked up to an IV and strapped to a gurney. As they ushered him out of the room, I caught a glimpse of a pale face, eyes closed. If he died ...

The Big Boss had been my North Star for as long as I'd been me.

Once they'd disappeared, and some of the staff started picking up chairs, putting the room back in order, my focus returned and the panic cleared. Many around me typed furiously on their cellphones.

"If I see a video of anything that happened here ..." I paused, shrugging away from Miss P, my focus returning. "Wait. I want to see all the footage you guys shot." I gave a high sign to all the staff. They knew what to do: round up names, contact info, and strong-arm the phones out of them.

A few of the men tried to sneak out. "Stop them," I barked at the two attendants closest to the door.

The men resisted, the situation turning ugly.

I'd keyed my phone to request security reinforcements, when Romeo arrived with a phalanx of uniformed officers. They ushered everyone back inside and organized the debriefing. Power and side arms, both attention-getters.

Romeo rushed to my side, emotions marching across his face and concern clouding his eyes. "You okay?" He rolled his eyes at himself. "Stupid question. I have an escort waiting at the front entrance. Two motorcycles to facilitate your trip to the hospital. I'll handle things here, but keep me posted."

"Get everybody's phone. They were all recording it."

Romeo barked at his officers.

I focused on breathing, and not speculating on what was happening with my father. Numbness seeped in, a haze of protective disbelief. "Did you get the shooter?"

The detective's lips pressed into a thin line, his eyes hard. "No. He ran through the casino. Got off some shots at the guards. Didn't hit anybody, but scared the hell out of everybody. At the first shot, they all ran—it was chaos. Apparently his car was waiting out front."

"Yellow Lamborghini, black dragon logos behind the front wheel wells."

Romeo's attention focused. "Yeah?"

I brought him up to speed on this morning. "Check with Security. See if they have a license number. How'd you get here so fast?"

"I was on my way to see you when the call came in. The uniforms got here right after I did, but we got tied up with the shooter." Romeo raised his head and searched the crowd. "Reynolds," he barked. An older man, a familiar arrogant disinterest on his face, looked up. Romeo motioned him over.

Trying to place him, I watched him amble toward us. "Isn't that the guy you used to work for?"

"He works for me now." Romeo didn't smile, but I heard the satisfaction in his voice. Reynolds jotted notes as Romeo told him where to go and what to do.

Reynolds nodded—whether he was angry or not, interested or

not, it was hard to tell, as he left to do Romeo's bidding. Another day, another attempted murder.

But this one was anything but every-day.

"You trust that guy?" The blood on my hands drying, I swiped at a couple of strands of hair tickling my eyes. My father's blood. It flaked and cracked where my hand bent ... like finger painting in grade school. Time folded. My father hadn't been a part of my life then. I'd felt his absence.

"He'll do his job," Romeo said. "But if I trip up, miss anything." He jostled me to get my attention. "If I let anyone go off half-cocked. He'll have my ass."

I met his stare. "Then I'll have to make sure I am fully-cocked, locked, and loaded."

Concern etched his features and his warning timbered his voice. "Right. Before you go, can you give me a quick and dirty?"

Miss P shouldered her way into the conversation, tucking a protective arm around my waist. "Let her go. I was here. I can tell you all you need to know."

"Between you and Kimberly, you guys saw it all."

"Kimberly?" Romeo asked, pulling his notepad out of his pocket, poising his pencil over a clean page.

"Yeah. She's right here. She's the one who told us about the shooter." I scanned the room.

Kimberly Cho was gone.

Raising my phone to my mouth, I pushed to talk. "Jerry. A young woman." I described her, Miss P weighing in on her clothing. I never noticed that kind of thing. "She alerted us to the shooter, led us here. And now she's gone. Find her." I felt Romeo's eyes boring holes. As I talked, I looked around the room. Everyone looked a bit confused, shell-shocked as they cooperated with my staff. Everyone except one, the man my father had been talking with. Arms crossed, head down, he glowered.

I shrugged away from Romeo. As I talked, I worked my way across the room, my eyes on the last man to speak with my father. Images, panic washed over me. My father turning, falling. I pushed the horror aside and tried to focus.

A man stepped into my path with his hand outstretched, stopping me. His size and the murderous look on his face would've been enough. "You can't talk with him."

Romeo, lurking behind me, flashed his badge. "Maybe she can't, but I damn well can."

"No, sir." The man-mountain shook his leonine head. "He doesn't have to talk to anybody—not until you're cleared through diplomatic channels."

Romeo glanced at me. I shrugged at his silent question. "Diplomatic channels?" he asked.

"Mr. Cho is a diplomatic attaché for the Chinese government."

"And he's in Vegas, why?" I said, preempting Romeo.

"To protect China's gaming interests." The man glanced over his shoulder. "But that's all I can say. It's common knowledge."

I could quibble—nobody had told me about a diplomat in the house, and that normally would be my responsibility. I'd love to know exactly why he was here and an answer to the larger question: why was he flying under the radar? If I hadn't been alerted, then nobody had been.

Curious. Cho was a common name in China, but the coincidence was too obvious to ignore. Mr. Cho. Kimberly Cho.

I needed to find that girl. So many questions.

Kimberly had recognized the shooter at the party and then again today. Was the shooter somehow connected to Mr. Chinese Big Shot? Were the three of them connected? If the diplomat, Mr. Cho, was the shooter's puppeteer, then there wasn't a law in the Universe that would stop me.

Maybe I couldn't save my father, but I sure as hell could kill whoever shot him.

I HATED hospitals. The smell alone unsettled my stomach, already tightened by fear. No matter how much Pine Sol, the stench of death and fear permeated the air. A protective disinterest dulled the staff's smiles. Hope and magic were my daily companions; death and despair, punctured by a few moments of joy, were theirs. Working here would shave my soul to nothing.

UMC, University Medical Center, was the best in Vegas at dealing with medical emergencies. That didn't make me happy to be here.

In fact, right now, I wanted to be anywhere else, worrying about anything else. A murder, even. That I could fix. This? Not so much. And if there's anything I hate, it's feeling helpless and powerless.

My only companion in the surgical waiting area was a young man with one tennis shoe, a misbuttoned shirt, and no belt to hold up pants that were at least three sizes too big. Lounging in a molded chair, his legs outstretched, he'd fallen asleep or passed out, his fist pressed to his face the only thing keeping him semi-upright.

Thankfully, the television hanging high in the corner was silent, its screen dark. To me, good television was an oxymoron, excepting the first four seasons of *West Wing*, of course.

Five cups of bad coffee had my nerves jangling and my teeth on edge when Mona rushed into the room. Her hair a mess, her face swollen with worry, her eyes brimming with unspent tears. In a pair of yoga pants and a tunic top, with ballet slippers, she lost her momentum when she stepped through the doors. When she caught sight of me, she wavered. I rushed to her. As her knees buckled, I caught her, easing her into a chair.

She held onto me tightly for a bit, until her composure resettled. Easing away, she curled back into the chair. "My God, Lucky! What happened?" She rooted in her bag for a tissue.

I handed her one of mine. "He was shot." Images raced through my head—my father falling, blood, everywhere blood, his pale face, no response. I squeezed my eyes shut, but I couldn't make them go away. I held up my hands, the blood long ago washed away, the stain remaining, a bad Shakespearean joke. A desperate need for revenge kept me from falling apart. "He's in surgery. They said he'd lost a lot of blood."

"His heart," Mona whispered. The Big Boss had almost died of a heart condition a few months ago. Teddie had been there to hold me, to help both Mona and me through it. Now we were all fighting for our lives, literally, metaphorically, and figuratively. While the outcome might be different for each, the pain was the same.

The world could turn on a dime. One of the Big Boss's favorite sayings. Funny how it was his life that took that turn, holding the future hostage.

"They know about his heart. Dr. Knapp is here. He's monitoring everything. Says the surgeon is the best."

Mona dabbed at her eyes. "The babies. They can't grow up without a father."

"The babies? Hell, I can't grow up without my father either." I lowered myself into the chair next to hers and took her hand in mine. Her skin, pale and blue, cold to the touch. I lightly brushed at a dusting of Baby Powder on her cheek then, tucked a wayward tendril behind her ear. "He has a lot to live for. You know what a scrapper he is."

JEAN-CHARLES pushed through the door, his face tense. A quick scan of the waiting room, then his eyes settled on me. His tension easing, he strode toward me. I rose, stepping into his hug. As he held me, I breathed him in. My world righted. Oh, I still wanted to be left in the desert someplace remote with the killer, a weapon, no witnesses, and a shovel, but it didn't have to be now. Tomorrow would do.

"And you are okay?" Jean-Charles spoke softly as he stroked my hair and held me close. Our bodies pressed together, his heat warming the cold snaking through my gut.

I could feel him shaking. "Better now."

"Your father?" His voice broke. He cleared his throat.

"No word yet."

"Hospitals, they are not good, *non?*"

"No, not good. But sometimes necessary." I raised my head off his shoulder and pressed my cheek to his. "Where is Christophe?"

"I am late to see you because I had to take him home. I could not bear to see him in a place like this. So much loss, it breaks the heart." His pain, though diminished by time, still vibrated under the surface. "You never forget. You find a way to live again, but it is there always."

"Of course."

He hugged me tight again. And yes, he was shivering. This was hard. Harder than he let on. "I could not lose like that again."

"Life, we don't call the shots."

"I do. As best I can."

I didn't want to tell him that was a recipe for heartbreak. The illusion of control could set you up for an even bigger fall. I should know. I'm the poster child for major crashes.

"What have the doctors said?" he asked, his face pale, his eyes haunted as if reliving his past. His wife. Death.

"They rushed my father into surgery. A nurse stepped out a bit ago and told me it would be awhile. And even after the surgeons are done, Father will be in recovery for a good bit. While they bring him back, she didn't think we'd be allowed to see him, but I'm not sure."

He included Mona in his look. "You both should let me take you home."

Mona shook her head. "No, I will be here when he wakes up."

Home. I so wanted to go home, to go back in time and start this day all over again. No, yesterday. If I could do it over. Maybe, just maybe, it would be different. "If I'd just listened to him."

"To whom? Theodore?"

"My father. He told me Irv Gittings would come after me ... that I could've handled."

"But you don't know."

"Oh, this has Ol' Irv's fingerprints all over it," Mona joined the conversation, her voice lethal.

I'd forgotten about her. Something that, before now, I'd thought impossible. She was like a rabid dog, able to kill with a small bite. That got me thinking.

She wilted under my stare. "What?"

"You and me. We got a murderer to put back in jail."

"Really?" She brightened a touch, the flush of revenge pinking her pale cheeks.

"You're going to be my secret weapon." She looked like the governor had commuted her sentence one second before midnight, which made me feel bad. We used to be the Two Musketeers. Adulthood ... mine ... had gotten in the way. Not a proud moment.

"You both are not going to do anything." Jean-Charles ordered.

"You will leave this to the police."

Behind his back, Mona winked at me, a tear-filled, still terrified wink, but she was made of stern stuff, and she was a Rothstein, even if only by marriage.

The Rothsteins were Old Vegas—you fuck with family, we fuck with you.

The automatic double doors whooshed open, admitting Dr. Knapp in scrubs and surgical booties, a sobering shot of ice water through the veins. He swiped the surgical head cover off, leaving his white hair standing in tufts in spots and flattened in others. Every one of his sixty-odd years showed in his creased face, his slumped shoulders, and his tired smile. He eased down next to Mona, taking her hand. I hadn't thought she could get any paler. I was wrong.

Jean-Charles pulled me tight. I wrapped my arms around his waist and braced for the blow.

"He's one tough cuss," Dr. Knapp started.

Mona smiled, ignoring the tear that trickled down her cheek.

"And he must've done something right. There were so many things that could've gone wrong had they been slightly different. The bullet nicked ... " At Mona's stricken look, he redirected and started again. "We were very lucky. If Dr. Ellis hadn't been assisting ..." He patted Mona's hand. "But we don't have to worry about the what-ifs. Albert has a long road, but he's tough."

"He's okay, then?" Mona's voice, soft yet tight, hoping yet not quite willing to believe.

"Resting right now. Coming out of it."

Mona grasped his hand in both of hers. "Thank you."

"Not me. Dr. Ellis. Man, that guy has seen some stuff. He had some work-arounds that saved a lot of time and probably saved your husband. Such luck he was here."

Lucky indeed. Life. Miss P's past, my father's future ... funny the synergy of life, the odd connections that make such a difference.

I was mentally trotting down the what-if-alley when the doors whooshed open again, this time expelling the doctor from the hotel, Dr. Ellis ... Cody.

Disengaging from Jean-Charles, I met Cody halfway. "I have no idea what to say."

"It's what I do, and this is why I do it."

His hand was warm, his smile relaxed. Tallish, he met me eye-to-eye, thin, with weathered skin and old eyes that reeked of adventures in faraway places. He exuded a quiet confidence that instilled a peace of mind. A rational thought in an incomprehensible situation.

No wonder Miss P had married him.

Miss P. As if on cue, she rushed in through the glass doors, cool air with a hint of rain sneaking in with her. She momentarily hitched when she caught sight of Cody, but then she motored over to me. "Your father?"

I deferred to Dr. Ellis.

Cody's eyes lit, but his smile dimmed when he looked at her, a sadness lingering under his carefully constructed expression. "He's in recovery. Probably a few days in ICU, but that depends on him. After that, we'll see, but he should be home by Christmas."

Miss P fisted a hand at her chest. "Oh, Cody, I'm so glad you were here." She looked bright, radiant, conflicted.

Her husband walked on water, or darn near, and the man I had thought would be mine was cooling his heels in jail. Somehow, I was happier with my problems than hers.

Life.

Standing between the two of them, I decided self-preservation dictated retreat. "Can we see him?"

Dr. Ellis nodded toward Dr. Knapp, who said, "For a few minutes. He'll be sleeping for awhile yet, and then we'll keep him comfortable, so he'll be in and out, probably won't even know you're there."

Mona rose, tugging her tunic into place. "Whether he knows it or not, we will be there."

"Only one of you can stay at a time."

Mona cast worried eyes at me.

"I'll go in with you, Mother, but you should be the one to stay."

Relief softened her fear. "When you go, would you mind stopping to check on the twins?"

JEAN-CHARLES folded the paper he'd been reading and rose to greet me when I stepped back into the waiting area. He was alone, except for Dane's man who sat near the door, leaving enough distance for privacy, but not so much he couldn't solve an issue if it arose. I hadn't noticed him before, but I was glad he was tailing my chef.

"Where are Miss P and Dr. Ellis?" I asked, trying to find my equilibrium. Seeing my father immobile, lacking a vital life force I'd taken for granted, hooked to machines to feed him, breathe for him, had shaken my foundation.

"They went to the cafeteria. Dr. Ellis wanted to stay close."

"Nice guy." Not knowing what to say and what to leave out. Not knowing whether I had the energy to explain even part of Miss P and Cody Ellis, I stopped there.

"Perhaps I shouldn't say anything, especially considering the wedding upcoming, but there is something between them."

"You have no idea." Needing his touch, the connection, I reached out and stroked his cheek. "But theirs is not my story to tell. Thank you for waiting. You didn't have to."

"But I did." He folded me into his arms and held me tight against this chest.

The tears I hadn't allowed myself threatened to spill. The fear past, the terror over, I'd let my guard down. The sleeve of my sweater, pulled over the heel of my hand, absorbed the tears before they could run unchecked.

Jean-Charles pulled a pocket square out of his jacket pocket, shook it out, and dabbed at the ones that escaped. "The last two days ..."

"Tell me about it." I eased back, but not so far that I couldn't feel his warmth, his love. For some odd reason, I was comfortable being myself with him. Just me. And something about him told me that was enough. "Let's do something fun, something life-affirming for a change."

He raised one eyebrow. "What do you have in mind?"

"How are you with twins?"

CHAPTER NINE

FLASH pounced the minute I stepped into the lobby at the Babylon. From past experience I knew I couldn't outrun her; tonight I didn't even try. As she began peppering me with questions, my phone rang. Romeo. I opened my arms in supplication toward Jean-Charles. "You'd think I could have a life."

He chuckled and leaned in for a quick kiss. "You do have a very nice life. A very nice and crazy life. I'll be in the Burger Palais. Call me when you want to check on the twins for your mother." He charged off with his security detail of one in tow. He pulled the man next to him and started chatting away—my chef, a master promoter, never knew a stranger. A cloud passed over that happy thought. Some strangers could be not so nice.

I watched Jean-Charles as he walked with purpose toward the entrance to the Bazaar. Many heads turned as he strode by. I could tell he was aware of the attention and indifferent to it. I wasn't so sure I was. Switching to work mode, I scanned the lobby, looking for problems to fix, as I pressed the phone to my ear. Stalling Flash mid-question with a raised finger, I handled Romeo first. "I sure hope you have some good news," I said to Romeo, dispensing with the niceties.

"I'm the one hoping for good news." Romeo sounded as tired as I felt. "How's your father?"

A young couple made it through the front doors, burdened with luggage and tugging more. I tapped a bellman on the shoulder. "Move. Go help them." He glanced at me, then bolted as if shot out of a cannon.

"Move where? Help who?" Romeo asked, but his heart didn't

sound in it.

"Not talking to you."

"Permanently or just right now?"

Whistling, I caught the attention of a Champagne server who had stopped moving. I circled my forefinger. She got the hint and returned to working the growing line in front of Registration.

"Dang," I said to no one in particular. I made a beeline for the Front Desk.

Flash dogged my heels trying to get a word in. "I've got some info for you, if you have a minute, but not here." She sounded proud of herself, which got my attention. I measured the problem in front of me and the one I still held to my ear. "Give me five to ten?" I said to Flash.

She seemed okay with that. She pointed to the side. "I'll be over there." I nodded and reengaged Romeo. "Sorry. Just walked into the lobby. A few things needed my attention."

"Using your job to hide from life. I know the drill. Your father?"

"My job is my life." Even I felt sorry for myself. Apparently, my act didn't fool Romeo. Not sure how I felt about that. Seems there were a lot of things in my life I was conflicted about. "Why can't life just settle into a nice rhythm?"

"Then you'd be bored." Fumbling sounds like he switched his phone from one ear to the next. "Are you going to tell me about your father, or do I have to call the hospital and pull rank?"

"In ICU. He made it through the surgery. Now Mona will make sure he makes it through recovery."

"Oh, boy, I don't envy him. She's probably really good at cracking a whip." Romeo chuckled.

"I'm not sure I can envision my mother as you seem to be and not be scarred for life." Mona terrified him, which I thought cute. And her former job as a hooker and a madam had captured his imagination.

Having been raised in her whorehouse in Pahrump, I was pretty much over it. The only time it really caused me any trouble had been on take-your-kid-to-work day, and the day Mona realized I was well past puberty. That was the day that I became me. Keeping the family affiliation to herself, she'd sent me to the Big Boss, and I jumped on the treadmill that now was moving too fast for my meager skills.

"Her bite is worse than her bark," I said, unable to resist adding fuel to his fire. "But really, although a major pain in the ass, she's pretty harmless."

"Right." Romeo scoffed. "You want to meet me in the Kasbah, Bungalow 7?"

"Mrs. Holt Box? I wouldn't miss it. On my way in a few. Wait for me." I re-pocketed my phone and eased my way to the front of the closest registration line. After a few moments, and I saw where the bottleneck was, fingers drumming on the countertop as the agents waited. I motioned the Front Desk Day Manager over, a newbie I didn't recognize. She apparently knew who I was. I never got used to that—it was weird being known by people I'd never met. "Having problems with the computers?" I asked.

"Really slow today, getting odd error messages." She brushed a wisp of blonde hair, tucking it behind her ear. Round face, competent manner, not harried but not happy either.

"Open the last line yourself."

"Yes, ma'am."

"I know that won't solve the computer issue. Have you called IT?"

"They're working on it."

Hit me where it hurt. Was I being paranoid, or was this part of a grand plan? I needed to find Irv Gittings and make a few connections, the last one hopefully being the one that let loose the two thousand lethal volts on Ol' Sparky. Of course, that was wishful thinking—death by electrocution was not available in Nevada. Pity. It'd be perfect for Ol' Irv. Regardless, it was a good metaphor and the thought made me happy... not proud, but happy.

After I carefully culled the waiting lines to populate the new one so we wouldn't have mutiny as the stragglers in the back rushed to get ahead of those who had been waiting, I made a few calls to get more registration agents and more servers to ply the unhappy with joy juice. I stayed until all that could be done was in place, then plotted my course for the Kasbah, running headlong into Flash's look of exaggerated patience.

"Remember me?"

"Seriously? Who could forget?" I felt fairly sure the last guy who had left Flash cooling her heels had found himself under-dressed in a very public place. Not something I aspired to.

"What about Mrs. Box? Is she a suspect?" Flash circled me. Dressed today in more subtle shades of neon, her red hair a cascade of curls that clashed with the particular pink she had chosen, which was probably intended, her lips painted to match, the gold hoop earrings, white ceramic J-12 on her wrist, and hunger in her eyes, she was the perfect predator—something I loved and hated about her in equal measure.

At five feet, she was under my line of sight by a good margin. Looking over her head at the throng, I plotted my course and hoped that, if I ignored her, she'd go away. That tactic had never worked before, but hope is a pretty big thing for me, my last tether to some semblance of sanity. "Have you found Jeremy?"

That stopped her incessant questioning. "What?"

Dead tired, and balancing perilously close to the edge of defeat, I decided to take the offensive, in every way. "First, you know I can't tell you anything about an ongoing investigation, so quit hounding me." She started to argue. I silenced her with a glare. She knew me well enough to know when I'd had my fill of bullshit. "And didn't I ask you to find Jeremy?"

She angled a sideways, narrow-eyed look at me. "Did you?"

"If I didn't, I meant to. He's not answering his phone." I'd dialed him several times on the way back from the hospital. Still voicemail. I didn't like it. He'd had more than enough time to pout. And I'd asked him to find someone who was proving to be very dangerous indeed.

Irv Gittings wasn't Ol' Irv, the old joke, anymore.

"If I didn't ask you, who did I ask?" I raked a hand through my hair as I scanned the lobby and tried to find myself.

Flash looked at me, eyes wide, blinking rapidly, a rabbit facing a fox. "Are you okay?"

"Of course. I'm peachy. Holt Box is dead. Teddie is in jail. Jean-Charles is pretending this isn't a problem. My father is in ICU with a real problem, so maybe Jean-Charles knows what he's talking about. Jeremy isn't answering his phone. Miss P, who is scheduled to marry in a few days, is married to someone else. And Dane ..." I clapped my hands. "Yes! Dane, he's the one I set off after Jeremy. I must call him. My hotel is due to open in time for New Year's. I'm sure there is a punch list a mile long awaiting my attention. Jean-Charles's restaurant opening has been ... delayed. So, of course I'm okay. No, no," I placed a hand on her shoulder and leveled a benign smile, "I'm better than okay. Why do you ask?"

Flash pulled in her reporter claws, probably more out of self-preservation than good intention. "Well, you don't have to be worried about Jeremy. He's got a stake-out going and is keeping on the down-low."

"Good to know." I thought about asking for more, but, if either Dane or Flash had anything I knew they'd tell me, so asking was wasted breath and time.

Flash darted a worried look at me. I half expected her to press a hand to my forehead looking for signs of imminent death. "Would I be able to help with any of the other stuff?"

"I just gave you the laundry list. Knock yourself out. Now, I've got a job to do and so do you."

"Come over here just a minute." She pulled me to the side, tucking us both into a small alcove. She pulled some papers out of her large messenger bag that she'd flipped around to ride on her back. Two photos. She handed me one. Irv Gittings and a woman I vaguely remembered but couldn't place. "Who's this?"

"Mrs. Holt Box."

The second one I knew. Kimberly Cho. "What do these mean?"

Two women. One man. All somehow involved in ... what?

But Irv Gittings was that connection I'd asked for. "A piece to the puzzle. Thank you."

Flash preened.

"Keep digging?"

"Couldn't stop if I wanted to." We both understood the meaning of work addiction. I made myself feel better about it by calling it diligence. Flash didn't see the problem so didn't need to explain it away.

"Now, could you please try to find Jeremy? Like actually talk to him? He won't take my calls thinking Miss P put me up to it."

Flash looked offended. "She would never!"

"You and I know that but men and their egos." She nodded as if I made perfect sense, which was sort of scary. "So could you try?"

She nodded, her look as serious as if I'd asked her to hide the Holy Grail or something.

I watched her as she cut a path through the crowd and disappeared over the bridge and into the casino. I dialed Dane's number, dodging and darting my way through the lobby.

The call rolled to voicemail, and I started to panic. Before I had time to completely blow a gasket, my phone vibrated in my hand, impossible to hear above the excited cheers and the canned music as I worked my way through the casino angling toward the Kasbah.

"You need to hear what Shooter has to say," Dane started in before I had a chance.

"What does Shooter have to say?"

"It's about that bayonet and the gun. He's got a lead on it."

I skidded to a stop, surprising the couple behind me who plowed into me. Thankfully, they weren't carrying drinks. I staggered. The man grabbed me, holding on until he was sure I had my feet underneath me—a stretch, all things considered. Rocking on my moorings, battered by the shit-storm of life, I seemed to be perpetually on tilt. I nodded my thanks. "He has a lead on the gun?" Had I told Dane about the gun?

"Got the info from Romeo. Figured I could work that angle. You've got enough on your plate."

Wow, help without hinder, go figure. "That's great. But what about Jeremy?"

"He's gone radio silent. Got a stakeout going. He said he'd be in touch."

"That sounds promising." I started walking toward the Kasbah again, this time a bit more aware of my surroundings. "How's he doing?"

"Not good, but he can do his job."

"It's not like she's in love with the good doctor."

"You don't think?" Dane's voice lowered, the timbre warmed with a hint of empathy. "First loves can be powerful. Make you do things."

I knew that song and could hum all the bars myself, even without Teddie's encyclopedic grasp of all thing musical. "I really don't need that problem."

"Hers or yours?"

"Hers. Mine's done, the show is over, curtain closed." How had I lost control of this conversation?

"You think?"

"Not your business." At one point in the past, I'd fought an attraction to the long, tall drink of Texas moonshine, but not anymore, at least that's what I told myself. There was that whole trust thing he'd managed to shatter. But, then, he could turn around and do the nicest things and make me feel like he could see inside, and worse, that he got me. How could I keep him as a friend, let him in, but not drink his brand of Kool-Aid? Why were men so damned difficult? Living, breathing, pheromone-reeking, emotional landmines. Why couldn't I just have one that I could hang in the closet, like an old coat, bringing him out when needed? I could dress him up, have him wine and dine me when my ego needed stroking, and other parts, too, then hang him back up when done and close the door. Unfortunately, the Rulers of the Universe hadn't been bright enough to ascribe to my vision. Pity.

"And Miss P's problems aren't yours to solve," Dane added, just in case I'd missed his point the first time.

"Can we stop talking about this?" I breezed past the same security guy at the entrance to the Kasbah. The fact of the matter was, I was much more adept at solving other people's problems than my own, something I probably should worry about, but my plate was full—sort of an endless logic loop that had trapped me.

The security kid jogged after me and stopped me with, "Excuse me, I need to see your room key."

I whirled. "Not me. I run this joint." At his grin, I relaxed. Life had me hardwired to the pissed-off position. "Sorry. Good job."

"What are you sorry about?" Dane asked in my ear.

"So much that if I even walked into a Catholic church, the priests would line up to take my confession. But I wasn't talking to you. Tell me about Shooter."

"You need to hear it from him."

Feeling my frustration starting to boil over again, I tried to slap a lid on it. "Dane, I don't have time for a side-trip to east-Jesus."

"Good thing both me and Shooter are at the Calibers and Old Coots Show setting up in the convention hall."

I'd forgotten the antique gun show due to start tomorrow! "I'll be awhile, but I'll meet you there."

"We'll be here for the rest of the night."

"What time is it anyway?" I glanced toward the curved drive fronting the Kasbah, surprised to see darkness. Either night had fallen or there had been a cataclysm of epic proportions. Either way, captives insulated in the casino wouldn't be aware, or care.

"Later than when we started talking." He rang off.

He had a point—this was Vegas, where time was irrelevant and sleep in short supply.

I dropped my phone in my pocket as I raised my hand to pull the bell at the door of Bungalow Seven. The door whisked open on silent hinges, revealing a disheveled detective looking like he'd stayed out way past curfew.

"Thanks for getting here so quickly," Romeo deadpanned.

Used to guff from everybody, I narrowed my eyes and tuned into my sarcasm radar. Nothing pinged. Romeo looked dead on his feet. I thought I'd seen the same clothes on him for days, but I couldn't be sure—the days were running together.

"After this, you're going home, or wherever it is you sleep these days," I sounded all motherly, which sort of appalled me. I'd always been the generation bringing up the rear in my family. Now, while still a part of the same branch on the family tree as my brand-new siblings, I was old enough to be a generation ahead, not something that made me feel like dancing. In fact, it made me aware of time flowing by. I didn't like that either. My youth, where time had seemed limitless, was now officially dead. And I didn't even have time to mourn.

At my reference to alternate sleeping arrangements, Romeo didn't reward me with his normal blush—pale apparently was his new shade and nonplussed his new attitude. He opened the door wider and stepped to the side. "The shooter in the Casino has all the Homeland Security guys lathered up like rabid dogs. And they've been chasing my tail for the better part of the day."

I resisted stepping inside, savoring just a moment more of not knowing. "Hmmm, it's a wonder I haven't heard from Agent Stokes."

Romeo motioned me inside, a matador tempting a bull, not that the metaphor fit me or anything—although there was that pissed off position thing.

"Agent Stokes is sitting in your office."

Homeland Security, could life get any more fun? "Another reason to buy that one-way ticket to a galaxy far, far away."

"Yes, well, that galaxy came with an evil empire, Darth Vader and a Death Star, as I recall." Romeo really was turning into a great friend.

"But that was a long, long time ago. I'm sure the Jedi have a handle on it by now."

"Good thing somebody does," Romeo said not sounding at all like he believed it.

I stuck out my chin, something that always worked for my father when heading into battle. "Let's see what's behind door number one, or door number seven, more accurately." Taking a deep breath as I walked, marshaling what little focus not scattered beyond repair, I shrugged into my normal business-as-usual mode, reaching for my father's badass attitude and hoped I could fake it until I became it.

The Bungalows at the Kasbah would make any major sultan feel right at home, well, forgetting the whole harem thing... although, this being Vegas ... *Focus, Lucky. Focus.* The short hallway decorated with original art by some of the lesser Masters, our footfalls muffled by hand-knotted silk rugs from Turkey, opened into a great room with soaring ceilings and a wall of windows draped in cascades of thick damask on the far side bracketing a soothing view of the private gardens that ringed a small private dipping pool. A couch, several wing-backed chairs and ottomans were clustered in the middle to take advantage of the view. A dining table with seating for twenty nestled at the front of the bungalow to my left, a wet bar beyond. Double swinging doors sheltered a small prep kitchen from view. Multiple bedrooms with bathrooms *en suite* curved from the left side of the great room, the master suite and media room replete with a one-hundred-ten-inch flat screen, theater seating and a baby grand for those with more refined tastes, curved off to the right. The Babylon's most prized accommodations—there were only twelve—the bungalows were reserved for the largest whales, most important dignitaries, and celebrities riding the wave of current popularity pandemonium. Everything in here was original, including, from the looks of her, Mrs. Holt Box.

A tiny slip of a thing, Mrs. Box had curled like a puppy in the sun, claiming every square inch of the winged-back chair by the window. Sunlight reflecting from the pool dappled her face. Not a good look. Hair so fine and lightly yellow, spun cotton candy around her head. Doe eyes, a button nose and bow-tie mouth were lost in a long, flat face, one my mother would ascribe to a certain farm animal that men rode into battle, but I was averse to the whole labeling thing. Frankly, I was afraid of being on the sticky end of that whole I-am-rubber-you-are-glue thing. Yes, a traumatic childhood event and the fact that only the transvestite section at the department store carried my size, but we won't go there.

Dressed in leggings and a red tunic top, her eyes dark, lightly shaded, and ringed in red, her lips a shade of translucent pink, her nails neatly manicured, the tips white, and the rest clear, she exuded a lost fawn attitude. Funny, I don't know why, but I was expecting more of a Texas don't-mess-with-me-or-I'll-bust-your-ass attitude. Her shoulders bowed in, her head hanging, she dabbed at her nose, then her eyes, a forlorn pixie.

Country music was all apple pie and pickup trucks, and love and loss, rowdy bar fights. Mrs. Holt Box was none of that—well, maybe a passing comparison to apple pie, but I couldn't see her in a truck with a shotgun or rifle hanging across the back window and a coonhound with its head out the window drooling in the wind. Maybe I wasn't the judgmental type, but I could ride a stereotype like the Pony Express guys rode their horses, until it collapsed under me.

"Mrs. Box, I'm Lucky O'Toole, Vice President of Customer Service at this hotel." I extended my hand. She didn't take it. Instead, she stared out the window looking lost. I fought an urge to call the ASPCA. Ineffectual women got my goat, especially today. Okay, I was being harsh—she had lost her husband. I needed to remember that. I worked to tap into a rapidly thinning vein of the milk of human kindness.

I caught Romeo's look out of the corner of my eye. I took a step back, crossing my hands in front of me. "Mr. Rothstein, who I believe was in contract negotiations with your husband, is my father. First, let me express my deepest sympathy for your loss, on behalf of my family and this hotel."

She gave me a cool look. "Curious. I didn't think a hotel of this magnitude would tolerate nepotism."

Oh, a pixie with a bite. Promising. "We don't." I gave her a carefully constructed, don't-fuck-with-me-smile. "We take advantage of it."

She seemed to wilt, sugar in hot water, disappearing as I stirred. I felt like I'd kicked a dog. "I'm sorry, that was rude." She gave me a quick once-over. "I can't believe you're standing here. It was your lover who killed my husband, right?" A tear leaked out and she dabbed at it with a shredded tissue.

I snagged another one from the box on the end table, handing it to her. "I believe you've been misinformed." I stood, awaiting her invitation to sit. When none came, I claimed an end of the couch. "The man they're holding is a former lover. But I'm not here about the who. I'm interested in the why."

"But the police seem to think they've got their man."

I leaned back, crossing my legs, and tried to act casual, despite the pounding of my heart jump-started by the mere oblique reference to Teddie and his predicament. "That's still in doubt."

Her posture changed. Switching gears faster that a NASCAR driver, she leveled a stony gaze that probably had eviscerated lesser mortals. "Then why is he being held? The police know what they're doing and they've stopped looking."

She had a bitch-streak after all. And apparently little experience with Metro. "A misunderstanding."

That got a snort, sort of a bark really, that made Romeo jump.

Mrs. Holt Box fixed an icy stare on me. "You're fooling yourself." She stared down at her manicure on her left hand, curling her fingers toward the palm. "He wore dresses for a living? Stooping awful low to bolster a mediocre music career. He clearly has some issues. I'm sure a man like that would be very jealous of Holt." She flicked her gaze back to me. "I certainly hope he is prepared to pony up a significant settlement. He robbed me of my husband, conjugal rights, all of that. And my children ... "

I half rose from the soft cushion, showing my rusty game-playing skills and confirming the pissed-off position. Teddie in jail. I couldn't help myself. "Your husband isn't even cold—"

Romeo rescued me, pressing me back down with a strong hand, squeezing my shoulder until I winced, and he was sure he had my attention. "Mrs. Box, we're very sorry for your loss," he intoned, even managing to sound like he meant it.

Maybe *he* was sorry. Frankly, it sorta looked like whoever had killed Holt Box had released him from domestic prison. Talk about doing a guy a favor ... in a backhanded way. I wondered: would being shivved in the stomach and bleeding out be worse than being married to the woman sitting in front of me? A toss-up for sure—the lesser of two horribles.

"We'd like to ask you some questions," Romeo explained, as if we all didn't know why we had gathered. "We need to make sure we have the right man in custody." He held me in place with a stern look. "Lucky?"

Teddie was the eight-hundred-pound gorilla in the room. Ignoring him was practically impossible, but I'd try. "My father mentioned that your husband was under contract to the Babylon. Am I right?" My voice was stony; I didn't even try to make nice.

Mrs. Box eyed me with disdain, a lioness viewing a mouse—unpalatable, less than satisfying, and no challenge to catch. That was where she was wrong. "Holt was coming out of retirement. He'd decided to return to touring."

"And he was launching his comeback at the Babylon?"

She sighed dramatically. "Vegas wasn't really Holt's kind of place, but your father insisted. And Holt being easily led astray ..." She shook off an ugly thought, at least that's what it looked like.

I'd love to know what that thought was.

Picking at the nail polish on her left index finger, she continued without making eye contact. "Holt wanted a smaller venue and low ticket prices so all of his fans could afford an evening with him."

Something in her tone pegged my bullshit meter. She was lying; I knew it, but how to prove it? My father wasn't in the best shape to set the record straight. "My father insisted?"

"He came after Holt, begging him to accept his offer. A very generous offer, I might add. One we were grateful to have. Holt had been out of music for some time and with five kids ..." She left the rest to our imaginations. From her tone you'd have thought she was hanging by her manicured fingernails to the very edge of solvency.

Frankly, I couldn't imagine how all the residual royalties on his songs that anchored every country-music song list I'd ever seen for license at properties like mine couldn't have supported them in fine style on their ranch in Podunk, Texas.

"That's why we were so shocked when your father wanted out of the deal."

My eyebrows shot so high they threatened to take flight on their own. As lies go, that one was a whopper, but again, the proof thing. "You're telling me my father wanted to back out of the deal?" Oh, man, the woman was good, but she was wading in deep. I wondered what her angle could be.

Reneging was so not the Big Boss.

But he'd bailed on Teddie. A frisson of doubt snaked through me.

And now in ICU, he couldn't tell me what the hell was going on.

My world tilted, angling as steep as the sand stage at KA. But this wasn't a Cirque show, although it was beginning to resemble a bad play. Where was my exit cue?

"Yes, your father said the numbers just didn't work. And while Holt would be great publicity for the Babylon, he didn't think the upside was worth the cost."

That was something the Big Boss would've analyzed backwards and forwards before inking the deal. "And he told Holt all of this himself?"

Her gaze shifted out the window as if there was something incredible to see. There wasn't. "I don't really know. All I know is Holt had this sweet deal at a very large venue in Macau—the Chinese are all over country music, you know. So American. Then next thing I knew, we were launching the comeback in a tiny theater at a Vegas strip hotel, of all places. I never wanted to come back here." Too late, she seemed to realize perhaps we weren't the most receptive audience for her denigration. She didn't apologize or even have the class to look chagrined.

Macau. A connection?

Kimberly Cho worked in our Macau property.

A Chinese diplomat was in town on the sly to "protect" his country's gaming interests.

We had some Chinese assassin on the loose.

As connections went, that one was lining up pretty tidy.

And everybody thought Teddie killed Holt Box? The punchline to a joke. I pulled the folded picture of our shooter, and suspected killer even if I was the only one suspecting him at this point, out of my pocket. "When were you here before?"

"What?" Her gaze stayed glued to the paper in my hand. What was she hiding?

"You said you never wanted to come back. When were you here before?"

"A long time ago. Holt and I barely married. Before he was somebody." She smiled a sad smile. Perhaps remembering better times.

"I think I may have met you then?"

Mrs. Box looked like I'd slapped her. "I doubt it."

As I watched her fidget, her face pale, her eyes haunted, the memories started coming back. "Irv Gittings."

She reared back. "Who?" She choked, then cleared her throat.

"Irv Gittings. He gave Holt his first Vegas stage, didn't he?"

She licked her lips and nodded. "Yes, the Rumba Room and the Moonlight downtown."

"It's coming back to me. The Rumba Room was a very good venue back then. How did Holt get the gig?"

Crossing her arms, she pushed back into the deep folds of the chair. "I don't know."

She glanced away at something in the garden over my left shoulder. Lying. "I think you do." She didn't argue; instead she kept looking out the window.

I unfolded the paper with as much dramatic flair as I could, then thrust it under her nose. The tension in the room was palpable. "Does this man look familiar?"

White dinner jacket, gold buttons, red bow tie, he hardly looked like a killer.

Mrs. Box's eyes widened. Her hand fluttered to her throat.

"That's Sam."

Well, she got his name right. "Sam?" Romeo asked.

I knew who Sam was; I didn't have to ask.

"Yes, he's Holt's assistant. The one who came back with him from Macau." She finally deigned to look at us. Okay, she ignored me, focusing on Romeo. "He's fabulous. Takes care of everything."

"SAM. Takes care of everything," I hissed at Romeo after we'd said our goodbyes and had been assured that Mrs. Box would have Sam contact us the moment he returned, which was, of course, if not a lie, a virtual impossibility. Sam might be bold, but he wasn't stupid. "I just bet he does. And she was lying through her teeth. That woman is horrible."

"She's like one of those frogs," Romeo said, sounding a like a boy watching his first *National Geographic* show on Africa—riveted and a bit horrified.

He'd taken a hard left turn, and I'd hit the wall. "Frogs?"

"Yeah, you know, the really cute-looking ones? Tiny, all pretty colors that make you want to just reach out and hold them? Then you find out they're like the most poisonous thing in the world."

What had started out as a bad analogy turned out to be spot-on. "Remember that when dealing with women. Brandy excepted, of course. I wonder where Mrs. Box fits in all this mess?"

"I know what you're thinking." Romeo shut me down with his best skeptical look. "She might be horrible, but that doesn't make her a killer."

"It's not too hard to imagine her and Sam, or whatever his real name is, conspiring to get rid of Holt. Or Ol' Irv Gittings. Boy, I'd love to see the two of them tangle."

"That's all great except for one thing: killing her cash cow seems pretty short-sighted. So, if she killed him somehow and I'm not saying I even consider that a viable theory—why?"

"Why?" I asked weakly. I hated people pointing out large holes in my theories. "Is Why in this game?"

Romeo laughed a bit. "Why plays left field."

"Everything with me is out of left field." That made me smile, breaking through the worry, the sadness, the outright terror of an imagination in overdrive. "But the shortstop is more my speed."

"I don't give a darn?" Romeo said, his voice pitching higher at the end in question. "No, that's your problem, Lucky. You not only give a darn, you care too much."

"It's a gift."

At the edge of the casino, I stopped. Hooking a thumb to my right, I said, "I'm going this way."

Romeo brushed down his jacket and straightened his tie. "I'm going to have dinner with my lady." He puffed a bit. "I'm taking her to Tigris."

Tigris was the Babylon's top chow hall, strictly five stars. "Wow. Special. Good for you. Every lady loves a little fuss to be made over her. Brandy could use a break, I'm sure." I didn't even want to think about the chaos in my office, including Mr. Homeland Security. "After that, go home, get some sleep."

"If you do the same."

"Sure." I was lying though my teeth, and we both knew it.

Until Teddie was sprung, Sam off the streets, my father out of danger, and Irv Gittings shot at dawn, shut-eye was not on the menu. I could try, and probably would, but it would be of little use. I knew myself pretty well even though I fooled myself more often than was good for my mental health and longevity.

But all that for later.

Right now I needed to see a man about a gun.

CHAPTER TEN

BY design, to get to the exhibit hall in the convention center at the Babylon one had to make the long trek through the casino, around through the lobby, then saunter past all the shops in the Bazaar, our ode to conspicuous consumption.

I picked up Agent Stokes of Homeland Security in the lobby. "You saved me a trip," I said as I shook his hand. "I was just going to stop by the office to grab you. Today is nuts. Would you mind if we talked on the way?" Before he had time to object, I grabbed his arm and pulled him gently along with me.

Tall, broad shoulders, blond hair cut short, and looking all business-like in a subtle blue jacket with Homeland Security in bold lettering on the breast, he shook his head and fell into step. "I'd like to talk to you about one of your guests." With my height, his mouth was ear level, which was a good thing, as he'd lowered his voice. "Not really something for public consumption."

I gestured to the crowd around us. "Look around. The public couldn't give a darn about us and what we're talking about. I know you Feds think everyone snaps to attention at the mere presence of Homeland Security, but to most of us Homeland Security is a rude agent with cold hands and an attitude at the airport." I darted a look at him. "Is the public at risk?"

"That's TSA." He didn't look worried. "Don't think so."

"Same difference." When he slowed down, captured by the smell of charcoaled beef wafting from the Burger Palais, I urged him on. "Glad you're on top of it."

"Are you particularly glad to see me, or do you treat everyone this way?"

I didn't think I was being that bad. "Sorry, I needed to offload some snark—being unctuous takes its toll. You drew the short straw."

He glanced around and apparently saw my point about nobody paying any attention, then he leaned into me slightly, his mouth closer to my ear. He smelled like gunpowder. "You've got a diplomat flying under the radar."

"Mr. Cho." I looked at him with renewed respect. "Have you shot anyone today?"

He gave me a wide-eyed look, then processed my question. "It's the jacket. Wore it at the range. I like the smell."

"Me too." Then I thought about yesterday. "Most days."

He faltered a bit at that remark but quickly regained his equilibrium. "Heard you had a shooting yesterday."

Agent Stokes hadn't made the family connection—no real reason for him to have. "Yes." I swallowed hard.

"I was with your Security man just now. We went over the tapes."

"Jerry?"

"Coughs a lot?"

"Yeah." I moved Jerry up my mental worry list.

"Have you ID'd the shooter?"

"Our LA office has been onto him for some time. He's a punk with some ties to criminally influenced gangs in Macau, and curiously, here in Vegas. We don't know his real name, goes by—"

"Sam, I know." We stopped at the entrance to the convention center. We'd left the crowd behind. Only a few stragglers, mainly couples, wandered down this far. The gun show didn't open until later. "Do you have any idea what's going on here, why Sam, or whatever his name is, shot Mr. Rothstein?"

"I was hoping you did."

Great, another misguided believer. "Not yet." In case I'd missed a detail or hadn't made the right loop to be included or there was something Agent Stokes might feel inclined to help with, I filled him in on what I knew and what I suspected.

It took him several moments to process. "Irv Gittings. If we could find him."

"Tell me about it. But whether he's jerking my chain or not, I still have to prove who killed Holt Box. Strong suspicion is your buddy Sam, but nobody saw him do it. Heck, I can't even place him in the kitchen for sure. I saw him the night of the party. He looked to be leaving the kitchen at about the right time, but I never saw him in there for sure. And a defense attorney would rip my testimony to shreds, given my past relationship with the accused."

"You think that crank call on your phone was from Irv?" He looked like he was warring with himself.

"My best guess is it was too coincidental to be anyone other than one of the actors in this play. But we don't know. Romeo is running the number, but I'm sure it's a burner phone."

"You got the number, though?"

I pulled out my phone and scrolled to it. "Right here."

Agent Stokes took my phone and made a note of the number.

"What good is that to you?"

He looked around like he was expecting a bolt out of the blue to fricassee him where he stood. This time he really did whisper. "You ever heard of Sting-Ray?" I shook my head. "You didn't hear it from me either, but I can find this phone. It might take me a bit, but I can do it."

"I'm pretty sure I don't want to know the things you can dig up. But if you can find him." I stopped; a thought pinged. "Can you also record what is said and texted and all of that, anything the phone is used for?"

Agent Stokes shifted from one foot to the other. "Yeah. I'm not telling you anything the major media hasn't sniffed out, but it's very controversial. The technology is very hush-hush, so no one can reverse-engineer it. The courts are all over the thing, dismissing evidence because we can't say exactly how we got it. So, if I find the guy, I can't guarantee any records can be used against him."

"Well, you find him, and I'll make sure the case is airtight."

"Just don't tell anybody we've got that machine here. Okay?"

"The cops?"

"They don't know. In the War on Terror, Vegas is in the bull's-eye."

Now, there's a happy thought. "You got it. Is there anything else?"

"No." He glanced over my shoulder and lust hit his eyes. "The gun show. I'd forgotten. I know it's not open but do you think I could take a look?"

"Knock yourself out."

MOONBIRD Ridgeway, Moony, to most of us, barked orders to forklift operators who worked for us and the installation guys, who didn't, as I followed Agent Stokes into the cavernous hall, then watched him stroll away—a kid overwhelmed by all the choices for his one piece of candy.

Overalls and a white T-shirt hid Moony's tiny frame, lending her a no-nonsense air, which she cultivated with an ever-present frown. Her steel-toed work boots had probably been broken in before I was born. Part Paiute, her large eyes and dark skin evoked American Indian, but silver now streaked her jet-black hair. Still, she wore it in a thick plaited tail down her back. Her face, a wide-open expanse, had never seen even a touch of makeup that I was aware of. Perhaps that's why her skin still held the luminous glow of youth. But, no matter how distant a memory her youth was, wrinkles had yet to defy the force of her vigor. With careful scrutiny, I couldn't find even the hint of a laugh line.

Often while they were building-out an exhibition, I'd sneak in to watch the amazing dance of men, tools, raw materials, and machines that transformed an empty hollow space into another world. The takedown part didn't hold the same magic. Watching them dismantle things was like being in on the illusion and none of it was real.

"The only folks allowed in here are those here to work," Moony barked as she gave me the once-over. "I'm thinking from those fancy duds that ain't you." Competent and to the point, Moony was as refreshing and as unexpected as a gully washer in July. Born in the saddle on a cattle farm outside Carson City, she was as mean as a prodded rattler, tough and apt to strike ... like now. She gave me a glare, then wrapped me in a hug, surprising us both. Shock on her face and pink coloring her cheeks, she jumped back as if contact with me could kill her, like I carried ten thousand volts or something.

Not wanting to add to her discomfort, I sailed right on as if a hug from her was an everyday thing. "I'm here to see a man about a rifle. I won't get in your way."

She snorted. "You always promise that, and, like a feral kitten, you never can help getting underfoot."

"Part of my charm. Over-promise, under-deliver."

She gave me a quizzical look—jokes weren't part of her warm-and-fuzzy personality, although she liked a bawdy tale better than most, probably due to being raised around mostly men. Her eyes slashed to a hapless forklift on a wayward path. "Next aisle over, Otis!" she shouted. "Dear God in Heaven, are we going to have to send you back to first grade to learn your numbers? Aisle seventy-seven, like I told you." Like a cowboy herding cattle, she ran her department with a shout and a whip; but she had the lowest turnover of any department head, so I stayed out of her way and let her do her thing. She liked that about me—she'd told me so on numerous occasions.

Otis, hunkered down in the seat of a forklift, didn't look our way as he spun the small machine and motored off.

Moony gave me a wry smile. "You think when you hire these guys you could make readin' and writin' part of the requirements?"

"Not my department. I handle them only after they become problems."

"Guess we're both lucky that way," she groused.

"You know Shooter Moran?" I eyed the rows and rows of booths in various stages of dress, some full fancy, others lean and mean, all sporting enough firepower to destabilize a small nation.

"Who doesn't know Shooter? That guy's got a machine-gun mouth and enough bullshit to fertilize half of Clark County."

"Only half?"

She gave me a snort. "He's holding forth over on Aisle fifty-three. In the back. That way I don't gotta deal with him—he's a pest, thinking he's so cute while hitting you up for something."

"I bet you give it to him, don't you?"

Her flawless skin, unadorned by makeup, creased slightly as her eyebrows snapped into a frown. "If he crosses my path once more,

I'm inclined to pepper his backside with buckshot."

"And I'd be your character witness at trial."

I found Shooter Moran holding forth to a few interested aficionados who gazed enraptured as he worked the bolt on a Winchester 70, my childhood weapon of choice. Tall, sporting appropriate military muscles, with dirty blond hair worn military short, he had an engaging smile that didn't hide the wariness in his eyes. Even though our paths had crossed through Dane, Shooter didn't ooze the warmth of a friend, but he didn't seem like a foe either. And he'd proven he could be useful, unusual for men with his attitude.

Like Dane. But Dane was different.

Shooter had served under Dane in the military, forging an allegiance that bordered on slavish, but that was my opinion and, as such, worth the paper it was printed on. His eyes flicked to mine as I walked up, but he didn't even hitch in his spiel. I did sort of stand out in the ruggedly male mercenary set.

Dane sat off to the side, his backside perched on the edge of a long table, his legs crossed in front of him, oozing an easy masculinity that was almost impossible to resist ... almost. Men who showed a lack of character then found ways to justify it were as plentiful and as painful as jellyfish in an August sea.

I parked my butt next to his and adopted his pose.

He looked unhappy when he saw me. "Where's your security detail?"

"I out ran him a long time ago."

"Lucky, having guys watch your back is a good thing. Especially considering yours has a target on it."

I stared down the aisle at the seeming endless array of tables and guns. "Bringing my own muscle has a chilling effect on my investigation."

He sucked in a breath. "It may come down to you or them."

"I'll try to be smarter than that."

Dane gave up the fight with a snort and a shake of his head.

Maybe he was right. Maybe I was being stupid or reckless. But I didn't care. Some things mattered more.

Teddie.

"So, what's so secret that I've got to hear it in person?" I asked.

"Shooter can give you the lowdown. It has to do with your buddy, Gittings, and a particular weapon with a bayonet."

As my cauldron of questions started to boil over, Shooter wound up, dismissed his acolytes, and sauntered over. He hitched up his pants and settled a long look on me like he was preparing for a summation at the end of a long trial. "Hey."

Talk about letdown—all show and no go, a man of few words, I'd forgotten. "Hey. Hear you got something interesting to tell me."

"Yeah. You know how awhile back you helped send down the casino dude, the big wig?" He rolled his eyes upward, like Mona, looking for a brain ... and a name.

"Irv Gittings."

"Yeah, that's the dude. Well, he started liquidating a bunch of stuff on account of his legal bills and all."

Or to pay for a hitman, but I kept that little stink bomb to myself. "And?"

"Well, Captain here,"—he nodded toward Dane who had been Shooter's captain in the military; once a captain, always a Captain, I guess—"he showed me the photo of the bayonet used to kill Holt Box." The way he said the singer's name reminded me of the penitent before the altar.

My patience on the pegs, I shot a look a Dane.

"He's almost there."

Shooter looked between us like he had no idea he was the subject of our brief discussion. "We okay here?" he asked.

"Hanging on every word," I said with a tight smile.

"Right. Well, you know I deal in guns, and a lot of people who need to liquidate in a hurry, well they look to me to solve their problems." Shooter looked a little uncomfortable.

"Look, what you do and who you do it for is your business. I'm just interested in Irv Gittings and his guns." I'd tap my foot in frustration, but it'd gone to sleep.

"Right. Well, I got his whole collection. And that gun, the one his granddaddy used in the Civil War?" He waited for my response.

"The one with the GG engraved on it."

Shooter's face lit. "Yeah, that's the one." He reached around behind him, scanned the guns lined up like birds after a hunt, then plucked one from the middle.

I leaned forward. "Is that the gun? Irv Gittings' gun?"

"Naw. This one's just like his except his was in better condition. "This here's a pre-Civil War Sharp's Carbine. A new model 1859—these were configured for bayonets."

He handed it to me. "A Sharp's, sweet gun." I worked the bolt, weighed the gun across my palm. "Perfectly weighted. You could knock a guy off a horse at over a thousand yards with one of these."

"Real badass." Shooter nodded, finally warming to me. He should remember I'm fluent in most calibers.

"So, what about Gittings' gun?" I handed the weapon back, holding it until Shooter's eyes met mine. "You had it?"

"Yeah, but I sold it." He didn't look like he was hiding anything, just sort of confused. "A guy came in, asked for it specifically, like he knew I had it. Weird thing was, I was just processing the whole lot into inventory. Hadn't even gotten to that particular gun."

"How'd he know you had it?"

"He didn't say; I didn't ask." He shrugged. "Sometimes it's better not to know, you know?"

Oh, boy, did I know. "If you don't know, then how is that helping me find the guy who bought the gun? I'm assuming he bought the bayonet, the murder weapon, as well?"

"Yep, bought the whole rig. I wouldn't sell it piecemeal anyway."

"I assume he had to register the gun?" Hope flared. "You have his personal information? You know how to find him?"

"No, he didn't have to register it. Antique gun rules and Gun Show loophole."

Anger burned; I couldn't control it. The last twenty-four hours had killed my normally low reserve of self-control "Dane."

This time Dane didn't put me off. "Shooter, quit milking it and tell the lady what you told me."

Shooter deflated. He'd been enjoying holding all the cards. "The guy paid with a pre-signed check. When you see the signature, you'll understand why I took the paper." He reached to the side, popped the drawer on the cash register, and slid out a slim piece of paper.

I barely resisted ripping it out of his hand as he held it out.

I scanned for the signature. I wasn't expecting this. "Seriously?"

I asked, looking from one man to the other.

They both nodded.

The signature was Irv Gittings', bold and brassy. The heading said "Irv Gittings Holdings."

"Why would he connect himself to a murder?"

"Unless he didn't know the gun or bayonet would be used that way." Dane said, delivering the blow.

Oh, yeah, Irv was playing a game, and he'd lie; he'd lie big. I just had to catch him in it. This was just the sort of stunt he'd pull—sin in plain sight. Do something so bold, so stupid, that no one would believe he would actually do something that would so easily implicate him. I pulled the now creased photo from my pocket and snapped it open, then stuck it under Shooter's nose. "You seen this guy around?"

He scrutinized the blurry image. "Not lately."

With a frown, I pulled the photo back and began refolding it.

"Not since he bought the gun."

I FOUND Romeo and Brandy huddled, holding hands, at a tiny table in the back at Tigris. Tucking a chair between them, I wiggled in and sat. Neither of them seemed surprised nor all that unhappy to see me. When the shit hit the fan, we all were on call twenty-four/seven.

"The steak is to die for," Romeo said, then cringed at his choice of words.

Had it even been twenty-four hours since a man died in Jean-Charles's kitchen? Seemed like a lifetime.

"How's your father?" Brandy asked. Young, beautiful, smart, and so much the master of some obscure martial art her hands had been registered as lethal weapons, my youngest assistant came to me with ambition, drive, and a former terrible taste in men. I was so glad she had listened to me and my whole do-as-I-say-not-as-I-do routine. Romeo—there weren't any better.

"No change, and no word, which is a good thing. Given time, he should be fine."

Roham, my favorite waiter, rushed over. "Miss Lucky, so wonderful to see you!" He set in front of me a double Wild Turkey 101, one cube of ice. "Will we be eating dinner or just drinking it?" he asked with a smile.

Sometimes it didn't pay to be so predictable. "Drinking. No time to eat." I took a long pull, savoring the whiskey's warm path down and the explosion of calm that came after. Then, I pulled the check Shooter had given me, after I'd promised one of my own to cover the amount, out of my pocket, pressing it on the table in between Romeo and Brandy.

They listened as I told them what Shooter had told me.

"Any idea where Gittings is holed up?" Romeo asked, after he'd taken a bite of steak and a moment to process.

"No, but I bet we can find out. Any idea who's holding his ticket?" Daniel had mentioned it, but I'd forgotten.

"Eddie V's Quick Stop Bail Shop." Romeo gave me a look, easy to interpret.

Oh, yeah—there was a good reason I'd not wanted to remember. "Likes attract."

Brandy pecked at her salad. "I know this is a bad time. But I really need you to sprinkle holy water on the holiday party for the whales. It's pretty important. I've never handled one by myself before, and, not to complain or cast aspersions or anything, but Miss P is a bit distracted. And, well ..." she wandered to a standstill.

"I've been shirking my duties. Yes, and thank you for stepping in. To be honest, I'm not at the top of my game. You've got to step up. Can I count on you?"

New, young, she swallowed hard and nodded.

Brave, too.

"When do you want to go over the setup?"

Brandy checked her phone. "We have time. Tomorrow afternoon? I can text you."

"Perfect." I agreed, even though I had no idea what the next hour held, much less tomorrow, besides a bail hearing.

"Agent Stokes." Brandy gave me a conspiratorial grin that lifted on side of her mouth. "I managed to get rid of him. Not forever, but you can worry about dodging him tomorrow."

"He found me in the lobby." She looked sort of crestfallen. "The shooting wasn't an act of terror, can't see why it raised his antennae, but I'm glad it did. I think he might be able to help."

"Spooks, they want to know everything," Romeo added through his mouthful of steak.

"Did you get any hits on the golden button guy?" Romeo had run his picture through the facial recognition thing, and I wanted to shift gears. I didn't want Romeo asking me how Homeland Security was helping.

"The photo was pretty grainy," Romeo reminded me. "Got a couple of hits, nothing definitive. I have some guys chasing the leads down anyway. You never know, right?"

"Right." I grabbed a knife and fork and carved a bit off of his hunk of meat. A bit well-done for my taste, but I couldn't resist.

"It's a long shot." Romeo wiped his mouth with his napkin, then motioned for the check.

"But it's a shot." I waved Roham off. "The check is mine. And there's nothing to do right now that I can't get done. Enjoy yourselves."

Romeo settled back in his chair. "Don't you want to find Gittings?"

"He could be anywhere. I'll check with his bondsman, but I bet Irv has jumped bail. He's got a plan. I'm thinking the only way we'll find him is to force him to show his hand."

"How are we going to do that?"

"Figure out exactly who he wants and offer that to him."

Romeo and Brandy looked at me, their expressions holding the same look of dread. Romeo found his voice first. "That sounds an awful lot like you plan to be bait."

"Only if it's me he wants."

I needed answers. For some reason, I felt Kimberly Cho was the key to unraveling all of this. And, if I understood anything about her culture, when the shit hit the fan, a good Chinese girl ran home.

JEAN-CHARLES caught me heading in his direction. "You look like you need a hug." He didn't wait for an answer as I fell into his arms. I felt like crying, but couldn't. My throat choked shut, the tears hidden. I worked hard to keep myself from falling apart.

Taking a deep, ragged breath, I stepped away. Too easy to be weak when propped up by his strength. "I need so much more than that."

"Do we have time to check on the twins? Your mother will be worried. Children, there is nothing more precious, and more terrifying."

"Tell me about it." I so got the terrifying part. Tiny little humans, so breakable, so foreign, like aliens. I swiped at my eyes and motioned for Dane's man to come closer. "We're going up to a private suite on the top floor. It's secure. Will you be comfortable with waiting here?" I answered a few questions that seemed to alleviate his concerns. We left him sitting on a bench watching the people parade.

As we rode the private express elevator to the Big Boss' and Mona's apartment, Jean-Charles held my hand, our reflections staring back at us in the polished metal of the doors. I loved the way his hand sought mine as if by its own will, or to satisfy its owner's unspoken need. We looked good together, Jean-Charles and I, and, despite everything, happy. Happy was good. Silence enveloped us, cocooning us from the outside world for a divine few seconds. Closing my eyes, I drew a deep breath, pulling this moment deep inside. Fortification against an indifferent world.

The elevator eased to a stop; I braced myself. New territory for me, dealing with babies, and siblings.

Jean-Charles gave me a grin and squeezed my hand. "They don't bite."

"They don't have teeth."

Wails greeted us as the doors slid open. Jean-Charles stepped out; I resisted.

"Come. Babies are easy. Wait until they are two." He pulled me after him as he followed the trail of cries to the kitchen.

A large room with white walls offset by a warm, burnished hardwood floor, open cabinets displaying a dizzying array of plates and stemware, a farmhouse sink, three ovens, two dishwashers, and a center island that housed a commercial Viking gas cooktop and grill.

A counter with orange leather stools arced around the island. Orange was Mona's favorite color. She'd replaced the tired granite countertops with quartz, translucent white marbled lightly with pale orange. Under lit, they were a nice touch. Mona, the happy homemaker. That label didn't jibe with the Mona I knew—one of her newer incarnations. But, she *had* been nesting. Hormones could do crazy things. Trust me. A pregnant Mona had been a weapon of mass destruction—an overwrought version of her already dangerous normal. I assumed, with the birth only a month ago, the hormonal stew still sloshed through her veins.

Two nurses, each cradling a swaddled baby, lightly bobbed and danced around the kitchen making soothing, crooning sounds. One of the nurses, a tall, black man, shot a wicked grin our way when we walked in. "Ah, just in time." He stopped bobbing and weaving, motioning to me. "Here," he extended his little blanket-wrapped bundle with oversized lungs, from the sound of her. "Take her. This one's Thing One."

I couldn't very well refuse. I folded my arms and accepted the package, trying to hold her as he had. Nothing about this felt familiar, but it all felt right—the barely-there weight, the little red face, and large blue eyes that stared up at me. She stopped crying, preferring instead to comfort herself by turning and attaching to my knuckle as I brushed her cheek, like a little suckerfish. "Thing One?" I asked, enraptured by the tiny form in my arms and the odd suckling sensations.

"Since they have no names, we've come up with our own solution. Your mother doesn't like it. On the other hand, I think it amuses your father." His face clouded. "How is Mr. Rothstein?"

"He'll be fine. Thank you." Some hidden instinct made me start rocking and bouncing my baby bundle.

Jean-Charles, his arms extended, took who I assumed was Thing Two from the other nurse, a harried, whippet-thin older woman with a soft expression and a halo of weariness that she wore with a smile. The baby instantly stopped crying. Of course, she did. She was female and in the arms of a very charming Frenchman. Clearly, the girl was no fool.

The older lady took a rest on a stool; raising first one foot then the other, she stretched and worked her ankles and her feet. "Those babies. Always active, they don't sleep much. I think they're missing their momma."

"A family trait," I said, hoping I sounded sympathetic. "Well, not the missing their momma part."

The male nurse whistled as he stepped to the stove, stirring a pot. "And they can eat!"

"Unfortunately, also a family trait," I admitted, making Jean-Charles smile.

While their formula simmered, and the nurses enjoyed two pairs of helping hands, I watched Jean-Charles with Thing Two. He gazed down at his little bundle enraptured, love lighting his face, softening the worry he tried to hide from me. Yesterday, heck the last few months, had taken their toll. When he caught me looking at him, I saw pure joy.

"Children. They find their way into your heart and they stay. You worry, you fret, you fear for them, and yet you love them to the very core of your soul. They become a part of you."

I felt those stirrings, but I wasn't ready to admit them. The whole parent thing scared the heck out of me. I wasn't sure I'd finished being a child. Besides, what did I know about how the world worked, about raising a decent human when I had such a hard time making my own way and meeting my own rather low expectations? Perhaps a conversation for another time, when I felt braver.

"Have you ever thought about having your own?" Jean-Charles asked, cutting right through my internal prevaricating as if he knew my heart.

"What?"

"Children? Any thoughts?"

We'd danced around the issue, of course. Jean-Charles had said he didn't have to have more, but he thought I should have at least one of my own. I know he wasn't pressing as much as he was curious if I'd given the topic any more consideration.

The nurses fell mute, watching our little drama play out.

I forced a steady voice. "With these two, Mona has done the deed for me." A dodge. Even I knew it was weak.

"It is not the same. The rope that binds you to them, not as strong." His eyes turned dark and deep.

Even though I wanted to avoid them, I couldn't.

"I would die before losing my son, or you." The words were strong, yet simple, forthright, like my Frenchman.

The female nurse gasped and clutched a hand to her chest as she gave me one of those *awwww* looks.

And for the first time I knew I felt the same. I stepped to him and gave him the best kiss I could, given the circumstances. Thing Two immediately started to wail. I stared down into the tiny face, scrunched in anger. "He's mine. Deal with it."

MISS Minnie's Magical Massage Parlor hunkered in a nondescript strip mall buried in the middle of Koreatown ... Chinatown apparently being too upscale for the likes of Miss Minnie. Blackened windows hid the small storefront. Most people would've sailed right by thinking nothing was there, except for the neon lights. Huge, pink flashing neon screamed, "Miss Minnie's. Let Us Rub YOU the Right Way." Since I'd last had reason to darken her doorway, she'd added a halo of white lights, in case anybody missed the neon. Subtlety was not one of Minnie's strong suits.

I'd left my Frenchman to go home alone so I could go slumming. Something was seriously wrong with my life.

The parking lot was packed, so I drove through neighboring lots, searching for a proper place for the Ferrari. At the far end, hidden in the shadows, I was surprised to see Jeremy's black Hummer and the moon of his face staring at me as I eased by.

This was his stakeout?

A parking space opened up further down the aisle. After ditching the Ferrari and making notations of the neighboring car's license plate number on the off chance of damage when I returned, I ambled back toward the Hummer, keeping to the shadows. Of course, I had no idea who I was hiding from.

Jeremy leaned across and popped the passenger-side door for me. He'd killed the interior lights, so I was feeling my way as my eyes adjusted to the dim light cast by a few distant streetlights. He scraped a mound of sacks and other fast-food detritus out of the seat onto the floor, then brushed any remaining crumbs away.

I slid in, trying not to think about grease on my silk slacks. "If I ask you why you're here, would I be prying?"

Jeremy rubbed his eyes. He looked like he'd been run over and left for dead. "Got a hit on your Irv Gittings. Rumor put him here, but I haven't laid eyes on the bloke. Lots of other comings and goings I wish I hadn't seen." He blew right past the innuendo that probably leaked over into reality. According to the small neon sign in the window, tonight's special consisted of a happy ending for everybody. Like I said, Minnie liked to hit you right in the face. Okay, that one turned my stomach. I shut myself down.

"He could've come in the back."

Jeremy shot me a disgusted look. "I'm a bit distracted, but even in my diminished state, I can hang onto that kind of detail. Got a colleague watching."

As if she knew we were talking about her, Flash's voice crackled through Jeremy's radio. "All clear. Still no sign of him."

Jeremy didn't look at me. "I asked her to report on the hour, even if she had nothing."

"Flash? You put a woman in the back alley behind Miss Minnie's, the sketchiest massage parlor in Vegas, and all that that implies, which is saying a lot."

"What? She's the second scariest female in town." Jeremy didn't sound defensive, so either I had slipped from the top spot on that list or he was beyond caring. "She's damn good in a fight."

"No argument from me. I was just momentarily caught off-guard." Once again, I unfolded the photo of Sam or whatever his name was. "You seen this guy or a bright yellow Lambo with a black dragon on the front quarter panel?"

"That sounds like a sweet ride, but no, haven't seen it." Jeremy held the photo down between his knees, and used a penlight in red, so as not to interfere with his night vision. "Didn't see the car, but I may have seen this guy. Hard to say. That photo the best you got?"

Considering the magnitude of Sam's apparent skill, I was glad we had this much. "Yeah. But you saw a guy who looks like him?"

"He came in the back." Jeremy raised his hand. "I'm assuming.

He didn't go in through the front, but he appeared at the desk, seemed to want to talk to Miss Minnie. The conversation got pretty heated."

I grabbed Jeremy's radio and pushed the talk button. "Flash. You seen an Asian guy in a yellow Lambo?"

"Sweet ride. Yeah, I've seen him. He was here about an hour ago, didn't stay long. Guess he was already primed."

"How long did he stay?"

"Five minutes, maybe ten, but no more than that." Curiosity pulsed through the connection, but she didn't ask. We were on an open connection; anyone could tap in.

"Did he leave alone?"

"Yep."

"Okay, thanks."

"You are going to tell me, aren't you?"

"Later." I handed the radio back to Jeremy. "Have you seen a young Asian woman?" I described Kimberly Cho as best I could.

"That girl, or one who could be her twin, I've seen. She went in several hours ago, late afternoon. Looked liked the Devil himself chased her."

"Run home to Mama, just as I thought. Am I good or what?"

"No, just lucky."

I didn't laugh. He knew better. "I'm going to go in and find her. She's got some explaining to do."

"Her mother is there?" Jeremy didn't sound surprised as much as quizzical. Vegas had already altered his reality.

"Kimberly and I have a similar upbringing; let's leave it at that."

"I can't even imagine what you two talk about."

"Kim doesn't know I know, but I make it my job to know as much as I can about those we rely on. She has a big job back in Macau. Wall Street is just catching up to the fact that Far East operations are adding more to the bottom lines of Vegas holding companies than the local properties."

"Perception versus reality. It's a bitch."

I couldn't interpret Jeremy's tone and didn't really want to. Problems I couldn't fix made me twitchy. "If I don't come back in thirty minutes—"

"I'll summon Romeo."

"What a Galahad you are." I almost said, I don't know what Miss P sees in you, but, wonder of wonders, my brain kicked in and overruled my mouth. First time ever. I squashed a cup with my foot as I shifted to get a better look at him. "How long have you been here?"

"Not long enough."

Subtext usually did a fly-by with me. Not this time. "Have you and Miss P hashed this out yet?"

He waffled a bit, shifting a load of guilt. "No, I sort of panicked and bolted. To be honest, I don't know what to say."

"Want to practice on me? It's easy," I lied. "Say what you feel." None of my business, but I had to try.

He stared out the windshield, gripping the steering wheel with both hands. "That would seem like cheating or something. But here's the deal—I love her so much, I want her to be happy." The strain, the emotion, stretched his voice tight. "I just want a fair suck."

I must've looked like a pinched-neck cat.

"What?"

"Fair suck? Interpretation, please, before my mind goes on walkabout and I get a visual I can't unsee."

Exaggerated patience leaked into his tone. "I want her to hear me out, listen with an open mind."

Apparently my attempt to lighten the mood wasn't appreciated. My vision started to swim, then I remembered to breathe. Awkward situations tend to override my autonomic nervous system. "Gotcha. And, then?"

"I want her to be happy."

"Even if that means she's not with you?"

"Of course. Not the outcome I'm hoping for. Would take some time for those wounds to heal. But why would I want her to be anywhere other than where she is happiest?"

I paused, closed my eyes, and offered a silent prayer. Dear God in Heaven and Rulers of the Universe, can you please clone this man? Womankind would exalt your name thorough the eons. Then, I said "Amen" out loud.

"What?" Jeremy glanced at me, looking as confused as a fourth-grader in chemistry class.

"Just agreeing with you." I put my hand on his. His skin felt feverish. "I haven't talked to her. You know how the past can come out of nowhere and knock you on your ass. Takes time to clear your head. She loves you more than you can imagine. You two are great together. Have faith in her."

"Easy to say, hard to do."

Man, I knew that song and could sing it myself. "Right. Hang in. Let me know if I can help."

"Your dance card seems a bit full." Jeremy hadn't asked about my father. He probably didn't know.

I didn't feel the need to add to the boulder he was already shouldering. "What else is new?" I grabbed the door handle and eased the door open. "Wish me luck."

CHAPTER ELEVEN

MISS Minnie must've seen me coming. She met me at the door, barricading the entrance with her tiny body. Tonight she wore a silk kimono and enough jewelry to have every cutpurse salivating. Her face, clownish with makeup, her dark hair swirled and lacquered on top of her head, even in five-inch platforms she didn't make my shoulder. Still, she wasn't one to be underestimated. Even though a small package, she packed a big punch.

"You not wanted here. Go away." Her voice could cut glass.

"I need to talk to Kim."

Her face turned to stone. "No know Kim. She not here."

I adopted a posture of exaggerated patience, which really wasn't all that exaggerated, my well bone dry. "Minnie, I know, okay. I know. You want to leave me out here to air your dirty laundry, or are you going to invite me in to talk with your daughter? If she's in some kind of trouble, I need to know. I can help. And I can also cause trouble; I think you know that as well."

Minnie made her bank on not attracting unwanted attention from Vice. To have survived and not ended up on the front page of the RJ being carted to jail spoke volumes about her savvy and cunning, two things I was counting on. She'd also been around long enough to have the dirt on well over half the players in the state, from high government officials to casino bosses.

"You be quiet." She stepped aside, allowing me past, but she didn't look happy about it. Still, I thought I caught a hint of relief; although, with all the pancake, it was hard to tell. "Men don't like big bossy woman."

"Unless they have a whip and are wearing leather," I muttered.

She gave me a haughty look. "What kind of place you think this is?"

"I know what kind of place this is. It's a Vegas kind of place. Everything is negotiable."

She narrowed her eyes. "You think you so smart."

"Far from it. But I've been around long enough to know how to play the game, just like you."

Miss Minnie caved. Things must really be bad. "She in the back."

Kimberly was curled up on a cot in the storage room in the far end of a hall that had doors to smaller rooms down each side. She bolted to a seated position, her legs bent in front of her, her arms encircling them. A defensive posture. She eyed me as I grabbed the back of a chair and spun it around to face her.

Minnie looked between us for a moment. "She help. You listen," she said to her daughter, then bowed and shut the door.

"How did you know I'd be here?" Kimberly's voice shook with fear or fatigue, I wasn't sure which. Probably both.

"I've been a part of Vegas for a very long time. Even though almost two million people live here, it's still a small town."

She didn't look surprised—she'd parlayed the same kind of access and info into a six-figure income and, she'd sat at the feet of her mother. "Macau, it is that way."

"Even more so. Much like Vegas in the past, a high-stakes game with no rules and no oversight. Money talks, and when somebody doesn't listen, bad things happen. Am I right?"

She brushed her hair back with a shaking hand. "The rules of the street are still more trusted than the rules of the law."

"So, you want to tell me how you ended up between an assassin and a Chinese diplomat?"

Her eyes dipped. "My father, he is old school."

"The diplomat who won't talk to me, the guy who's in town on the QT? He's your father?" I knew he was a player in Macau; and with the last name Cho, it would've been easy to jump to conclusions, although Cho was as common a name in China as Smith in this country. I'd considered the possibility, so I wasn't surprised as much as amused. Miss Minnie and a diplomat, the stuff Hollywood or at least those tawdry tell-all shows would salivate over. This could be good, or really, really bad … like international incident bad.

"Yes, and he is not happy. I have shamed him."

Shame. Keeping face. Esoteric concepts for us Americans who tend to cover ourselves with ignominy to feed the insatiable appetites of reality television. But for the Asian cultures, appearance really was everything. "Can you give me a hint?"

Her face colored, her eyes sought the floor. "I have been very stupid. And with a married man."

"You're pregnant?"

Still staring at the floor, she nodded. "It is worse."

And I had an oh-shit moment. "And Holt Box is the father."

More nodding. She seemed to shrink away from me, as if I was beating her with a cane or whatever horrible thing it was they did to "sullied" women in the Dark Ages and still in the not-so-Dark-Ages in far horrid corners of the universe. "That's why Holt left Macau and broke his contract?"

"My father threatened to kill him."

I eyed her. She was scared. "How did he know any of this?"

"I don't know." Crossing her arms, she tried to keep eye contact but couldn't. "I didn't even know he was my father until a few years ago. My mother, she worries."

"Is that why your father is here? To kill Holt Box?"

Tears leaked down Kim's face. "It is possible. My father has diplomatic protection."

"But Sam, or whatever his name is, does not." I bolted to my feet and began pacing. Three strides across the small room, pivot, three strides back. As I tried to think, I made several circuits.

Kimberly remained a mute statue, but she couldn't muffle totally her quiet sobs.

I paused in front of her. "Why is your father still here, and why does he want my father dead, assuming he does? Is signing Holt Box really enough to warrant death?"

"You do not know my father."

I resumed my pacing. "I'd really like to know the shooter's real name. I've been told he worked for Holt Box."

She raised her head, swiping at her eyes with the back of her hand. A tissue was in desperate order, but I was fresh out. Scanning the shelves, I found a fresh box amid the bottles of antiseptic and sanitizer, boxes of condoms, latex gloves, and cases of massage oil and handed it to her.

"His name is Sam, Sam Wu." She dabbed her eyes as they followed me back and forth across the small room. Who told you he worked for Holt?" Her voice hiccoughed.

"Holt's wife."

"She is lying."

Now that was an interesting little tidbit. I so wanted to believe it that I had to caution myself to keep on a rational plane. "How do you know?"

"Do you know her?" she asked, her feelings showing.

"Instant dislike." I said without thinking, but not regretting my honesty. At her slight brightening, I added, "But that doesn't mean she's lying."

"She is. I was with Holt a lot. I helped him with his business, like I do for you. Macau ..."

"Takes an inside man, I know." Tired, my brain completely out of sugar and alcohol, its fuels of choice, I couldn't think anymore, and didn't want to. With thinking came feeling. "That's all you know?"

"My father's business is not known to me."

"The shooter was just here. Did he come to see you?"

Her eyes grew wide with fear as she tucked into herself. "Sam Wu was here?"

"Yes. He spoke with your mother."

That seemed to rock her a bit. "Kim, if you don't tell me what's going on, I can't help you."

"Nobody can help me." She sounded like she believed it.

"Please, out-of-wedlock children are all the rage these days. Your family will get over it."

"You don't know my family. My brother—"

A sharp word from the doorway stopped her. "Kim!" Miss Minnie had been listening.

Kimberly once again stared at the floor, her dark hair hanging like a curtain shrouding her face.

"Minnie. There is bad business going around. You need to tell me who that man is who came to talk to you. The one in the yellow Lambo. The one who shot my father."

"He shot Albert?" Her voice cracked. "He okay?"

I nodded.

"Albert, he made things right for me. Long time."

Sounded just like him. "Now you make things right for him."

Miss Minnie sat next to her daughter and pulled her close. "Kim my daughter. Sam, he also my child. Sam very bad. That man you look for?"

"Irv Gittings?"

"Him. He pay Sam lots of money to do bad things."

"How do you know this?"

"Sam tell me."

"Why would he tell you?"

"He try scare me. Scare Kim."

"Do you know what Irv is after?" I got the whole Cho family saga, but where and how did Irv inject himself in it?

"I know you both know Irv Gittings. Did either of you pull him into this?"

"No." Miss Minnie dropped the word like a bomb. "We no stupid."

Kim nodded in agreement. "I did some PR work for him a long time ago. I was just getting started; he was a pretty big player."

I remembered that version of Irv, the façade I'd needed time to see through.

Kim finally met my eyes. "But, if you learned my heritage, it would be possible for Irv Gittings to learn it as well."

And it'd be just the sort of info he'd leverage to his advantage.

LOST in a fog of hatred and frustration, my heart hurting for everyone and my trigger finger itching for an opportunity, I left Miss Minnie's through the back door. Jeremy was about as functional as I was, but danger was his business. Flash was ill-suited to handle herself against the Sams of the world.

I felt sure Flash was keeping her eagle eye on the back door, probably recording the comings and goings for a future exposé, so all I had to do was walk through the door to get her attention. Minnie hadn't said anything more as I left. She and Sam had argued—she'd been a bit vague as to over exactly what, leaving me with the impression that what she had told me was only part of the story. She didn't even hurl one of her ubiquitous insults. Pain lurked under all that makeup. And desperation.

Her kid was hurting; she thought I could help. The burden of her expectations rested heavily on my shoulders. A lot of folks seemed to think I could untangle some of these Gordian knots. A case of misplaced confidence, I feared.

Funny how we choose to protect ourselves from the cruelty of life. Makeup, sarcasm, self-deprecation. The comparison made me uncomfortable, so I shoved it to the bottom of the worry pile which teetered, a house of cards threatening to bury me if I didn't solve some of these problems.

Flash whistled from the darkness. I followed the sound as far as I could. She stepped out of the darkness into the dim light from the light over the backdoor to Miss Minnie's. "Man, the things I've seen."

"I don't want to know. Not unless it's pertinent to my immediate problems. Any idea where the yellow Lambo guy went?"

"No."

"Can you tell me anything about him?"

"He was pissed, and, I don't know where he'd been in the Lambo, but it was covered with dirt."

"Dirt? We're surrounded by dirt."

"It's all I got."

I gave her a hug. "You be careful. This isn't some white-collar exposé. These guys..."

"I know. They're wild animals with the scent of blood in their noses."

I laughed. "Good one. You should be a writer."

Keeping to the shadows, I worked my way around the far end of the building, then headed for the Ferrari. Head down, I ignored Jeremy hiding in the dark, but I felt him watching, and I felt his hurt.

Holt Box could shed some light on Kimberly's situation, but her little bombshell did provide some understanding of Holt's bolt from Macau. There was something there that warranted further digging. But not tonight. If I even hoped to remain semi-functional, serious shut-eye needed to be my next stop.

Climbing into the Ferrari, I fired the engine, which settled into a low growl. Pausing for a moment, I considered which bed to sleep in; then I pulled out of the parking lot and headed for home ... my home. This time I remembered to alert the dealership I'd bring the car back in the morning. Last time I forgot, and they put out an APB, damn near causing my father to stroke out.

A short drive, I used the time to check in with my mother. ICU frowned on cell phone usage, so our conversation was brief. I told her about the babies; she told me about Father. All were in good hands and holding their own. I thought about making her go home, even if I had to swing by and drag her out of the hospital myself, but then I realized she was where she needed to be.

I parked the car in one of the guest spaces in front of the Presidio, then tossed the keys to Forrest on my way through the lobby. "If anyone has a beef, would you have someone move the car to my spot, please?"

His face a mirror reflecting all the questions he wanted to ask, Forrest nodded and wisely didn't comment. "The plumbers were in your place today working on that leak."

"Thank you." I didn't remember a leak, but that wasn't unusual. Given the events of the past few days, something that trivial wouldn't have hit the radar, much less imprinted the gray matter. The neighbors below had probably called it in and arranged for it to be fixed. "Have them send me the bill."

The maw of the elevator stood open to receive me. I shoved the card into the slot and hit my floor. Facing the front, I propped my shoulder against the wall and rested my head as the floors ticked by. My last ride in this elevator. Mona. Teddie. Holt Box had still been alive and life had been irritating rather than its current state of terrifying. The elevator slowed, the doors opened, and I stepped out, breathing deeply of my space, my own home.

"Bitch! Bitch! Where you at, bitch? Hungry." A shrill voice from my roomie, Newton, a very foul-mouthed macaw who had fluttered into my life one day and never left, despite my offering him plenty of opportunity.

Shucking my sweater, I tossed it on the couch and headed toward the kitchen. The great room was dark, the multicolored lightshow from the Strip the only illumination. It was enough, and it was my favorite. Those lights, the magic we created, kept me going through the dark times. And even though problems mounted—serious problems—I just refused to get sucked down that rabbit hole. My life, on the whole, was damn good.

I flicked on the light in the kitchen, scaring the bird who flapped madly, raising a cloud of feathers.

"Asshole." His best word. And he said it with such relish, putting a song in my heart.

"So, you're hungry?" Hands on my hips, I gave him the eye. "Join the club. I'm so hungry I'm considering roasted parrot. What do you think?"

"Fuck you."

"Stand in line, big guy. Stand in line." I found an apple in the bottom bin of the refrigerator. Amazingly, it hadn't turned to mush or started sprouting things. I peeled it, sliced it, and dropped the slices in a bowl to brown while I foraged for food. Nothing in the fridge. The cabinets were pretty bare as well. Not even a very inventive cook, which I was not, could make a meal out of the sparse boxes and one can of tomato paste. What to do?

With food so close, Newton was apoplectic. I stuffed one slice through the bars, careful to keep my skin from getting between his beak and his enthusiasm. He'd sidle over, snatch the morsel, then skitter away, eying me while he devoured it. Watching him eat had me salivating. Where could I get food? Pizza sounded like a stomachache in a box. If Teddie were home ... he always had food.

I eyed the back staircase. A trip down memory lane. Could I handle that?

Everybody said I needed to face him, deal with everything. Funny thing was, I could deal with the man. But handling the memories and the what-could-have-beens was much more difficult.

I girded my loins, figuratively speaking, and marched up the stairs, letting my mind take me back. On my way up, I passed memories of Teddie coming down, a smile lighting his face, full of stories ... he was great at stories. And when you're a straight male making a living dressed in women's clothing, you have stories. At the top of the stairs, I paused. Teddie's kitchen was a mirror of my own, on steroids. He liked to cook; I liked to eat. A perfect pairing, he used to say.

My appetite under emotional assault, I opted for a banana from the bowl on the counter—they were still green. Life. How quickly it could turn. I peeled the fruit and took a bite as I wandered into the great room, passing the media room where we'd shared our first kiss. Well, actually our second. The first had been in Delilah's Bar and had surprised the hell out of me.

We'd bonded over our mutual love of all things Rogers and Hammerstein here. And we'd taken a great friendship and ruined it with sex.

I tried not to look at the white baby grand in its own alcove. Without Teddie, there was no music. The French doors leading to his patio opened easily, with a twist and a nudge. The night air held a chill and a hint of Christmas. I dropped the banana peel in the trashcan by the door and walked to the edge where the high hedges parted and I could drink in the Strip. I breathed deep, letting my town, its resiliency and ever-evolving skyline, center me. Change. Under pressure, either you grew and changed or you broke.

I had changed.

Teddie had broken.

With aches and bruises and hurts in places I didn't even know could feel pain, I had half a mind to fire up the hot tub. A relaxing soak sounded like the perfect antidote to a dismal day. But not here, not with the echo of Teddie reverberating from every corner.

We were really good.

And then we weren't.

The clash of dreams and reality. Teddie wanted to be a rock star, and he should be, he was destined to be. And I fit in Vegas; my soul lived here. My friends, my family, my life, where I found value and felt needed. Teddie had wanted it all and he'd been left with nothing, but only he could fix that. I could get him out of jail, but he'd have to find a way out of his prison.

Two lives that crossed, two futures that diverged.

If word on the street could be believed, it happened every day. Dreams killed nascent love, and I guess the reverse as well. But dreams killed by love sounded like a recipe for resentment.

I really had moved on. Teddie seemed like a teenage crush; Jean-Charles like a man with whom to run the race, weather the storm, walk the path, and every other cliché I could think of. There was a difference, hard to articulate without sounding like a bad poet. But it was real; I felt it in my heart.

Teddie would always be my first love, but not my last. A special place in my heart always, but only a small corner, a warm memory.

Just to test my mettle and prove my theory of being totally and completely over Teddie, I wandered into the bedroom. His scent surrounded me, taking me back. His touch. His kisses. The memories, almost tangible, shuddered through me.

A profound sadness tugged at me as I sat on the bed. His things were still on the nightstand: a novel splayed open, print side down, as if he'd just paused and would be right back; a tablet with some hastily scrawled notes on lines—Teddie always had a melody running in his head; his guitar within easy reach.

This place was his heart.

I'd lived there for a little while once, wrapped in his songs.

I lay down, curling into myself, hugging a pillow. Perhaps the one he'd slept on night before last. I felt sad, so profoundly sad, but not for what was or even what could have been. I simply felt sad for Teddie ... his dreams shattered.

I closed my eyes and breathed deep. He'd dream new dreams, write new songs.

And my heart would let go.

AT exactly 2:37 a.m. an explosion rocked the building, bolting me out of bed. I knew the time because, oddly, my first reaction was to look at the clock. The explosion was close, very close. Like an earthquake rolling through, but with smoke. And another smell ... acidic. These things registered viscerally, bypassing logic and pounding my flight response. Staggering, trying to get my bearings, I rushed to the window, threw open the sash, and leaned out. Smoke billowed as shattered glass caught the wind and the light in a sparkling shower.

The explosion had been directly below, one floor down.

My home.

My bedroom.

Where I should have been sleeping. Death tickled the back of my neck.

Sirens sounded in the distance. The building fire alarm wailed an ear-splitting shriek, jolting my body to action as my brain spun.

What to take? Finally, I focused on my surroundings.

Teddie's place. Nothing of mine here and I had no idea what he would want. I grabbed his guitar, then bolted through the great room toward the back stairs. Funny. Nothing here looked out of place other than maybe a few paintings hanging off kilter. No smoke. No damage that I could see.

The smell of smoke was stronger in the kitchen, growing more acrid, stinging my nose and eyes as I took the stairs down as fast as I could. Stupid, I know, but Newton would be terrified.

I couldn't leave the bird.

He flapped and fluttered as he shouted, "Fuck, fuck, fuck!"

"Couldn't have said it better myself." I popped open the door and presented my shoulder. "Hop aboard, no time for arguing."

Wild-eyed, he did as I asked, his claws puncturing cloth and the skin underneath. I couldn't take him down the stairs and risk him bolting for safety, only to be caught in the stairwell. Grabbing his feet, I carried him through the great room. The fire licked through the doorway to my bedroom. Smoke trickled in, the majority of it funneled through the hole where my bedroom windows had shattered. But, hungry and with plentiful oxygen, the fire would spread. Knowing I would help that cause, I threw open the French doors to my balcony, and tossed the bird out. I had to watch, make sure he took flight.

Sensing fuel, the fire flared to my left. I slammed the doors, grabbed my purse off the couch, and paused to glance around. There was nothing I wanted here. An odd and sad thought—I'd take time to process that later. I hit the door to the stairwell behind the elevator. About halfway down, I heard feet pounding up. Two more turns and I met Romeo leading the fire brigade. Catching sight of me, he sagged against the railing. Dropping his head, he sucked in lungsful of air. I joined him, letting the firemen stream past.

"Heard the call go out," he gasped. "Damn near died."

"You and me both." Realization eked through the fissures in the dissipating cloud of my panic. Emotion rattled my bones, shaking me from the inside.

"Scared?' Romeo asked.

"Pissed."

He gave me a weak smile. We turned and started down through a gap in the firemen, careful to avoid the hoses snaking as they pulled them from the hook-up two floors down. Romeo followed me, a hand on my shoulder. He needed the physical reassurance as much as I did.

One small choice.

And I lived.

At the bottom, we pushed through the door, the cold air slapping us with life.

I grabbed his arm. "Make sure everybody is out of there. Then find Forrest. Pull the surveillance video for the last couple of days." Questions lurked in his eyes. I cut them off. "Do it now before we lose it."

He turned, caught sight of his target, and rushed off.

I drifted across the street where my neighbors huddled, but stood apart. I felt guilty for this little exercise even though I wasn't, not really. Not in any way that I could be held accountable, but people were my business, and I knew I'd be the lightning rod for their fear and discontent. I wouldn't blame them. My fight had followed me home.

This had Irv Gittings' stink all over it.

Revenge. As a motivation for murder it was almost clichéd.

Now to prove it.

And avoid using the same justification for the same action. I really didn't need a cell next to Teddie or a bed next to my father. The damage Irv had already wreaked was more than enough. I had to get to him before he hurt anyone else.

My neighbors, still feeling the euphoria of having brushed up next to disaster yet remained untouched, closed around me peppering me with questions and sharing their delight that I hadn't been hurt. Long on suspicion and short on fact, to be honest, I was still gob-smacked that weakness, emotional wallowing, had led to my being alive. There was an interesting metaphor in there somewhere, but I was too shaken to devote the energy to find it.

"The firemen have cleared the building," Romeo announced, as he shouldered through the crowd. He waved several small HD tapes. "The system also backs up to the cloud, for future reference. Glad the fire chief owes me one."

"You got enough strong-arm capital left to convince them to let me get my car out of the garage?" I asked, my mind coming back online but still pinging a bit randomly. More fire trucks screamed into the driveway, then disgorged their human cargo dressed in full protective gear. Men pointed and scrambled, unfurling hoses, joining the fight.

"Doubtful. The chief is a tough nut. And I'm not sure I'd play my last card for that car." Romeo didn't sound all that hopeful. "I can't believe out of everything you could've grabbed you took Teddie's guitar and the keys to that rattle-trap that probably should be parted-out."

"Hard to explain." My neck hurt, but, transfixed by the fire, I stared skyward. "It's like you know you should grab something that has some value, especially something with emotional resonance that can't be replaced. But you can't think, so you just grab. In my defense, I didn't grab my car keys. I leave them in the car."

This time I could feel his incredulous look; I didn't have to see it. "You leave your keys in the car? In the car-theft capital of the universe?"

"Car won't start for anyone but me." I met his smile with one of my own. "Loyalty. Priceless." I gave him a quick hug. "Thank you." Newton chose that precise moment to flutter to a landing on my shoulder.

"Shit!" Romeo leapt back, then recovered.

Newton gave me a look and said, "Bitch." The word held a hint of ownership that made me laugh.

"I can't lose you," Romeo whispered, then recovered. "You keep life interesting."

A kindred sufferer of emotional constipation. "Comic relief, my best thing."

"Weren't you wearing those clothes yesterday?" he asked.

"Yes, Detective, I was."

He glanced at the guitar as he chewed on his lip. "You going to tell me how you survived that?" His eyes once again shifted to the inferno leaping out of my bedroom window.

"No," I sighed. "Let's just say it was a stroke of luck."

So, there I stood, with a guitar in one hand, my purse over one shoulder, a parrot on the other, and an arm around Romeo, both of us looking up as fire consumed everything I owned.

JEAN-CHARLES, in the middle of the late-night burger rush, had dropped everything and run from the Babylon to the Presidio. He'd been my first phone call. Out of breath and red-faced, he brushed the bird from my shoulder, handed the guitar to Romeo, then grabbed me tight, rocking back and forth. Sharing love, a heady thing.

"You're making me hungry," I said into his neck, relishing his nearness, the feel of him, the emotion that vibrated through him into me.

"Hungry? Why is this?" He didn't loosen his hold to look at me as he usually did.

"You smell like hamburgers."

He chuckled and still didn't let go.

I wiggled a bit, giving him a hint, and he reluctantly eased his hold on me. One arm remained around my waist as he stepped to the side and took in the crowd, the fire trucks, the men hauling hoses, the debris of my life floating down, swirling as the wind caught it. "How?" he started, then shook his head. "It is a miracle."

As he pulled me tight, I could feel him shaking. "Come, let me cook you something." My chef considered food to be the panacea for all ills, a theory I heartily embraced.

"**D**EAR God in Heaven, you're all right!"

Jolted out of a deep sleep, I bolted upright. "Shit! I wish people would stop doing that." I stared into the angry, worried, terrified face of Miss P. Finding her attitude no fun, I took a look around. My office. My couch. I remembered. Jean-Charles. Dinner. I left him at the Burger Palais handling some crisis. I couldn't remember exactly what. He said he'd come get me.

I fingered the blanket covering me. He must've come and decided not to awaken me. The thought warmed my heart, then the cold arrow of reality, of the fire, pierced it.

"Why didn't you call anybody?" Her eyes shot daggers. Not a good look.

I gently eased her out of my face. "I called everybody. Romeo helped. Check your phone. When I called you it rolled to voicemail. I left a message." Gently, I put my feet on the floor, but I didn't have the energy to stand. "What time is it?"

"Eight o'clock." She punched at her phone, her brows crunched together.

I took the offending device out of her hand. One look and I thrust it back to her. "This is my old phone. It was in your desk drawer."

"What?" She glared at the thing as if she could scare it into giving up its secrets. She bolted into her office, making scratching sounds as she rummaged in her desk.

I tested my legs; they held. One hour of sleep, not counting the hours I'd slumbered in Teddie's bed. To be honest, my sleep last night totaled more than my average, so I wasn't feeling too bad. I wandered to the small bathroom in my old office. Searching the closet, I was a bit disappointed in my clothing options—I usually kept several changes of clothes there for exigent circumstances. "Is this all of my clothes?" I called to Miss P in the outer office.

No answer. I peeked through the doorway.

Miss P looked up, her grin a mile wide. "I found my phone. Voicemail full. Jeremy called."

"Of course he did. My clothes?"

"I sent them out to be cleaned." She stuck headphones in her ears, and was lost to me. "For that, you get to take care of the bird." She didn't hear me. And apparently she hadn't noticed him in the small cage in the corner. They had a love/hate relationship.

Ain't love grand?

CHAPTER TWELVE

MY shrilling phone caught me just toweling off. I leaned out of the shower, retrieving it. I heard the bird shouting obscenities in the front office and someone slamming drawers.

A glance at caller ID. A number I didn't recognize ... I almost didn't answer. If I didn't know them, I didn't want to talk to them. Especially not today. Although I did have a lot of balls in the air. Curiosity killed self-preservation. "O'Toole."

"Squash Trenton here. You are coming to the bail hearing." It wasn't a question.

"Of course." I tried to sound functional, an impossibility without mainlining caffeine—next on my to-do list.

"We're on the docket in forty-five. Third on the list, so you've got some time. But, O'Toole, get a move on."

I started to ask why the hell my presence was so damned important, but he'd hung up. There was no time to indulge my irritation.

Thirty minutes. A new record. Five hundred horses, light traffic, and unadulterated panic made short work of the trip to the courthouse. I didn't need to go to the gym; my heart rate got a good workout just dealing with my life. The firemen wouldn't let me have my car, doing me a favor, but they had let Forrest go inside and get the Ferrari keys. Today I was especially grateful for the Ferrari—functional, fast, and not at all temperamental.

Security at the courthouse took time I hadn't planned. I slipped into the courtroom and silenced my phone as the bailiff called Teddie's case, "The People of the State of Nevada versus Theodore

Kowalski." A packed house. Not a good sign. Media, fans, the curiosity crowd that traveled from one public train wreck to another, packed in tight, giving off a charged vibe. An uneasy hush fell over the crowd, leaving a low-level crackle of salacious appetites needing to be fed. Even the glare of the judge and a threat of contempt couldn't override the nervous excitement.

Daniel, entrenched at the opposing counsel's table, turned and scanned the crowd. Gauging sentiment, perhaps—lawyers, nothing more than actors in a bad farce playing to the crowd. The best actor, the cleverest storyteller, the meanest pit bull usually won. An American spin—he with the most money wins. Despite lawyers' myopic belief in the system, all us folks who counted on justice being served, yet rarely saw any, knew the system was broken.

And Teddie's life hung on the horn of this dilemma: play the game or cut your losses.

Squash Trenton, in wavy hair, calm expression, and easy manner, sported a cowboy vibe in creased jeans, a white shirt, bolo tie, and fringed suede jacket that conjured either Wild West justice or a spaghetti western—a Champion of the Everyman. Daniel, all spit-and-polish in a three-piece suit, waged war on behalf of the government. In theory, justice was the goal, but I didn't have a lot of confidence that anyone else saw it that way... only me.

Thankfully, Teddie didn't have to appear in jailhouse orange. In a sweater and button-down with the tie I'd given him last Christmas, and creased slacks, he looked like Teddie; yet he was somehow diminished, as if the music had stopped. Stress highlighted his large eyes and high cheekbones. His hands crossed in front of him, he tried to look solemn and not shatter under the pressure. I knew him as well as I knew myself, sometimes I thought perhaps better. I could read every nuance. Seeing him this way, in this situation, with iPhone photos being surreptitiously snapped, judgments being made, hurt me more than it did him.

The judge pounded his gavel and scowled from on high. Judge Biggerstaff, a friend of my father's since the both of them had been young and stupid enough to have big dreams that stepped on the toes of the Mob. They'd both lived through it, which said a lot. Not sure what, but I hoped it meant that Judge Bickerstaff knew bad when he saw it and knew bullshit when he stepped in it.

"No cameras. No photographs in my courtroom." He motioned for a policeman standing off to the side to remove a few who ignored his order, then got down to business.

I half-listened as they went through all the preliminary stuff. Then we got to the juicy part. Squash stepped from behind the table and made an impassioned plea for bail. Powerful, strong, persuasive, yet collegial, no wonder he was considered the best. Everyone seemed to hang on his every word. Squash sat, and I resisted the urge to applaud, bad form in a courtroom where decorum reigned supreme. The crowd shifted and stirred. I held my breath.

Daniel rose, buttoning his jacket. Would he or wouldn't he?

Oddly, he glanced back at me, stopping my heart. Icy and cold, I couldn't read his expression.

Then he faced the judge and said, "Your Honor, the People believe that Mr. Kowalski is not a flight risk at this time. While bail is not normally available in this circumstance, we feel, based on the evidence gathered so far, that the case warrants a consideration of bail."

Stunned murmuring.

The judge silenced the crowd with a glare. "Mr. Kowalski, do you have someone who can speak for you?"

Squash turned and stared straight at me. When he turned back to the judge, he said, "Lucky O'Toole will stand for the accused, your Honor."

Terrific. So nice they'd asked. Heads turned, necks craned.

Awkward in the spotlight, I pressed down my slacks, an old pair of Dana Buchmans in soft bronze wool, and straightened my matching sweater over a metallic-threaded silk camisole. When I'd dressed I'd had work in mind, not a photo spread in *People*. Of course, I hadn't had too many choices, piecing together this outfit from random pieces in my office closet. Too late, I realized I had on two different shoes, one leopard-print, one zebra, both flats. I resisted patting down my hair, too Hollywood, too self-indulgent. I didn't matter here.

Teddie, the flush of anger climbing his neck and face, leaned into Squash and whispered in his ear. Squash brushed him off.

The bailiff called me to the stand. As if somnambulating, I

walked up the aisle, through the little gate separating the gallery from the participants, then found myself swearing on a Bible and then speaking as a character witness for a man I wasn't sure had much left, although I was pretty sure he wasn't a murderer.

I didn't look at Teddie. I didn't know what I would do. I stared straight ahead and pretended I was somewhere else.

The judge turned to the bailiff. "I want a freeze on all Mr. Kowalski's assets. Have him turn in his passport, and get an ankle bracelet on him." Then he looked out over the courtroom. "Bail in the amount of a million dollars is granted."

My knees weakened. The crowd gasped. Some outraged murmurs, some relieved sighs. Teddie had his fans, too.

Before he let me step down, he leaned in, putting a hand over his mic. "If he flies, I'm holding you personally responsible." My heart leapt in my throat. My job was to stay out of the news and keep the hotel from being sullied through my association. And if he thought I had any control over Teddie, well, he was grossly misinformed, but the joke was apparently on me.

"How's your father?" he asked, switching gears and leaving me in the dust.

"Okay," I stammered.

"Serious business, this," he growled. "You get to the bottom of it before anything else happens, you hear?"

"Yes, sir." I sounded like a cowed schoolgirl.

Why the hell did everyone think I had the cipher to this code?

*T*HE media pressed around me, hurling loaded questions like Molotov cocktails. Squash caught me wading through the throng. He grabbed my elbow, "I see you know the drill; ignore them and keep moving."

"Early in my career, I stopped once." I shot him a look as, shoulder-to-shoulder, we formed a human plow, carving a trough through the crowd. "I was lucky to get out alive."

"This is a rabid bunch. And equally divided from what I can tell."

Shouts to our left. A fight erupted, shifting some of the attention. We charged through the gap in the crowd's attention. Bolting through the door, we both cringed against the assault of a new day. "I really get sick of the sun sometimes," I admitted, apropos of nothing, but an interesting metaphor when I thought about it.

"Glare of the spotlight; it never gets old." Squash slowed only slightly, as if waiting for a steer. "Where's your car?"

"Why?"

"I need you to post bail."

I yanked my elbow out of his grasp. I wasn't really mad—desperate times and all of that—but I hated being railroaded. "If you just asked, this would go down a lot easier. We're on the same side, and, whether you know this or not, Teddie is very dear to me. I'll do what it takes, stay the course."

He gave me an appraising look, then throttled back. "Sorry. Sorta comes with the territory."

I didn't want to think about his normal class of associates. "I bet. The car's this way." I led him through the parking lot.

When he caught sight of the Ferrari, he smiled like he knew something I didn't.

"What?"

"I play this game with myself," he said as he opened the passenger door and settled inside. He waited until I'd gotten the horses under control. "I had you pegged as a fast car kind of gal."

"Sorry to disappoint. This is a loaner. My real car is a 911 that predates me and is far more unpredictable."

"Classy."

"Where are we going?"

"Have any relationships with any bail bondsmen?" he asked casually as if he thought I actually might.

"Not since a rebellious college phase, but I would like to put the thumbscrews to Easy Eddy V." I shot him a wicked smile.

"Thumbscrews. I like your style. Eddie V it is."

Eddie V operated out of a cinderblock one-story building that he shared with a lawyer, Jesus Morales, also known as Freddy, who made most of his freight selling forged IDs and other documentation somewhere on North Rancho—he moved around, but was easy to find if you knew who to ask. He thought Jesus Morales had a classy ring to it and gave off sort of a saintly air, so he immortalized it on his business cards and painted it on his window. We all still called him Freddy and knew his invoking the Almighty wouldn't come close to balancing his ledger when he arrived at the Pearly Gates. His mother, Mrs. Morales—no one dared refer to her by her first name, if she even had one—ran not only her son's shop, but Eddie V's as well. And she pinched pennies so tight she made Lincoln scream. Just the person I wanted to have me over a monetary barrel. But, I had leverage.

"How are you at negotiation?" I asked Squash as I wound through the maze of downtown. Eddy V's wasn't far. Like wolves encircling their prey, the bail bondsmen rented space as close to the courthouse as they could get without overdoing tacky. Okay, that was my take. From my few brushes with them, bondsmen never worried themselves over presentation.

Squash pressed a hand to his chest. "I'm offended. They devote at least two years in law school to how to be an asshole and get what you want."

"Good to know. Explains a lot. But you are about to meet your match."

"Who?"

"Mrs. Morales, Eddy V's money man."

A happy look settled over Squash's face as he hummed a snatch of a catchy tune. Silly man. Clearly he had never met Mrs. Morales.

I hid the Ferrari around the corner. Even if I didn't hold the pink slip, flashing that kind of bling wouldn't help our side. Squash took the lead as we pushed through the glass door, a single bell announcing our presence. The front desk stood empty, as were the offices we could see. Cheap, mismatched furniture, two chairs, a square coffee table, and a fake plant so old the leaves were faded white decorated the waiting area.

"No expense spared."

Squash ignored me, preferring to follow his nose. "Dear God, what is that smell?"

We found Eddie V and Mrs. Morales seated at a round laminated table, the laminate so thin in spots the particleboard showed through. A fridge groaned and hissed in the corner, leaking Freon. A ptomaine breeding ground.

Mrs. Morales was a large woman—so large that I couldn't think of an adjective that sufficed, so I went with the catch-all. She glared at us from under a unibrow. Eddy glanced at us, a hopeful expression which flared as recognition dawned on his nondescript face. Eddy was one of those guys who just seemed like there was nothing at all distinguishing about him—sort of the wallpaper of life. He had slicked down hair and an oily manner to match. "You here to bail out your boyfriend?" a question that sounded like a statement of fact.

My stomach roiled a bit as I watched him stuff a bit of fried mystery meat into his mouth, then slowly lick his stubby fingers. "Depends. He's not my boyfriend, so I don't have a lot of skin in this game. And there're lots of guys like you lining up to write this paper."

He dabbed at his mouth. "Let's talk turkey." He pulled out the chair next to him.

Ignoring his gesture, I remained standing. "You want to talk a million over ... that?" I nodded to the pile of whatever-it-was, the grease soaking through a thick layer of paper towel underneath.

"Want some?" Eddie V asked, clearly immune to insult. "Your father did bigger business on the back of a napkin."

He had a point. I pulled out a chair. Delicate sensibilities had no place at Eddie V's table.

Squash honed in on Mrs. Morales, remaining outwardly unfazed. Ignoring Survival Rule Number One: never get between a wild animal and its food, he leaned over the bowl in front of her and breathed deep. I'd seen Mrs. Morales in action—she once hefted a guy who'd jumped bail and missed his hearing over her shoulder, tossed him into the bed of her pickup and drove him to the courthouse herself. Badass to the bone.

"Green chili. My favorite," Squash said, a reverent tone sneaking into his suck-up. "You could put that stuff on shoe leather and I'd consider it a feast." He gave Mrs. Morales a golly-gee-whizz kind of look.

I threw up a little in the back of my mouth. While I prided myself on having good game, I had my standards. So I remained on the sidelines, even though Eddy V was drooling. His lunch couldn't have caused that, so it must've been the thought of a million-dollar bond. Stewing in his own juice for a bit would soften him up. Yep, never met a metaphor I didn't enjoy torturing.

"You made that yourself, didn't you?" Squash asked.

Mrs. Morales actually beamed as she nodded. "Do you want some?"

"Really?" Squash gushed. "I'd be honored."

Wow, he must enjoy courting death, or Teddie was that important. The latter gave me a warm fuzzy, so I went with it.

"How about you?" Mrs. Morales leveled a glare at me.

"Love some." Yes, Teddie was that important.

She put steaming bowls in front of us—apparently they used the microwave as a culinary autoclave. One bite and both Squash and I groaned. If this stuff killed me, I'd die happy. My stomach leapt to life, hunger on overdrive. The meager fare I'd scored recently insulted my stomach. It growled in protest, earning a smile from Mrs. Morales. I'd never seen her smile, and I knew better than to let it lull me into a false sense of complacency. I had a feeling I wasn't the only female at the table playing games.

Eddy V waited until we'd all finished, Squash practically licking the bowl. "I'd take you guys into my office, but some guy blew chunks in there yesterday. The gal who cleans the carpets got picked up by Vice last night. I'd have her out already, but it's her third. I tell her to work the high-class joints like yours," he nodded to me, including me in this lovely conversation, "but she don't feel right there. Been a Monday."

"Doesn't," Mrs. Morales corrected.

"She's trying to class me up," Eddy frowned. "I need to attract a higher-class business. That way I don't have so much of the cream going to the bounties."

I nodded, as if classy was even remotely within Eddy V's reach, but to me, high-class and bail bonds seemed like more of an oxymoron than he realized. "A reasonable plan."

Eddy V rose, taking his greasy towel and my bowl to the sink. "Premium on your guy will run you twenty percent on top of the ten percent I need to write the paper."

I leaned back in my chair. The games had begun. "Five percent premium. I'll go with the ten down." That was pretty standard for the insurance companies to write the bond, and I didn't have time to fight a battle I wouldn't win just to beat him up for my own amusement.

"Fifteen." Eddy plopped back in his chair, a look of sincerity as fake as the tans that paraded through the Babylon. "I want to help your guy, you know I do." Arms spread in a grand pleading gesture. "I want to help *you*."

He was as transparent as a French negligée. I leaned close to him. "No, you want my money and to gouge an innocent man."

He leaned back, tugging his threadbare jacket closed, a tight fit across his potbelly. "It's business."

A justification, but I let it slide. The Big Boss had tried that on me recently, and it had left the same bitter taste in my mouth. "I've got something you want."

His face shut down. "What?"

"Not what, who." And yes, right now I had no problem being the Grinch.

"What's the largest bond you've written recently?" I asked, breaking the know-the-answer-before-you-ask-the-question rule, a calculated gamble.

"A million five." At the mention of it, Eddy paled.

"Let me guess, Irv Gittings." How I managed to keep the smug out of my voice, I don't know. "And I'd be willing to bet his collateral was nothing more than a shell of empty corporations holding fictitious assets." That was on the insurance company, but Eddy'd be out a chunk of change.

Eddy wilted.

"Who fronted the cash?"

"A young Asian girl showed up with it. Pretty, looking a bit scared."

I didn't see that coming. "Kimberly Cho?"

Mrs. Morales harrumphed.

I took that as a yes. "And now," I pressed, "Irv's jumped bail."

Eddy looked like I was sticking pins under his fingernails. "I'm not sure."

Mrs. Morales weighed in. "Cut the crap, Eddy. He's missed his call-ins, one hearing, and nobody can find him."

"I can." Okay, that was a tiny bluff, a step out on a limb, but this was business and I had their attention. Squash's, too, as he eyed me with a hint of a smile as he tucked into the second bowl of green chili

Mrs. Morales had dished out for him.

"Here's how it's going to go. Eddy, you write the bond, pay the court the million. We'll give you the deed to Teddie's penthouse at the Presidio as collateral." I got a slight nod from Squash.

"No, I want the deed to your place. Your guy would be less likely to run if he knew you would lose your home."

"Forget it." I guessed he hadn't read the morning paper. Better for me. Besides, I wouldn't invite him to dinner, much less risk having him move into my place. The Homeowner's Association would have me shot at dawn. "Teddie's place is worth more anyway." I almost said, "Especially right now," but stifled myself. If he didn't know about the damage, all the better. "Do you want Irv Gittings or not?" *That* question I knew the answer to.

"What about the ten down and the premium?" Mrs. Morales asked, giving me her best glare, which was pretty darn good. Lesser men would turn tail and scurry back down their holes.

I stood my ground. Teddie was that important.

"Take it out of my bounty for delivering Irv Gittings."

"WHERE'D you learn to negotiate like that?" Squash asked as we headed back to the car. He'd presented the deed, and Teddie should be out by nightfall.

"Life is negotiation, but I'm in the casino business ... a woman in a man's world."

"Gotcha. My partner, she's got some of the same stories, I bet."

"Same song, different verse."

His eyes met mine as he opened my door, holding it for me. "It doesn't piss you off, playing the same game but with different rules?"

I pushed the start button and the engine growled, reverberating through me like a peak sexual experience. So easy to please. And so shallow, but I owned it. I looked up at him and gave him my best smile. "Never get mad, get even."

That got a laugh, a big, bold, throaty laugh. "My motto exactly." He smiled down at me.

Great. I thought we'd just bonded over a dish of cold revenge.

"Can you really deliver Irv Gittings?"

"Done it before. This time it might be in a body bag." I'd travel to the ends of the Earth to ensure Irv Gittings spent the rest of his life fighting off unwanted attention in the slammer.

Light dawned. "That was your place that got torched last night." I didn't need to confirm. "Wow, you're lucky."

"Seriously, that's the best you can do?"

"Hey, I'm really sorry."

"I know. And you have no idea how right you are."

He shifted to lawyer mode. "So you think this is personal?"

"Couldn't get any more personal," I growled.

"Gittings?" he asked, following the breadcrumbs.

"He's the top of a very short list of people who have me in their sights and have the ability to do something about it."

"And Teddie got caught in the crossfire?" I nodded. "But why kill Holt Box?" he pressed.

"I'm working on that angle."

"You prove it, Teddie walks."

He didn't have to tell me.

"Just remember, it'd be best if you leave the folks who did this alive."

"No promises." I pulled my door shut. "You getting in?"

"No, I'll walk. Fresh air does me good. I've got more cases on the docket and some clients to see, and I've got to keep pushing on Teddie's bond—the wheels of Justice grind slowly. I'm sure you're ready to have him home."

Home. A name with no place. As much as I loved turning phrases on their heads, that one didn't give me any pleasure at all.

The magnitude of the loss nipped around the edges, but I pushed it away. Nothing would change that, other than a rifle, my finger on the trigger, and Irv Gittings doing something stupid. Although, what he'd done to me so far might justify homicide, it would be best to catch him dead-cold certain.

I watched him until he reached the corner. Looking back, he gave me a small wave, then rounded the building and was gone. I took my time heading to the Babylon, winding through the streets of old Vegas. Small clapboard houses, some behind bright white picket fences, showcasing new touches of proud owners: fresh paint, window boxes, new sod, and bushes decorating the postage-stamp yards.

The original Andre's, a famous Vegas chef's first eponymous restaurant, had started in one of these small houses in a mixed-use neighborhood. Idling at the curb, I stared at the little building, abandoned for the bright lights of the Strip and a primo spot atop the Monte Carlo. Forlorn, weathered, unloved, the small space still held magic. In my mind's eye I restuccoed it, and fixed the roof tiles; trimmed the hedges and relit the trees with tiny bright lights. Closing my eyes, I could hear the trio tuning up, then launching into a Sinatra set. Andre greeting everyone at the door. The bartender fueling the merriment with heavy pours. The upholstered walls, the wood floors, the dim lighting that made every woman look fresh and young. Most of the big events of my life had been celebrated there. Andre had closed the location not too long ago, devastating many of us natives.

Teddie had taken me there. A special evening—he could be so thoughtful, so fun. His smile lit my heart; his touch lit a fire.

When had it changed? Maybe I'd grown up, grown into me. And Teddie still played at life, chasing one dream, only to be distracted by the next bright shiny object. Who knew?

A couple of kids eyed the car, and, not having time to indulge their interest and regale them with all the attributes of fine Italian iron, I checked the rearview, then punched the accelerator, getting grins as I flashed past them.

I checked in with Jeremy. Flash had answered. She was pulling stakeout duty while Jeremy went home to lick his wounds and get some shut-eye.

And still no Irv Gittings.

The dealership had been relieved to get their car back. At some point, I thought perhaps I should either buy one or adopt a Porsche mechanic, but I'd been unwilling to pull the trigger on either. Life was in flux.

I needed to call Warden Jeffers and get out to Indian Springs. Too bad cloning or teleporting had not been perfected yet.

Today, I stepped into the service area and took the non-public route to my office. Staff, hurrying on their duties, giggled and chatted as they passed each other or occasionally shared a stretch of hallway together. I loved this part of the hotel, too.

I loved making people happy. Sometimes that led me to put myself last, which didn't always lead to good decisions. But recognizing the problem is the first step to solving it, right?

Miss P waited for me in the office, pretending to work, the look on her face telegraphing her heart was elsewhere. Calm and collected on the outside, she presented a perfectly polished corporate executive exterior. Makeup in place, hair short and spiky, her curvy body displayed beautifully in a just-tight-enough form-fitting royal blue stretch dress, she looked the part, except for the red-ringed eyes and the tremor in her smile. Brandy was off making the rounds, I assumed. "Any fires to put out?"

She pulled her shoulders back and jutted out her chin, doing battle with a bad mood. "Not really. Brandy's got a handle on the holiday party for the whales. You're going to meet with her later?" Just like old times, she eyed me over the top of her cheaters. I really should hire my own assistant—Miss P was the Head now ... the me I used to be. But we all seemed to be clutching at the status quo right now. Normalcy, a rope as the quicksand threatened to suck us under.

"Yep, she's going to text me." The whales and their baubles seemed so far removed from important right now. Of course, they were the wax on the gaming skids, and, as such, needed to be coddled. I just wasn't in the mood.

"The media are leaving us alone for the moment." She lost some of her stuffing.

"What?"

"I have a wedding to plan. Poor Delphinia is beside herself." Delphinia planned all the weddings at the Babylon's Temple of Love, and she'd agreed to help with Miss P's even though Cielo would be hosting the festivities. "There are still more decisions to make, colors, flavors." The normally efficient Miss P wound down, looking totally overwhelmed.

"And the groom?" I pretended to be interested in a pile of messages in my in-box.

Miss P knew I'd rather pet a rattlesnake than flip through missives from people who all wanted something. She slapped my hand. "Working on that. Finding out I'm still married is a bit of a complication."

"Yes, well, let's talk about that. But not here. Come with me." I turned the tables, catching her hand, then easing her from behind her desk. "We both need a little dose of reality."

She resisted. "Reality? Where's the fun in that?"

"Having two hot guys, both incredibly accomplished and in love with you? Your reality looks pretty damn good from where I'm sitting. Don't let a little blast from the past tie you in knots."

She shot me a look. "You think so?"

Clearly, her look was meant to remind me of Teddie and Jean-Charles. "Take your shot. You know I can be relentless, so you might as well humor me."

She grabbed her sweater from the back of her chair. Shrugging into it, she followed me out the door. "It's not the past that's giving me so much trouble," she said, as she matched my stride toward the elevator. "It's the future."

Holiday cheer echoed through the lobby, the crowd in full family and fun mode. The Vegas vibe shifted at the holidays in a subtle way. The whole naughty thing moved toward nice. Hooking my arm through Miss P's, I drank in the joy. We'd made it across the lobby before I hazarded a look at her. The sadness I'd seen in her face had faded a bit.

"It's going to be okay." I squeezed her arm, pulling her close.

"I know. Somehow."

We let the crowd carry us into the Bazaar, the great Hall of Conspicuous Consumption, which jibed perfectly ... this being Christmas and all, when present buying reached unparalleled heights. Not in any hurry, and with no real plan or destination, we wandered, indulging in window-shopping and other lollygagging that would never be part of a normal business day. But these days were anything but normal, and sometimes just slowing down helped put the train back on the track.

"What are you going to do about your place?" she asked as we perused art neither of us could afford in one of the two high-end original art galleries.

"I don't know what's left. Romeo said maybe later today I could get back inside and get a few things. But, if my supposition is true, the explosion occurred in the bathroom and was rigged to blow out, taking not only the bathroom but also my bedroom with it." I shrugged, thinking about what all that was. Jewelry from the Big Boss, my collection of vintage designer clothes—which had taken all of my adult life to pull together. My shoes. That was a punch to the gut. I had some great shoes, also collected through the years. Limited styles, commemorative pairs, irreplaceable. The Manolos Teddie stretched out. The Chanel he wore better than I did. All of that hurt my heart but, in the grand scheme, not too important. I could've lost so much more. "You think life is trying to tell me something?"

"Let go?" Miss P gave voice to what I knew in my gut.

It was time to move on.

"Enough about my problems. Let's start tackling your pile." I steered her deeper into the Bazaar. "I know just the place."

The Daiquiri Den was a small thatched-roof stall off to the side in the Bazaar across from the Temple of Love. We both took stools and plenty of time to make our decisions. With yards of daiquiri in hand—mine strawberry, peach for Miss P—we turned our backs to the counter so we could fully appreciate the flow of holiday cheer ambling by. Neither of us spoke until we'd each made it a foot into our drinks.

"I believe we left the story in Africa?" I prompted, feeling a rum glow.

"Yes. Kenya." Miss P took a long pull on her drink. "We were just kids. Me straight off the farm. Cody a bit more worldly ... from Mason City and three years older than my twenty-one. Cody wanted to be a doctor and was getting some practical experience before committing fully to medical school. I was getting off the farm. With my basic knowledge, I could stitch up cuts and all of that, so I handled nursing duties."

"How'd you learn how to do that?"

"In the middle of nowhere, help is hard to come by. You need stitching up, a calf delivered, or a bull neutered, I'm your go-to gal."

"A few of your impressive list of talents." I'd worked my way through over half my drink and was feeling flushed with the milk of human kindness ... that's what they call rum, right? "Okay, so you guys got together, I can fill in those gaps." Being visual, I usually shied away from too much detail. "But why does Cody think you guys are married?"

"It's really not clear. We got caught up in a tribal wedding ceremony—things there can be very harsh with the young women traded for cattle and the like. One of the elders wanted to marry me. It was a bit dicey."

"So, to avoid that, Cody stepped in."

"Yes. It was a long time ago." Miss P's cheeks flushed—the alcohol apparently having an effect. "He was very dashing but such a child in so many ways."

"He was what, twenty-three?"

"Twenty-four."

"Scientists have proven that the center of the brain in males responsible for judgment doesn't mature until at least twenty-five, and that's an average." Teddie was working on the far end of that bell curve.

"Really?" Miss P, for all her farm knowledge, couldn't hope to compete with the education in all things male earned by a young woman raised in a whorehouse.

"It's true," I nodded like the oracle of Pahrump. "He's still damn impressive, though." I know, not helping, but it was the truth. He'd saved my father's life. Enough said.

"Isn't he, though?" The words rushed out on a sigh.

"After all these years, you've not married and neither has he." An interesting observation, I didn't like where it led. "Connection in the past can be a heady thing. It can make you think that just because the past was fun, the future could be, too. Problem is you both are two different people now."

"It is nice to share some history with somebody," Miss P acknowledged.

"Don't get caught up in the past and lose sight of the future." Spoken like the true fraud I was.

"I could tell you the same thing." Leave it to Miss P to call me out.

Teddie could pull all those strings, and did, and we didn't even go back that far. But it was enough. I could only imagine how strong the pull was for her with Dr. Cody Ellis. "So why is he here now?"

"After Kenya, we both went our own directions. I'm not sure either of us thought of the tribal ceremony—we thought it was a quaint bit of partying. Cody went off to medical school, and I wandered a path that brought me here. My parting words to him were to look me up when he grew up." She laughed, which sounded a lot like self-deprecation. "Looking back, it wasn't Cody who needed a bit of maturity."

"So, back to my original question: he's here because?"

Miss P looked at me with wide eyes as she sucked on her straw. "He grew up."

"Indeed." Sucking on the bottom, I ordered us another round. Probably not a good thing, but I considered it medicinal.

Miss P accepted her new yard of daiquiri, then eyed mine. "I'm peached-out. Want to trade?"

"Sure." I took a sip of the peach and understood—totally pucker-worthy.

"Cody turned out way better than I imagined, and back in those days I could imagine a lot." Miss P had been a Deadhead, following Jerry Garcia and his crew to the ends of the Earth, which spoke volumes about her imagination, perhaps not in a good way.

But who was I to judge? "Are you feeling that old attraction?"

She gave me a self-conscious glance. "Between you and me, right?"

I was only slightly offended. "Of course."

"Jeremy is perfect. A total dream. We were so happy." Miss P shifted on her stool, glancing around to double-check no one was eavesdropping.

I could've told her that, while this story was riveting, most everyone else had far bigger problems than an old boyfriend, now a dishy doctor playing God, showing up claiming to be her husband. Wait ... on second thought. I backed up her scan. Nobody listening. "Wait, you were happy? Haven't you guys talked it out?"

"Of course."

"And?"

Miss P sighed and stared down into the tube of her rapidly diminishing drink. "He says he understands. But I still feel like I've really let him down."

I blew at the bangs that had crept onto my forehead, tickling one eye. "Welcome to my world. Hell of a fall for you off your self-imposed perfection pedestal, but take the leap, jump in. The water is nice down here where mere mortals splash and play."

She gave me a dirty look.

"I'm serious. You are way too hard on yourself. We all make mistakes. If we don't, we're not really living, sticking our necks out, reaching for the golden ring—"

"I get it."

I gave her a gentle, one-armed hug. "The trick is to not make the same mistake twice."

CHAPTER THIRTEEN

SQUASH answered on the first ring. "Have you heard?" He didn't sound happy. In fact, he sounded pissed and scared.

"From the sound of your voice, I think not."

"Judge Jameson?"

"The asshat who sprung Irv Gittings?" I didn't know him personally, but anyone who let a murderer walk on a technicality, even tasting freedom for a moment, had to be an ass.

"Yeah. Someone punched his ticket. A car bomb in a parking garage downtown. Just happened."

"Shit." I tried to compose myself. "Irv's special way of saying thank you. Did you know the judge?"

"We sparred from time to time. He loved to put me in jail for contempt. A bad judge, a not-so-nice man, but to be blown to bits? Harsh."

"But poetic, a bit of Vegas past." Irv was tying up loose ends. Not good. Yet interesting. Did he really hope to cover his tracks and use a claim of false imprisonment and whatever to leverage a new career? Ego knows no limits. I'd kill him myself before I let that happen.

Squash sighed. "So, you didn't call about the judge. Teddie'll be out by dinner-time."

Leaning back in my desk chair, I considered the fact that Miss P lurked within earshot. I'd re-installed her back at her old desk, although I wasn't sure she should be allowed near the phones. After two daiquiris and not nearly as much tolerance as I'd managed to accrue, she was feeling pretty loose.

Next item on the office punch list—an office door. Privacy is underrated. "What do you know about the validity of marriages conducted in other jurisdictions?"

"Why ask me?" he sounded surprised, but not too. "You must know lots of attorneys. Family law is a bit out of my area, I'm a criminal attorney."

"The only other attorney I know is in entertainment law. I figured marriage is somewhere between a bad play and a crime, so I flipped a coin. You won."

"My lucky day."

"In so many ways." Okay, I get peeved when others make bad puns out of my name, but sometimes doing it myself kept me entertained.

"You have turned up pretty regularly today. Not that I'm complaining. You do keep things interesting." A chair creaked in the background.

I could picture him leaning back, putting his boots on a big mahogany desk somewhere. "You're the second man today who has told me that. I'm beginning to feel insulted."

"Trust me, interesting women are hard to find."

"And sometimes more trouble than they're worth."

"Never." He sounded sure. "So, about this marriage thing, why don't you give me what you got?"

I told it to him straight.

He didn't even laugh. "And I didn't have to wait, what, a minute, for you to prove my keeping-things-interesting theory. This woman isn't you, is she?"

"You've got to be kidding. I'm not the marrying kind." I twirled the five-carat diamond on the ring finger of my left hand. "Well, not yet."

"Smart woman." There was a history in the way he said those words, sparking a curiosity. As if I needed any more OPP—other people's problems. A twelve-step program for those addicted to sticking their noses in other people's business should be at the top of my Christmas list.

"Only for you." The lawyer agreed. "My partner handles this sort of thing, but she's in court right now."

"This sort of thing?" Even with my immunity to most everything, this pegged my meter.

"In Vegas? You've got to be kidding."

I developed a new appreciation. "Mr. Trenton, you and me, we play in the same sandbox. I get the rookies; you pick up the championship crazy."

"Keeps it interesting."

"You're big on that." Briefly, I thought he and Flash would make an incendiary pair, then I thought better of the idea. The fallout would register high on the Richter, far beyond my meager coping skills. "Friends and family discount?"

"Everybody gets one free ride."

I wasn't sure I wanted to be indebted. Squash Trenton hid a killer instinct underneath his comfortable cowboy exterior. I could see it in the hardness in his eyes, the set of his jaw.

But, no matter what, I wanted him on my side.

Teddie was that important.

THE pile in my in-box reduced by two-thirds—okay a generous half—I was feeling a little less pummeled by life and a bit more in control when my phone both dinged a text and started ringing. Mona calling, the text could wait.

"Is everything okay?"

"Oh, Lucky," she started, stopping my heart. Weariness filled each word. "Your father is a fighter. He's holding his own. That Dr. Ellis, he's been here all night. What a life-saver."

"Literally." Miss P and her problems. "Have you been home?"

"That's why I was calling. I need to go check on the babies, take a shower, and pull myself together. But I don't want your father to be alone should he awaken."

I checked my watch. Still time before Brandy would be ready for me. I was running out of day to go out to Indian Springs. "I'll be right there."

The burden she shouldered echoed in her sigh. "I don't know

what I'd do without you."

Mona, never one to be the emotional type, so her comment, granted in an unguarded moment and paid for by my presence, put a nice little happy note tucked deep in my heart.

"Oh, Mom, you still there?" I heard her sharp intake of breath. I'd never called her mom before, always mother, one of those cold, distancing words. Her heart was in the right place, even if her brain was a little cockeyed. We all did the best we could, and that's all anybody could ask.

"Yes, dear."

"Who is the doctor that all the girls in town see?"

"Well, I've not been in the business for a while." I smiled, letting her have her fantasy of complete respectability. "But I can ask around. Can you tell me why?"

"Yes, there's a young woman. She says she's pregnant. I want to know if the doctor agrees."

"Has she seen a doctor?" My mother sounded intrigued.

I contemplated Kimberly Cho and her predicament. If I was Holt Box, I'd want some proof of her claim. "Not sure, but if I was a betting woman I'd put all my money on yes."

"Okay, how do we find this doctor?" I hint of doubt crept into Mona's voice.

"Miss Minnie referred her. And since prostitution is done under-cover, so to speak, here in Clark County, I figure the girls all have one go-to guy. Can you help me? It has to do with the man who shot Father."

"I don't think the doctor will share confidential information with you."

"I'm sure he wouldn't. But, he'll share it with you."

She paused, theatrical pretense if I knew my mother. Forced by life to reinvent herself over and over, she knew how to play a part. "Okay. I can do this." Mona sounded happy to be included.

I wondered if she really could pull it off. A long shot at best. But most of us often underestimated my mother. "Thanks."

"Before you ring off, Lucky, are you ever going to call me mom again or just when you want something?"

She didn't quite cover all of her vulnerability. A new side to my mother. Perhaps it had been there all along and she covered it up with all the bravado. "Of course I'll call you mom. What else would I call you?"

I heard her smile before I rang off—don't ask, I just did.

The text dinged again. Jean-Charles, another happy note in my heart, luring me with promises of leftovers when I stopped by Cielo. We made a date for a couple of hours hence, and I launched off to be a part of my family, a family that needed me.

MY father looked much the same as he had yesterday when I took Mona's place in the chair by his side. I shooed her away with a quick kiss and a smile. "Paolo is waiting. I brought a security guy with me. He's to stay with you wherever you go. No arguing."

Curiously, she nodded, and gave me a hug. "Thank you. I love you, you know."

Had the Earth tilted on its axis? "I love you, too."

My father lay immobile, almost like he'd been laid out for a viewing. Of course, the hospital gown wouldn't be my choice for his funeral dress. His pink tie, white shirt, power suit. *Jesus, Lucky. Get a grip. He's not going anywhere.* "Hell no, he's not. He can't." I often spoke to myself—sometimes I was the only one who'd listen to me.

His hand felt cold in mine as I squeezed it. Machines beeped out a heart rate; a pressure cuff inflated periodically, recording his blood pressure. A plastic cup over his mouth delivered oxygen, but, thankfully, he breathed on his own. Shallow, but regular. "Father, I need you to wake up." I leaned into him, self-conscious. "Bad things are happening. I don't understand the connections. No one is safe. I need you to fill in a few of the blanks."

He moaned and stirred. The beeping of his heart rate accelerated.

I squeezed his hand harder, as hard as I dared. If I could only transfer my will osmotically somehow. "That's right. Come back. Reach for my voice. I need your help."

"Keep talking to him. That's good." Cody Ellis breezed into the room.

Embarrassed at being caught in the act, I leaned back. "I heard that, even though they can't respond, they hear."

"It's been proven, anecdotally." He slipped his cheaters from the top of his head to the bridge of his nose in one quick nod, then pulled up my father's chart on his iPad, flipping the pages with a swipe of his finger. "You know the medical establishment, they won't accept anything as valid unless it's been proven in a double-blind, controlled study." He looked up, catching me staring. "But I believe comatose patients can hear. I've seen it. I had a patient once who woke up and remembered whole conversations that had swirled around him while he was out."

"How is he?" My gaze shifted to my father, bringing Dr. Ellis's attention with it.

"He's a tough old coot. What a fighter. It was close there for awhile, but he's on the right side of the power curve."

"Nothing but full power from here on," I said, finishing his analogy. I'd taken some flight lessons, and I loved internal combustion more than most men. I must've shown more relief than I'd thought because he gave me a knowing smile. "You look pretty darn fresh for someone who's had no sleep," I stammered, knowing what I needed to say, but not sure how to say it. So, being me, I beat around the bush. "I need to know your secret."

"Catnaps. They have a lounge." He stepped to the other side of the bed, scanning the monitors. He looked as he had yesterday, graying hair pulled back, thin, tall, mustache neatly trimmed, handsome in a comfortable and kind sort of way with a magnetism he seemed unaware of. By the looks of him, the complete package.

"Why did you come back? Why now, after all these years?"

He paused, looking at me over the top of his cheaters.

Just like Miss P often looked at me. I shut down that thought or pretty soon my mind would take me places I didn't want to go.

"I never stopped loving her. Nobody else compared with the young woman I remembered."

So now Miss P had to compete with a memory of herself that had been perfected through the years. Memory was a tricky thing, the bad stuff falling away until only perfection remained.

"And the reality of who she became?"

"Even better." He stopped, tucking the iPad under his arm, then crossing his hands in front of him. "I know what you must be thinking. After all these years, I show up and throw a bit of a wrench in everything. I just had to see her. I had to know. I figured we deserved that chance."

I didn't want to like him as much as I did. "I get it. I certainly wouldn't want Miss P marrying Jeremy if he wasn't the right one."

He gave me a grin. "Miss P? Is that what you call her?"

"She won't tell us her real name." The light dawned and I attacked. "But you know it."

He raised his hands, catching the iPad in a deft move. "Oh, no. I'm not playing that game. If she doesn't want you to know it, she must have a reason."

I couldn't read one thing in the look on his face. "Is it just horrible?"

"Not playing." His eyes sparkled with merriment as he shifted seamlessly. "We've been backing off on your father's sedatives, trying to bring him back slowly. Keep talking to him. I sense him there, listening, just out of range. You can bring him back; make him want to come back."

"I am not an old coot." The voice was weak, muffled. My father.

Tears sprung to my eyes as I grabbed his hand in both of mine now. "You're absolutely right, but the doctor doesn't know you well enough to use the appropriate adjectives and noun."

His smile was hidden, but it lit his eyes that blinked furiously. He swiped at the plastic breathing thing. "Get this damn thing off."

Dr. Ellis hopped to. Nice to know the mighty doctor wasn't immune to the Big Boss's authoritative grumblings. He gently removed the breathing thing and untangled the strap that kept it tight to my father's face. "Better?"

My father took a deep breath as his gazed traveled the room, absorbing, looking for a connection, continuity. "A tumbler of twenty-five-year-old Scotch would go a long way toward improving my mood." His voice was husky but stronger than I expected. Breathing tubes, bullets, they each did their bit of damage. But time would heal.

Dr. Ellis and I both laughed and said, in unison, "Mine too."

Cody patted his shoulder as he put the oxygen thing away and turned off the flow. "I'll see what I can do." He caught me giving him a surprised look. "Medicinal. In other parts of the world, alcohol has many uses besides getting shit-faced. A little won't hurt."

"When I need a doc, I want you." I thought about the doctors I knew, afraid to stick a toe even close to the line for fear of litigation. How had we managed to litigate the humanity out of sickness and pain, life and death?

"Hopefully, I'll be around." He gave me a tentative smile and a shrug, then he turned his attention to checking my father's vital signs and all of that.

Miss P was spoiled for choice, and I didn't envy her one iota. Her heart would have to decide, because no way could logical thinking whittle this embarrassment of riches down to one.

My father handled the doctor's poking and prodding with a slight scowl and veiled patience.

Apparently happy with what the monitors told him, Dr. Ellis shuffled, backing away from the bed. "I'll go scare up some firewater, leave you two to talk."

I didn't watch him go. Instead, I focused on the struggle shifting across my father's face. For the first time I realized, while still handsome and vibrant, life had taken a toll. Of course, a bullet to the chest could have something to do with it. I lowered myself back into the chair, keeping myself at a comfortable height to see my father and not have him twist uncomfortably to see me. "You gave us quite a scare." Stupid. He had nothing to do with anything other than battling back from a horrible injustice. "Never mind. An inanity to offload stress. What the hell happened?"

That got the hint of a grin, then it fled. "Mona?" His voice gaining strength; his brain sorting memories and priorities, finding the present reality.

"She's fine. I've got a security detail dogging her heels. I'm probably going to have to spring for hazardous-duty pay, but she's protected as best I can."

He squeezed my hand with remarkable strength, considering. "I could always count on you to do the right thing, take care of everybody."

Well, if this wasn't warm and gooey family day. I loved it. My family had been too attenuated for far too long, almost to the point of distance and cynicism, especially on my part. I didn't want to be that. "Do you remember what happened?"

He moved, shifting the pain.

"Do you need something for that?"

He gave a quick dismissive shake of his head. "A little pain is good. Lets you know you're alive."

"Good point." I didn't know what I could do to ease his pain, so I patted his hand and felt helpless and homicidal in equal parts. "Can you tell me what you remember?"

He stared at the ceiling, running the video reel from ...yesterday. Had it really only been twenty-four hours? I'd aged a decade.

"I was arguing with that fathead, Cho. Damned ass. So arrogant." My father rolled his head over to look at me through both eyes. "I really hate that man."

"Good to know. We won't put you at the same table."

He gave me a long look. "You must've gotten your smart mouth from your mother."

"Oh, I think I got the worst of both of you, so don't piss me off."

That got a belly laugh, cut off when he winced, his hands reaching to hold his chest. "Don't make me laugh."

"You find me funny. What am I supposed to do with that?" At his sharp look, I tried to get a handle. "Okay, Mr. Cho. What were you arguing about?"

"Holt Box." That sobered us both.

"Can you give me a context?"

"Yeah, Cho accused me of poaching. Me! Poaching! Like I'd have to undercut somebody else's deal. Give me a fucking break." Anger accelerated the heart rate monitor to a pounding rhythm.

"So, he thinks you stole Holt Box's comeback? How did you end up doing the deal with Mr. Box?"

"His people approached me." He closed his eyes for a moment. When he reopened them, the anger was gone. "I should've known he blew in on a troubled wind. Enough years, enough mistakes, you get a sense. My grandmother used to warn me about those kinds of things. Course, she was referring to your mother." He gave me a sly grin.

"She was wrong there."

His grandmother? I knew nothing about my extended family. My parents acted like they'd been hatched from eggs, rarely mentioning parents, siblings, grandparents. Having the two of them was enough for me, so I hadn't pushed. But part of me really wanted to know. My great-grandmother had known my mother. Had she been wrong about Mona? My father thought so, but their path to happiness was a bit more tortured than I hoped for. Years and years, a lifetime of watching each other from afar, unable to have, unable to touch. And I got lost in the shuffle, not knowing the Big Boss was my father until a few months ago. Mona, an underage hooker, was the kind of wife that would've landed my father in jail, a huge detour off the fast track. Mona had lied about her age and cost both of them years together.

"So, you inked the deal with Holt Box?"

"Yeah, it was pretty generous. I bent to his demands and was happy to do so. Lots of interest in his comeback. We would've gotten a lot of traction out of that. Good for everybody."

We were getting a lot of media traction, but I didn't think it was what the Big Boss had intended, so I didn't mention it. "So, why'd you want out of the deal?"

He captured me in a traction beam of intensity. "Who told you that?"

"Mrs. Holt Box."

"Ah, yes, the viper in a pretty package." He shook off some memory with a shudder, a horse dislodging a fly.

"What?"

"She was after the money, acting as her husband's manager. Had this sleazy guy ... I got the impression he held her leash. They brought me the deal."

"Really?" Once again, I pulled the photo out of my pocket. "This the guy?" I held the photo so he didn't have to strain or move to see it.

"Looks like him, but I wouldn't swear to it in court. Who is he?"

"The man who shot you."

My father thought about that. I could see him working through the angles, the plays. Finally, he bit his lip and shook his head. "I don't get it. What don't I know?"

Holding out on him never worked. He had this sixth sense or something. "Mr. Cho's daughter."

"He procreated? Dear God."

"Worse. His daughter, Kimberly Cho ..." I urged him to the obvious conclusion.

He didn't disappoint. "*Our* Kimberly Cho?"

I nodded.

"A traitor? Is she working against us, using her inside track? She's incredibly important to our success in Macau. I'm counting on her."

"I have no reason to believe she is anything but loyal to us. She is estranged from her father. Her mother lives here."

Something in my tone must've hit his radar. "Her mother? Here?"

"Mmmm."

"Do I know her?" asked the man who had made it his life's work to know all the players, and those who influenced them. And Miss Minnie was an influencer—the things powerful men would do for a good blow job.

"Yes, but I hope not too well." There are some things about my father even someone like me couldn't handle. Paying for sex was one of them.

"Quit leading me down the path; it only pisses me off," he growled, as if he believed he could scare me like one of the other minions at his beck and call.

He could. Sorta. "Miss Minnie."

He didn't seem surprised; in fact, he seemed to gloat. "Smart men, stupid choices. It's a cliché."

Valuing my life, I didn't point out the parallels between him and Mr. Cho. Funny how most of us never recognize our own foibles when they manifested in others. "I talked to both of them. The man who shot you is Miss Minnie's son, last name Wu. The women told me Kim introduced him to Irv Gittings, and he's paying the Wu boy, Sam, to do his dirty work."

He eyed me. "You don't buy it?"

"The women seemed scared, their stories too pat."

"Any theories?"

"Nothing that has gelled. I'm still trying to get all the information. So you thought you were dealing straight up with Holt Box? Anything unusual in the negotiations?"

"No, just the usual shuck and jive." He reached for his glass of water. "Getting sort of dry." I helped him maneuver the straw to his mouth. He took a few sips, then continued. "After we inked the deal, Holt did come back for more once he had the chance to speak with me directly. He cornered me at the party the other night."

"What'd he want?"

"He wanted to negotiate some weekends off and the private transport back to his ranch. He said he had some healing he had to do with his family. Something about recognizing too late what was really important." He didn't add, "Like Teddie." He didn't have to.

I understood and I could forgive, but my heart had slammed the door. Some things can't be repaired.

"Did you give it to him?"

"I told him we'd talk." He winced and shifted, pushing himself up higher in the bed. I tried to help without hurting, hard to do when you don't know where all the hurts are. "I was inclined to give it to him. Family comes first."

I squeezed his hand. "You and Mr. Cho were arguing. What about exactly? What did he say?"

"Nothing really other than he was pretty steamed about his big name running back to Vegas."

"Did he happen to mention that his daughter is pregnant?"

That got his attention. He eyed me, a hawk following a rabbit. "No. Who's the father?" He held up a hand as a weary acceptance settled over his face. "Let me guess. Holt Box."

"Ding, ding, ding. You get the prize behind door number one. Holt is the father, at least according to Kimberly. I don't need to point out that all of this is he said-she said, everybody pointing fingers with no hard proof of anything."

My father gave me a long stare. "Just the sort of mess Irv Gittings loves to play to his advantage."

DR. ELLIS had run me off with some lame excuse about my father not needing to be overtaxed. Frankly, I thought he didn't want any witnesses to the firewater he'd promised. Understandable. He was still on the outside when it came to our family and lacked a full understanding of just how loose our rules could be, especially when it came to primo hooch.

Given my exercise allergy, I decided not to walk back, calling a cab instead. The car, painted in screaming yellow and emblazoned with foot-high sevens down the side, eased to a stop, the smiling face of River Watalsky peering at me through the open window.

He jumped out and opened the door, almost knocking me to the side to do so. Sporting his ubiquitous Hawaiian shirt, creased khakis and sandals despite the chill in the air, he flashed his high-wattage smile. His hair looked like he'd grabbed a high voltage line; perhaps the two were related. Wattage and voltage, they were related, right? "Ms. Lucky, our paths cross again. What are the odds?" Southern manners and his Mississippi accent still in place.

I slid into the back seat, self-conscious at the fuss. "You would know."

A professional poker player, River rode the highs and lows with equal equanimity. He slammed the door, then retook his position behind the wheel. "No upside to calculating them."

"I think I'm hurt," I feigned insult. "The Babylon," I said, probably unnecessarily.

His gaze flicked to mine in the rearview, his eyes echoing his smile. "So, you been hanging out at Miss Minnie's since I last saw you?" He'd taken me there once before not too long ago, another rescue mission.

I listened for subtext. Did he know something? "As a matter of fact, I have."

"Really?" *There* was the subtext: surprise.

I leaned forward to talk through the opening in the Plexiglas shield. "Look, I got something I need your help with."

"Sure thing," he said, serious creeping into the Southern.

"You and the other cabbies, you guys talk, right, share info and stuff?"

"Depends on what it is. Who's giving kickbacks and stuff, we keep that pretty much to ourselves." If a fare didn't know which strip club or whatever, cabbies would recommend one, usually one they had a kickback agreement with. Twenty bucks for delivery of a paying customer, that sort of thing. I knew about it, but it wasn't a slippery slope I wanted to step out on. Tips were the oil that kept the Vegas engine running. Well, tips and alcohol. "Why?" River didn't try to hide his interest.

"I'm looking for a couple of guys. One has skipped bail. I'm pretty sure he's still in town. All his assets are gone, and he's got to get around somehow."

"Who's the dude?" River asked, his gaze on me unwavering.

"How do you drive while you look in the rearview?"

"I got one eye on the road. Man, with the kind of trash I can get in my back seat, being able to do that is a life skill, if you know what I mean." He braked hard, following the car in front, proving his level of skill.

"Remember Irv Gittings?"

"Dude tried to frame your father for murder." His tone turned sharp enough to eviscerate.

"One of his lesser transgressions." As I mentally ticked through the list, I realized that one of my jokes actually was no joke at all. We all were capable of murder, even me. The right moment, the right circumstances, Irv in the sights, I could pull the trigger and never give it another thought. On one hand, that horrified me, on the other, it made my inner super hero proud. Nothing like ridding the world of evil to add a bounce to one's stride. If only... "Anyway, can you put the word out? I don't know how you're going to do it. You need to be selective."

"Don't want to let the bear know the hunters are in the woods, I got it." Stopped at a light, he turned to look at me, complicity written on his face. "We'll find him for you, Ms. Lucky. You said two? Who's the other guy?"

I didn't give him any background, but I felt the need to warn him as I handed him the photo, a bit worn from all the recent usage. "This guy is not afraid to shoot somebody in cold blood with witnesses.

He's not above shivving somebody or setting bombs. Sky's the limit with this dude."

"Gotcha." A honk had him stepping on the gas before he'd fully turned back around, sending my heart into my throat.

In my defense, the last day or so had me jumpier than my normal cool, calm, collected, and delusional self.

As if some dim light in the dark recesses lit, River gave me a sharp look. "Who were you visiting in the hospital?"

"Big Boss. That guy in the photo buried a bullet in his chest."

"He okay?"

"Yeah, but things like that change you." I could feel things shifting inside of me. I could only imagine what the Big Boss was feeling. He'd call in markers on this one. I hoped he didn't do something stupid. And I hoped he'd leave the guy alive, assuming, of course, his guys found him first. I prayed that didn't happen. Punishment could be worse than death. Something inside me sang as I contemplated the possibilities.

"I know that," River said, sounding for the world like he did.

"Watalsky, find that guy. Bring him to me. I'll make it worth your while. Oh, and you can break him a bit, but leave him breathing, okay?" said the apple who hadn't fallen far from the Rothstein tree.

CHAPTER FOURTEEN

THE energy in Vegas grew as the daylight waned, as if the sun gave some of its wattage to light the nighttime revelry. The Babylon had added significantly more horsepower to the low rumble in the lobby. I drank it in as I texted Brandy and headed to the Golden Fleece Room, site of this year's whale party.

During the last of the cab ride, Watalsky and I had retreated into our own thoughts. It made sense actually, my father's theory. Irv, playing both ends against the middle, could get everything he wanted: revenge against me and my father, and an influential Chinese diplomat in his back pocket. A man perfectly set up to offer Irv a new stake in the gambling business in Macau. Oh, it was slick and just like him. I knew in my gut he was the puppet master jerking everyone's strings, forcing their hands or simply setting life and human nature in motion. All of us dancing to his whim.

But how to prove it?

I beat Brandy to the Golden Fleece. A few whales wandered among the toys that we'd give away at the party, so I joined them, drooling just the same. A Ferrari 458 Speciale whetted my greed, but the Porsche Boxter Spyder won my heart. Brand-new on the market, I'd pulled teeth getting one for the party. Normally a Porsche purist, 911 or nothing, this car punched all my buttons.

"Nice car, yes?" said a voice next to me.

Mr. Cho. I wasn't sure how I felt about standing this close to the man. The last person I'd seen in his company was now in the hospital. "I'm sure you can think of a better opening line than that."

He seemed a bit taken aback at having a female speak to him so frankly. "Your father, he is okay. I spoke with him."

"Really? When?" I didn't try to cover the sarcastic tone. The guy hit me the wrong way in every way.

"Ten minutes ago, no more. He told me you had just left."

Okay, maybe he had talked to the Big Boss. "Care to share?"

"He told me you could help me." Mr. Cho looked uncomfortable.

"I'm sure he didn't tell you whether I would or not."

He gave me a fleeting smile. "He said you wouldn't."

"More accurately, I'm sure he said I wouldn't want to." I angled a look at him as I crossed my arms. "To be honest, I don't know enough to have a beef with you. So, why don't you come clean with me, then I'll decide?"

"So, you will help me?"

"Depends on what you have to say and what it is you want."

"I want my daughter back."

Not what I expected. And he'd said perhaps the only thing that could've opened my mind a crack. I opened the door to the Porsche. "Get in. Let's talk."

He climbed in the passenger side; I took the wheel. It was a tight fit. My kind of car—one I had to wear. "Did you order the hit on my father?" I asked when we were both settled and the doors shut. I didn't expect honesty, but I figured going on the offensive was a decent strategy.

"No. Why would I want him dead?"

"Holt Box?"

"I didn't know until I arrived here that Mr. Box had agreed to relaunch his career here."

"How did you find that out?"

"Everyone knows." His shoulder against mine moved in a shrug. "It is no secret."

Even I'd heard the scuttlebutt. "You came for your daughter? You expect me to believe that?" I did, actually, but I didn't think I needed to show all my cards at once.

"I don't care what you believe. It matters not to me." He paused, apparently deciding to make nice. "Kimberly and I have not been close. Her mother, she did not want me to have influence on her and did not want people to know she is my daughter. I agreed. My enemies are powerful."

Miss Minnie's life's work had been the study of men. I'd be a fool to doubt her assessment of Mr. Cho's character or his situation. "Is Kimberly your only child with Miss Minnie?"

"I know only what she tells me."

"Your life depends on knowing things." I gripped the steering wheel tight, imagining. "If experience is the best teacher, then you and my father are more alike than you think."

"I want Kimberly."

"Why?"

"She needs to know her father."

I didn't like the way he said that. In fact, I didn't like much about him at all. Maybe his taste in cars, but that was it. "I just can't shake the feeling that you, my father, Holt Box, Teddie, me, we're all pieces on a board, pawns to be used to take the king."

"What are you saying?"

"Somebody is playing us." I angled a look at him. "Is it you?"

"What do I stand to gain?"

I shook my head slowly as I thought. "I don't know. Why did you come here?"

"I told you, to get my daughter back."

"And Holt Box? What motivation was he? Enough for murder?"

"He went back on his word, he stole my daughter, and," he paused, looking a bit uncomfortable., "it is not good for business to let these things happen."

"We have lawyers, the law and the courts. You have Sam."

He didn't seem concerned that I knew. "Sam has worked for me, yes."

"Is he working for you now?"

He focused on the car as he fingered the leather, the woodwork, the fine detailing. "This is a precision machine. It is built for one purpose, and it is brilliant at that one thing. Sam, he was built for killing, and he is very good at it. A machine. But I am not directing him."

"Even if you were, I can't touch you. Not unless China revokes your diplomatic privilege, which they won't do. You run the money pipeline that feeds them."

"Even the men who define my world have their limits. I am not here to kill anyone."

"And we're back to the first question: why are you here?"

"I am here to make things right; to get my daughter."

"Did you order the hit on Holt Box?"

"No, but no one will believe me. And I will not deny that whoever ordered his killing did me a very large favor."

Saving face. With Holt Box's death Mr. Cho looked like a man who took care of his business. "How did you sign Holt Box? As far as we knew here, he was retired on the farm, hanging with the wife and kids."

"Kimberly brought me the deal," he began.

Mental note: fire Kimberly. I touched the controls, and marveled at all the whistles and bells.

"Your property expansion is still in the construction phase, and he wanted a place soon for his big comeback. And he wanted it to be China. The Chinese people are in love with everything American, and country music is quite popular. I made him a very good deal. He seemed quite taken with it." He spoke with British intonation, and his word choice and cadence matched. I always found that odd, the non-British sounding like the British. Of course, he wasn't American either, so who was he supposed to speak English like? Clearly I hadn't thought it through.

"In addition to being quite taken with your daughter." I gripped the steering wheel, wondering what it would be like to hit the road in one of these. My car would bring a good price in trade; it was a classic.

His face darkened. "Yes. They met here in Vegas, became good friends."

That's why I didn't sleep with friends—well, except for the Teddie thing, which proved my point. Kimberly and I were the poster children for the pitfalls of friends with benefits.

"She wanted to help him. I hadn't seen her in ages. I enjoyed negotiating with her. She's a remarkable young woman."

Too bad it took him this long to figure that out. "Yes, that's why we hired her."

"She can be trusted," he said, like a true businessman, and a father trying to repair his daughter's image.

"In this country, we believe in innocence until guilt is proven. So you sign the deal with Holt Box. Then what happens?" I looked out the side window at all the other cars lined up to give away. Several Ferraris, the requisite Bentley that made me curl my lip, a few Lambos. They wouldn't miss the Porsche, would they?

"Next thing I know, a man comes to me, tells me Mr. Box has shamed my daughter and then has walked out on the deal and fled the country. And, worse, your father is the one behind it." He stopped there.

I stopped pretending and paid attention. I knew a clam-up when I heard one.

"Who?"

He weighed his words. "Sam."

I could see he was coming around to my theory. "And you got angry and decided to get even."

"No. I did not. You must believe me when I tell you I did not ask for him to shoot your father, even though in my country it is how business is done."

"I don't have to believe anything," I spat. "Besides, what I believe doesn't matter. It's all in what we can prove. You can go back home with no resolution, no consequences. But my friend will be charged with murder and tried for it. His life for a crime he didn't commit."

"What do you need?"

"I need Sam." I turned toward him and pressed my back against the door so I could watch him. "Can you get in touch with him?"

"Not directly. He changes phones, always untraceable. I usually get the word out I'd like to talk with him, and he gets in touch with me."

"Might be worth a try. There's money in this somewhere for him, and, according to you, he isn't on your payroll." I waited for Mr. Cho's confirmation, then continued. "See if you can find him, but, remember, you're not in China anymore."

"And then?" He looked at me as if I didn't matter.

A chill chased through me. "I don't know. Twenty paces at

dawn? I need Sam in order to free an innocent man who will pay for Sam's crime if I fail."

"You don't know what you are asking." A hint of warning cooled his tone.

Teddie.

"A dance with the Devil, I fear." I pulled out my phone and scrolled through some newspaper articles on the *Review-Journal* site until I found the one I wanted. "Does the name Irv Gittings ring a bell?"

Mr. Cho frowned. "No."

I shoved my phone under his nose. "Does this help jog your memory?"

He pursed his lips and shook his head. "No. Who is he?"

I sighed as I shoved my phone back into my pocket—hard to do with my head touching the roof of the tiny car. "I think he's the guy behind all of this. Only one problem, though."

"And that is?"

"I can't prove it."

*M*R. CHO had left me with my thoughts. I realized he'd agreed to nothing. Of course, so had I. Was it possible to agree to nothing? Brandy had rescued me from that tortured conundrum and was now reaching the end of her spiel when Romeo called. I nodded to Brandy. "Great job." Then I answered the call. "Tell me you've broken the case, Irv Gittings is either dead or behind bars, and the balance of the universe has been restored."

"Well, not quite, but you might like this."

I didn't think there was anything that came close. "What?"

"The fire chief called. I'm on my way to meet the arson investigators at your place. Want to come?"

He sounded like he was inviting me to the prom. "Do I get dinner and a corsage?"

"What?"

"Never mind. Want to pick me up, or should I meet you there?"

"I'll swing by. Meet me out front."

I LET myself into Romeo's unmarked, ignoring the squeaky hinges and lumpy seat. For the short ride, I didn't bother with trying to fish the seatbelt out from between the seats. "What'd they do, rescue this thing from the crusher at the junkyard?"

"Still working my way up." Romeo looked a bit fresher and he'd changed clothes. "I won't be sorry to turn this one in. Maybe I'll get one that doesn't require two quarts at every fill-up."

"Still, you'd think the department could spring for cars manufactured in this decade." As a fan of classic cars, I was torn—criticizing what was probably two years from being a classic felt like a betrayal. Romeo and I filled each other in on what we knew. It didn't take long, which didn't make me happy. We suspected a lot but knew very little. In this sort of game that was akin to having our ears to the ground and our asses in the air—not a defensible position.

"We have the button and the photo." Romeo ran through the high points, summing up. "But no jacket and no tape placing the guy, Sam?" I confirmed with a nod. "We have nothing placing him in the kitchen where Holt Box was killed."

"Eyewitnesses?" I knew there were like a million people in that kitchen.

Romeo blew out a sharp breath. "Very unreliable even if they did remember something, which, in this case, nobody does. Everyone was wearing a white jacket and was busy with their own tasks."

Nothing but loose ends, questions with no answers. Speculation with no proof. "What about the tapes Forrest gave you? Anything there?"

He darted a glance my direction. "Rented van, abandoned on the west side. Trace in it is overwhelming, as you can imagine. Trying to match a set of fingerprints or anything to this crime will be a half-inch short of a miracle."

"Clever. But expected." I shifted as an unruly spring poked me in the butt. "Any shots that can help us identify the guys? Do you smell gasoline?"

"Yeah. Got a full tank and there's a leak in there somewhere. No facial shots—they knew where the cameras were."

"Pros." I expected that too, but that didn't mean I wasn't disappointed.

"Weird thing, though. After watching the two of them, I got the impression one was a woman."

That I wasn't expecting. "Really? Anybody we know?"

As we approached the Presidio, I rolled down the window in Romeo's rattletrap, having to press the glass down the last few inches. I stuck my head out and peered up at my apartment. A huge hole gaped where my bedroom used to be. Curiously, one curtain billowed through the hole, only partially burned. Soot and smoke blackened the building above, but it looked like the fire had been contained quickly, my apartment taking the brunt of it.

"Like I said, they were careful." Romeo, looking like a kid behind the large steering wheel, turned up the drive to the Presidio, parking in the same spot I'd left the Ferrari in yesterday. He killed the engine and pocketed the key. "I gave the tapes to our forensics staff. They have this gait analysis that might help us."

"Is that admissible in court?"

He had the door open and one leg out, catching the breeze and letting in more of the stench that still perfumed the air and clenched my stomach. "At this point, I don't care. If we have an idea of who, I'm sure we can catch them clean."

"Since we're doing such a great job as it is." Hanging back, I let Romeo lead us up the drive. Unlike the rubberneckers on the highway, I never liked seeing the aftermath of an accident. Although the fire was no accident, it was a loss just the same, perhaps worse. And witnessing the devastation made it hurt.

Forrest rushed to greet me the moment I stepped inside the foyer, his face, his whole body crumpled with distress. The smell of smoke lingered here, subtle yet noticeable. "Miss Lucky, I am so sorry. This is all my fault." He blocked my way, taking both of my hands in his huge mitts. "I let the plumbers in. It had to be them." His gaze shifted to Romeo. "Right?"

"I don't know yet." He moved to step around Forrest, subtle in his hinting.

Subtle was no longer a tool in my toolbox. I disengaged my hands. "Forrest. It is what it is. I've called servicemen before and forgotten to tell you. Why would you think this was any different? Perhaps we need to change that policy, but that is for later consideration by the Homeowners Association. I don't blame you. I blame myself."

His shoulders turned in. With his head hanging low between them, he looked like a chastised puppy.

I didn't know what else to say, so I did what I always do—I changed the subject. "Have the other tenants been allowed back into their homes?"

"Yes. They got the fire out pretty quickly, containing it to your place really. There's enough smoke damage to Mr. Teddie's that he won't want to stay there until it's been cleaned. No structural damage, just cosmetic." Again, his face scrunched; he looked like he wanted to cry.

I knew exactly how he felt.

Romeo steered me by the elbow around Forrest, propelling me toward the elevators. "They've restored service. We won't need to use the stairs."

That was a good thing. Thirty flights of stairs. After having survived the blast, I didn't want to meet an ignominious end dying of apoplexy halfway home. Neither of us said anything, and I studiously avoided looking at Romeo's reflection as I tried to ignore the stronger smell of smoke and fire.

The elevator slowed. I prepared myself, but nothing could've prepared me for the sight that greeted me when the doors opened. A blackened shell. That's all that was left. Acrid dark water pooled in the low spots on the floor. My furniture reduced to piles of cinders. The color erased from the walls, the artwork gone. As if my life had disappeared.

"Wow," Romeo whispered.

"Not exactly the word I was reaching for, but, yeah, wow." Hurt unfurled in my belly, squeezing my heart. I'm sure in the days to come I'd reach for something, forgetting it was gone, rekindling the incredible sense of loss that overwhelmed me now, stealing my voice, and erasing me. I'd thought I was prepared.

I was wrong.

Not wanting roots to grow, I moved slowly though the great room, pausing, remembering where furniture was placed, hoping for the comfort of a memory and finding none—as if the memories had burned with the inanimate objects that triggered them. It was all gone, a clean slate, the past reduced to smoke that drifted away on the wind. A part of me, defined by the space I'd created, was gone now too. Did that leave more space for the me I was yet to be, or simply a hole that would remain, a testament to who I used to be?

Sadness weighed on me; yet, underneath I sensed buoyancy unconstrained by the tether of past choices. Romeo walked beside me, a reverence in his posture, quiet and reflective.

"It's just things," I told him.

He glanced at me, unsure. "Things."

"They can be replaced." I took in the devastation, imagining the heat that tore through my home, turning everything to cinder and ash. "Could've been me in here. Or one of my friends."

"I still can't believe how close you came."

He had no idea. One decision to walk down memory lane, to deal with the ghosts, the what-ifs and the why-nots. Had I just gone to bed, I'd be dead.

In a way, Teddie had saved me.

Now it was my turn to return the favor. "Let's see what the pros have to tell us."

The investigator with the Clark County Fire Department looked about as old as Romeo, both of them kids dressing up for Halloween. Slicked down, carefully cut dark hair, a fresh face yet to be introduced to a razor on a regular basis, piercing blue eyes that looked older than the mountains—interesting pieces to the puzzle of an investigator that stood eye-to-eye with me. "Fred Stone, Fire Investigator." His voice was unexpectedly deep, like a spirit speaking through a medium and as unnerving. "You're Ms. O'Toole, the owner?"

"Yes."

"You're lucky."

"Yes."

Knowing the guy wasn't following, Romeo looked uncomfortable.

He knew my wise-ass, and this wasn't it.

"In two ways," I explained, taking pity. "My name is Lucky, as in Luciano, but I also am aware that being alive today makes me very lucky indeed."

"Yes, ma'am," the inspector intoned like Sergeant Friday.

A bad day, and a bad act. How lucky could I get? "Any idea what caused the fire?"

"Yes, ma'am." As he led us back through the bedroom into the bathroom and dressing room, I tried not to think of the things that were no more. The clothes could be replaced. The shoes, too. But the jewelry, each piece a memory, a celebration of a life event, a milestone. That I would miss.

The investigator—Stone, was that his name?—knelt down next to the melted mound of my former jetted tub. "They planted the device here, a charge carefully designed to blow straight out." We followed his gesture into the bedroom and out the window. The bed was in the direct path of the blast. "If you'd been taking a bath, getting ready for bed, sleeping ... any one of those things and you'd ..." he trailed off not wanting to state the obvious, I guessed. "You were home?" he asked me.

"Yes. Well, sort of." I waffled, then decided the truth was the only way to go. "I was upstairs."

I felt Romeo look at me. I thought maybe he might understand, but I didn't know.

I explained about the back staircase, passing off my foray upstairs to checking on the place, since I knew Teddie wouldn't be home for a bit. The investigator didn't ask where he was. Maybe he knew. It didn't matter.

"Perhaps you could tell the owner there was some pretty serious smoke damage?"

"Will do." Teddie was coming home today, at least that's what his lawyer had promised. And, somehow, I felt Squash Trenton didn't welch on his promises. So Teddie would have to find a new home to come home to.

Apparently, Romeo and I were riding the same track. "House arrest at the Babylon? Your old apartment?"

"Doable. Set it up with Jerry, but you're going to have to clear it with Mona."

Romeo looked like I'd asked him to donate an organ or something. "Don't worry," I assured him. "Mona and Teddie are tight. She'll be nice."

Romeo's disbelief was written over every square inch. He'd have to grow a set sometime when it came to Mona and other pushy women, myself excluded, of course. But I wasn't going to tell him that.

"Do you have any idea who might have done this?" Investigator Stone's expression didn't change, his monotone consistent despite the gravity of the topic.

One way of coping, I guess. But spontaneous self-combustion could be a future downside.

Romeo and I filled him in on what we knew and what we believed. It took a while. He listened without speaking, only occasionally tapping a note or two into an iPad. When we'd finished, he tucked his pad away, and then reached into his pocket, pulling out a plastic bag he handed to me.

A gold button. With a familiar crest embossed in the metal. It still gleamed, unadulterated by the fire.

"Where'd you find that?" I asked, transfixed by the audacity.

"In the drain of your tub, affixed to the grate with a wire. I'm assuming it's not yours?"

"Do I look like the kind of gal who does gold crested buttons?" Both men looked at me like I'd just asked them if my slacks made my butt look fat. "Not a trick question. No, the button is not mine."

"Then we can assume someone put it there on purpose," the investigator stated, causing Romeo to roll his eyes.

I jumped before Romeo could trot out the surly lurking behind his benign expression. "We have a pretty good idea who put it there and who it belongs to." I turned to Romeo. "I'll leave you two to trade secrets. I'm assuming you're done with me?" I asked the investigator.

He nodded. In any other circumstance, I'd work to see if I could get just one grin out of him but I didn't have it in me today.

"Where are you going?" Romeo asked.

"I have a date."

"Don't you need a ride?"

"No, I'll take my car." I motioned with one arm, taking in the devastation. "This is why I leave the keys in it." Well, that and the fact they were always hiding from me, but I didn't feel like admitting that.

THE garage was dark, the motion-sensitive lights failing to pop on. Either maintenance needed a swift kick or I was having a Bruce Willis *Sixth Sense* moment. Today, that thought had some appeal. What I would do if I could influence life and no one could see me! Of course, the whole being dead part wasn't that attractive. The shadows taunted me, tickling my fear, sending a chill racing down my spine. Something scratched in the dark. I jumped. *No one is here.* The garage is locked, gated, and guarded.

My ride, a sweet classic 911, waited for me where I always left it: in Teddie's parking spot. His was closer, and he didn't have a car. I wouldn't have one either except this car had been with me for almost as long as I could remember. And she was getting as creaky and as temperamental as her owner. Couldn't really blame her; it'd been a bumpy ride.

I knew I was alone. Still, the frayed ends of my nerves crackled. I hurried, my mind playing tricks.

Another rustle.

I hurried for the car, opened the door, dove in, then slammed and locked it behind me. Taking a few moments to catch my breath, I chastised myself. *Way too pansy-ass, O'Toole. He's got you jumping at shadows.* I pulled air deep into my lungs, then reached for the ignition with my left hand.

No keys.

I knew I'd left them here.

Something glinted, catching a weak light from the next row over. Hanging on a string from the turn indicator.

A gold button. Embossed crest.

It hit me like a sucker punch. My head snapped up, my eyes scanning as I yanked the door handle.

A man; a face swam into view, half-hidden in the shadows.

Irv Gittings.

He smiled.

I ripped open the door and ran, then dove behind the nearest pillar.

The air around me erupted in flames.

CHAPTER FIFTEEN

*T*HE deafening echoes of the blast reverberated, lessening with the distance. Sitting, with my knees tucked to my chest, my arms around them, my head tucked between my elbows, afraid to move, I smelled singed clothing and hair. My ears rang, my head pounded, I must be alive. But I was afraid to move.

Silence settled. I sensed it more than heard it, my ears screaming in protest to the assault.

Scuffling.

Irv Gittings. That thought propelled me to my feet. I'd seen his face. I know I had. His mocking smile. I cast around wildly, swiping my hair out of my face. Footfalls reverberating. Running. One set. Which way?

The cement walls created a great echo chamber. I whirled one way, then the other. No one.

I thought I heard a laugh, evil and taunting.

Then the single footfalls were drowned out by many. People running. Growing louder, I thought. Hard to tell with the ringing.

Romeo rounded the corner coming down the ramp from the outside. Forrest and the investigator with the unremarkable name and flat affect followed behind.

"Shit. Lucky are you okay?" He skidded to a stop in front of me, grabbing my shoulders.

Emotion welled from a deep primal place. Relief. Anger. Energy burned through me. "Did you see him? Which way did he go?"

"Who?" Romeo stared hard into my eyes.

"Irv Gittings. He was here. I saw him."

"Where?"

"There." I motioned to the aisle that I would've seen as I sat in the car. "You didn't see him? He had to go out the ramp. The door inside is locked." And then I thought of my keys. The car keys. There was a building key on the ring. And they'd been gone when I'd reached for them. "He had a key."

"How'd he know we'd come down the ramp?" the investigator asked.

"He didn't," Romeo answered for me. "He waited, then used the entrance we didn't."

"Fuck!" I shouted it because if I didn't, I'd explode. "I'll kill that man." That I said much more quietly.

Romeo shook his head. "We've got to catch him first." He gave me a half-hearted smile as he relaxed just a bit. He probed my arms, touched my face, then shook his head. "All parts accounted for." He tried for a smile.

Forrest punched his phone. I heard him calling in the auto-cide. The investigator went over to the car, or what was left of it. "Hell of a thing to do to a Porsche."

"How could you tell what make it was?"

He pointed to an emblem, the Porsche shield, resting neatly on top of the pile, as if someone had put it there. They hadn't. I'd been here the whole time. And Irv Gittings couldn't drift into smoke anymore than I could, although his skill thus far bordered on otherworldly.

Romeo folded me in a one-arm hug as we watched the investigator probe the smoldering pile of twisted metal and scattered parts.

"Scared the hell out of me," Romeo said. "When that thing went, it shook the whole building."

I stuck my fingers in my ears to try to stop the ringing. It didn't help.

"You're really testing the whole cat theory," Romeo continued.

Even though my brains were scrambled, I thought I followed. "Just don't tell me what life I'm on, okay?" His smile confirmed I had.

The investigator stood, putting away the pen he'd been probing with. "Still hot," he said as he wandered over. They guy had a knack for the obvious.

"Their backup plan." I could play the obvious game as well, but I had an excuse. "My poor car."

"Your poor car?" Forrest sounded incredulous as he joined the conversation; he'd rescued me more times than I could count after having lost an argument with the temperamental hunk-o-junk. "Fire department is on its way."

"That car did have an Italian personality cloaked in German equanimity, but we've been together a long time." I fought the urge to grab the steering wheel from the smoldering pile. Hardwired to hold on when letting go was the right choice. Would I never learn? Now the Fates, with a little help from Irv Gittings, had taken all I owned. A sign, of sorts, perhaps. "After this, I have a feeling the Homeowners Association is going to vote me off the island."

Nobody disagreed as we stared at what remained of a very sweet little ride. Funny how we remember the good things. That car had stranded me all over town, but I remembered her fondly. If anyone else had done that to me there would've been serious bodily harm involved.

Sirens sounded, closing in. Romeo shepherded us up the ramp and outside. "Let's give them room to do their work."

We sat on the grass, close to where we'd sat last night as we'd watched the fire consume my life's possessions and, thankfully, not my life. Today was anticlimactic in a way, although I'd come much closer to meeting my Maker.

"How do you feel?" Romeo asked. He'd wandered off, and I hadn't noticed until he loomed over me with a cup of water in his hand. "Here. Wish it was 101."

"Not me." I closed one eye and looked up at him, trying to hide the glare of the floodlight behind him. "Not yet. I've got a score to settle."

Romeo dropped down beside me, his legs out straight, his back against a pole. "You have an uncanny knack for surviving the unsurvivable. Last night it was a trip down memory lane that saved you. What was it today?"

"Arrogance."

"Yours?" He sounded disbelieving, which made me feel good.

"No. Ol' Irv's. I'm speculating here, but I'd be willing to bet they put the bomb in the car when they planted the other one."

"In case they missed you the first time," Romeo nodded, warming to my story.

"This isn't hypothetical. I almost died."

He shrugged. "You didn't. Go on."

I knew he was trying to keep me from getting too close to the emotional ledge, but he was seriously pissing me off. I tried to ignore his act. "But they were pretty sure the first bomb would do the job. And they really didn't have enough time to wire the car bomb into the ignition. The risk of someone driving into the garage grew the longer they stayed, and that would've taken more time."

"So it was remote detonation." Romeo nodded.

"I wish you'd stop doing that. Just let me finish." He met my glare with a smile, but did as I asked. "That's why Irv had to be here, had to be watching. He'd know he didn't get me last night; it was all over the news. And he'd know I couldn't keep my nose out of the investigation." I beat Romeo to that punch line.

"So, he waited." Romeo apparently bought into my theory. "Where was the arrogance?"

I looked off in the distance, but I was seeing Ol' Irv's face, his grin. How the hell had I ever slept with him? Love blinders on. Young and stupid—wouldn't go back there on a bet. "He had to let me know it was him. I had to see him, to realize what was about to happen. And, in that fraction of time, I moved fast enough, thought well enough, that I survived." I put my finger in my right ear and wiggled it. "Although this ear is pretty much shot. The ringing is loud enough to call the townspeople to Sunday services."

"In Vegas that'd have to be loud enough to wake the dead, or the seriously hung-over. Like one of those air-raid sirens."

"Pretty much."

"Well," I eased myself to my feet, still testing all the parts. They seemed to be sound, if a bit wobbly. "About that date." I extended my hand and pulled Romeo to his feet. "I'm going to need a ride."

ROMEO insisted on escorting me through Cielo and up in the elevator. I pretended I didn't want him to, but he saw through to my thinly disguised appreciation. Reality had tamped down the adrenaline rush, and it was starting to hit me just how close I'd come. My nerves quivered from some deep place inside, working their way out. Romeo handed me off to Dane, who sat at the entrance of Cielo under the Van Gogh as he had before, two masterpieces. I gave Romeo a squeeze and Dane a smile, ignoring the question in his eyes, and went off in search of a hug and a stiff drink, in that order. It didn't dawn on me that I might look a bit worse for wear.

I followed my nose to my chef, who was absorbed in a culinary masterpiece. Pausing in the doorway, I drank in the sight of him, letting this reality overwrite the memory of the past couple of hours. This was good. He was good. We were good. Solid in a way I'd never had before. With him I could be me. And I needed a hug in the worst way.

Stepping behind him, just before I touched him, before I dove in for that hug, he sensed my presence and turned. His shock registered in widened eyes. As I tried to snake my arms around his waist, he grabbed them.

"What?"

He couldn't talk. Instead, his eyes roamed over me, drinking in the details. With two fingers, he touched my cheek softly, a world of hurt creasing his face. My hurt.

I hadn't thought. "Just hold me." I buried my face in the crook between his shoulder and his neck, breathing him in as his arms wrapped me tight. "It's not as bad as it looks," I said, my voice muffled. "Scratch that. It is as bad as it looks."

He held me until my shaking stopped. When I could find the words, I told him everything.

After I'd finished, he parked me on my stool next to the stove, then brought me back a whole bottle of Schramsberg. He popped the top, took several long swigs, then handed the bottle to me. He tended the meal as I watched him wrestle with his emotions, searching for control. The words would come. I focused on my bubbly—I needed both hands to steady the bottle to my lips.

I'd had enough alcohol to begin to thaw the ice inside when he spoke, his voice tight and soft, filled with emotion. "I cannot lose you."

"We can't control that."

He slammed a spoon down on the counter next to the stove. "Yes, yes I can. You must stop this."

"I was getting in my car." I wanted to argue, to fight, but my fight wasn't with him. And logic never prevailed over emotion. Logic could win only when the emotion was gone.

Jean-Charles vibrated with anger, and perhaps fear. Hadn't Desiree warned me the one thing he was afraid of was losing someone he loved? I had my way of coping. I'd let him have his.

"Please don't burn whatever that is." I said, wishing today was a normal day. Then it struck me: all things considered, this was par for the course in my corner of the Universe. I didn't know how to reconcile with that, so I didn't. "It smells amazing and I'm starving."

The anger left my chef. I saw it in the slackening of his posture, the rigidity of anger melting. "I cannot ask you to be who you are not."

Relieved, I took another pull on my bottle, not feeling the least bit embarrassed. I thrust it at him. "Bubbles make everything better."

He drank greedily—the first time I'd seen him slug the good stuff, or any stuff for that matter. He polished off the rest of the bottle, then wiped his mouth with the back of his hand and gave me a knowing smile. "I am learning American ways, yes?"

"Boardinghouse manners, but American, yes."

I could tell he wanted to ask me what I referred to, but banter wasn't in his repertoire right now. "I'd be a fool to ask you to change—I am in love with you the way you are. But perhaps I can ask you to be more careful?"

"For you, anything." I contemplated which to feed first, my growling stomach or my still unslaked thirst. I decided neither. "I'd like to ask you something about the night Holt Box was killed."

"Not the sort of romantic whisperings I'd like, but okay." He put two beautifully marbled pieces of meat on the hot grill.

They spit and sizzled, making me salivate. "Detective Romeo is having a hard time placing the man with the white dinner jacket with the gold buttons in the kitchen. I know he has questioned you, but is there anything you remember, anything at all that might place the guy in the kitchen?"

He stirred and tested, then held a spoon out for me to try. "Careful, it's hot."

I licked at the sauce, then took a full taste and groaned. "What is that?"

He gave his patented Gallic shrug; he knew it irritated me. "A secret."

"Of course."

His grin faded to serious. "I am sorry, I was not in the kitchen much once the party started. I could not say if the man of whom you speak was in here or not. Theodore says so."

"Yes, but he is the only one, and he has the most to gain." I slipped off my stool, feeling a bit more energetic. Nothing like having a murder to investigate and an old love to pin it on to make me feel like myself.

Love and hate, a fine line between them, like a tightrope strung between two tall buildings. One slip and terminal velocity was a surety as you plummeted.

With the bubbles warming my insides, I tried to picture the kitchen as it was when I'd walked in. I stepped to the middle. Jean-Charles glanced at me. "Teddie was here, Holt sagging in his arms, my father next to him." I closed my eyes. *Details, Lucky. Remember the details.* "Blood."

"Where?"

I pointed at the floor. "Here. Drops. A trail." I followed the remembered path deeper into the kitchen, then around the corner to the walk-in. There was a door to the left of it I hadn't focused on before. "This door, it goes to the service area, right?" Jean-Charles wasn't going to leave his meat, so I raised my voice a bit.

"Yes. To an elevator we use to bring in supplies. It's always locked but can be opened from the inside."

I pressed the bar and pushed the door open, sticking my head out. A small vestibule and an elevator that right now stood open. Another door led from the vestibule, and from the orientation and more than passing familiarity with the architectural plans, I knew it opened into the public corridor leading from the main elevator to the front of the restaurant. I stepped out of the kitchen, letting the door shut behind me, then I turned and tried to open it.

Locked, just as Jean-Charles said it would be.

I pushed out into the public space and came back into the kitchen through the restaurant as I had before. Dane hadn't said a word as I'd strolled by; he'd seen me in action before.

"Either the gold-button guy came through the swinging service doors from the restaurant itself, or someone let him in through the service entrance and he left through the restaurant," I said when I'd rejoined Jean-Charles.

He flipped the meat carefully. "You like yours medium rare." A statement that only needed correcting if he was wrong. He wasn't. "How do you know he left through the restaurant?"

"I saw him."

"Are you sure?" Tongs poised above the sizzling beef.

"Pay attention." I motioned to the grill. "Don't overcook my steak."

He raised one eyebrow, then turned to tend the meat. "And yes, I'm sure. Something about him caught my eye. Ol' Irv used to dress in that dinner jacket and he would always pair it with a bow tie; red was for special occasions."

"Why do you speak of him this way: Ol' Irv?"

As one of the more difficult second languages, English and its peculiarities had captured my Frenchman. "He has this very irritating habit of referring to himself in the third person. Instead of using 'I,' he would use his name, Ol' Irv."

"And this is irritating?"

"And arrogant. Like he considered himself royalty." With Ol' Irv directly in my sights, I looked around the kitchen with fresh eyes. If I could find a gold button... But they wouldn't be that arrogant, that stupid. Oh, yes, they would. They had proven that at my place. So where would they hide it? He'd probably do that before he stabbed Holt Box. And he'd place the gold button where the police wouldn't look for it.

I scanned away from the probable hiding place in the walk-in and the path Holt had followed after he'd been stabbed, eventually falling into Teddie. A drain under the dishwashing line caught my eye.

They'd used a drain once.

Would I be lucky?

Squatting, I tried to peek into the hole, but it was too dark and in an awkward spot under heavy equipment. My cheek pressed to cold metal, I reached back, probing the drain with my fingers. The grate moved when I pushed it, letting my fingers search deeper. The drainpipe was narrow, a tube from one of the pieces of equipment, presumably the dishwasher, feeding into it. Packing had been pressed around the pipe, creating a ledge. Working from nearest to farthest, then back around again, I felt for something that shouldn't be there.

I found it on the second pass, pressed into the packing material. Something metal. Not smooth. Using a fingernail, I pried it up, careful not to let it go down the drain. Stuck tight, it popped loose. Adrenaline spiked. I thought I'd lost it. At the last minute, I flipped it into the palm of my hand, then clenched my fist tight around it. And I was stuck—like the monkey and the cookie jar. Using my legs as pistons, I put my shoulder into the machine and pressed, careful to ease it only as far as I needed.

Heavy and bolted to the other machinery, I couldn't move it quite far enough. Jean-Charles squeezed in next to me, adding his strength to mine. It was just enough, and I wiggled my closed hand out. I held it between us, palm-side up, then slowly opened my fingers.

A gold button with an embossed crest.

"Better toss on another steak," I said, probably grinning like a fool. "Romeo likes his medium."

ROMEO had polished off two steaks in between crowing about the button and giving me grief about not preserving fingerprints. I doubted there would've been any useful fingerprints—Irv was arrogant, not stupid—but I the detective fuss. All of us on emotional overload, some of the steam had to vent or rivets were going to pop. Fussing, especially at me, was Romeo's way of offloading.

For me, I thought perhaps some animal sex with a delish

Frenchman would be just the thing to bring my stress load back into line, or as close as it ever was.

Sex is interesting—it's also pretty silly when you think about it, but at the moment I was fixated on the interesting aspects.

We'd shooed Romeo away and had done a cursory cleanup. On the way home, we'd swung through the Babylon, and I'd grabbed a few clothes from the office. I also had some I'd left at Jean-Charles's house. Together they were the sum total of my worldly possessions. I couldn't quite get my mind around that and didn't want to try, not now, maybe not ever. But some retail therapy was definitely in order. But that, too, could wait. Although, this being Vegas, the dark of night was the perfect time to satisfy all your needs and desires. I opted for the carnal over the tangible.

During the drive home, we both had been quiet. Apparently we'd been thinking along the same lines. The house was dark, quiet, when we let ourselves in through the garage. I stepped on something soft that squeaked, making us both giggle.

Jean-Charles put a finger to his lips, stifling a laugh. "Shhh. Christophe, he is sleeping. Chantal, too." Chantal was his niece who lived with him while in culinary school, following in her exalted uncle's footsteps.

"Where is Desiree?"

"Here or the Babylon, I am not sure." He grabbed my hand and pulled me through the house. Tiptoeing like thieves, we advanced on his bedroom. Once secure behind locked doors, he gathered me into his arms. My nerves raw, my heart sore, my body thrummed at his touch, a touch that awakened all the senses, sharpening, feeding. His mouth captured mine, feasting. His tongue darted, sending bolts of desire arcing through me.

Tonight, life stripped to its most elemental, I met his demands, reveled in them, then feasted of my own. I took what I wanted. Life had taken from me. Anger fed my desire, fueled my passion, and I claimed him for my own.

I think he liked it. Okay, I know he liked it; all the signs were there.

Lying spent on the bed, the covers ripped and strewn on the floor, our bodies slick with sweat, satiated for now, I had no idea what time it was. Darkness settled soft and warm around us, my head on Jean-

Charles' shoulder as he wrapped me into him. I think I slept, or maybe just drifted, but I awakened, warm where our skin touched, but cold where it didn't.

He felt me shiver. "You are cold. Let me get the duvet."

He untied the knot of our bodies, untangling our limbs and moving away. I didn't watch him; I didn't need to. With my eyes closed, I retraced every peak and valley of his body as I remembered it, my fingers, my lips recording every square inch. When he returned, pulling the feather comforter over us, I checked my accuracy.

He remained still under my touch, his quickened heart rate when I pressed my lips to his chest, the sharp intake of breath when my hand roamed lower, the only evidence of the effort it took. Finally, he broke. With a growl, he flipped me over and made me his own.

Light tinged the sky when I awoke the second time, comfortable, warm, complete. And life had refilled all the empty places inside.

His arms around me, he brushed a kiss on my forehead. "We must sleep a bit more. You are my life, my heart. And that scares me."

As I drifted, I thought love shouldn't instill fear. Love should be savored for however long you have it. To have known its gift even briefly was beyond what most are given. I didn't say the words.

I wished later that I had.

A pounding on the door jarred me awake. Jean-Charles bolted out of bed.

A small voice. "Papa. I am sick."

CHAPTER SIXTEEN

THIS time a different hospital, but it was hard to distinguish it. Perhaps a bit newer than UMC, the waiting room had more comfy furniture, and a Keurig coffeemaker and a snack station. But it held the same air of despair, of frailty. Unable to sit for long, I held up the wall and watched Jean-Charles pace.

"He was burning up." The worried father hurled the words, weapons against the unthinkable. Worry creased his face as he raked a hand through his hair and glanced at me, not pausing in his pacing. A caged tiger, feral, angry, needing only a hint of an opening to lash out, ripping flesh, fighting for his life. "The doctors, they are worried."

"They'll get his fever down."

He whirled on me. "How do you know this?"

"Because it's what doctors do." I crossed my arms, a small shield in an unwinnable battle. No matter what I said, Jean-Charles would not find comfort. I'd had enough years dealing with all kinds of trauma; I knew the signs. "And I have to believe."

"You are a—." His face reddened as he searched for the idiom.

"Pollyanna, yes."

"Yes, this." He stalked across the room.

I understood his anger, his fear. A control freak finally faced with the reality that we have no control over the most important aspect of our lives. Those we love, those whose loss can cut us open, leaving our entrails to rot, they can be taken from us in the flash of a gun, a moment's indecision, a poor choice, the indiscriminate callousness of life. I'd been there, railed against the Fates, fought for control, and failed, just as he would.

The doors to my left whooshed open, admitting a worried Desiree, with Chantal behind her. Jean-Charles had dispatched the girl to go fetch her mother, surrounding himself with the comfort of family. We clustered in a worried knot as Jean-Charles told them what we knew. "He has a very high fever. They don't know what caused it. The important thing right now is to bring it down so there is no damage. They have put him in ice." Jean-Charles flinched at the memory, the tiny body red with heat, his hair slicked with sweat, as the doctors placed him in the tub and began packing ice around him.

I reached to comfort him. He shrugged away. Worry rooted us to the spot; fear kept us apart. Indecision ate at us. Finally, the doors from the back opened, expelling the doctor. A young man with a worried expression and kind dark eyes pulled down his mask. "Chef Bouclet, your son, his fever is coming down slightly, but not as fast as I'd like. He's not out of the woods, but he is improving."

"May I see him?" He fought to control himself, but desperation prodded him.

The doctor waffled for a moment. I thought Jean-Charles would grab him and shake him until he agreed. Thankfully, he agreed before Jean-Charles ran to the end of his rope. "Okay. But just for a moment. He is hallucinating a bit. This is not unusual with fevers this high. Your voice should calm him."

The doctor shot me a worried look as he eased Jean-Charles toward the door. I knew that look.

"Fuck," I whispered, wanting to shout it, but afraid of arousing Death's attention.

"Yes, this," Desiree added, sounding just like her brother. "He cannot lose the boy."

"None of us can lose Christophe," I said, anger leaking through. It'd been one hell of a day. One I would never forget. And one I would have revenge for.

"*Oui,* but for my brother, his heart will die and he will be lost. We almost lost him once before. If it hadn't been for Christophe ..."

She let me fill in the rest. Jean-Charles was a man who lived a life of passion. And with passion came fear.

We sat, the three of us, silent soldiers paralyzed by our inability to have any effect on the outcome, our weapons useless. Perhaps only ten minutes or less had passed, but it seemed like a lifetime before Jean-Charles reappeared, disgorged by the same door that had swallowed him, but this time alone. He seemed less, his energy sucked away, his face haggard, his eyes pained. He slumped down in the chair next to me. "He is so small. But so brave." A tear leaked out of his eye ,and he pinched the corners near the bridge of his nose, working for composure. "The fever, it is very bad. They are thinking meningitis." He looked to his sister. "They will know shortly, but it is bad, very bad. The bacteria can go through his system. He could die." Jean-Charles picked up a coffee cup sitting on the table and hurled it across the room, spraying cold coffee in an arc. "If he doesn't die, he could have deafness or brain damage; they don't know."

"He could also be okay." The moment I said the words I knew I'd made a mistake. Like moving when the bear is standing over you.

Jean-Charles whirled on me, a cornered animal, his eyes wide and wild. "What do you know of loss? You are a silly woman always thinking the best will happen. It won't. Bad things happen every day, horrible painful things that rip your heart out, leaving you bleeding out with no way to stop your life, your joy, from leaking away."

"I'm sure you're right."

He gave me a haughty look. "You are too afraid to risk your own heart, to have children." He didn't add "you pathetic thing." He didn't have to.

Some of it rang true. All of it hurt.

"I cannot marry you." He flipped his hand at me, a rude, dismissive gesture. "You need to go."

He rose and fled down a hallway I hadn't noticed. I didn't follow him.

Desiree put a hand on my arm and gave me a wan smile. "He doesn't know what he is saying. He speaks from fear. It is better to push you away now than hold you in his heart only to lose you later. I have told you, he fears loss more than life."

"Then loss is what he's asking for."

A spark of life hit her eyes. "You understand. He will regret his words, and he will do all he can to make them up to you."

"Words, the most vicious weapons we have in our arsenal. They can cut deeply, inflict almost lethal wounds, but the wounds heal." I gave her a long look. "The words, however, once spoken, can never be unheard. Verbal splinters that work themselves in deep."

"Only if you let them," Chantal said, injecting herself in the conversation for the first time.

"True." I gave her mother a thin smile. "She is wise."

"An old soul."

Feeling the need to move, to run, yet not wanting to leave, I had a moment of paralysis before gathering my purse and buttoning my sweater. A chill had burrowed in deep.

There comes a moment in life where everything is stripped away. Now was my moment. I felt as exposed, as stripped bare as if I were walking naked down Las Vegas Boulevard on New Year's Eve for all the world to see.

I thought about staying, but my presence didn't lend comfort. I couldn't cure Christophe. I would keep close watch from afar—well, maybe not too far afar. I gave the two women long hugs and told them to take care of Jean-Charles. My heart cracked more than a little. I wanted to be the one he turned to, the one who comforted him.

But that wasn't what he wanted. I understood, but that didn't lessen the hurt.

Logic pounded once again by emotion.

Waiting for my cab, I grabbed my phone, searching for the number.

Cody Ellis answered on the first ring. "Cody, I need another miracle."

WHEN the cab eased to a stop and I let myself in the back, I was relieved to see the driver wasn't River Watalsky. I didn't want to take a friend on this ride. "High Desert State Prison, please."

The driver turned around, a young woman with a shy smile and hard eyes. "Indian Springs?"

"Yes." I settled back for the ride.

"That'll cost you."

"In so many ways." I leaned my head back as she put the car in gear. "You can wait for me, right? I won't take long."

"Meter and a half to sit in the jail yard." She watched in the rearview, gauging my reaction.

"I'll pay the meter; the rest is at my discretion. Don't push me, not today."

She caved at my pushback. The fare would be the best she'd had in months; we both knew it.

I must've dozed for part of the ride north—we were there before I was ready. Even though less than thirty miles from the Strip, Indian Springs was a world apart. A small town squatting amid sand, rocks, scrubby angry brush fighting for life, and mountains that looked like they'd been picked clean by a life-consuming cloud of locusts. The Mojave, a desert as bleak and as beautiful as any, and the last place any sane man would envision a place like Las Vegas.

Vegas, an insane vision of a delusional mobster. It fit. But it was home.

Nevada had always welcomed the outliers.

The Tonopah Test Range was out here, the site of atomic testing back in the days before anyone understood the effect of exposure to radiation. Yucca Mountain, the abandoned national repository for nuclear waste, was out this way too. So it fit that the largest correctional facility in Nevada, a one-hundred-and sixty-acre site of low buildings hunkering in a remote corner of the desert behind electrified fence, rounded out the neighborhood. Guards with automatic weapons watched from towers that dotted the fence line. Their eyes on us as I presented my ID at the checkpoint raised the hair on the back of my neck. Even my cabbie with the attitude seemed subdued. The guard directed us to the Visiting Center.

The warden was waiting for me when I finally got through all the security checkpoints, the double-door hallway—my least favorite part, where they let you in then lock the door behind you before unlocking the one in front, all the while watching you from behind thick glass, gauging your every movement, weighing all possible motives. Every time I passed down this hallway I felt guilty of something. And I worried they would discover my transgression through some unconscious tic or something and would never let me out.

Warden Jeffers greeted me warmly with a firm handshake and a smile. He probably didn't get too many visitors who didn't have a rap sheet or love someone who did. A tall man with a shaved head and a kind manner, he hovered a hand behind the small of my back as he motioned with the other outstretched. "Here are Irv Gittings' visitor logs. I made copies of the pertinent sections."

I scanned the sheets. Nobody I recognized. Darn. My hope was hanging on someone being stupid. I should know better. I folded the sheets and tucked them in my pocket—Security had relieved me of everything else.

"Tell me what you're looking for." The warden seemed interested. "I'd love to have Mr. Gittings back." He shook his head. "A bad judge, now dead. Got Gittings' fingerprints all over it."

"I'm trying to connect Irv to the two high-profile shootings recently."

He nodded, his face serious. "Holt Box and your father. I'm very happy he's okay. He's a good man."

"He is, thank you." We stood awkwardly in the hall, neither knowing which way to turn. "Anything you can tell me about Irv while he was here? Did he make any friends?" I had the unnerving feeling that every move we made, every word, hell, every thought, was being recorded, monitored, and evaluated. A bit too much scrutiny for my comfort.

"We kept him out of the general population, although he seemed to figure out his way around pretty quickly."

"No doubt." I thought about the Irv I'd first met and the man he became. Of course, that man, the one who'd thought murder was a viable business strategy, had always lurked inside the suave pretender. I'd been too young, too easily impressed, too foolish to peek under the veneer. But I took a bit of solace in the fact I wasn't the only one. Irv Gittings had cut a wide swath.

"Did he have a cellmate or anyone he might have traded confidences with?" If I knew Irv, he'd find someone to use, even in this place where brawn trumped brain.

"No cellmate. We thought he needed to acclimate, lose some of the refinement before we turned them loose on him."

I shot a glance at the warden. He met it with a level gaze—he'd meant what he'd said. The thought put a song in my heart. As my father said, there are worse things than dying.

"I checked with some of the guards who spent more time around Mr. Gittings. They said he had one friend. They hung together in the yard, that sort of thing. His name is Frank, and he's actually a pretty good kid. Did one stupid thing. Rode a motorcycle into the casino at the Starlight. Grabbed a bunch of chips from the cashier. He didn't know the casinos chip the high-dollar ones. He didn't get far."

"I remember. Made the national news—a prime-time stupid criminal spot." I glanced up at the camera in the corner and its blinking red eye and fought the urge to stick my tongue out. One of those irrational urges, like hurling oneself into the void from a high balcony.

"Yeah, he got slammed. All the publicity made it worse for him. Like I said, he's a good kid. Stupid, but not bad."

"There ought to be another place for us to rehabilitate stupid. In here, they just get mad and learn all kinds of bad tricks. Can I talk to Irv's little buddy? It's Frank, right?"

"I thought you'd ask that." He stepped back and motioned down a side hallway. "This way."

We walked shoulder-to-shoulder down the hallway as I fought the urge to drop breadcrumbs. Institutional setting, everything looked the same, each hallway a mirror of the others, all connected in a maze. I felt like a dog in Pavlov's lab.

"He's waiting for you in room six." I must've looked uncomfortable as he added, "A guard will be with you at all times, and Mr. Wu will be restrained."

"Wu? His name is Frank Wu?" Had the Fates finally decided to open a window?

Visiting Room Six reminded me of the interrogation rooms at the Detention Center in Vegas. Same gray paint, same metal furniture, same anger lurking in the corners. The warden held the door for me, then stuck his head in long enough to make sure the prisoner and guard were as he said they would be.

The door closed and I turned, locking eyes with a nightmare. "Sam?" I stared into the face of the dinner jacket guy, the guy who'd shot my father.

He eyed me, a predator eyeing a future kill, with a look that told me he knew what I was thinking, what I was experiencing. But he didn't quite pull it off. "It's nice to meet you, Ms. O'Toole." He angled his head. "I've heard so much about you."

The guard stood close, ready, making me feel crowded and wary. "Funny, nobody has told me about you at all."

A prick to the ego that drew blood. I saw it in the slight narrowing of his eyes. "Irv, he really hates you."

The resemblance between the man who sat in front of me and the guy who'd shot my father and mocked me from across the casino was amazing. Not quite identical, but close enough to warrant a double-take. "Tell me something I don't know." I eased into the chair across from him, which put me at eye level with the guard's gun and his crotch, both unnatural bulges. "What did he tell you?"

"He would get even." Frank crossed his arms, adopting an arrogant air I knew pretty well.

"Your brother has that same look."

Shock focused his stare. "I don't have a brother." He swallowed hard, his eyes moving from mine—not a good liar. Apparently not a good hood either, considering his current address.

"Well, you've got somebody out there pretending to be you, looking like you, doing all kinds of interesting things on camera." I leaned forward. "And I have a feeling he's working with Irv on that revenge thing. What did Irv promise you for connecting him?" I pressed, my voice hard, my patience short.

"I don't know what you're talking about."

"I've done some stupid shit in my day; allowing anyone like Irv Gittings within fifty yards was among one of my more stupendous follies. But," I leaned forward and gave him my best badass, which I'd been told by those who should know, was pretty good. "I am far from stupid."

Frank's mask slipped a little, giving me a glimpse of the kid pretending to be bad.

I leaned back in my chair and crossed my arms. "So let's see how I do. You got this brother, he's the real deal, mean, ruthless, a killing machine. And your father, he's no Boy Scout either. But you didn't get those genes. You weren't the kid torturing animals and knifing his friends. No, that was Sam. And your father was proud of Sam, could use somebody like him. So you tried to fit that mold. And you got caught." I angled my head and gave him a raised-eyebrow look. "How'm I doing so far?"

He shifted uneasily.

"Your sister worried about you in here. So, when her friend Irv Gittings got an invitation from the State of Nevada, she got word to him to look you up, take care of you."

I hit Frank's soft underbelly. I saw it in his face, his eyes especially; they were a lot like his sister's. "You might look like Sam, but you favor Kimberly."

He broke. "She worries about me."

"Did you set Irv up with Sam?"

"No." The last bit of artifice shattered, and I saw the real, frightened, sad kid. "I would never hook anyone up with Sam." Frank licked his lips and looked away. "Sam is..."

"I know. A coldhearted killer."

"When he left, did Irv say anything to you?"

"He said he'd get me out of here, which I shrugged off. A lot of guys make promises, and Irv didn't strike me as the kind who keeps many."

Smart boy. Smarter than me. But he'd had a different kind of education.

"You need to be careful. He has it out for you. Never seen anything like it."

"Revenge. It'll eat your soul if you let it."

"Assuming you have one in the first place. He did say he had a lady waiting for him, which was rubbing it in."

"That's Irv. Hold out a carrot while he stabs you in the back." I patted Frank's hand, and the guard harrumphed. I'd forgotten about him. I turned and ran headlong into his crotch again. I looked up at him. "Could you back away a bit?"

He just stared down at me.

Frank gave me a look. "You get used to it."

"When will you be out?"

"Long time. Around here they take messing with the casinos

seriously."

I would've thrown the book at him, too. That thought gave me something to think about. Snap judgments—perhaps I was guiltier than I thought.

"You got the warden's ear, right?" he asked. Hope, even in this place.

I didn't agree or disagree. "Why?"

He glanced at the guard, then found his courage. "I'd really like a drawing pad and some colored pencils or anything. I really like to draw." He clutched himself, both arms across his chest. "I'm going crazy in here without my art stuff."

I had to play this hand, but I was going to hate myself a bit in the morning. "Okay, I'll use what I got, but you've got to give me something, anything to get the drop on Irv Gittings. He and Sam, they're doing some serious damage. Shot my father, tried to kill me twice. I need some leverage here."

Again, he glanced up at the guard. Nobody liked a snitch, especially not here.

"I get it, kid."

A smile lifted one corner of his mouth. "Home. Have a nice trip home."

*T*HE cabbie had been true to her word. She fired the engine when she saw me. I'd stopped to chat with the warden. Frank would get his art supplies. Hadn't taken long. The warden was a good guy.

The ride back passed in silence, with me lost in thought and the cabbie leaving me to it. We rolled through the desert, the miles clicking under the wheels. On the north side, just as the first of the suburban sprawl crawled over the hills, we passed the turn-off to Mt. Charleston sporting its mantle of snow—most folks were surprised to find out one could ski in the morning and sunbathe in the afternoon. Vegas winters, as many distinct faces as the city itself.

When we hit the edge of town, I leaned forward. "Can you reach another cabbie?"

"The dispatcher can find anybody."

I gave her River Watalsky's name, then wrote my number on a slip of paper which I handed to her. "Ask if he can call me at that number."

I watched my city slip by outside the window. When we passed the turnoff for Summerlin Parkway, my breath caught. Jean-Charles's neighborhood.

Home.

Irv and I had one thing in common—neither of us had a home. I had no idea where I would call home. But the more important question was, where would he?

I had options. What were his? He'd lived at the Athena.

It was gone.

My phone vibrated in my hand.

Jeremy. "Hey. Got anything?" I asked, hope flaring. I knew the pieces were there, but how was all this going down? How could I prove it?

"No sign of your man at Miss Minnie's." Jeremy's voice was tired, but had a hint of happy in it. "I left Shooter out there, and Flash is still hanging in. She is relentless."

"One of her best qualities and one of her worst. Depends on the context."

That got a chuckle. "I got that."

"Any idea where the young Asian woman is? Is she still there?"

"No, she left, but she didn't come back. Took her mother's car, or at least I assumed it was her mother's."

I heard a female voice in the background. "Thanks. Where are you?"

"Home." He was being intentionally oblique; I could hear it in his voice. Jerking my chain. Why not? Everybody else was.

"Get some sleep." I wanted to ask him so much more, but it was none of my business and not a problem I could solve. Sticking my nose in would only make things worse. Amazingly, I took my own advice and hung up.

Waiting for River to call, I was at wit's end. Frank had said Irv had a lady waiting on the outside. He'd said it casually, but could it have been another hint? A female accomplice? Given Ol' Irv's appetites, that would be consistent.

Papers crumpled in my pocket as I shifted, looking for a more comfortable position. Tugging them loose, I unfolded them. The visitor log for Ol' Irv. Not many names for a guy known for his glad-handing. One name caught my eye. Dani Jo. No last name. On a whim, I rooted through my purse and found the registration form Mrs. Holt Box had signed.

One look and I laughed out loud, startling the cabbie, who darted a worried look at me in the rearview. "I'm okay. In fact, I'm better than okay."

"Good to know," she said in a voice filled with indifference.

Different names; same handwriting down to the left-handed slant and the closed-loop letters. Granted, I was no expert. But the similarities were enough to warrant paying the grieving widow a call.

WITH the help of security and their cameras, I found Mrs. Holt Box at the private pool in the Hanging Gardens. Carrying the Babylonian theme to the max, the Big Boss had created Las Vegas's very own jungle under glass. The Hanging Gardens, fashioned after the seventh wonder of the Ancient World, were a riot of large draping trees, flowering shrubs, trailing greenery, and all manner of plants clinging to the banks of meandering streams filled with tubing tourists. The streams flowed through three distinct pools—one family-friendly, one adults only, and one private, tops-optional.

The original gardens, as described in ancient texts, consisted of steps of flowering plants, like a giant pyramid or mountain. Nobody knows for sure and many speculate the gardens were purely mythical. Not in Vegas. Here, we make it our life's work to turn the magic and mythical into reality.

And with the gardens, the Big Boss had exceeded himself.

Yes, the Babylon had the only tropical climate in all of Nevada. And it took an enormous amount of energy, electricity, and manpower to sustain it. Two acres of climate-controlled wonderland.

Mrs. Box lounged by the top-optional pool, availing herself of the option. She needn't have bothered—by Vegas standards, anti-climactic. But, my assessment ... and to be honest, I didn't make a habit of evaluating boobs. A couple of strings and a tiny triangle completed her ensemble.

Apparently today was my day to be small. Something the two of us had in common, albeit in different contexts. However, I didn't think pointing that out would be a good icebreaker, so I bailed.

Instead, I dangled the visitor log from the jail in front of her face. "This is you, right?"

She shaded her eyes from an absent sun with a dainty hand. "No."

I dangled the registration form she'd signed next to the other.

"Oh." She moved herself to a seated position, swinging her legs over the side of the lounge chair so she faced me, knees to knees, as I plopped down on the lounge chair next to hers.

I could tell she was trying to assess my bullshit tolerance level. "I'm tired of playing games. Your buddy, Ol' Irv, and Sam, a buddy of his you know, have tried to kill my father once and me twice. They killed your husband, which you seem really broken-up over, by the way. You better tell me what's going on. If you're honest, I can help you. If not, I'll see you buried in a shallow grave where the crows and rats and other desert critters can get to you, ripping your flesh from bone."

She swallowed hard. "Is that a threat?"

"No. It's a promise." My inner Robert De Niro cheered. I had always wanted to say that ... and to mean it. Okay, I was faking it, but as they say, fake it 'til you make it.

She knotted her hands in her lap. "Me, and Holt ... we haven't been so good for a long time. We have a big house, him on one end, me on the other, the kids in the middle. We're doing it for the kids, but I got to the point I couldn't stand it. Being married to somebody who has a bazillion gals waiting to bed him every night takes a toll, you know? We were just kids, nobodies when we got married. Irv gave him that stage and everything changed."

"Big lights. How'd that happen? That was a pretty big gig for a nobody, as you say."

Her face closed. She plucked at the edge of a towel as if there was a thread to pull.

Not in a Babylon towel, thank you. I wanted to slap her hand away.

"I slept with him." Her voice came out small, defeated.

"You slept with Irv?" I wasn't surprised. Back then, Ol' Irv was at the top of the Vegas heap, and apparently at the top of his game.

"Shhh." She glanced around as if a microphone could be in the bushes. Came with the territory, I guessed. "It was a huge opportunity. Holt was good enough—I think that's been proven. Look what happened."

"But Irv needed a bit of extra incentive."

"Yeah. I'm not proud of it, but you could say I opened the door for Holt. He ran through it, but still." She looked sad. A plain gal from a small town—simple wants, simple needs, caught in a celebrity maelstrom.

I sorta started feeling sorry for her. Sorta. I still sensed a piranha lurking under the boots and Levis act. "Irv has proof?"

"Pictures and a video." She shivered. "It's awful."

"You've seen it?"

"I was there, and yes, I've seen enough." She wouldn't look at me.

I didn't blame her. "That was a long time ago. What could it matter now?"

"Yeah, several lifetimes, it seems. But I was married. And now we're getting divorced, or were. The press didn't know yet. Nobody knows really—our lawyers, my mom."

Holt's death just increased her wealth by a hundred percent. "Irv?"

"Irv," she affirmed, her voice hard and cold—a tone I remembered from our first meeting. "I'd kill him, you know."

I had no doubt. "How'd he find out?"

She adjusted the tiny string on her bottom half, untying one side with a yank, then redoing it in angry, jerky motions. "Who knows? Can you ever keep something like that totally quiet? People were all over the new tour, coming out of retirement. Why now? That sort of thing. Lots of questions, people guessing. Some guessing right."

"So, if it came out you'd had an affair, you stood to lose a lot in the divorce."

"My kids, enough money to go back home, start over. Nobody knows, and I couldn't risk it. I got scared. I didn't want anyone to know. You can imagine how it would be, fighting the Holt Box publicity machine. I'd be labeled a tramp, unfit for everything."

She had a point. The Court of Public Opinion—a free-for-all where the media sacrificed the truth for the salacious and incendiary. "So, what did Irv want?"

"He wanted the Babylon to hire Holt for his comeback."

"That's all?" Seemed like a bad bet for a trump card.

"That's what I thought." She quit picking at the towel. With a delicate gesture she caught the eye of a roving server. "Veuve, please."

"A glass?" She looked between the two of us.

"A bottle." Mrs. Box raised an eyebrow. I shook my head. "One glass."

She might be from a small town, but she'd acquired big-city tastes. "And Sam?" I asked once the server had moved away. "Why was he bird-dogging you?"

"Insurance. Irv put him onto me to make sure I did as I said I would. Totally unnecessary. It seemed so easy. All I had to do was open the door, and I knew your father would jump at it. Anybody would."

"And you get Irv out of your life." She was naïve if she believed he'd go away so easily. Blackmail, the gift that kept on giving, like one of those white elephant gifts you keep re-gifting every holiday. Easy money. "And the tapes? The pictures?"

"He gave me a copy, said they were the originals."

"But we know how that goes." Mrs. Box could be lying through her teeth. That was the whole problem with all of this—everyone had something to gain from seeing Holt Box dead.

Even Teddie. "Did Irv approach you again?"

"Not yet." At least Dani Jo had a bit of insight.

Maybe that really was all he needed from her—a way to turn a killer onto the Big Boss. So that took care of the revenge thing as far as my father was concerned. I was still a loose end. But, knowing Irv, I knew that wasn't his end game. He had to find a new gig. "Did you know about Kim Cho?"

"What about her?" No anger. No jealousy.

The server came back with the Champagne, and filled a flute, handing it to Mrs. Box, then nestling the bottle in a silver ice bucket in the shade. I eyed, the Champagne, regretting my decision no to partake.

"Holt hired her to do some publicity and things. I think she's the one who facilitated the Macau contract."

"How does she fit with everything else?"

Maybe she didn't know the down and dirty. On the off chance she didn't, I wasn't going to be the one to deliver the blow. "No idea. Any idea why Holt went back on his deal there?"

"We didn't have time to talk about it, not that he was sharing. We didn't talk much, as I said. Things had turned..." She searched for a word as she sipped her Champagne, savoring it like it was her last meal or something.

"Distant?" I guessed.

Her tight smile told me I'd underestimated. "What about my father? You said he wanted out of the deal."

She gazed at the other people lounging by the pool, turned in to each other, or heads together as they cuddled in the cabanas, her expression turning wistful. "I'm not sure that was quite right. I know Holt went back to your father with more demands. He's a tough negotiator; he didn't just roll over." She smiled a satisfied smile. "Holt wasn't used to that."

"The money was important?"

She tossed back the rest of her drink and reached for the bottle. "When is it not?"

She sounded like the money was the only thing she had left to fight for. Maybe, after all this was over, I'd tell her what her husband really wanted—if it would make things better. Would I want to know if the roles were reversed? I wasn't sure.

Shadows fell across us—the looming figure of Detective Romeo. He took in all of Mrs. Box and instantly reddened. Stepping from behind Romeo, Agent Stokes didn't have the same problem enjoying the view.

I tossed Mrs. Box a towel. "I don't even know your first name, not really. I'm assuming it's Dani Jo."

She covered herself with the towel, which was large enough to completely hide her. Her brows crinkled. "Dani. Dani Jo." She said the words as if conjuring a long-ago past. "Nobody has called me that in a long time. I'm always just the bimbo, Holt's wife. A hurdle for other women to climb over."

"No one can relegate you to inconsequence unless you let them. What does your mother call you?"

"Pickles." She blushed.

"Mothers." I angled a look up at the two men who stood there looking all official and uncomfortable. "Can we help you?" I speared Romeo with a look. "We were just having a nice chat."

Agent Stokes took the lead. "We found that phone."

My hope would've taken flight, but his tone and expression shot me down. "Where?"

"Bungalow seven," Romeo said, glancing at Mrs. Box, then settling his gaze on me.

I could tell he didn't want anything with me in particular; he was just searching for a comfortable place to rest his eyes. There was something so guileless about the detective that was completely endearing. Vegas could make you forget the rest of the universe had sensibilities a bit more delicate.

"I'm assuming you had a warrant?" Mrs. Box refilled her flute, then slammed the Veuve.

Romeo pulled the paper out of his inside jacket pocket. Nobody reached for it.

Dani Jo finally gave up on the Champagne, setting the glass on the ground with careful finality. "I'm guessing it wouldn't make a difference if I told you I had no idea what phone you're talking about?"

Agent Stokes tossed a plastic bag across her towel-draped legs. The white dinner jacket minus a bunch of buttons. "The phone was in the pocket."

She looked at me with big eyes. "Lucky, I've never seen that jacket in my life."

I stood so I could stare down the over-eager public servants. "Did Sam have access to your bungalow?"

"He had a key." Dani Jo pretended to be interested in her wiggling toes.

"Why?" I beat the detective and Agent Stokes to it.

"Irv insisted. Until the contract was signed, sealed and delivered."

The contract was still open, or at least she thought it was. Good to know.

"I can confirm he had a key," I said to the enforcement types standing there, looking all official.

"How do you know?" Romeo asked, doing his job.

I wilted a little under their scrutiny. "I don't know *know*, but when I was chasing him, he waved a key at the security guard at the entrance to the Kasbah."

"So you know he had a key, but you can't prove what to?" Agent Stokes had no problem saying what Romeo wouldn't want to.

He was right, so I couldn't exactly shoot the messenger, which I was conflicted about. "You're thinking she killed her husband? Haven't you already made one bad arrest for that?"

Agent Stokes fell silent, leaving Romeo to handle the not-so-easy part. "I just want to talk to her."

"At the station?" Why I was feeling defensive, I couldn't fathom. The woman had triggered every preconceived notion I had. Maybe that was why the defensive thing had kicked in—feeling a bit judgmental and not liking myself for it. And I wanted the right person to fry for one murder and three attempts. Everybody was still on the list, but some were leading the race. Dani Jo wasn't one of them. "I think you're overlooking one thing. No one saw her at the party."

"There's that, but she was in town. You said so yourself." Romeo shut me down.

And I had the registration log to prove it. So I didn't argue.

Romeo continued, shifting to Mrs. Box. "We'd also like to record your gait, Mrs. Box, the way you walk, and compare it to one of the people who planted the bomb at Lucky's place. Would you agree to that?"

Dani Jo stood, wrapping herself in the towel and whatever dignity she could muster. "If you'll let me change, I'll be glad to go with you. I've nothing to hide, but somehow I don't think the truth is going to set me free." Before she left with her guards, she paused, looking up at me. "You know what they say about things being too easy."

Guess she knew Irv better than I thought.

CHAPTER SEVENTEEN

MONA'S call caught me wandering the lobby looking for a problem to solve or someone to shoot. Nothing worse than knowing who and not being able to prove it.

"Oh, Lucky, I did what you asked. Lying is so easy." Her voice breathless through the phone.

With Mona, there was always a yin to her yang. But I blew by that anyway, so I deserved to pay a price. But lying wasn't a good thing, especially considering her dipping a toe in the political scene. We had enough lying politicians already. "But, Mother, remember, lying is normally frowned upon except when a matter of life and death."

"Oh, I know that."

I pictured her waving her hand, slapping away my concern as she would a pesky gnat. A heart of gold, but a brain wired to get her ten to twenty.

"So what did you find out?"

An exaggerated sigh. "I thought you were not going to the mother thing."

"Only when I'm running low on patience."

She didn't take the hint. "Well, I'm a bit disappointed, I must say."

"I must say, haughty suits you...Mom." She went all giggly. "Now that we've got that out of the way, can you fill me in on what you found out about Kim Cho?"

"I couldn't possibly talk about something that delicate over the

phone. You must come up. You're in the lobby; Jerry told me so."
She went quiet. I'm sure he'd told her not to tell me, which made me
smile. "You won't get mad at him, right?"

"Nobody has any secrets in this hotel. We all know that."

"So, you'll come up?"

I heard babies giggling in the background. "I wasn't aware I have
a choice."

"We'll be waiting." She rang off before I could ask who "we" was.
I charted a new course, worrying about what kind of storm I'd be
walking into. With Mona, one never knew and could never anticipate.

The private elevator was the first peace and quiet I'd had. Even
my brain stopped spinning for a brief moment—without that force, I
struggled with equilibrium. And tried not to listen to the Christmas
music. I so did not need an earworm of *Jingle Bells*. And nobody
hates *Feliz Navidad* more than me. The first strains prodded me
through the narrow opening as the elevator came to halt.

I skidded into the great room.

And ran headlong into Teddie holding Thing One or Thing Two,
who could tell? Even with a baby in his arms, he looked relaxed,
casual, like he hadn't a care in the world ... except for the ankle
bracelet.

"Aren't you supposed to be home?"

"Home. Interesting word. My place has a bit of smoke damage.
They worked out for me to stay next door in your old place. I thought
you knew."

"I did. I forgot. Been a little distracted lately."

He shifted the bundle in his arms. Seeing him with a child had
my belly feeling funny. I had no idea what that was about. "Sorry
about your place. That was a really close call."

He gave me a look. "Thanks for saving the guitar."

He didn't ask me how all that came about, which was good
because I didn't want to lie. "Anything new that might make me feel
better?"

Mona talked in the kitchen, using the clatter of pans to punctuate
what sounded like a speech. "What's she doing?"

"Practicing." He cooed to the baby, singing a snippet of *Some
Enchanted Evening*. When the baby settled, he looked up. "Your

father is sleeping; they moved him out of ICU. She's cooking."

"Two signs of the coming apocalypse." I glanced toward the kitchen. "You don't think she's cooking up a way to get Father a couple of roomies at the hospital, do you?"

Teddie grimaced. "Could be." His bundle started whimpering again, so he started bouncing it. "You got any news?"

Wandering to the bar, I fixed myself a glass of single malt in honor of the Big Boss—the fifteen-year-old stuff. I saved the twenty-five for his return. "I'll tell you what I know so far, not that I can prove any of it." I started at the beginning and tried not to leave any detail out.

"So, you think Irv Gittings is behind all of it?"

"Up to his ass, but everybody stands to gain somehow. Some proof that would help point a finger would be great. I'm sure once forensics gets through with the jacket we can prove Sam killed a couple of folks, maybe even planted a bomb or two. If we catch him, maybe we can charge him. He is Mr. Cho's son. I wonder how far China is willing to extend the diplomatic privilege." I stepped to the wall of windows and stared out at the Strip. I could just see Cielo far down to the left at the south end of the Strip. The opening was soon. I'm sure I had a punch list a mile long; the thought paralyzed me. "I'd really like to see him hang. Frankly, I'd love to see Irv, Sam, and Mr. Cho dangling in the wind. They mess with my magic." I turned around and caught Teddie looking at me, sadness and longing arranging his features. I knew the feelings.

"I'd love to see him hang, too. That'd get my ass out of a crack, although repairing my career will be impossible."

"Please, I'm the PR person, and I can tell you there is no such thing as bad publicity." I'd disputed that little truism with myself earlier, but decided to trot it out here. Maybe I could lighten Teddie's load.

"You're customer relations, and you're just trying to make me feel better."

Yes, we were the best of friends, could finish each other's sentences, read each other's minds. That thought made me sad. I saw it mirrored in Teddie's face.

"My career is pretty much fucked."

"Don't say that. Talent will out."

He didn't look convinced and I had nothing to give him.

Mona breezed into the room dressed in slacks and a crisp white shirt, her hair pulled up, and looking all businesslike. I almost didn't recognize this incarnation of my mother. But the frilly apron that said "WILL COOK FOR SEX" gave her away. "Hey, Mom." I met her halfway and gave her a kiss. "What were you doing in there?"

"Practicing a speech. I'm not very good at speaking in public, so I hired a speech coach." She kept moving, walking back and forth.

"Peter Paisley the fourth?"

"How'd you know?" She looked crestfallen as she paced by me.

"It's my job to know. Where is your off switch?"

"Moving helps not to get brain-freeze when you're giving a speech. That's what Peter tells me."

I grabbed her arm and rooted her to a spot in front of me. "You're not giving a speech now."

She paused, then started pacing again. "I know, but I need to think to get it all right."

I gave up and tried to not let the pacing bother me. "Why all the secrecy?"

"I thought maybe you and Teddie ..."

I motioned her to move on—figuratively, but she took it literally. "We've made nice, now could you tell me what you found out about Kimberly Cho?"

"Well," she swooped in, relieving Teddie of his little package as if she couldn't be in close proximity and not have a baby in her arms. She cradled her child with a casual ingrained deftness. Her voice held a conspiratorial whisper. "I had to work through the girls. Turns out I have more friends than I thought. All that lobbying I did." At my look, she motored into the meat of the matter. "I found the doctor Miss Minnie's girls use."

"Skanky, right?" I wrinkled my nose thinking of all the possibilities.

"No, actually very upscale, treats all the Summerlin moms. While I believe in what he's doing, I know he could get in a bit of trouble, so I won't say who or where."

"Okay, if you just tell me what he told you."

"Kim Cho is lying. According to the doctor, who would have no reason to lie to me, Kim came to him wanting some complicity in her ruse. Apparently Holt Box wanted to see some proof. The doctor said she got pretty ugly."

"I'm sure she felt, with Miss Minnie's weight behind her, she could get some help from a doctor, especially one with something to hide. I like the fact he drew the line."

"Just because something is illegal doesn't make it wrong," Mona said, parroting her daughter.

"And the reverse is true as well, something Father needs to be reminded of." I glanced at Teddie. He got it.

For Mona, it was a fly-by. But she'd given me a lot to think about.

Kimberly Cho wouldn't be the first to try to trap a celebrity. "Mom, you've been a great help. I really appreciate it." I gave her a peck on the cheek.

Teddie wandered away as Mother and I finished up, taking my former spot in front of the windows. He looked like someone who once had had it all only to lose it. And some of it hadn't been his fault. I stepped in next to him. "Life changes. We move on. It won't ever be the same, but it can be as good or better."

He nodded, but didn't buy it. Like I said, I knew his nuances.

"How's Jean-Charles. You guys good? I'm asking because I sincerely care. All I ever wanted was for you to be happy."

I didn't remind him of the fracture in time where all he wanted was a career as a pop star and the roadie girls that came along with it.

He must've sensed more in my pause.

"Tell me. What's going on?" He asked as a friend—I could read that all over him.

That was the part of us I missed the most. So, I told him. Just saying the words tore my heart in two.

When I'd finished, he turned to look again at the Strip, the lights fully illuminated now, a rainbow of dancing color against the Stygian darkness of a winter night. "Do you love him?"

He'd asked me that once before. I'd answered in haste, hurling the words at him to draw blood. Not a proud moment. This time I took better care—of his feelings and of my own. "Yes. It feels solid, permanent, in a way you and I weren't. He knows who he is and what he wants."

"Do you?"

"Yes. But what he wants apparently doesn't include me."

Teddie raked a hand through his hair. For some odd reason I got the impression he was warring with himself. He knew I was open and wounded right now. I wondered how he'd play it. To his advantage or as a friend?

Teddie gave a shrug, his posture losing the hurt. "Here's the deal with Jean-Charles. Take it from a guy who knows, okay?" His reflection stared at mine. "He's just a guy, one who has already suffered a huge loss. And there he was faced with losing the one person who had brought him back, made him want to live again." Teddie held up a hand. "I might be overstating, but I don't think so. I get the Frenchman. I'm not his biggest fan, but for selfish reasons. He's a good man with a good heart.—one you have filled, much to his amazement and horror. The risk probably terrifies him. Better to push you away now than to risk losing you later."

"That is so messed up."

"He's a guy."

"Point taken. But why wouldn't you just grab each moment and squeeze the juice out? None of us know how much time we have or how things will work out. Got to grab it while you've got it."

I hadn't realized I'd shifted to "you" until I saw the look on Teddie's face. "Truer words were never spoken." He smiled and gave a rueful little noise. "That's so like you. Others aren't quite as brave."

Brave? Me?

He turned to me and took my hands. "He's scared. Trust me, I know. If you love him, fight for him. Go to him. Show him you are strong enough to fight for both of you right now."

I could see how the words cost him, and I loved him all the more for it. He'd picked the friend path. And he'd been right—he wasn't the man I'd feared he'd become.

"Okay." I nodded. It felt right. His words were true.

"You deserve to be happy, Lucky."

"Don't know that I deserve it, but I'll fight for it." Looking at him made me sad—all that could have been. But perhaps it really couldn't have. We'd never get that chance. "Thanks."

I gave him a hug, one he returned. None of the sizzle and pop—that was gone, but my friend was back. "I gotta go. The construction guys at Cielo want to do a walk-through; I have a race to officiate at in the morning; my assistant is up to her ass in alligators of her own making, which doesn't mean it's not my problem; I either have a wedding to plan or a divorce to facilitate; and then there's that whole pesky killer-on-the-loose thing."

That didn't even get a smile.

ONCE again, I borrowed the Ferrari and headed out to Cielo—the valet hadn't even bothered to put the car away. Instead of taking the back way, I turned down the Strip. This time of night cars packed the road, Hummer limos with pretty young girls standing through the sunroofs drinking in all the possibilities. Boys whistled and shouted from the sidewalks and other cars, vying for attention. Couples, some decked for the evening obviously taking in a show, others still casual, roaming from property to property, contributing to our economy along the way. Vegas was about fun, about magic, about escape, even if only for a few days. It was also about reinvention, rekindling, and maybe a bit of creative rewriting.

The city pulsed in my soul.

The phone rang. Cody Ellis. I put him on speaker. "Tell me you have good news."

"Christophe is out of the woods. His fever broke. He spent most of the afternoon with his father. A good man, by the way. We gave the boy something to help him sleep for a while. His aunt and cousin are with him. His father went to his new restaurant. The opening is imminent, yes?"

"Yes." A flood of emotions rolled through me. The boy was safe, his father's heart whole.

"He seemed sad when he left." Cody spoke volumes with those simple words. He knew. And he understood.

"Cody, thank you … for everything."

"It's what I do."

"Roam the world healing people?"

He paused. "I never thought about it that way, but, yes, that's exactly what I was meant to do."

"And you do it well."

He was Miss P's Teddie—both of them roamers. I only hoped he didn't break her heart.

I MUTED my ever-present Luis Miguel CD as I absorbed the beating heart of Vegas in all her finery. Even the fountains shot green and red as they danced.

One thing was bugging me—like an itch just under the skin, I couldn't shake it. I dialed Jeremy.

His voice sounded better. And he was once again taking my calls. I chose to se that as a good sign.

"How good are you at delving into bank records through the back door?"

He didn't even laugh—Miss Goody Two-Shoes, he used to call me. I bet I just shot that out of the water. "Whose?"

"Kimberly Cho and maybe Mrs. Holt Box while you're at it." I watched families and couples gathered around the Bellagio fountains. And thought about how innocence can live right next to guilt and you'd never know it. "Can you do it? It's for a good cause."

"I know somebody. It'll cost you."

"I'll pay, just ..."

"I know, don't let anyone trace it back to you."

I tapped on the steering wheel in time to the Andrea Bocelli Christmas song that wove its way in through the rag top as I accelerated past the Bellagio—the fountains had to have music to dance to. "You know what? I don't really care." *Teddie was that important.*

"Don't worry," he chuckled as he said the words. "I won't let them throw you in the slammer."

"If I go, we all go, so I'll be in good company." Friends bound by felonies. The wrong thing for the right reason—I could live with that.

CIELO was still humming as the crews worked to put the last minute polish on. The foreman met me as I came through the doors. A small man with a bark like a drill sergeant and an air of efficiency completely negated by the too large hardhat that almost covered his eyes, handed me a hat as he started reading from the punch list like he was giving orders.

I set the hat aside as I listened.

He glanced, then barked, "This is still a construction zone. We haven't had the final nor been green-tagged, although I expect it any minute. The inspectors are here. There was as slight glitch with the HVAC. It's been remediated."

I smiled and left the hat where I'd put it.

He'd seen my signature in the lower right corner on his checks, so wise man that he was, he said no more. Only a few things on his list needed my personal attention. I asked about the others, giving orders of my own. When we'd worked through the list, which hadn't taken anywhere near as long as I feared, I said, "I'm going to swing through JC-Vegas. I want to gauge the status myself." I shut his smirk down with a look. "Give me half an hour and meet me at the suites."

"Yes, ma'am."

A seventies playlist accompanied my ride to the top floor. Mental note: change that. The Athena had been retro, not on purpose, though—one of the last of the original properties to be repurposed. Cielo was a far cry. Savory smells greeted me as I stepped off the elevator. When Jean-Charles was upset, he cooked to calm himself, center his emotions.

Instead of following them through the public sections, I used my owner's privilege and master key to let myself in through the back. Rinaldo at the stove, Jean-Charles next to him, taking notes and giving instructions. Each dish would be detailed, the recipe available, but the chefs would be expected to have it all committed to memory. Plating instructions by the service station. Prep instructions across the kitchen where I stood now. Opening night, the kitchen would be like a symphony, everyone playing their part in the melody, blending into an artistic masterpiece.

Absorbed, neither man noticed me. I slipped behind Jean-Charles and put my arms around his waist as I always did. My heart pounded. How would he react? He'd said he loved me. He made me believe it.

He stiffened, then put his free hand on mine and leaned his head back. From behind, I pressed my cheek to his. I caught Rinaldo's amused glance as he kept cooking. "Kids," he muttered.

"You are here," Jean-Charles whispered as if he couldn't believe it.

"Of course." I brushed my lips against his skin, savoring the tingle. "I never should have left."

"I was an ass."

"Yes."

He turned into my arms, wrapping his around me, after he discarded his notepad. "I have been thinking of you from the moment I sent you away. I am so sorry. I wanted to tell you; I didn't know how."

"You just did." I buried my head into the crook of his neck. "I'm sorry, the most powerful words."

"After I love you," he whispered, his breath warm, his arms home. "Sometimes, I am a fool."

"Aren't we all?"

There was no let-go in his hug. "You left. My words were horrible; yet, you sent the doctor."

"Of course. I can be stupid, but God willing I'm not petty. I love you. I love Christophe. How either of you feels about me won't change that. And, since all Dr. Ellis has done since he showed up is work miracles, I asked him for one more."

"He took over and instantly everything changed, everything was better. Christophe, he is okay." His voice hitched.

"I know."

He leaned back but didn't let go. "I was out of my mind with fear. Can you forgive me?"

"For what?"

He pressed his forehead to mine, savoring, drawing strength from the connection, I thought, since that's what I was doing. "There is something I want you to see." He grabbed my hand and led me out of the kitchen into the hallway. He presented an owner's card at the elevator. He met my cocked eyebrow with a smile. "Sometimes I can get what I want."

Way more than sometimes, I thought. A charming Frenchman in America, he could write his own ticket.

While Cielo had thirty public floors, it actually had one more. Two apartments comprised the entire floor. The larger of the two was a guest suite for dignitaries and others with security concerns. I'd spent countless hours reviewing every detail of that suite. The other, the owner's suite, I hadn't thought about at all. Jean-Charles stopped in front of this suite, waved his card, then depressed the handle when the lock clicked. He pushed the door open slightly, then stopped, reaching back to grab my hand. "Close your eyes."

The set of his jaw told me arguing was futile, so I did as he asked. I held his hand with both of mine and took baby steps, trusting him to lead me. I felt the space around us open. Maybe it was the echo, or the air, but I felt the expanse. He wormed his hand out of mine, then with both hands on my shoulders he positioned me as he wanted, then let go. "Okay, open them now."

I waited for a minute; I could feel the smile tickling my lips, the frisson of excitement at the surprise that tingled through me. I always pretended not to like surprises, but that wasn't honest. I was a better giver than receiver, but still, who didn't like to be surprised with a gift?

I eased my eyes open, then gasped out loud as I moved slowly in a circle, drinking it in. This was no overnight surprise. They'd finished out my apartment. We stood in the most perfect room—a great room with a wall of windows that invited the magic inside. The magic mile of the Strip stretched to the horizon, the Babylon bookending the view on the far end. A small kitchen gleamed behind the arc of a counter against the wall opposite the windows. Apparently, no expense had been spared. "It's perfect. But commercial appliances?"

"I will cook for you, in private." He had a gleam in his eye that would be fun to explore. "You like it?"

I turned once more before answering. The furniture mimicked

my own in my apartment-that-was, the artwork by the same artist, but there was room for new treasures, new memories. "It's perfect."

His enthusiasm infectious, he reached for my hand. "Come."

Laughing, I let him pull me along. "When did you do this?"

"Miss P, she did most of the work. We knew you would not pay attention to your place, so we did that for you." He stopped at the entrance to the bedroom. "This is a place for you, but it is not your home. Your home is with your heart." Pressing his hand over his heart, he had a moment of doubt. I saw it in his eyes.

"With you and the children."

A smile banished his worry. "Yes, this." He pulled me into the room.

Again, perfection, from the bright colors of the duvet, to the hardwood floors, to the hidden window coverings.

Jean-Charles gently tugged me forward. "The bathroom, as you say, is to die for."

"In light of recent events, I'm seriously considering eliminating that tired phrase from my vocabulary."

"A very wise thing." A hint of serious. "Worry only brings what we most fear."

Another man who knew but didn't apply the philosophy to himself. He and my father needed to go on a personal discovery retreat. Just the thought made me cringe. Maybe it was just the curse of the Y-chromosome, since I saw myself so clearly and all. Maybe we all needed a kumbaya weekend.

He opened the door with a flourish. "Just like home." A jetted soaking tub built for two, a shower that could also handle multiples, a vanity with two sinks, twin mirrors, and face-friendly lighting. A CD player sat between the sinks and I couldn't resist punching play. Then I laughed out loud. The theme from *Thomas the Tank Engine*. A special memory. "That isn't going to become our song, is it?"

Jean-Charles leaned against the doorjamb, arms crossed, looking irresistible. "Perhaps." He was teasing—I hoped.

I narrowed my eyes. He had better be teasing.

"But it can be our own private memory," he added, not sounding that convincing.

"Care to give it a spin?"

In one stride he captured me, holding me close, then kissed me. His kiss held all the promise the future could hold.

"I am thinking our minds might be a bit distracted," he whispered against my hair. "Your foreman has been pacing the lobby half the day. I'm sure he is not done with you."

"Just gotten down to the good stuff." I breathed him in, making a memory, one that would hold me for a few hours. "And you need to get back to the hospital."

"I must be there when my son awakens."

"No argument here." I eased away from him. "Go. And thank you for this lovely place."

"It is not just for you. I will be working so close." He pointed upstairs.

"Convenient."

"Yes, this. And you will sleep at our home tonight?"

Home. "Where will you be?"

"I cannot say. It depends on what the doctors tell me."

I tried to imagine Jean-Charles's house without him in it. Home? Maybe. But without him, it wouldn't feel like it. "You tend to your son. I will stay here."

His frown crinkled the skin between his eyes. "But will you be safe here?"

"The building will be locked and the guards patrol."

"And there is security?"

I didn't know the exact operational status of out eye-in-the sky, but no need for Jean-Charles to worry. "Sure. Don't worry. Do what you need to do., but let me know where you are and how Christophe is doing, okay?"

"Of course."

We both lingered in a last kiss.

MY foreman was waiting for me at the rear of the property where we had our own mini version of the Kasbah. A private drive, private suites, private chefs, everything private, but no bungalows with private pools. Space wouldn't allow. But there would be no skimping on the pampering.

"Everything okay?" he asked, giving me a poorly hidden smile.

"The owner's suite is amazing. When did you have time to do that?"

"Your Miss P, she is a taskmaster, had us all hopping. But, to be honest, the project is so large it was easy to roll that into the plan. And given the explosion the other day ..."

"It's very much appreciated." I raised my finger. "Give me one more minute?"

"Sure. It's your dime."

Literally, times like ten million. Miss P answered on the first ring. "Customer Relations."

"Thank you."

Her voice lost its crisp edge when she realized it was me. "It doesn't begin to cover all that you've done for me. And your things are on their way over. You should be functional inside an hour, but some serious retail therapy is in order."

"Find me more time in the day and you're on."

"Not a problem."

"Have you heard from Squash?" I thought I slipped that in there pretty seamlessly.

"Yes."

"And?" Two could play my game—I was always doing this sort of thing to her.

"Thank you."

"Cute. Okay. We'll talk." With everything else, I hadn't even had time to swing by and grill Delphinia about wedding plans and all of that.

Miss P's voice switched gears. "Remember, you have the race in the morning."

"At oh-dark-hundred, I remember." My voice held a bit of a whine, which violated my own rules.

I punched the end button. Personally, I liked it better when I could flip the thing closed with some flair. But the iPhone was pretty darn amazing, so, a small price to pay for cool. A deep breath fortified me for the game of pay now or pay later with my foreman that would take up the rest of the day.

Daylight had given way to dusk, a softening that provided the backdrop for the lights that defined this city. This was my favorite time of day—like being at a magic show waiting to be teased and tantalized and totally amazed by the illusion.

We'd been through all the suites but one, saving the best for last. Well, the best besides the one on the private floor. This one, called Cloud Nine, had its own back entrance for added privacy. Three bedrooms, a game room with a one-hundred-inch flat screen and a full bar, and three *en suite* bathrooms large enough for a football team—okay a basketball team. The suite had been booked for the next year, even at thirty-five thousand dollars a night. While that might sound steep, the suite came with a twenty-four-hour chef on call, a dedicated Bentley limo, and a helicopter waiting on the roof, so there was a bit of extra bang for the buck.

The place looked pristine, already set up for its first guest. The living room area was decorated in light Asian style, bamboo floors stained dark, overstuffed white pillows with embroidered green leaves on minimalist couches and chairs. The walls painted vibrant green, adding warmth to the white. Clean, white Caesar Stone countertops in the bar, stainless and white marble in the baths, accented with bright green and orange towels. I fingered one as I walked through, taking in every detail. Still damp.

Like I said, working to the wire to get the place ready.

The game room was next. A counterpoint to the minimalist décor of the main rooms, the game room resembled more of a man cave with dark leather recliners, tastefully disguised of course, theater-style seating, and a wooden bar straight from Scotland. The designer or one of his minions had even monogrammed the Steuben tumblers. The antique gun in the lighted case above the bar was a nice touch. "That doesn't work, does it?"

"Not unless you have a cap, wad, and black powder."

I didn't share his confidence. Many of the pre-Civil War guns had been retrofitted to take shells. "Put a lock on it anyway. I like the touch, but still, I'm a bit gun shy these days. And alarm it too."

He made a note.

The bedroom was fit for I don't know who, but somebody with fine tastes and a ton of money. This room alone had cost several hundred thousand dollars, each suite over a million. The electronics alone required a dedicated closet and around-the-clock IT staff. The toilets could do everything for you except sing a song—that was extra. And since our music system was state-of-the-art, I didn't spring for the song part. It still made me giggle at all the personal hygiene the toilets could be responsible for. I couldn't picture myself sitting still while a machine made a fuss over my nether regions. The whole idea sounded fraught with peril, but apparently this sort of pampering was *de rigueur* with the well-heeled set.

My foreman and I made a few notes—the finishes that were missing were minor.

"Overall, very impressive job," I said, as we wandered back to the front of the property where the average millionaires would play. Staff training was winding up—everybody put in long hours as we got closer to the opening.

"You want me to have the guys get on these things tonight?"

"No, it's almost Christmas, it's late. We don't open until New Year's Eve. We got this. Tell everyone thank you and go home to their families. Tomorrow is Christmas Eve. I'll see everyone on the 26th."

He looked grateful, only now letting me see his fatigue.

Man, were we rowing the same boat. I was about dead.

MISS P had been as good as her word. I'd hung my meager possessions in the owner's apartment closet, mourning the loss of my shoes the most. My toiletries from the office, including makeup and other lotions and potions had been laid out on the vanity. Too tired to sleep. Too wound up to think. I decided a bath was in order.

The hotel ... my hotel ... settled in around me. The windows brought in the whole of the Strip to keep me company. I dimmed the lights and left the window coverings up. The tub was huge, and I longed for my Frenchman to help me fill it, but that could wait. As if he knew I was thinking about him, my phone lit up.

"Hi," I said, as I took a seat on the tufted cushion in the boudoir and shucked my shoes. "How's Christophe?"

"He has charmed all the nurses, and they are filling him with ice cream."

"As you have charmed me, but I'm not feeling the ice cream. Maybe whipping cream?"

"You are not being nice."

"Naughty is so much more fun. I'm spending my first night in the owner's apartment. Would you like to come take advantage of me?"

"*Oui.*" His voice dropped, turning husky.

Liquid heat through my veins.

"I will see you tomorrow. They say perhaps I can take Christophe home."

"That would be wonderful. Make him happy-face pancakes and think of me."

"I think of you always."

Shucking clothes—how long had I worn these? Long enough they ought to be incinerated, but since most of my wardrobe had met that fate, I thought perhaps a good fumigating might do. I cranked open the taps to the tub, turning the hot to barely short of scald. Warm bubbles on the outside to soak the day away. If only I had some bubbles for the inside. I smiled and wrapped myself in the thick bath sheet hanging on the warming rack.

Padding to the bar, I opened the fridge and bent to peer inside. A bottle of Schramsberg Brut Rosé. They'd thought of everything. I made short work of the cage, popped the cork, and eschewed the dainty flutes for a more robust delivery vehicle—a double old-fashion glass. Cut crystal, it felt heavy in my hand, its quality complementing the primo juice. A creature used to her comforts. Pausing in front of the huge, windows I absorbed the view—a very high-priced view even for Vegas. The fact that it was mine was still something I found hard to comprehend, much less truly believe.

Brand-new surroundings, but they felt right. Each of us grows into our own destiny. Perhaps I'd made it to mine, setting my foot on the first brick of the path meant for me. The tub was filling nicely, and the bubbles warmed me from the inside as I dipped my toe in the water and pushed the button for the bubbles. Dropping my towel, I slid into the luxurious warmth, feeling it pull the hurt, the fear, the loss, the anger out of me. Okay, not so much the anger. That still wrapped around my heart, a black poisonous snake demanding revenge. I would have it, even if it killed me. But not tonight, not now.

I'd brought the bottle with me, so I refreshed my glass and lay my head back, using the rounded edge of the tub for support, everything submerged except from the nose up. Occasionally I came up for a drink. I stayed until my fingers ridged like prunes.

Sleep pressed on me, a demanding suitor not to be denied. A brief towel-off, then I slipped between the sheets, nestling in the softness as I listened to the hotel settle around me. The whir of the elevator as staff tidied up and left for the holidays. The creaks and groans of a building adjusting to the cold night after absorbing the warmth of the sun. Random noises of my hotel, a lullaby to sleep by. Desiree had felt a frisson of fear at staying alone with only Christophe. Not me. I let go and succumbed to the reality of what had been a grand dream.

The day grew distant as I fell into sleep.

*S*OMETHING prodded me awake. A noise?

I bolted upright in bed, startled out of a dream, a nightmare. But what had awakened me? I pushed back my hair from my eyes and tried to focus. For a brief flash, I hadn't known where I was. Then the memory flooded through me. My brain fuzzy—I'd been down deep—I tried to think, to process as I scanned the room. The Glock waited on my nightstand. I grabbed it, knowing it was ready to go.

And I was ready to use it. I stilled, listening. I thought I heard the faint whir of machinery. The heat? The elevator? The guards patrolling? The police? Something in my gut told me this was foe not friend. They'd tried twice. Maybe third time was their charm. But not without a fight.

The night had deepened, the noise quieted. Six a.m.

I'd been dreaming—a gun, a killer, an old hotel ... running.

My subconscious worked the puzzle, fitting the pieces. I bolted out of bed.

The gun—Irv's gun in the case downstairs. I'd been too tired to pay much attention—I never expected his gun to be hanging in my hotel.

The damp towel. Someone had used it.

Home. Irv had lived at the Athena.

The Athena had become Cielo.

Home, Frank Wu had said. Irv was going home.

As I shimmied into a pair of pencil jeans and Teddie's old sweatshirt, the one with Harvard on the front, the one that still smelled like him despite numerous washings, then stuck my feet into a pair of silver sequined flats, I thought I heard the distant whir of the elevator. Brushing the hair out of my face, and wiping the sleep from my eyes, I grabbed the Glock.

Irv was here, and he was looking for me.

CHAPTER EIGHTEEN

IF Irv wanted me, he'd have to find me. As Father always said, the best part of defense is a good offense. And taking the offense would add an element of surprise, which I hoped would help even my odds.

Taking a deep breath, I killed the lights, stuffed my phone and my master key in my pocket, and moved toward the door. I didn't call Romeo, probably should have, but I had to be sure. Last thing I needed was the cavalry screaming back to Cielo looking for a killer and once again landing us a primo spot on worldwide social media. With a hotel to protect, perhaps I wasn't thinking clearly.

Keeping to the shadows, my back against the wall on one side of the interior hallway, I pressed the door handle and thanked myself for buying top-of-the-line locks and hinges. The door moved silently, opening wide enough for me to ease my head around. The lights had dimmed as they were scheduled to do just before dawn. Still light enough to see and for the cameras to record, but a subtle touch for those who staggered to sleep or were awakening for a Grand Canyon tour. Catching a killer hadn't been a part of the decision-making.

Gun at the ready, I looked both ways, several times. I cocked an ear, trying to override my pounding heart, listening for any hint of movement. My mind played tricks. A new place, new sounds. Pulling my head back, I leaned against the wall, both hands around the butt of my Glock.

I took a deep breath, then ran.

Movement behind me. At the corner, I dove to my right. The shot missed me by inches. Keeping my momentum, I rolled. Back on my feet, I bolted through the door to the stairs. Flashing my keycard in front of the pad, I punched in my number, then locked the door. The bolt engaged just as someone threw their weight against the door from the other side.

How the hell had he gotten a key to the private floor? Security not fully online, construction workers flowing in and out. Not hard to imagine, but it still pissed me off. This was *my* hotel, dammit.

I pressed back against the wall. The door absorbed three shots; then the firing stopped. Taking the stairs two at a time, I realized how lucky I was that my apartment was one of only two on the private floor. The building code allowed us to have only one stairwell instead of the normal multiples to handle a large crowd. For the moment, I had the jump on my pursuer. He had to take the public elevator—if the last person out had done what they were instructed to do and locked the service elevator.

After putting ten floors between me and my apartment, I hazarded a look into the hallway. The elevator motor whirred to life. Crouching, listening, gun in front of me, I kept to the side as I moved down the hallway toward the elevators. When I could see the displays, I tucked into an alcove, straddling a vase.

The middle elevator moved upward. I'd have the jump on him. Then the far elevator lifted; then a third counted up the floors. Smart man. Now I wouldn't know which one he took.

Since I wanted to stay above him, I watched them all. They reached the private floor—I had no idea how he'd gotten up there unless he'd ridden up with the workmen, blending in, then hidden and waited for everyone to leave. Right now, the how didn't matter. The why, I knew. The who, I suspected. And the what was I going to do about it was still a toss-up. Shoot to kill or shoot to punish? Jury was still out.

While I waited and watched, I took the time to call Romeo. Curiously my hand wasn't shaking and my voice was deadly calm. I quickly filled him in, then finished with, "Seal all the exits before you come looking for me. I can stay alive that long." He didn't agree or disagree, but he was a good cop: he'd do the right thing. Best of all, help was on the way. My well of courage was only so deep.

The elevators each paused at the top floor. With four elevators, he'd have a hard time launching them all at once. Narrowing my eyes, I waited for the lag.

He'd taken the middle one. I had to wait, watch where he went.

He stopped at every floor.

If that's the way you want to play it.

Arms straight, gun in front of me, stance wide, my back braced, I watched, and I waited. My heart galloped as I closed one eye, sighting down the short barrel. But my eye was steady, my hands firm, my finger light on the trigger.

The elevator stopped at twenty-two. Two floors higher than my position.

A pause.

Twenty-one.

I held my breath.

Twenty. The bell dinged and the doors slid open. He'd killed the light inside.

Nothing. No movement. No head peeking out.

I didn't dare move. He was baiting me, trying to get me to disclose my position.

The doors slid shut. The elevator continued its floor-by-floor descent.

Keeping my gun at the ready, I breathed, slowly, deeply. He had to have been in there. Trying to lure me out.

Where would he get off? Not the first floor. Even now, sirens sounded in the distance. What would he think I would do? I bet my life on his thinking I was a typical female and would run for safety the minute I heard the sirens.

My guard up, I made my way around the floor and down the far hallway to another set of stairs. With five to choose from, I figured the odds were still in my favor. I guessed he'd get off at the mezzanine—from there he could shoot up a floor toward the Spa level or down into the lobby. Stepping lightly, I muffled my steps as best I could. I'd chosen one of the original stairwells from the Athena built when concrete was the norm and those twangy metal steps we used now, unheard of.

At the third floor, I eased the door open. I knew this hotel inside and out, every twist and turn committed to memory by this time, the architectural plans burned on my brain. The architects had seen to that—I didn't even argue with Mother that much. Nobody fired. I pictured the hall to my left—a small hallway angled off to the right. Pushing the door open, careful it didn't bang against the stops, I bolted for the hall. I skidded around the corner.

After listening for a moment and not hearing anything, I risked a look. No movement. I sidled to the railing—Cielo's lobby ceilings topped out at twenty-five feet, the mezzanine ringing the atrium—a fact I hoped my would-be killer didn't know or hadn't paid attention to. Halfway around, I caught movement one floor below.

Red and blue lights strobed through the glass front, painting the lobby. The sirens whined as they fell silent. Momentarily distracted, the shooter eased a bit further out from his position, exposing a nice target.

I lined up, held my breath, and brushed the trigger.

The gun jerked.

I heard him grunt as he whirled, raising his gun in one motion.

Cringing back, I tucked into myself.

His shot chipped plaster six inches from my head.

When I stepped out again and fired, he was gone.

"Fuck."

As glass broke, I heard the bang of the backdoor as it clanged against the wall, then slammed shut on the bounce back.

He was gone.

The police, in full tactical gear, crouched, automatic weapons at the ready. Small groups ran, found a fortified position from which to cover the next wave.

I shouted down to them. "The shooter went out the back." When I'd decided nobody had a happy trigger finger, I stepped into the light, my hands raised, my gun visible. I identified myself. "He went out the back." I motioned which way. "You'll find a blood trail to follow. I winged him, damn it."

Some of the police went after him, others stayed, their weapons trained on me, none of us moving, until Romeo skidded into the lobby. He assessed the situation with one look. "Stand down," he ordered his men. "You okay?" he shouted up to me.

"Have your men check the Cloud Nine Suite." I pointed. "That way."

With a nod from Romeo, half the group peeled off and

disappeared in the direction I'd pointed.

Help had arrived. I started to relax. Then I saw him. Movement behind Romeo.

Sam.

I raised my gun and fired as the light fixture over my head shattered. The remaining geared-up cops whirled but didn't fire. Romeo was in the line.

The guy was gone as quickly as he'd appeared, the police in full pursuit.

Romeo hadn't even ducked. Rooted, he waited for me to join him. Close up, I could see he was rattled despite the calm, cool and collected bit. "Irv?"

"No. Sam Wu dressed as a member of the construction crew." I was disappointed that it hadn't been Irv.

Romeo whistled. "You're lucky, then." He glanced out at the brightening day. "Wonder why he waited so late?"

I nodded at the construction crew that was already assembling. Although I'd told the foreman no work today, with his reputation on the line, he'd have them here at least half the day. "So he could blend in and disappear, maybe?"

"If you were dead, who'd he have to run from?"

"The guards? Your guys? A good killer always has several exit strategies," I said like I knew what I was talking about.

"I don't even want to know how you know that."

"Another reason could be timing."

He scratched his head, then mussed his already mussed-up hair. "I'm not following."

"Irv is tidying up loose ends. I'd say he's getting ready to move to greener pastures." I motioned the construction crew to wait just a bit. "Did you get anything out of Mrs. Box?"

"No, not really. And the gait thing didn't line up. It wasn't her helping the bomber at your place."

"That leaves Kimberly Cho."

Romeo shot me a surprised look.

"Something's been bothering me, and I just couldn't put my finger on it. But it dawned on me: that whole thing with the shooter and my father getting shot. It's like he was waiting until I showed up."

"How'd he know you'd be there?"

"Kimberly came to get me."

Romeo took a moment. "What's in it for her?"

"Maybe she got a bit tired of a working stiff's salary and wanted a piece of her father's pie? I don't know. I've never really understood what motivates the bad to do what they do. That'd just be way too much trouble for me."

"You'd suck at it," Romeo nodded in agreement.

I was only slightly miffed. I punched my phone to life as I tucked my Glock away. I dialed the main number at the Babylon. "Front desk manager," I said, when the operator answered.

"Sergio Fabiano."

I cringed. Anyone who sounded that bright after a night shift, and a holiday night as well, should be shot at dawn, or promoted. I'd consider it—if Sergio would just be a bit less unctuous. "Sergio, Lucky O'Toole. Has Mr. Cho's delegation checked out?" He was supposed to stay for the whale party, but I had a sinking feeling.

"No. His party is booked through the holiday."

"Thanks." I stuffed my phone back in my pocket, careful to disconnect the call or Sergio was going to be listening to my stomach churn. "Mr. Cho seems to have dug in."

"You don't think he had anything to do with this?" Romeo seemed a bit skeptical.

"He's the one everyone wants us to believe is behind it. His reputation precedes him, and everyone makes snap judgments. The Big Boss gets it all the time. I think he got wind of his daughter pulling a few fast ones and he came to get her, and perhaps get Sam if he could."

"A nice theory."

"True. But I've got a couple of folks working on some things." Romeo started to ask. "You don't want to know."

He clammed up.

"And then there's a couple of other things that have been bugging me. If Irv was supposedly paying Sam for all this dirty work, where'd he get the money? He was totally tapped out when we sent him up.

Mr. Cho wouldn't be quite that stupid, I don't think, but I could be wrong."

"So, you think Kimberly—your Kimberly—is working with Irv."

"I'm willing to bet she thinks she's pulling the strings. But, messing with Irv is like holding a viper by the tail." My phone vibrated. "O'Toole," I said, as I pressed it to my ear.

"Hey, you awake?" The Southern strains of River Watalsky.

"I'm talking to you." I bit down on a grin, I don't know why. This whole thing was serious business.

"Right."

"Whatcha got? Any sightings?" I shut my eyes and crossed my fingers. Tired, but wired, my brain stuck in overdrive, long on problems, short on answers, I could really use a little bit of help.

And I got it. "No, no sightings, but something one guy said struck me as odd. He said he had a pickup at your new place at like two in the morning. A gal, young."

"Asian?"

"How'd you ... never mind. Anyway, when he said it, it got me to thinking. Your joint isn't open yet. So what business would she have there at that time of night?"

"What business indeed?" During the day, Cielo was busy as a beehive with the buzz of last-minute prep and training. But at night... I thanked him, and told him to come by the hotel tomorrow.

"On Christmas?"

"We all need a little Christmas, don't you think?" I grinned at Romeo; I couldn't help myself.

"Kimberly Cho has been hanging out around here at odd hours of the very early morning." I started to pocket my phone, but it vibrated again.

This time, Jeremy. "We've been rooting through digital documents half the night. Hope you're happy."

"Only if you got something." I paused. I heard him take a breath. "Wait. Kimberly Cho, right?"

"Yep. I don't even want to know how you know. It's just not fair."

"Nobody promised fair, only that you had a spot in the race. Thanks. Thanks a lot, Jeremy."

He got the sincerity. "You got it. Anytime."

This time I got my phone back in my pocket.

Romeo shook his head. "What made you finger Kimberly Cho?"

"The white dinner jacket." At his big eyes, I kept going. "It's stupid, really, and a total gut call. But why put the dinner jacket in Bungalow Seven, Mrs. Box's bungalow? If Mrs. Box had anything to do with all this mess she wouldn't have stashed it there. She isn't that that stupid."

"Neither is Sam." Romeo joined the discussion, nodding his head but still looking like he was on a long leash.

"So, who would put it there? Irv? He wouldn't be caught dead in the Babylon—that's aggressive even for him."

"Process of elimination?"

"No. Planting that jacket ... that would link Dani Jo Box to a bunch of bad shit. Knowing the publicity shit-storm, that was just plain mean. It has hate written all over it." I grabbed Romeo's shoulder. "And that, my friend, is exactly something a scorned woman would do."

"Your father said Holt wanted to fix things with his family, right?"

"Leaving Ms. Cho out in the cold."

Romeo looked a bit stricken.

A worker stuck his head in through the broken door. "Excuse me, can we come in and get to work?"

"Wait until the police clear the building; then the police will check you in." I looked to Romeo for confirmation. "Then you can do what you need to do, but make sure you're out of here by noon and home to your families. Family comes first." Parroting my father—this apple didn't fall far. A thought hit out of the blue. "What time is it?" I asked Romeo.

He glanced at his phone. "Six-twenty."

"I gotta go." A text chimed in. Miss P reminding me of the race. I typed back a hurried response telling her I was on my way.

Romeo squeezed my arm tighter, as if he could hold me there through physical force. "You can't go. This is redundant, but they're gunning for you."

"Your guys are chasing the shooter. Irv's not getting his hands dirty in all of this, so I'm not worried he'd actually find the balls to shoot at me. Have the bomb squad check the dais and surrounding areas if that'll make you feel better. But, I think that bit of business is over. I winged him; you'll catch him. Life as we know it has been restored." I threw an arm around his shoulder. "Now, my valiant Galahad, let's go find some Christmas spirit."

A LARGE crowd had gathered for the Elf Run; this year's turnout looked to be a record. It seemed all of Vegas had donned elf costumes or the occasional Santa outfit and packed in to the south end of the Strip for the start of the run, which would take them past all the big hotels, through Naked City, then finishing under the lighted canopy at the Fremont Street Experience.

Thankfully, the start was close to Cielo, so a short jog had me in the thick of the crowd. As I elbowed my way through, I did my best to straighten my hair and pinch some color into my cheeks. In my jeans and torn sweatshirt, I wasn't exactly the well-turned-out corporate executive, but given the last couple of days I thought perhaps I might get a sympathy reprieve from scrutiny.

As I approached the dais, I kept my head on a swivel, looking for an out-of-place construction guy. The organizer, a thin nervous young woman wearing no makeup and a Santa outfit, clutched a clipboard as she barked into a microphone arcing from her ear. When she caught sight of me, she staggered, as if ready to crumple with relief. I paused at the bottom of the steps. She motioned me up. I scanned the crowd, then waved her down to join me.

She paused on the last step, which put us eye-to-eye. As I gave her the short-and-sweet, her eyes grew wider and wider until she did a perfect Marty Feldman imitation. I stifled a giggle—it would be impossible to explain and most likely misinterpreted.

"But we're counting on you," she whispered. "You're like a rock star."

"Hardly. I'm sure there is no real danger, but I want to be on the safe side. I'll still be the starter, but you must clear the dais." The words sounded removed, the reality distant. I really didn't think Irv would show himself. Oh sure, he'd let his presence be known right before he tried to blow me into the next adventure, but that carried a small risk of detection. After all, I was virtually dead, by his way of thinking anyway. My phone vibrated in my back pocket. Romeo. I pressed it to my ear, putting a finger in the other so I could hear over the buzz of the crowd. "You got him?"

"No." His voice crackled with worry. "What we got is a runner who was mugged by an Asian guy in construction gear."

"Shit."

"It gets worse. You know anything about a gun in a gun rack in the suite you said someone had been using?"

My heart stopped. "Yeah."

"It's gone."

"And the shooter wasn't using it to shoot at me," I said, thinking out loud.

"So that means there's someone else wandering around with a gun looking for you." I moved up a couple of steps and scanned the crowd, my hand shading my eyes from the brightening morning sun. "Is the construction guy okay?"

"Yeah, just a little cold. The dude stole his costume."

"Who was he dressed as?"

"Santa. The full outfit, except for shoes."

"Got it. I'll be on the lookout." Of course, there were thousands of Santas, but he knew that. Finding one with work boots on? What were the odds?

"We need to cancel the race." Romeo said.

"Ms. O'Toole?" The race director tapped my arm. "We're about ready."

"Too late." I sucked in a deep breath. "He's gunning for me. With that Sharp's he could knock bug off my nose. Nobody else will be close to me."

"Lucky ..."

"Get him, Romeo. He'll be up high." I rang off.

Six SWAT Team members filtered out of the crowd and surrounded the dais, their presence and their weapons both comforting and alarming. Apparently only to me, though—nobody else really paid much attention. One of the SWAT addressed me. "We have snipers placed on the rooftops. Lookouts all around. With the crowd, we've got to be super careful, but we've got you covered."

"As long as no one else is at risk."

"Yes, ma'am." He cleared the dais, then escorted me up. "The bomb squad cleared the dais before you got there, so no bombs."

"Good to know."

Teddie.

Right now I was standing a good four feet above the crowd—a lightning rod. Talk about feeling exposed. I grabbed Mr. SWAT. "You get the asshole, you hear?"

"Yes, ma'am."

"Don't ma'am me, just do it." I tried not to scan the crowd, leaving that to the police. I had to put my life in the hands of my most-vilified Metro. Talk about ironic.

The crowd quieted as the race director started into her spiel over the loudspeaker. I only half-listened. Then it was my turn. I gave my usual rah-rah Vegas rally cries, added a bit of Christmas cheer and thanked everyone for coming.

The crowd roared, clapping and cheering. I felt like the city's mascot or something.

Someone pressed a gun into my hand. I must've recoiled.

"Starter pistol." a cute kid in an official race T-shirt said. "Just point it up and pull the trigger when the countdown gets to zero."

The gun felt light, cold and lethal. "What's it loaded with?"

"A whole lot of bang powder, meant to make an impression."

"That's a technical term, is it?" I weighed it, turning it from side to side. It looked real, felt real, and was real except the barrel had been obstructed with an internal cross piece that prevented a projectile from leaving but allowed the gases to escape. It would be just like Irv to substitute a real gun, have me shoot it and have the projectile drop on somebody, killing them, leaving me to deal with that. *Not today, Ol' Irv. Not today.*

"If I knew the real name of the stuff, I'd tell you." The kid grinned, easy in his ignorance.

"Gunpowder," I provided, thinking people were too comfortable not knowing.

"Seriously? Like the real stuff?" He seemed genuinely surprised.

"The real stuff. Just no bullet."

I glanced at the cop standing next to me. "It's loaded for a big bang. Are you thinking what I'm thinking?"

He whispered into his mic.

Everyone quieted. The countdown began. "Ten." I scanned the rooftops. "Nine." Then the crowd. Still nothing stood out in the sea of thousands of elves and Santas. "Eight." The fast runners toed the line, bending, poised. "Seven."

The cop's radio crackled. "Rooftop. Southwest, one hundred yards."

"Six."

"Raise your gun, Ms. O'Toole," The race director directed.

"Five."

I did as she directed, my other arm creeping protectively around my stomach, my hand finding the butt of the Glock under my sweatshirt.

"Four." I found myself looking at feet. Lots of Nikes, some Adidas, Reeboks. And one pair of steel-toed construction boots, in the back, shifting. "There." I pointed, alerting the cop next to me.

"Three."

Sam Wu. Standing slightly apart from the runners, he looked up, staring right at me.

The SWAT guy pointed and spoke into his mic. "Man on the roof. Westside parking garage."

Sam swiveled and stared at the rooftop.

Metal glinted in the sun. The man on the rooftop had a gun! I squinted trying to make out who was on the rooftop. It had to be Irv. "Shoot him," I barked at the cop.

"Two."

"Do you have a clear shot?" The cop asked into his mic.

"Negative," came the reply.

The man on the rooftop sighted on the crowd.

"Everybody down," I shouted. A few complied, not many. Most simply stood there, looking around like lost sheep.

Exposed, Sam Wu raised his gun, pointing at the rooftop shooter. A pistol, he'd never make that shot. Why would he even try? I assumed he was here to shoot me.

"One." Instinctively, I pulled the trigger. A loud boom. The pistol jerked in my hand.

I flinched.

Sam Wu fell.

Irv was covering his tracks.

The first wave of runners launched.

Screams. The middle of the crowd stopped, then moved back, ringing the fallen man. Some looked at me.

I scanned the rooftops.

The gunman was still there. Now I knew it was Irv. I could feel his evil. He paused, looking at me, then he shouldered the rifle, sighting on me. Anger short-circuited thought and rooted me where I stood. *Take your best shot, asshole.*

Where the hell was SWAT?

Hiding, shielding myself wasn't an option—that would put me closer to innocent bystanders. Up here, I was by myself and no one else would be hurt.

I couldn't tear my gaze from Irv, the gun. I could imagine his finger tightening on the trigger as he held his breath. Irv lifted his head once, then refocused his aim. Games. Ego games that I prayed would get him killed.

"Somebody shoot him," I growled through clenched teeth.

The SWAT guy was resituating his people for a clear shot. Time we didn't have.

As I narrowed my eyes waiting for the pain, a body hurtled from the side, tackling Irv. I squinted. *Could it be?* The cops pulled me off the dais, and I lost sight of the struggle.

The race went on—the cops thought it the best way to disperse the crowd. With the rooftop cleared, I wandered over to Sam Wu. I motioned to one of the cops standing there. "Give me a look?"

"It isn't pretty."

"It never is."

I stood over the body as he knelt and peeled back a corner, lifting it so only I had a clear view.

Irv was a good shot. He'd hit Sam mid-forehead. A small hole in the front, but I'm sure the back of his head had been blown wide open. I didn't ask to see that part.

Death. I'd always thought it stole our humanity. In Sam's case, a look of peace had settled over him, the twisted evil no longer present. Perhaps we all really were restored when our journey was over. A nice thought.

But he'd been my best hope of clearing Teddie.

Teddie.

That had been him I saw on the roof, tackling Irv. I'd know Teddie anywhere. All I had to do was close my eyes and I could remember his every curve and angle, all his expressions. I was trying to save Teddie and he'd saved me.

Funny how life works. Good things from bad situations.

I nodded at the cop and he once again covered Sam.

At a loss as to how to help or what to do, I wandered. I thought about calling Romeo, but he probably had his hands full with Irv and Teddie.

ROMEO found me sitting on the edge of the fountains at the Bellagio, dangling my toes in the water. Totally against the rules, but the cops had larger problems. "Hey," he said as he stood over me.

"What are you doing here? I thought you'd be busy with photo-ops and all after catching the shooters that have the city on edge."

He sat next to me. He didn't look happy. "You like breaking the rules, don't you?"

"Don't we all?" I knew what his no-so-happy look meant. "You didn't get them, did you? Irv and Teddie?"

Despite the chill, he shucked his shoes and stuck his toes in. "It's warmer than I thought."

"I'm sure physics could give you the reason why."

"No. They were gone when my guys got there."

"You just confirmed my low-regard for Metro, present company excepted, of course."

"I have no idea how they got away."

"Irv is good at pulling a disappearing act."

My words finally registered with the young detective. "Teddie? How'd you know?"

"I'd know him anywhere."

Romeo pulled Teddie's ankle bracelet out of his pocket. "You were right. We found this on the roof."

I stared over the water at the Bellagio, one of my favorite hotels in Vegas—next to mine, of course. "He saved my life." I wondered if that would balance the scales of justice. "I couldn't save his."

"Not yet," Romeo said.

"So you didn't get either of them?"

"No."

"Not, yet," I said, taking my turn at the encouragement game. Irv was still on the loose and he had Teddie. And I had no idea what to do about it. I felt like scouring the alleys myself, but that wouldn't do any good. "You've got to find them, Romeo. Find them now, before something bad happens to Teddie."

Numb, I didn't even flinch when the fountains shot their first salvo.

"Wow." Romeo flinched back. "We're doing all we can."

Considering it was Metro we were talking about, that didn't make me feel any better.

Mist rained down on us as we hugged our knees and watched the show.

The music died, the water quit dancing, and reality returned.

"Teddie's gone." The reality stole a bit of me.

Romeo pushed to his feet then extended a hand. "Let me walk you home."

*L*OST in negotiating with the shyster glass company that wanted a fortune to make the front entrance look presentable—a replacement for the custom glass door would take weeks—I didn't notice Eddie V until he pounced.

"You owe me." He shook a finger under my nose, which was like waving a lit match close to a fuse. "You promised Irv Gittings." He gestured dramatically around the lobby, gathering an audience. "I don't see him," he said, using the exaggerated cadence of a nursery rhyme.

The Glock rested warm against my stomach. I really wanted to shoot him.

"And now Teddie's run."

"You don't know that." I didn't feel inclined to letting him in on the facts as I knew them.

Giving me a smirk like he knew something I didn't, he leaned in close. "I believe you promised the judge you'd make sure he stayed around to face the charges against him. The judge is going to be super pissed."

I thought Eddy understated. But he knew that. He looked like he was enjoying this far too much.

I left the gun where it was and whirled on Eddy V. "Look, you little parasite, I'll bring you your man. We didn't set a time frame. So, do what you need to do, but get the hell out of my hotel."

He cowered but kept a shred of backbone. "Sure, fine. Then you and me, we're going to be neighbors. Unless the judge finds you in contempt or something."

I didn't think a broken promise was contemptible, but I wasn't well versed in judge's powers. "Get out, Eddy."

"Sure. Sure." He straightened his ugly jacket, then ran a hand over his slicked back hair. "You know Freddy?"

Something in his voice stopped me from breaking his nose. "Yeah. What about him?"

"Your boyfriend, the one with the ankle candy, he paid him a visit. Ordered some new docs, if you get my drift."

My heart sank; I got his drift. A new ID. Teddie had planned to leave. But why? And then it hit me: the one thing he could do to make things right was to catch Irv and bring him back.

Teddie. My music man. Against Irv Gittings, Kim Cho and God knew who else.

My eyes went all slitty. "You got a name?"

"You friend is now known as Ima True."

I burst out laughing. Of course he'd run as woman. And he'd just let me know I was right—he had a plan, not a good one, but a plan.

I prayed Metro would find them both and soon.

And it frustrated the hell out of me that I couldn't do anything to help. I had no idea who was leading whom and where they'd go. I knew Teddie would get word to me, he had to. So, for now, all I could do was wait.

And show up at a very important wedding, assuming it was still on.

As far as I knew, nobody had called it off, but it was anybody's guess what or who we'd find when we showed up.

Either way, I planned to be happy, to celebrate.

Now, what did I have to wear?

I didn't have long to ponder that imponderable.

Romeo burst through the door. "We've got a problem."

"I hate it when you do that. Nothing good ever comes of it."

I hated being right.

CHAPTER NINETEEN

"WE'VE got a dead guy in Mr. Cho's bungalow," Romeo announced, his breath coming in gasps. "One of his. Everybody's gone."

The same thought propelled us as we both turned and ran. They were running, and Mr. Cho was their ticket out. And Irv was leaving as part of Mr. Cho's team. But where did that leave Teddie? I shut my mind to the possibilities.

"Where's his plane?" Romeo asked, as he slipped into the passenger seat in the Ferrari.

"Right around the corner. McCarran."

He got on his phone to rally the troops as I negotiated the throng of milling runners. The Strip was still closed to traffic. We were stranded in a sea of people. "We gotta run for it."

Romeo and I bolted, leaving the car marooned. I did remember to take the keys. The north end of the airport was only a couple of blocks away, but it seemed an eternity.

"Any idea how long they've been gone?" I huffed at Romeo.

"Long enough."

And if they'd been smart enough to call and have the plane ready, the engines spooling up, we'd miss them.

We rounded the fence, raced across the parking lot, then skidded into the FBO. No cops yet. I guessed they'd found the same traffic as we had.

One bored gal sat behind the counter. She tried to perk up, but she didn't pull it off. I got it. I wanted to tell her I hadn't had a vacation or a holiday in decades, but I didn't have the time, and didn't think it would make her feel better.

Romeo took the lead, flashing his badge, which was great, because I had no air left to talk. "Chinese diplomat and his contingent?"

"Taxied out ten minutes ago."

"Are they still on the field?" I managed to gasp.

The girl looked at Romeo.

"Call the tower," he barked.

She jumped and did as he asked. She gave them the tail number. Covering the mouthpiece, she said to us, "First in line. Cleared to go."

"Stop them," Romeo ordered.

She spoke quickly into the phone. "Stop them. The cops are here." She listened, then slowly hung up the phone as a plane roared overhead. "Too late."

Romeo reached across her desk and grabbed the manifest. He scanned quickly then looked up, meeting my gaze with worried eyes. "Everyone else in Mr. Cho's group is accounted for. No additions other than Kimberly Cho."

"So Irv is masquerading as the dead guy and Kim's paperwork would be in order as she is a Chinese citizen and travels to Macau frequently." They'd thought of everything.

But where was Teddie?

As if he could read my mind, Romeo put a hand on my arm. "Don't worry, we'll find him. He's got to be here somewhere."

Yes. But was he alive?

CHAPTER TWENTY

MY job came with a few perks—the long hours and getting shot at were not two of them. But being able to call the boutiques in the Bazaar and have salespeople rush over, arms laden with beautiful finery, was most definitely one of the best. It took a couple of hours, but finally I had the bare bones of a functional wardrobe.

But even the retail therapy couldn't put a dent in my worry.

I missed Teddie, missed his eye; he really could dress a woman. And undress her, if memory served. I thought he'd approve of my choices. Alone for the moment, I wandered to the windows in my new apartment. Vegas spread at my feet, the Strip stretching north to the horizon like Dorothy's yellow-brick road. Teddie had shared my emerald vision of Vegas; then he'd found another Oz. He kept telling me he'd come back, realized his mistakes. But he didn't understand that coming back was not the same as never leaving.

His absence carved a piece of my history away. Bottom line, I missed him, all of him—his talent, his sense of humor, the way he got me. We'd been the best of friends. And I had yet to truly mourn the loss.

And now he was gone. Maybe dead.

My heart broke as I tried to hold myself together.

I had to keep believing he'd be okay.

With old lovers, I guessed folks could mourn them, resent them, wish they'd been different, wish you had. But lovers carve a piece of your heart to take with them and fill the hole with a bit of their own. I worked to find my smile and focused on what I could do right now. Now I could be a friend.

Miss P deserved that.

Showered, dressed, and coiffed, with face appropriately painted, I tucked my feet into a pair of strappy silver Jimmy Choos, the only pair of fancy shoes to have survived. They'd been secreted in my desk drawer at the office for dress-up emergencies. Before I headed out, I took a quick look in the mirror. Somehow, I looked like a more-adult version of me. Light brown hair softly curling on my shoulders, blue eyes accented by angled bangs, high cheekbones Mona always took credit for, I looked like me, but something had changed. Something subtle. Peace—no contentment—had settled into my features, smoothing the worry. I liked the look. Smoothing down my new silver sheath that crossed one shoulder then delicately touched my curves, ending in a hem shorter in the front, I delighted in the new style for the new me.

Tucking my keycard in my bra, making sure it didn't show, I left my purse, my phone and my gun. Tonight it was my turn to be a friend.

Christmas greeted me when I stepped from the elevator into the lobby. A great tree festooned with gold ... I loved gold ... regal below the Chihuly glass, which looked like an explosion of colorful fireworks. Apparently the foreman had relented and let the decorating crew start early. They had tucked Christmas into every corner with small trees laced with lights. Garlands wound around all the desks. Even the music reflected the season.

Our official opening still a week away, I probably could've ignored Christmas. We'd have to take the decorations down by New Year's anyway or Mona would faint, sure we all were going to perish of some superstitious peril. But this was my home now, or one of them, and Christmas was big for me.

I'd managed to arrive ten minutes early so I took the time to wander, savoring, moving the knickknacks, straightening pictures that didn't need it, and rearranging furniture an inch one way or the other, claiming my space, putting my little mark on it. On the second pass around the tree still looking for something that needed tweaking, I spied an envelope, my name scrawled in a familiar hand on the front, tucked in the branches. Teddie.

I read the lines twice:

My dearest Lucky,

By now, I've gone. Don't try to find me. I don't know if I will come back, but I will send you an important package. Knowing you, you won't be angry and you'll find a way to not hate me. Perhaps you should. I've let you down in every way possible. I'm sorry, so sorry, for everything. Know that I take you with me in my heart and you will always be my true love, and the one who got away.

Yours,

Ted

He was alive!

Warmth and hope rushed through me.

I carefully refolded the note and stuffed it back in the envelope.

*An important pack*age. Irv Gittings.

Teddie would try to head to Macau. Should I alert the authorities, wise them up to his ruse? Teddie would be pissed, but telling the police was the only way to keep him alive.

A kiss behind my right ear fractured logical thought. I leaned back. "I love you."

"How did you know it was me?" Jean-Charles seemed surprised that I could do that.

I turned, stepping back to get a good look. Resplendent in his tux with a festive red cummerbund and a gold tie, he said easily but with feeling. "I love you, too. You must know this."

My heart tumbled—I wondered if he'd always have that effect on me. A lifetime was a tricky thing. My ring flashed as he took my hands, kissing each one, then folding me in for the real thing. I never wanted him to stop.

Someone tried to get our attention. A light throat-clearing—I guessed they thought we'd been at it long enough. Brandy, looking like an angel dropped among us, except for the pink coloring her cheeks. "Sorry."

Jean-Charles loosened his hold, but didn't abandon it.

I gave her half of my attention, which was all that was available with my body pressed to the Frenchman's. "We're about ready." She glanced at the papers in my hand. "I see you got your note."

"You put it in the tree?"

"It was on my desk with instructions." Her brightness dimmed a bit. "I did the right thing?"

"Of course."

Happiness returned. "People should start moving toward the chapel."

"Okay." I stopped her with a touch on the elbow as she moved away. "Do you know where Romeo is? I need to talk to him."

"On his way."

"Good. And about this wedding: any idea what's going to happen?"

"Haven't a clue. Miss P has been locked in the dressing room with Delphinia for hours. The only person I've let in is Mr. Trenton. He had a handful of papers and a judge in tow. Jeremy's laying low, and I haven't seen the doctor either." She spied Romeo stepping through the doors. "Excuse me," she said, as she rushed to greet him.

I followed her with Jean-Charles in trail. "Romeo, we have to stop Teddie. I know what he's going to do." I filled him in. He stepped to the corner and got on the phone.

"Come." My young assistant motioned for us to follow her. "It's time."

Jean-Charles and I waited to bring up the rear.

As we were about to enter the chapel, Agent Stokes grabbed my elbow, pulling us aside. "We need to talk." He darted a glance at Jean-Charles.

"He's one of the good guys," I explained as we all stepped to the side. "Can't it wait?" I asked the über agent.

"Your friend, Theodore Kowalski exited the country on a flight to Macau. Caught him on the security cameras. He was dressed as a woman, so we didn't catch him in time. We will try to intercept him, but our power in a Chinese province is limited."

I interpreted for Jean-Charles, "They have to depend on the locals, and they don't like to play nice."

Agent Stokes dropped the formal manner. "I just thought you should know. He's running into a minefield."

"I know. And now I'm sure he's done something stupid, or, if not yet, stupidity is imminent."

Romeo joined our little group; apparently he'd overheard the last bit. "We don't have any pull over there."

"Well, maybe a little. I happen to be an executive with one of the largest properties there. We contribute heavily to the local government."

I set my worries and my thoughts aside as Brandy hurried us inside and we took our places in a pew on the bride's side. I couldn't do anything right now. At the moment, Teddie's fate was up to him and the authorities.

Now Miss P deserved my attention. Of course, I had no idea who the groom would be. Who would her heart choose?

The officiant stepped to her position as the music started.

No groom. No groomsmen.

We all rose when the processional started. The first down the aisle, Dane and Flash.

Then Miss P, flanked by Jeremy and Cody Ellis, an arm hooked through each of theirs.

I whispered in Jean-Charles's ear. "Seriously? Talk about a flair for the dramatic."

One arm around my waist, he pulled me tight and whispered, "Soon it will be us."

That thought chased away all the worries, all the second-guessing, and all the attempts to control the path.

Life, what an adventure.

Miss P looked beautiful in an off-white, tea-length lace gown that hugged her in all the right places, shoes to match, and a million-candlepower smile. She also looked a bit incredulous—I knew the feeling. To be loved by someone incredible is a humbling, awe-inspiring thing. She had two. Who would she pick to walk with her through eternity?

The anticipation was killing me.

A thought zinged in out of the blue. I reached around Jean-Charles and tugged Romeo's sleeve.

We both leaned in, meeting in front of Jean-Charles' chest.

"We still have the good brother," I hissed.

"What?"

"Frank Wu, Kimberly's Achilles heel. She wants the good brother out of prison. She got rid of the bad brother—used Irv to do that. She brought her father here under false pretenses. But, back home, it will look like he didn't take care of his enemies. His control will weaken.

She needed someone to stick in as a figurehead."

"Gittings."

"She may have met her match, but in Macau she will have the advantage."

"And Teddie?" Romeo asked, worry already clouding his smile.

"He'll never see it coming." I motioned Romeo back, then I leaned back and looked at my love. "I need to go."

He smiled, seeing all the way through to my heart. "I know. But you must take Mr. Dane and his friend."

"Shooter?"

"Yes. And could you wait until tomorrow? Christophe so wants you there for Christmas."

"Of course. But could we also go celebrate with Mona and the Big Boss?" I had no idea if they'd let us all in the ICU, but we'd give it a shot. "Maybe we can pick up the babies on the way over?"

Jean-Charles smiled and squeezed my hand. "You will be careful when you go." That wasn't a question. "And you will be back for New Year's? That's your birthday, you know."

"I'll be back. I promise."

Miss P paused at our row, tapping my shoulder for attention. "Stand up with me?"

With a thousand-candlepower smile, I followed the trio, then took my place to the right of the officiant. I still had no idea what was going to happen and I didn't care. I just wanted the look on Miss P's face to stay there forever.

"Who gives this bride in matrimony?" The archaic words grated but seemed appropriate in this instance.

"I do," said Dr. Cody Ellis. He bent and kissed her cheek, then stepped aside.

THE END ... sort of ...

Thank you for coming along on Lucky's wild ride through Vegas. For more fun reads, please visit www.deborahcoonts.com or drop me a line at debcoonts@aol.com and let me know what you think. And, please leave a review at the outlet of your choice.